"There are only two ways to live your life. One is as though nothing is a miracle. The other is as though everything is a miracle."
— **Albert Einstein**

"Darkness cannot drive out darkness: only light can do that. Hate cannot drive out hate: only love can do that."
— **Martin Luther King Jr**

ACKNOWLEDGMENTS

The Magdalenes has taken me years to complete. There are so many people who helped me write this book. I am grateful to each and every person who held my hand and, kindly, help edit all my mistakes. I hope I don't forget to mention anyone who was part of this endeavor. Please forgive me if I did.

My wonderful critique groups: Jill Sayre, Adrienne LaCava, Mandy Montane, Jean Reynolds Page, Ian Pierce, Mary Turner, Kathy Yank, Lou Tasciotti, Chris Smith.

My readers: Donna Holmes, Nina Flournoy, Angela Sheets, Michael Dee, Lily Davis, Jane Mcgregor. My best muses: Cherryl Duncan, Brigitte Kelly (you are missed, but I'm sure you had something to do with "*Mags*" getting published).

To Mom, who I'm sure also helped edit from heaven.

Sarah Martin McConnell who gave me the seed of this idea years ago with her tireless work with nonprofits.

Thank you, Susan Humphreys, and editor Vivian Doolittle with Black Opal Books for taking me on.

And, of course, my family. Terry who puts up with me (and my writing) and my daughter, Alex who inspires me every day.

The Magdalenes

Jeanne Skartsiaris

A Black Opal Books Publication

GENRE: WOMEN'S FICTION, CATHOLIC FAMILIES, ADOPTION, MYSTERY

This is a work of fiction. Names, places, characters and incidents are either the product of the author's imagination or are used fictitiously, and any resemblance to any actual persons, living or dead, businesses, organizations, events or locales is entirely coincidental. All trademarks, service marks, registered trademarks, and registered service marks are the property of their respective owners and are used herein for identification purposes only. The publisher does not have any control over or assume any responsibility for author or third-party websites or their contents.

THE MAGDALENES
Copyright © 2023 by Jeanne Skartsiaris
Cover Design by Erin Dameron-Hill
All cover art copyright © 2023
All Rights Reserved
Print ISBN: 978-1-953434-84-5

First Publication: AUGUST 2023

All rights reserved under the International and Pan-American Copyright Conventions. No part of this book may be reproduced or transmitted in any form or by any means, electronic or mechanical, including photocopying, recording, or by any information storage and retrieval system, without permission in writing from the publisher.

WARNING: The unauthorized reproduction or distribution of this copyrighted work is illegal. Criminal copyright infringement, including infringement without monetary gain, is investigated by the FBI and is punishable by up to 5 years in federal prison and a fine of $250,000. Anyone pirating our eBooks will be prosecuted to the fullest extent of the law and may be liable for each individual download resulting therefrom.

ABOUT THE PRINT VERSION: If you purchased a print version of this book without a cover, you should be aware that the book is stolen property. It was reported as "unsold and destroyed" to the publisher, and neither the author nor the publisher has received any payment for this "stripped book."

IF YOU FIND AN EBOOK OR PRINT VERSION OF THIS BOOK BEING SOLD OR SHARED ILLEGALLY, PLEASE REPORT IT TO:
skh@blackopalbooks.com

Published by Black Opal Books **http://www.BLACKOPALBOOKS.com**

DEDICATION

For Mom.
Who could take a punch
and still get dinner on the table.

Chapter 1
Texas

Jude took her seat at the gleaming conference table. Her reflection, mirrored in the wood grain, appearing distorted, as if revealing her soul. She turned to the window and gazed out. Twenty stories up, a dull haze hung over the Dallas skyline. The scorching sun was like heat steam from hell blurring the sharp edges of the buildings.

"Let's get to work," Drew said, as he strode to the head of the table and sat. The attorneys became quiet when he entered. Drew exuded power yet fought with compassion for each client. That juxtaposition is what attracted Jude to his practice. "We got hired on a big truck wreck case. *The* truck case," he emphasized, opening a file as he slipped on his reading glasses.

"The one where the girl was under her dead mom for an hour before the paramedics found her?" a senior associate asked. "I'll take it. It's going to pay huge." He made a ka-ching sound, exploding his pudgy hands out like tiny fireworks.

Drew looked sternly over his glasses. "The victim is thirteen. We don't need your bull in a china shop approach."

"Jude." Drew slid the file to her like a bartender sending a beer. "This will be the biggest case you've handled.

You can do it. Your success on the airline case proves your skill." He winked. "Took some big *cajones* to take on Delta."

"You mean, *ovarios*," Jude smiled, reaching for the thick folder. She sat forward, eager but unsure. *Always unsure.* She sucked in a deep breath. Fear of failure constantly nibbled like hungry piranha. She felt like a hack, though she'd handily won each case she'd worked. "I won't let you down." Drew had been a solid force in Jude's law career, like the guy who held her bike after the training wheels were off.

"You're ready." He nodded brusquely.

Opening the file, Jude tried not to flinch at a grisly photo of a woman's decapitated head next to a body as if it were from two different people. Barely visible under the woman's torso, Jude saw a small, blood-soaked arm tangled in the seatbelt. Holding her breath, Jude quickly flipped through the gory photographs.

"Tell me about the girl," Jude swallowed shock at an image of the bloodied child strapped on a gurney and being loaded into an ambulance. Tears glistened through thick gore on the girl's cheeks.

"Tiffany Carmen. She's recovering from her physical injuries which are detailed in the medical record." Drew pointed to the file, "not to mention the psychological damage. The paramedics weren't aware she was in the car until she screamed, nearly an hour after they worked to extricate her mom." Drew took off his reading glasses and rubbed his eyes. "Mom's divorced. She and Tiffany were living with her mother. Grandma watched Tiffany while mom worked and went to college." He shook his head sadly.

"What about her father?" Jude closed the file, scribbling notes on a legal pad.

"He's a deadbeat. Not in the picture." Drew sat back in his leather chair. "We need to make sure the son-of-a-bitch doesn't get a cent." He leveled his gaze at Jude. "*Capisce*? If he comes sniffing around, give him the boot."

Jude looked Drew in the eye. "I understand."

"I'll work lead, Jude can assist," the other attorney persisted. "Especially if the father tries anything." He looked Jude up and down as if he held power over her.

"I'll handle him," Jude remarked sharply, anger burned like acid on her tongue. She swallowed it down and sat straighter. *I've got this*. She knew about son-of-a-bitch fathers. Her own father booted her out when she was only fourteen, and innocent.

And pregnant.

"I have more experience," he groused. Reaching for the file, he grunted as he bent forward, making Jude think of accordion bellows.

"You have enough to finish before Christmas," Drew said. "Jude will knock this out of the park," He nodded to her. "We need someone who has the silent sense of a shark. Sink your teeth into it. Draw blood."

"Roger that." Jude stacked her files neatly, ignoring the other attorney. She wished she was as sure of herself as Drew thought. *Pretend, act.* She pulled her files closer.

"I'm here if you need anything," Drew said, tapping the shiny conference table with a finger. "The father has already called sniffing around."

She nodded, remembering her own abusive father. Of course, Jude would never bring up her history here. No, she held the kink tight on that hose. Jude was determined not to let her broken past derail her future. She'd sealed off that part of her life, as if with brick and mortar.

Jude clenched her fist under the table, her fingernails biting the fleshy part of her hand, no doubt leaving half-moon marks. She wished she'd had the courage to take on her own father all those years ago. That sink-stone still wrapped heavily around her neck, kept her gasping at the surface. Now, her job was to find justice for her clients.

She could play in the big leagues and take a punch with the best of them.

And had taken many.

Chapter 2
New York – Christmas Day
17 Years Ago

"If I find out you're pregnant, I'll kill you," Judith's father sneered shoving her against the wall in their living room. A lit cigarette dangled from his lips, its ash glowed hot fire.

"Wh...what?" Judith sputtered, cowering from his raised hand.

"Whore!" He slapped her face so hard she heard, more than felt the pain. "Just like your mother." His thick New York accent was dense with spit. He grabbed her arm, shook her until her long hair tore loose from its ponytail. Judith reached for her hair to hold it in place before thinking to dodge his fists.

"You're worthless," he slurred. That priest said you're running with boys." He threw Judith down, her ribs slammed into the arm of his greasy recliner before she landed on the wood floor gasping for air. A full pedestal ashtray fell, scattering the remains into a pile of empty beer cans. His evening shrine. Christmas decorations tinkled from the force.

"I should'a known you'd be just like your mother." He ground his cigarette on the top of a can, the hot ash sizzling like burnt bacon.

Still on the floor, trying to make herself small, invisible, Judith closed her eyes and steeled herself for another blow, fought to think of something else as his foot landed in her back. A shot of pain tore through her chest. *Tramp, whore, slut*—all words her father used to describe her. He called her mom those names. An image of her mother came to her mind's eye. Her smile, her strength, her bruises.

Judith stayed down and held her breath as pain pulsed in her face and back where he'd struck her. He paced, cursed, picked up a thick glass vase, and threw it. She flinched as it landed by the Christmas tree. It didn't break. She tasted blood from his first punch.

"I work my ass off," he yelled from the doorway. "If you'd listen, maybe you'd learn something from the goddamned nuns and priests at that school instead of carrying on the family tradition and opening your legs to any dick that wants it."

Pinching her eyes tight, Judith refused to cry. Tears made him madder. Most of the time he wasn't happy until he saw blood. She didn't want to give him the satisfaction. She buried her face in his chair and wiped bloody snot in the rough dank upholstery praying he'd leave.

No matter how hard she tried to be good, it was never enough. One minute he could be decent, then like a time bomb, explode at the smallest trigger. Was there a difference between fear and love?

How did he know? She wasn't sure. Didn't want to know. Her period had never been regular. She'd only just gotten it last year. Judith hoped her constant upset stomach was from a virus or cancer or anything but what she feared.

At school, Mary Toby, one of the bad girls, talked about French kissing boys and where babies came from. At fifteen, Mary was a full year older than Judith, having been held back in the second grade. Mary used her extra year of experience to teach the younger girls. She seemed to feel a need to tutor what the nuns didn't talk about. Judith was appalled, especially since Mary knew how to *do* everything. Judith never wanted to learn about such things, wanted to stay pure for Jesus, secretly hoped to be a nun. The sisters at St. Francis Academy, especially Sister Agnes, took her under their wing. Made her feel special and, sometimes, normal.

"I should'a sent you to public school and saved my money," her father seethed. Judith snuck a glance as he stood near the front door, hand on the knob. The lights from their Christmas tree gave his face a reddish, evil glow. Cracks in the plaster seemed to radiate out of his head.

Judith knew he wouldn't open the door until he was done screaming. She reached under his precious chair and felt the stuffing, like cotton candy. She slowly, quietly ripped open a seam.

"I don't want you here when I get back. Go live with the bastard." He opened the door, sharp, cold wind whipped through the room. Leaving, he slammed the door so hard the house shook. Judith's favorite glass angel ornament, the one with the sweetest bell, fell from the tree and shattered. Its song silenced forever.

Judith tried to muster the strength to get up. *Go live with the bastard.* His words echoed in her head. If he only knew who the *bastard* was. Judith didn't have the courage to tell anybody. Who would believe her? Sister Agnes seemed to realize what had happened, but nothing had been done. As Judith counted the days since her last period she thought about that evening. She'd been in church on a Friday at dusk, alone. Judith often ducked out of the house on weekend nights when her father was home. His alcohol-fueled temper lashed like the crack of a whip. Judith found peace in the solitude of the sanctuary.

The street noise on Thirty-first Avenue in Astoria was

muffled through the oak doors of their small duplex. Across the river, Manhattan's lights brightened as the evening sky dimmed. Christmas lights cast a festive glow through the window.

If Judith could have known what would happen in the church that night, she would have gladly taken whatever her father doled out. Instead, sitting in the quiet sanctuary, as she watched silhouettes of shadows playing off the stained glass, her rosary entwined in her fingers, she never expected the old priest to be there. Life would again twist her dreams, her future, wrung out like an old sheet.

Judith stayed on the floor counting each pulse of pain, prayed her father wouldn't come back. She tried to take a full breath, but a sharp stab in her chest and sickness in her stomach clutched, turning her inside out. The smell of his oily chair clung in her nose. Listening to the noise outside, she thought of families sitting down to Christmas dinner. Today's Christmas dinner here, with the old priest, had been a nightmare. She prayed the floor was quicksand and would suck her through.

The taste of blood and the odor of the rancid chair brought another kick of nausea. Painfully, she rolled on her back. She didn't want her mother to find her like this. Her mom fought like a tiger when she saw her babies getting hurt and paid a heavy price for it. Her father beat her mother often, thought she "deserved" it. He usually saved hitting the kids until mom was out. Judith's older brother took the beatings without crying. Judith wondered why he never fought back. He'd been big enough for years. Stephen never raised a hand to their father. Knocked to the floor, he'd take each blow, each kick, his face strained and red as he fought tears. Instead, he tried to deflect the blows with his hands to shield his face.

Judith gingerly hugged her knees to her body fighting sickness. The thick hardwood floors absorbed the smell of her father's cigarettes and stale beer which also lingered in the throw rug. Her mother spent hours cleaning, even after work, but her father could trash a room in minutes. He was the king of his house and could do whatever he damned well pleased.

Occasionally, if they were lucky, he was on the road. Judith lived for his business trips. It saved her from having to crawl on hands and knees to avoid him.

She'd gotten pretty good at being quiet.

She sat up and touched her bloodied face, praying her father's fists had taken care of the baby inside her. Judith wiped a tear away, or was it blood, and felt her upper lip. It was starting to swell. She squeezed hard on her lower abdomen. No bruises, no pain. Damn, why couldn't one of his punches have landed there?

Judith pushed the hurt down, swallowed bile, and stood on shaky legs. Wiping her face with her shirt, she wavered and grabbed a sturdy bookcase for balance. A statuette of St. Jude stood prominently on the shelf. The patron saint of lost causes.

Her namesake.

His image beckoned, but she knew better than to pray for help, for hope. As a child she'd blow bubbles, watch the rainbow-tinted spheres float toward heaven. She imagined each bubble filled with prayers, and when they popped it meant an angel had taken the message to God. Now, Judith could see each prayer fallen, unanswered.

Chapter 3
Present Day

The Texas sun bore relentlessly through Jude's windshield. The visor was no match for the late afternoon blaze. Her black BMW absorbed heat like a sponge. She squinted, determined to find the building in this southeast Dallas neighborhood. The street signs didn't help since most had been pulled down or bent. She suspected the ones left standing had been turned in the wrong direction. Pawnshops and used car lots mingled with apartments and wood-frame homes, all in varying states of disrepair. A contrast to the beautiful deco architecture of nearby Fair Park.

Jude watched children play on rickety stairwells and couldn't help but think of premises liability cases waiting to happen. As a plaintiff attorney, she saw the world as a backdrop for potential accidents.

The building Jude looked for was an old hotel or was before the city condemned it for being used as a drug and flophouse. Now Jude had been tasked to handle the estate of a woman who'd left it to the Catholic Church. It was like a Samurai sword to her gut dealing with anything Catholic, though she couldn't let work know about her deep hatred of the church. Drew had pulled Jude aside after the attorney meeting with this new "special" assignment.

Her phone rang as she tried to drive and decipher directions. GPS had taken her around the same block three times. Siri liked to screw with her, Jude knew, could almost hear the mocking tone in her voice.

Jude scrambled to answer, dropping her notes on the passenger seat before checking caller ID. "Jude Madigan."

"Hey, Jude…don't make it bad…take a sad song…" Rick's off-key voice cut through her.

"I hope that's you singing."

"Of course, why? Did you mistake me for John Lennon?"

"No, I thought I ran over an animal and killed it."

"Where are you?"

She heard Rick shuffling papers.

"Looking for an old flophouse hotel in a bad part of town."

"Planning to invest in some real estate?"

"Nope. It's a probate case Drew gave me. Our client left money and property to the Catholic Church." Jude fought an urge to chew up and spit out the word Catholic. "Drew wanted me to deliver the paperwork in person."

"Why're you working a probate case? You do personal injury. I told you, you should've gone into real estate law. I just closed on a sweet deal—some bleeding heart lost his family business. I brokered his building top dollar."

Jude wondered if she was attracted to assholes, or, like a magnet, did they find her? "You must be proud."

"I am."

"Drew takes cases to help the community." Jude glanced at the GPS on the phone which was dinging alerts. "I'll call you back. I need to figure out where I'm going."

"I'll come over later."

"No, I'm working. Oh, shit, I just ran a stop sign!"

"Hey, I told my mom you're my plus one to Sis's wedding. You *are* coming?" It was both a statement and a question.

"No. Besides, you'd have more fun if you went alone."

"Jude, you're my number one."

"Number one? See if two or three are available. You know I'm not about commitment." Rick was charismatic and handsome, but he had a fuse that stayed lit and ready to explode.

"And who better to help you with your career but *moi*? Besides, I need a hot piece of arm candy."

"That's enticing. Plus, I don't do the church thing."

"Come on. Otherwise, my sister will try to fix me up with one of the fat bridesmaids."

"Maybe you'll get lucky. Look, Rick, I've got to run."

"Dinner then." He demanded. "I want to celebrate my big windfall."

"No. I'll be late. That is if I ever find this damned place. Gotta go, ciao." She disconnected. Rick was like a big fish stretching the line taut. Jude was ready to cut him loose. Catch and release, a metaphor for her love life.

Jude hit the brakes and did a fast U-turn, trying not to attract attention. Her sleek BMW had already caused some heads to turn.

Bumping through cavernous potholes, she found the property. A chain-link fence surrounded a three-story, dilapidated brick hotel, that was missing most windows and chunks of bricks. Jude could see it had been a beautiful building once. It tried, like a soldier who'd lost the war, to stand proud through defeat. Neglected, boarded-up strip centers, and a large Baptist church flanked the old hotel.

A few cars were parked in front, and people were clearing debris around the periphery. Jude figured she was at the right place when she saw three nuns, dressed in dark robes, supervising the workers. She wondered how they were able to bear the Texas heat in the heavy black habits. They worked pouring water into cups and handing them out.

Jude's tires crunched over gravel and debris as she parked next to a construction truck. She grabbed her briefcase from the passenger seat and struggled to keep her short skirt over her legs as she got out of the car. The uneven terrain was tough to manage in heels as she walked to one of the nuns serving water. The older sister had a gentle, friendly face. "Hi, I'm Jude Madigan. I'm looking for a Sister Elizabeth."

"Oh, yes." The small nun smiled, clasped her hands together, and looked at the sky. "She's there," she said, fluttering her fingers at the blistering sun.

Jude looked to the heavens, shielding her eyes. "I just spoke to her yesterday!"

The nun chuckled and waved her hands as if shooing away tiny cherub angels. "Hello, I'm Sister Bernadette." She grabbed one of Jude's hands with both of hers. She glanced up, and, in a loud sing-song voice, said, "Lizzie! Where are you? You have a visitor." She continued to laugh as if in on a secret joke.

Jude's Catholic roots had been ripped from terra firma many years before. Though she'd lost her appetite for Catholicism, nuns still held a special place. But to see a nun talking to the sky seemed weird, even for a former devout believer.

"Over here." A voice from the heavens.

Sister Bernadette pulled Jude to the side of the old hotel. A woman's head popped over the roof, her hard hat slipping forward.

"Sister Elizabeth. This is Miss Madigan; you were expecting her?" Sister Bernadette covered her eyes from the sun as she looked up.

"Give me a sec. I'll be right down. Help yourself to some water." Her head disappeared behind the structure.

"That was a nun? On the roof? Wearing a hard hat?"

"Yes, Sister Elizabeth holds a master's degree in structural engineering. She's the project coordinator of this wonderful building." Bernadette walked ahead of Jude, took in the scene happily as if it were the first time she'd seen it. "Isn't it grand?" She held her hands out and turned, her robes swirled around her. "Did Trudy Wells tell you what we're using this building for?"

"No, I've never met Ms. Wells, although my boss had. He asked me to handle the execution of the estate."

"Oh, Trudy was an angel on earth," Sister Bernadette sang as she led Jude to the front of the building.

The nun from the roof walked toward Jude in a cloud of dust, wearing faded jeans, a dirty chambray shirt, and steel-toed construction boots. "Hi, I'm Elizabeth. You must be Jude."

Sister Bernadette interrupted. "Saint Jude! You know, he's the patron saint of lost causes."

"Yes, I know. My mother's favorite." Jude clutched her briefcase to her chest.

"How special." Sister Bernadette clapped with the enthusiasm of a child meeting Santa.

Sister Elizabeth offered a grimy hand. "It's nice to meet you."

Jude took the nun's hand and looked closely at her. Graying hair was cropped short, and fine laugh lines creased her expressive eyes. She seemed at home in dirty work clothes.

"You know, I'd never imagined a nun working construction," Jude said.

"Oh, we all have our talents." Sister Elizabeth gulped a cup of water offered by Bernadette. "Our order has Sister Doctor, Sister Car Mechanic, Sister Electrician, and, of course, Sister CPA, who will be helping us with the money Trudy so generously left. Nuns were saturating the market on nursing and teaching, so we thought we'd diversify our education and our talents." Her eyes twinkled as she talked. "Come on, let's find a cool place to sit."

Jude's silk suit and high heels were painfully out of place as she stumbled over broken pieces of wood and brick. "My boss, Drew Winslow, asked me to come to you every month with the structured payments," she said, as she tripped over a broken chunk of cement. "I guess Ms. Wells wants the money paid out in person and over time."

Sister Elizabeth strode ahead. "She wanted to make sure this project was a go before she gave us the whole sum. She was also concerned about other groups laying claim to it." The nun turned to Jude. "This organization meant a lot to her."

Jude read a sign at the entrance to the site. A broken piece of plywood hand-painted with a cross and neat block letters spelled THE MAGDALENE HOME. "What will the building be used for?" Jude asked as her heel caught in a hole and twisted her ankle. "Dammit! These shoes…Oh, I'm sorry, Sister." Jude rubbed her sore leg.

Sister Elizabeth laughed and waited for Jude. "Don't apologize. I'm sure I've said worse after hammering a finger or two. Thankfully, God is not only forgiving, but He also has a sense of humor. I think that's why He invented high heels." Sister Elizabeth raised an eyebrow at Jude's shoes." She turned and began walking again, too brisk a pace for Jude's heels. "To answer your question," the nun said, "this home is being constructed as a halfway house to rehab former prostitutes and sexual assault victims. The sisters plan to offer shelter and education, as well as counseling to build up the women's self-esteem."

"That would be Sister Psychologist?" Jude limped along beside her.

"Right." Sister Elizabeth laughed again and took a long drink of water. She surveyed the building. "Ms. Wells had a special place in her heart for girls in need."

"Really." Jude's feet throbbed with pain and her expensive stockings were shredded.

Sister Elizabeth shrugged and threw her cup in a trashcan. "She felt sympathy with women struggling to get off the streets. Especially ones who had kids taken from them."

Even in the oppressive hundred-degree heat, Judith felt a cold chill tingle down her spine remembering the night her own child was pulled from her arms.

Sister Elizabeth continued, "Trudy saw firsthand how quickly a woman might wind up selling herself. She became a very wealthy businesswoman and decided to help them. Pretty amazing, huh?"

"Yeah, amazing." Jude's lunch curdled in her stomach. She looked away.

"Hey, are you okay?"

"I'm fine. I think the heat and these heels are getting to me."

"Come on, let's get you out of the sun." Sister Elizabeth took Jude by the arm and walked her around the front of the building. As they passed the entrance, Jude again read the bold print on the homemade sign. THE MAGDALENE HOME. Mary Magdalene, Jude thought, wayward woman or a trusted disciple of Jesus?

Sweat trickled down Jude's back and soaked through her delicate shirt. Why had Trudy Well's path crossed with hers? Jude was not prepared for her past to rear its ugly head. No, she'd worked too long and too hard and wanted to leave the remains of that life behind her.

Chapter 4
Seventeen Years Ago

When her water broke, Judith was getting out of bed. Fear gripped her because she thought she'd wet the bed and would be punished. Even though the coaching nurses told the girls this would happen, it was still a surprise. She felt sweaty, hot, and sticky. August in Texas was, she imagined, how the devil set the thermostat in hell. The heat and humidity could bring her to her knees.

She was in a home, *no* an institution, that took care of "girls like her:" The Aurora Home for Unwed Mothers. This was a place where "nice Catholic girls" went to have a baby. Even now, when high school students were openly attending classes with bulging bellies, Judith's parents sent her here. Her father had dropped her off, alone, at Grand Central Station seven months before. Judith vowed never to see her family again. She still couldn't believe her mom would allow her to get on that train, to abandon her. Her good Catholic mother only told her to go, have the baby and come home. Her mother's spirit and body had been shattered too many times to question Jude's father.

Obedience was easier.

Judith turned, quickly pulled the sheets off the bed, and felt a warm trickle of fluid course down her leg. It was early and no one was up yet. As she bent to bundle the linens, her baby moved, seemed to turn completely around in her.

"Soon, baby. Soon." Judith patted her round abdomen. She'd talked to her child throughout the pregnancy. After the first flutter, the hate she'd had for the pregnancy vanished and she began to feel love. Now, she didn't want to give her up. She feared the lifeline of the umbilical cord being cut from her protective womb, leaving her newborn alone. Motherless. Papers had been signed for adoption early. Now Judith felt part of this child.

A girl.

When Judith saw her baby's hand flutter on the sonogram, all five fingers waving, she fell in love. The thought of handing over her perfect child terrified her. But so did taking care of her.

Judith had never questioned parental or school authority but while staying in this place she'd considered ways to escape—just her and the baby. Now the wet warmth of amniotic fluid spilling out told her it was too late. Judith hadn't acted on her dream, never knew how, she just complied like the good girl she'd always been. Waited to let things happen for fear of rocking the boat. She'd hoped her daughter would give her the strength to fight back.

"It's not laundry day, why are you stripping the bed?" Her roommate turned toward Judith a protective hand rested over her distended abdomen.

"My water broke." Judith cried quietly. "I'm scared, I don't want to give up my baby."

"Let me get someone!" The girl moved as quickly as her seven-month bulge allowed, rolling out of bed, barely landing on her feet.

"No, wait." Judith hugged the wet sheets close. "I'm not ready."

"Too late for that. Are you cramping?"

Judith shook her head. "It doesn't hurt."

She hurried from the room as Judith called after her, "Don't leave me alone."

∽∾∽

The hospital room was ugly. Linoleum floors had been scrubbed to a dirty yellow. The walls were painted to match. Dingy curtains hung on the wall, and Judith wasn't sure there were windows behind them. A nurse instructed Judith to walk soon after labor began. Her plans for escape vanished when the first painful contraction hit.

The nurses mostly left her alone, occasionally checking to see how dilated she was. In bed, no position was comfortable. Constricting pain was mixed with fear and uncertainty. Who was going to adopt her child? Between the contractions, Judith knew she wanted to keep her baby.

A nurse barged through the half-opened door. Her uniform reminded Judith of an old Girl Scout dress worn a lifetime ago. The ugly green material hugged her plump rolls and was too short for her fat legs. "Let's see how far you've gotten."

As the nurse glanced at a chart Judith noticed a course mustache sprouted over her upper lip. She thought of her Italian aunts in New York.

"Your name's Judy?"

"Judith."

"Judy, what?" The nurse looked at the chart again.

A drop of sweat trickled into Judith's ear. "Jude, just call me Jude."

"That's a weird name for a girl." Hearing the nurse's Texas accent made Judith realize how far she was from home. The woman showed no kindness or gentleness as she pulled the sheet aside, exposing Judith. The nurse did a brief, rough exam.

"You're just about there. I'll check on a delivery room." She turned to go, leaving the sheet half covering Judith's legs.

"Can I get some medicine for pain?" Judith used a corner of the thin sheet to wipe sweat from her face. "It really hurts."

"Childbirth hurts." The nurse walked to the door and gave her a look that said maybe you should have thought of that before you got yourself pregnant. "You're too far along to get an epidural now."

Another grip of pain wrapped around Judith. She squeezed her pillow hard to fight off the contraction. "Please!" She sobbed. "It hurts." The nurse had already left the room.

The labor room was nothing but a surgery suite with pink-and-green wallpaper borders peeling at the edges. Judith looked around for something to focus on, but everything she saw was a medical tool. The lights were too bright, tubes hung limp along the wall, and a broken IV stand was pushed into a corner. A cart against the wall reminded her of an oversized toolbox. She pulled the sheet tight over her mouth, smelled the burnt dryer scent of it.

"This will be over soon." A gentle hand touched her shoulder.

Judith couldn't see who'd spoken. "It...hurts." Her voice came out staccato. "Please, help...I need to push."

The voice moved to her line of sight. "I know, dear. But don't push now. The nurses will tell you when."

Judith was shocked to see the woman was a nun. She turned away, reminded of the church, that night, the priest. The reason she was there.

"Hey, Sister. You're in the sterile field. Stand here and stay put." Another nurse, masked and wearing a paper hat moved the nun next to the head of Judith's bed.

"Of course!" The nun smiled as she moved out of view. She leaned down to talk to Judith. "Almost time now, dear. You can do it."

Suddenly, a pain hit that was so intense it knocked the breath out of Judith. She lost any sense of self; wasn't aware she'd cried out until someone shushed her.

"Don't push! The doctor's not here yet." The nurse who'd spoken to the nun squeezed Judith's leg.

"I can't help it. Ohhh…!"

The nun held Judith's hand tight. "Breathe, try not to push."

"Please, I don't want to give up my baby. My…daughter," Judith sobbed. "Help me keep my baby." Conflict spiraled through the pain. She craved the comfort of the nun but hated the church.

"But you're just a child," the Sister said gently.

"I can take care…" Before she could finish the sentence, a contraction grabbed hold of her whole body, the pain felt as if it would knock the life from her.

Judith pushed and screamed.

Chapter 5
Present Day

Jude fought the impulse to scream as she drove from the Magdalene Home. This place was too close to home. She'd never forget the images or smells of the institution she'd been sent to. She was fourteen and pregnant when her father put her on a train from New York to Texas with a one-way ticket. Jude had never felt so alone, scared, and worthless.

Sister Elizabeth may have thought that God had a sense of humor, but Jude never saw the amusement or reason for the pain she'd endured. Now, by some weird twist of fate, Jude was forced to work with a group of nuns delegating an estate for a woman with a kinship to prostitutes. Did God really think all this was funny? Did he chuckle heartily, years ago, when Jude fought the excruciating pain of labor? Had he been slapping his knees in delight when Jude heard the first cry of her newborn? Did he find humor in the fact she'd only held her child, drank in her scent for a moment before the baby was taken from her?

Jude's heart had long since shut down, but the past always crept back like a leech on blood. A submerged corpse, no matter how well hidden, rot and decay always float it to the surface. Jude learned it was best not to dwell, she only wished she could forget it. *Move forward*, her mantra.

By the time she pulled into her garage, it was almost nine o'clock. She wanted to burrow in her home, her cocoon, to escape the false composure she'd maintained all day. Hell, the facade she'd lived for almost twenty years.

Walking into her kitchen, she angrily threw her keys across the room. Her cat, Tommy, jumped out of the darkness and ran across her feet before scrambling down the hallway to a safe hiding place. "Great," she thought as she looked into the dark den for her keys. "I'll never find them." She took out the cat food and called for Tommy. "It's safe, you can come out." Jude filled his bowl with a heaping portion.

Her feet ached, her blouse was ruined, and she was starving. She debated between eating first or showering off the day. Instead, she decided to pull dinner out of the freezer to defrost and shower while her meal—a pint of Häagen-Dazs Coffee ice cream—thawed like thick gumbo. She walked to the den and stopped at the doorway. As she flipped the light on and looked over the shiny hardwoods for her keys, Jude figured they'd slid under her overstuffed couch. A piece of furniture that would be difficult moving. Too bad they didn't land under the rocker. No, that would have been too easy.

Glancing at her bookcase, her eyes rested on the statuette of Saint Jude, one that had been in her home in New York. Her mother sent it when Jude graduated from college, thought it would bring her luck. Jude leaned against the doorway and smiled. "Okay, Saint Jude, maybe you can help me find my keys before work tomorrow." As pagan icons went, Saint Jude seemed harmless. For now, he stayed busy holding a stack of paperbacks upright on the bookshelf.

She laughed. "Now I'm talking to little statues. Somebody help me." She headed to her bedroom for a hot shower, but before she made it to the hallway, she noticed a glint of keys peeking out from under the rocker. "This is too weird." Bending to pick up her keys, she gave St. Jude a sideways glance.

After a comforting shower, and clad in soft sweats, she checked the consistency of dinner. "*Perfect*," as she put a heaping spoonful in her mouth. Turning on the speaker of her landline's voicemail, she listened to messages. Her legal assistant, Katie, called to make sure she was prepared for her deposition against the trucking company tomorrow. Jude knew that she'd have hours more research for the truck driver's depo. She'd gone over witness statements and the accident report. All I want to do is enjoy dinner and go to bed.

Rick had called twice to let her know he'd bought enough Chinese food for both of them. She shook her head. Jude kept her relationships at arm's length. As soon as her beaus came too close, she flitted away like a hummingbird. Rick was an auger, digging too deep.

She took her briefcase and ice cream to the den and fell into her double-sized chair. Tommy sat in a corner quietly preening himself. He didn't look at her as she sat.

"Are you mad at me for tossing my keys?" Jude pulled out paperwork from her case.

Tommy glanced at her, indifferent, his bobbed tail ticked side to side. He'd lost it by some trauma when he was young. Jude wasn't sure how. The SPCA found him in a scummy home where dogs were bred for fighting. He was filthy, skinny, and sported a festering wound where his tail had been. Jude adopted him as soon as he could leave.

He was still neurotic, skittering away from any human contact except Jude. And even then, only at his bidding.

The one time her brother, Stephen, came to visit, Tommy spent the weekend under Jude's bed.

She arranged her files on the ottoman and began reading about the truck wreck. An eighteen-wheeler had run a stop sign and hit an SUV, the mother had been killed, decapitated by the carriage of the truck, but not before she pushed her daughter down on her lap, saving the child from the same fate. The girl was trapped under her mother's body for almost an hour before the paramedics cut her out of the mangled wreck. Initially, they didn't know she was in the car. It wasn't until she screamed that the first responders found her. Jude kept the photos of the accident scene sealed in a manila envelope. "I need to find a happy job," she said out loud. Tommy looked up uninterested then curled back to sleep, obviously still pissed about the keys.

Immersing herself in work, she put thoughts of the Magdalene Home out of her head. At midnight, she rested her eyes and recalled the meeting with Sister Elizabeth.

In an air-conditioned trailer, they had gone over the terms of the settlement. Though Jude had no experience with estate law, the agreement was easy to define. What Jude couldn't figure out was why Trudy Wells asked for her to personally deliver the structured settlement. Jude couldn't imagine why she was required to hand carry the monthly payments to the home. She'd never met Trudy, had only found out about her when Drew handed her the case. Apparently, Trudy had paid the firm a considerable amount of money and specifically asked for Jude to work with the sisters.

"Why?" Jude whispered, stirring the melted soup of ice cream. She decided to get a few hours' sleep before the deposition.

※

Though raw-eyed and exhausted the next morning, Jude managed to make mincemeat out of the truck driver during his deposition. He had a history of driving offenses, and the trucking company had been cited by the Department of Transportation for numerous violations of mechanical failures and doctored driver's logs. Plus, two eyewitnesses clearly saw the truck driver run the stop sign.

On the phone with Katie after the deposition, Jude gave her a rundown. "These guys are sleaze. Make sure you get the video transcribed right away. I want to shove this case up their malfunctioning tailpipes."

"I'll take care of it."

"What else do we have today?" Jude zipped in and out of downtown traffic as she made her way to the office.

"Drew wants to see you when you get in, and your sister called. I didn't know you had a sister."

"I don't."

"Elizabeth?"

Jude laughed. "*Sister* Elizabeth from the Trudy Wells estate. She's a Catholic nun."

"Oh, Jesus, I hope I didn't say anything to offend her."

"I'm not sure you could. What did she want?"

"For you to call her sometime this afternoon. What's the deal with this case? I've never worked on this kind of law."

"Me either. I'll have to dust off some old law books."

"Oh good, more homework." Katie laughed.

"Anything else?"

"Nothing urgent—except don't forget to see Drew when you get back."

"Okay, I'm going to grab a quick lunch, see you about two." Jude disconnected.

❧❧

As usual, Drew was on the phone. "I won't consider an offer until I get all the facts." He motioned for Jude to enter his massive, oak-paneled office. "Actually, Jude just walked in." He peered over his reading glasses at her; his expression indicated that Jude should know who was on the other end of the call. "Good, then let's set up a mediation soon." Drew rang off and smiled. "That was Jack Barrone, apparently, you scared the shit out of them this morning. They're ready to talk about settling the Carmen case."

"That was quick." Jude sat in a high-backed leather chair in front of his desk. "I'm starting the demand at five million."

"Barrone's going to flip. He'll say that's excessive because the mother wasn't making a lot of money."

"Tell that to her daughter, who, by the way, is dealing with some tremendous emotional damages. It's tough to go through teenage years without a mother." She tried to sound more confident than she felt, remembering her life as a foster kid.

"I like your tenacity, are there any hiccups in this case? Like the mother had a drug problem or slept with every guy in town?"

"No, and even if she did it shouldn't matter."

"It will to a jury, and Barrone will eat us alive with any dirt."

"Tell him I'll have our orphaned client in court."

"I intend to."

"Thank you. Is that all you needed?" Jude stood to leave.

"I also wanted to ask you about the Trudy Wells estate. Did you meet with Sister Elizabeth?"

"I went out there yesterday. Why in God's name did you give that case to me? I don't handle estate law."

"Trudy called the firm, said she'd heard of you and thought you'd do a good job executing the money."

"How had she heard of me?"

Drew shrugged and took his glasses off. "I don't know, maybe from the news on the aviation case. But, hey, she offered to pay the firm a huge chunk of change." He paused. "You'll also be responsible for some pro bono work with these women."

"Why me?"

"I'd have some of the male associates do it, but with prostitutes, they'll probably be more interested in pro *boner* work. Plus, I thought you wouldn't mind an easy case. Really, all you have to do is advise and counsel a few of these girls and deliver a check and a letter every few weeks or so."

"A letter?"

"Yeah, she has a file of handwritten, sealed envelopes with special instructions for delivery. Weird, but she's the paying customer. You know, Jude, it means a lot that your name is bringing in new clients."

"Even if I don't know what I'm doing?"

"You're doing great."

Drew's secretary beeped his intercom to tell him he had a call. "Okay, tell them to hold a sec." He turned to Jude and smiled. "I'll call Barrone and let him know you've dismissed me from the case." He nodded. "Follow your instinct, take care of that little girl. And keep me updated every step. I'm trusting you with this, it's the biggest case we have."

She left Drew's office thinking about representing these women. She didn't have time for this. Not with a full docket and the truck case, which required most of her attention. Jude wanted to settle this lawsuit with a bang. It was important to her career, and to the little girl.

She thought of Tiffany Carmen, the young child she represented, and tried to push down memories of her own motherless years. After her father sent her to "the home" Jude always thought her mother hadn't called because she was ashamed of her. Jude didn't find out until years later that her mother had fought so hard to find out where Jude had gone, she wound up in the hospital, beaten severely by her father. By that time, the baby had been born and Jude was living with strangers. After, Jude had no interest in going back to New York. Instead, she stayed in Dallas, became a teenage foster, and enrolled in school.

When her mother finally came to visit, for Jude's high school graduation, Jude was shocked by how much her mother had aged. Jude learned later the beating she suffered trying to find Jude had fractured her hip and shattered two vertebrae. She walked with a limp now, tilted slightly. The pain was visible, her face was different, strained. Jude begged her to leave New York, and move to Texas, but her mother wouldn't leave her other child and grandchildren, and, besides, Catholics don't divorce. Plus, her mother knew her father felt awful about putting her in the hospital, she knew he'd change after that. She just *knew* it.

Jude tried to picture her mother as a young woman, wanting to go out on a date with Jude's father.

"He wasn't always so…oh, I don't know, honey…angry all the time," her mother had once said.

When she was about nine or ten, Jude asked her mother how they met. Her mom leaned over the kitchen counter to slice potatoes for her father's homemade fries. He demanded a T-bone steak and fries every night. The rest of the family usually had mac-n-cheese or fish sticks. The fries smelled delicious, and Jude watched her mom shake the grease out of the first batch in a brown paper bag.

Sometimes she shook the oil sodden bag so hard, Jude imagined her mom wished her husband's head was in with the hot grease.

"My father was hard on me, so I was ready to move." She held the saturated bag thoughtfully and looked through the dirty kitchen wall as if she saw something Jude couldn't. "Your father could make me laugh. Plus, he begged me to marry him."

"How old were you?" Jude played with the plastic salt-and-pepper shakers on the table.

Pain flashed across her mother's face as she gave the bag another good shake. "Sixteen." She glanced at Jude. "Thought I knew it all back then." She smiled and the light came back on in her eyes. "You know, honey, you can do anything you want. Don't get married so young like me. Live some, then settle down." She opened the greasy bag and a puff of steam escaped. Then she looked hard at Jude. "Promise me you won't ever depend on a man for anything." She poured the fries on a platter and smiled bitterly. "Make sure you can take care and support yourself. I didn't even know how to open a bank account when I married him."

Jude refocused on her young client, Tiffany Carmen. She wanted to help her be strong. The child would carry the burden of loss, regardless of how much Jude settled the case for. Divorced from the mother, the girl's father was only interested in the money. He rarely saw her, didn't know "how to talk to her anymore." For now, Tiffany's maternal grandmother was providing a stable home. Jude felt a strange need to protect the child from the emotional devastation of living without parents.

Jude walked into her office, closed the door, and recalled the last time she saw Tiffany at her home after being assigned to the case. The girl came and sat next to Jude on the couch while she'd been going over documents with Tiffany's grandmother.

"You're pretty, like my mom." Tiffany looked away. "She had long hair too. Browner than yours." Tiffany glanced at Jude.

Jude wasn't sure what to say. "Thank you," Jude replied, uncomfortable with the affection. She was never sure how to act around children.

"Are you going to get the truck driver?" The girl scooted closer.

"I'm going to try." Jude put her hands in her lap. "To help take care of you."

"I miss her." Tiffany started to cry.

"I know you do, I'm sorry." Jude wanted to do something to make her feel better but wasn't sure what.

Tiffany reached out to hug Jude.

Jude edged back and patted the girl's head.

It often surprised Jude when people told her they admired her, that she seemed so together. Jude was glad they couldn't see her from the inside. She imagined an Escher-like maze with the path going nowhere.

Chapter 6
New York

Judith didn't have close friends in high school. Always on the periphery, she'd observe others giggling and talking. She wished she was able to join but was afraid she'd say something stupid.

Mary Toby, always demonstrative, waved her hands wildly. "Ewww, Monsignor Callen is such an old prick. Doncha' know he's always behind the altar whacking his weenie."

Judith wasn't sure what Mary meant.

"My parents saw him when they went to Rockaway. He was wearing a bathing suit. Yuck!" She screeched.

Grace giggled. "Gross, he's such an old geezer. He probably looked like a freckled hairy prune." The girls laughed.

Judith couldn't imagine the priest wearing anything but his holy robes. Was he even allowed to?

"I saw Matthew Roberts there last summer." Grace clasped her hands together. "He is *so* cute!"

"Did you talk to him?" Mary Toby asked.

"No, way!" Grace shrieked.

"You're such a chicken." Mary Toby looked at Judith. "So, who do you like?"

Judith, who hated to be singled out, shrugged. "I don't know."

"Don't be such a prude. Have you ever kissed a boy?" Mary Toby leaned close.

"No!" Judith was taken aback. "Have you?"

Mary Toby smiled and deviously addressed the group. "I'll tell if you tell."

Grace giggled. "You've kissed a boy? No way!" She looked around to see if anyone was listening, then squealed. "Shhh, there's Matthew now." She blushed.

Mary Toby stood up. "Watch this." She walked to Matthew. "Hey Matthew, ya wanna play dress up?"

The boy stopped. "Huh?"

Mary lifted her skirt and exposed her white panties. "Dress up!" She laughed loudly as she dropped her skirt down.

"Miss Toby, come here this *instant*."

Mother Superior's voice shot fear through Judith.

Mary Toby's head snapped around as she looked at the stern nun. "Yes, ma'am." Mary walked toward the girls to get her books.

"I said this instant." The nun stood tall, menacing in her long robes.

"I'm getting my books." She rolled her eyes as she bent to pick up her stuff. She whispered to the girls. "Can you believe the old bitch saw me?"

Judith was appalled. Mary not only showed a boy her panties, but she also talked back to Mother Superior *and* called her an awful name. Judith would be beaten within an inch of her life for even thinking such behavior.

The girls were silent as they watched Mary trudge toward the nun. Mother Superior harshly grabbed the girl's arm and pulled her inside the building. Mary shot her friends a look but also winked and smiled. *Winked?* Judith couldn't imagine not quaking in fear of the old woman.

She tried to calm her own trembles. Would she get in trouble for talking to Mary Toby? Judith worried about it all afternoon.

Later, Mary told the girls about what happened. "She paddled me with this huge stick. It still hurts like crap. I won't be able to sit down for a week." As she proudly showed the girls the red welts along the back of her legs, she pulled her skirt high enough for the world to see.

Chapter 7
Texas

For two weeks, Jude avoided calling the nuns. But as the date for a check drop loomed closer, she knew she'd have to deliver the goods. Jude called Sister Elizabeth late one afternoon. She flipped through files on her desk while the phone rang.

"Jude." Sister Elizabeth answered with a confidant, yet light tone. "I'm really glad you'll be helping our residents with legal advice, and I wanted to invite you to our open house next month—a sort of pre-Thanksgiving get-together."

"Thanks for the invite. But really, that's not necessary."

"I won't take no for an answer."

Jude dodged the bullet about the party by asking, "What sort of legal help will these women need?"

"For starters, one of the women, Sangria, is trying to get custody of her kids. I know she'll need to prove to the courts that she's sincere in her rehab. Do you think you can help her?"

"I've never done family law *or* estate law for that matter."

"These women can't afford an attorney, I'm sure they'll appreciate any help you can give them."

"As long as they don't get their hopes up. I may be slow

trying to figure out what's needed." Jude wadded a sheet of paper into a tiny ball.

"I'm sure you'll do fine. How about I get some of the legal documents to you next week so you can look them over. Then we can set up a meeting at your convenience."

"Okay. Let's take one case at a time, though." Jude looked at the pile of work on her desk and thought the last thing she wanted to do was take the time to give free legal advice to a group of prostitutes. But Drew made it clear she had no choice. If she wanted to make partner, she couldn't argue with him about the caseload.

Elizabeth's voice was cheery. "Thank you. I'll help with anything I can."

"By the way, how are you going to get the home ready by next month?"

"We have a wonderful contractor who has done an amazing job. And we have many volunteers paying off their guilt tabs. So you better plan on coming. You know Trudy asked I keep an eye on you. Make sure you're okay."

Jude put a hand to her forehead. "Who *is* Trudy Wells, and why is she in my life after her death?"

"What do you mean? I thought you knew her."

"I've never met her. I'd never heard of her until this case was dropped in my lap."

"That's interesting. When she asked for me to look after you, I assumed you two had a relationship."

Jude leaned her head back and closed her eyes. "No, we didn't." Again unsure about how she got involved in this mess.

"Listen, when we get together next week, I'll tell you about Trudy. Really, it's too bad you didn't know her. She was a wonderful woman."

"I'm sure she was." Jude hung up more confused than before. Every time she talked to Sister Elizabeth her inner balance tilted.

Jude remembered another nun from her past. Sister Agnes who, many years ago, had found her in the church, bloody and shaking from shock. The nun held her for a long time, praying in a soft whisper. *"Hail Mary full of grace. The Lord is with you. Blessed art thou amongst women and blessed is the fruit of thy womb..."*

At that time, Judith wasn't sure what "womb" was. Only knew it had to do with a baby. It was later she understood.

"...Now and at the hour of our death."

Part of Judith had died that day.

Sister Agnes listened to her, held her, took her to the girl's gym, and helped her clean up. She didn't say much, just continued to pray quietly for Judith as she gave her a clean uniform to put on. She walked Judith out of the church and whispered so softly it was as if a breeze moved the small sound from her lips. "I'll talk to Mother Superior."

Judith shook her head and cried. Sister Agnes took Judith's face gently and said, "God is with you. Give Him your burdens. I will help you here."

Judith tearfully ran home and tried to forget. Tried to convince herself it hadn't happened. Months later, in the confusion and terror of realizing she was pregnant, Judith went back to ask Sister Agnes for help and was shocked to find she had been sent to a convent in Central America. The black hole continued to suck her in. Mother Superior summoned Judith.

"Child, one must atone for sins committed. You may ask God for forgiveness, but you must do penance for the lies you've spoken. It is God's way of guiding you toward heaven."

Guilt. It had been Judith's fault.

The ring of her phone jolted Jude back to the present. "This is Jude."

"Come by for dinner?" Rick asked.

"I was up late getting ready for a deposition. The only thing I'm doing is going home to bed."

"Okay, that sounds good."

"Alone."

"Don't try to play hard to get with me. I love a hunt."

"Thanks for thinking of me as prey, but I'm tired."

"When will we get together? Sometimes, Jude, I think you're trying to avoid me."

"I've been busy." Jude did not want to get into their usual argument that he liked her more than she liked him.

"I told my mother you'll be at the wedding even if I have to blindfold you, tie you up, and throw you in the trunk."

"Was she impressed that was the only way you could get a date?"

"Jude, I need you to go."

"Oh, you know what? That's the seventeenth, right?" Jude remembered her conversation with Sister Elizabeth. "I may have to attend a work party that night." It seemed the lesser of the two events.

After a tense silence, Rick said, "I know how important work is, Jude, but I asked you a month ago."

"I know, but this case is important. Besides, don't you think you'd have more fun with your family and friends?" She felt like she was running a maze smacking into a wall at each turn." I'd just be baggage."

"You'd only be baggage if you were fat." He laughed at his joke. Then his mood shifted. "You owe me."

"Raincheck," Jude said. She wasn't sure why she'd started dating Rick. Convenience probably. He said he wasn't ready to commit—which appealed to her. But lately, he drove the relationship harder than she wanted. Like most of the men she'd dated, the closer she became to each, the more their insecurities surfaced. The more distant she became, the more needy they became. Each time one got too close, the door to her past opened, the raw pain ripping open her soul.

It was best to keep it small, far away.

Chapter 8

The next Wednesday, Jude met Sister Elizabeth for drinks and dinner at a Mexican restaurant. She was surprised when the nun ordered a Margarita.

"A Margarita? No water to wine?" Jude was relieved Elizabeth wasn't wearing her habit. Instead, she dressed casually in a black turtleneck and jeans. The only sign of her calling was a large silver cross on a chain around her neck.

"Nah, I'll leave that to the big guy. Thank God the Catholics can drink with the best of them." Elizabeth laughed and pushed a lock of hair off her face. "Really, most Catholics are not as stodgy as you think."

"I know, I am one. Fallen, perhaps, but I know the routine."

"I thought you might be." Elizabeth sat back in her chair and looked at Jude. Her gaze seemed to pin her like a butterfly splayed on a board. "Actually, I thought that's how you knew Trudy."

"You know, it's interesting, I'd never heard of Trudy Wells until she died. All of a sudden, she's become part of my life." Jude broke a corn chip and lightly swirled it in the hot sauce.

"I'm surprised." Elizabeth shook her head. "She spoke as if she knew you. But Trudy knew many people." Elizabeth ran her finger around the edge of the salty glass.

"Well, let's see, what can I tell you about Trudy? For one, she was determined at whatever she did. She'd dig her heels in, with spurs, and never let go."

"Why was she so dedicated to helping prostitutes?" Jude nibbled her chip as she talked.

Elizabeth scooped a chip loaded with hot sauce and crunched it before she answered. "She was raped when she was a teenager. Wanted to help women who'd suffered abuse.

Jude choked her drink down in one gulp and motioned to the waitress for another.

"Eventually, Trudy became a wealthy businesswoman and decided to help other less fortunate women get on their feet."

"Was she married? Children?"

"Trudy never married." Elizabeth, said. "She was young when diagnosed with ovarian cancer and couldn't have children. She adopted a baby when she was in her thirties with Bernadette's help. Trudy and Bernadette have been crusaders for the underdog since." She bowed her head as if in prayer.

Jude fearing Elizabeth would become lost in prayerful meditation over her tortilla chips changed the subject, "Trudy certainly did well."

"Yeah, Trudy's first restaurant opened in the early nineties." Sister Elizabeth segued easily from her reverie. "It became so popular she opened several more. Before she knew it, they were in practically every city. Now it's a national chain."

"I know. Trudy's are everywhere. The best chicken fried chicken in town." Jude sang their tag line.

"Then she invested well in the stock market and real estate." Again, Elizabeth ran her finger around the edge of the glass and licked her finger.

The waitress brought Jude a fresh drink. "How old was she when she died?"

"Mid-fifties. Much too young." Elizabeth shook her head. "I hate that her daughter will go through her adult years without her mother."

"Yeah, I understand." Jude recalled her teenage years alone, away from her mother. A foster family that took her in was okay, but Jude always felt as if she were on the outside looking in at their life. Jude didn't feel like she belonged with any group. She kept a guarded distance from any emotional attachments and immersed herself in school.

"Hello, is anybody there?" Sister Elizabeth waved a hand in front of Jude.

Jude snapped out of her memory.

"I was asking about your family."

"Sorry. My family? There's really not much to tell." Jude sipped her drink and folded the wet paper napkin that had been under the glass. "Irish Catholic father, you know, bad temper type. My mom is Italian, and beautiful, but lets her husband call the shots. At the expense of...oh, never mind."

Sister Elizabeth gazed calmly at Jude as if looking inside to read the rest of the story. "Are you from Texas?"

"New York, originally. I moved here when I was a teenager to go to school."

"Did you go to parochial school?"

"Yeah, until the ninth grade in New York. Then I skipped a year and moved to Texas. Went to a public school here, in East Dallas."

"And law school?"

"Southern Methodist University. I got in on a scholarship and grants. Did my undergrad there, too." Jude fractured a chip in the hot sauce, the questions were getting too close. Jude tried to shift gears. "What about you? What made you decide to become a nun?"

Elizabeth shrugged. "Many reasons. What school did you attend in New York? Maybe I know some of the nuns."

Jude laughed. "How would you know since you all change your names to saints? When I was young, my mother told me I was named after her aunt, a nun. I could never figure out why her name was Sister Claire and mine was Judith."

"We try to carry on the good work of our predecessors."

"It's like you're covering up your real identity."

"I can assure you we aren't covering up anything." Sister Elizabeth looked at Jude and smiled. "Nor do we hide behind our patron saints. Most of us are very committed to our work."

"I didn't mean to offend..."

Sister Elizabeth held up her hand, "I know you didn't, no offense taken. My skin is much thicker than that. Really, I love what I do, I get to travel a little, build, meet interesting people, and try to redeem them. I have learned well, Jedi." She bowed and laughed.

Jude couldn't help but laugh. "As a child, I'll bet you played priests and nuns instead of cowboys and Indians?" She sipped her drink and thought of her own childhood dream of joining the sisterhood. "Do you have any regrets about becoming a nun?"

"None." Elizabeth smiled. "I've been inspired by some great women. Sister Bernadette for example. She's dedicated her life to serving others. I hope to do as well as she." She bent to retrieve a large manila envelope. "Speaking of helping others, here's the information on Sangria." Elizabeth handed the envelope to Jude. "She's the woman who's trying to get custody of her kids. The paternal grandmother has her daughter, and a foster family has the son. Sangria wants to get them back. Can't stand having someone else raise her children. She doesn't think they're doing a very good job with them."

"Worse than a prostitute?" Jude leaned the envelope next to her chair without looking at it. "What makes Sangria think she could do better?" Jude couldn't keep the skepticism from her voice.

Elizabeth looked directly at Jude. "You have to understand none of these women ever planned on becoming prostitutes or victims of trafficking. They were forced to make money. Sangria did it for her kids."

"I don't mean to be unsympathetic, but I can't imagine she couldn't find another line of work." Jude used her fork to tear the wet paper napkin and said sarcastically, "It would make for an interesting career day at her kid's school though."

"Have you ever tried to support yourself, much less two kids, on minimum wage?"

Jude could hear controlled anger in the nun's voice. She answered the challenge. "Yes, I've taken care of myself *and* I busted my ass to get an education." She stopped short of saying anything about having a child but twisted a little inside. "Nothing was handed to me." She finished her second drink in one gulp. "I'm sorry, I have little patience with people who can't help themselves." Remembering her own child pulled from her arms and now, being obliquely compared to a prostitute made her defensive. The alcohol made her bold.

"Maybe you don't understand their lives because your bar was already set higher."

"How could you know? I managed with no help from anybody." Jude's guard was up, but she wouldn't tell the nun her story. "Trust me, it wasn't easy." Jude squirmed under Elizabeth's thoughtful eye.

"You're right, I don't know what you've been through." Elizabeth sat back in her chair, easing the palpable tension. "I admire you for accomplishing so much, and I hope to have the opportunity to get to know you better." The nun raised her glass for a toast. "To the Magdalene Home. And to new friendships."

"New friendships." Jude felt a flutter of hope, light and delicate. An inner desire made her want to confide in Elizabeth, unburden her secret, as if in confession. Or maybe it was the alcohol sparking those feelings. Good sense and years of experience reminded her it was better to keep quiet. Hide the past in her hardened heart.

⁂

Driving home from the restaurant, Jude was surprised she'd allowed her emotions to get so close to the surface with Sister Elizabeth. There had been a curious desire to tell the nun about her past. Damned Catholic upbringing, always feeling the need to confess.

Bitterly, she remembered when she was young and wanted to be a nun. She spent as much time as possible in the quiet church. It was her comfort. Being a nun had been her dream since she was seven when she watched *The Song of Bernadette*. Back then, she wanted to be just like Bernadette. Hoped and prayed that she, too, would see a vision of Mary. That was her favorite daydream as a child. There, in the church, she could get away from her family. Her life. She'd always felt safe and secure in the quiet sanctuary praying the Rosary.

That was before Monsignor Callen raped her. Before everything in her life changed. The colors in her rainbow dream pooled to a dirty gray.

Chapter 9

Jude's bed was heaped with most of the clothes from her closet. Tommy, displaced by her wardrobe, sat on a chair near her bed and glared indignantly at her.

"Oh, don't be such a sourpuss." Jude reached down and stroked his back. He responded by arching his back in ecstasy before grabbing her hand and biting. "Ouch! You little shit." She picked him up and scratched behind his ears, something he couldn't resist. "I'm gonna love you whether you like it or not." When he'd had enough, he squirmed from her grasp and jumped out of her arms.

Jude couldn't decide what to wear to the opening of the Magdalene House. Why was she stressing about her outfit when she only planned on staying for twenty minutes? Just enough time to hand a check and some legal documents to Sister Elizabeth.

The only item left hanging in her closet was a blue dress she'd bought in case she went to Rick's sister's wedding. Angry that she declined, Rick had called her daily threatening to bring a hot nasty blonde instead. Good, Jude thought, please do. Not only was she not ready to meet his parents but the ceremony included a Catholic mass. Too bad his sister wasn't marrying a Methodist. Thankfully, the Catholic event tonight was at the restored home and not a church.

As she sifted through the stack of clothes, she remembered the last time she'd been to a Catholic church. It had been a disaster. A college friend asked her to be a bridesmaid. Only nineteen, Jude hadn't thought twice about going. It wasn't until she walked past the altar that chills swept her body, and she suddenly felt exposed in the strapless flamingo pink dress she wore.

Looking for a bathroom, she went past a row of confessionals. When the light went red over one door, Jude stopped, held her arms tight around her body, and began sobbing hysterically in front of the wedding party. The mother of the bride, herself ready to jump out a window, hissed at Jude. "Pull yourself together. Don't smear your makeup. This is *my* daughter's wedding don't you *dare* ruin it!" Jude ran out, crying. Since then, she'd avoided any church. She had to, at least, make a showing tonight at The Magdalene reception. She would escape as soon as she could get away.

༺༻

A valet opened Jude's car door. She stepped from her car amazed at the transformation of the building in a matter of weeks. Light blazed from new windows, the brick had been cleaned of graffiti, and the arched doors of the entrance gleamed with fresh paint. Shiny brass letters over the door spelled out *The Magdalene House*. New shrubs and trees were freshly planted, and the air smelled of turned soil and wood chips. Incredible, she thought. God may have made the world in seven days, but this place was a close second for getting the job done. She grabbed the envelope for Sister Elizabeth from the car seat as the valet handed her a ticket.

Inside, the rooms were bright, clean, and inviting. The anteroom's floor was honey-maple and a high arched cathedral ceiling made it appear cavernous. Three large rooms opened from the foyer. Jude saw Drew speaking with Sister Elizabeth, who was dressed in black Dominican robes, in the wood-paneled entry of the dining room.

"Here she is." Drew's booming voice welcomed Jude. "Sister Elizabeth and I were just wondering when you'd get here."

"I can't believe how different this place looks since I was here last. I'm impressed." Jude accepted a glass of wine from a young woman who looked uncomfortable in a starched shirt, she seemed barely old enough to serve alcohol. "Thank you."

"You're welcome." The young woman turned to Sister Elizabeth. "Sister, I'm dying in this outfit. Can't I wear something more comfortable?" She switched the drink tray to her other hand and pushed a long lock of red hair out of her eyes.

"You're doing great, Bandee. These are our guests. I know you can do it." Elizabeth's tone was firm but polite.

"This is way harder than I thought." The girl turned in a huff and spilled some wine on her sleeve.

Sister Elizabeth watched her go and confided to Jude and Drew. "We asked some of our residents to help out tonight. We want them to feel as if it's their home."

"She doesn't sound happy about it." Drew said, eyeing her rear end as she sashayed out. He turned back to Jude and Elizabeth, seeming unaware they'd been watching him. "Did you bring the check?" he asked Jude.

"Right here." Jude reached in her purse and handed the envelope to him.

"Good." He gave it to Sister Elizabeth. "I also have one of Trudy's letters to read to the group whenever you think it's time."

Sister Elizabeth slipped the envelope into the pocket of her habit. "It will be nice to hear her voice again, if only in a letter. Give me thirty minutes or so, then we'll get the group together for a speech and prayers."

Jude glanced discreetly at her watch, had planned to leave before then. Elizabeth must have noticed the gesture because she said, "Don't try to slip out early. You should stay and meet the gang."

"You caught me." Jude smiled. "I have some documents for Sangria to look over and sign. I can't get any of her past records until she gives me permission. They're in the envelope with the check."

"Thank you." The nun squeezed Jude's hand affectionately. "Since you're so impressed with the renovation, let me introduce you to the contractor who made it all happen."

Elizabeth excused herself from Drew and took Jude into a spacious, bustling kitchen. A group of women were arranging food and taking trays of wine into the main party. "Has anybody seen Reece?" Elizabeth asked.

A statuesque black woman with the face of a fashion model spoke up from behind a tray of appetizers. "Yeah, I see him every night in my dreams." She laughed and popped a stuffed mushroom in her mouth.

"Sangria, you're welcome to eat, but save some for our guests." Elizabeth went to her, rearranged the tray, and gave it to Sangria. "Go hand these out. Then later I want you to talk to our friend, Jude."

"Okay. I'm going. I'm going to find Reece first and see if he'll let me eat these off his body."

"Just save some for the company," Sister Elizabeth said, unfazed by her remarks.

"That's Sangria? Jude asked. "She's not what I imagined."

Elizabeth smiled and shook her head as she watched Sangria squeeze into the crowd of people. "She's a gifted singer. Unfortunately, it was easier for her to be a prostitute. She's got two small children who need her." Elizabeth watched her offer food to the guests. "She's trying. I hope you can help her."

Jude looked at the beautiful woman and wondered how she became a prostitute. What event made her turn? Jude remembered how hard it was to finish school and realized, with a sharp level of discomfort, she wasn't far removed from these women. "How many live here?"

"So far, we have five. Sangria and Bandee," Elizabeth looked toward the woman who served Jude's wine, "were the first to move in. I'll introduce some of the others when we see them."

"Bandee, Sangria? Are those professional names?"

"Actually, no, those are real."

"How long are they here?" Jude picked up a mushroom from the pan sitting on the counter and popped it into her mouth.

"We give the women time to find direction, look for work, or start school. I know some will start the program but wind up back on the streets. But we're here for those souls who work to save themselves."

They'd walked through the massive kitchen and a stunning refinished oak-paneled breakfast nook.

"This house is beautiful. Elegant. I would never have imagined it was possible after seeing it only a month ago." Jude stopped to look through a large bay window next to a dining table.

"This was a pretty fancy hotel back in the early 1900s. Luckily, vandals didn't damage the inside too much." Elizabeth stood with Jude and admired the room. "That, and having a contractor interested in restoration instead of demolition helped...speaking of great contractors." Elizabeth waved to someone in the next room.

A tall man with fine angled features excused himself from a group. Jude didn't want to stare but couldn't take her eyes off him. His hair was thick and dark, flecked with bits of gray. He wore a black jacket with faded jeans and looked as if he'd fit in anywhere.

"Lizzie." He gave Sister Elizabeth a hug. "Great party. I just hope no one flushes the toilets tonight, I'm not sure the plumbing was finished."

She laughed. "Just don't tell me the water fountain is really a bidet."

The contractor glanced at Jude as he chuckled at Elizabeth's joke. He raised his eyebrows and whispered, "We may have to pray to the patron saint of toilets."

The nun waved his comment off and said, "Reece, I want you to meet Jude Madigan. She's the attorney Trudy asked to handle the estate."

Jude suddenly became uncharacteristically tongue-tied. "It's nice to…um, meet you."

Elizabeth touched his arm. "Reece and I went to college together. He decided to get his hands dirty working as a contractor, while I decided to stay pure." She bowed dramatically.

Reece laughed. "Don't let her fool you about being pure. Believe me, I've seen dirt under her fingernails many times. The habit is a good disguise." He turned to Jude. "Elizabeth told me about you. You're helping with the estate?"

Jude blushed and nodded.

"She speaks highly of you."

"Really? I'm flattered." Jude felt herself staring into his striking blue eyes. For an awkward moment they stood together, not speaking. Reece looked away and put his hands in his pockets. Jude felt her cheeks blossom. She was uncomfortably shy.

"Can I have everybody's attention, please?" Sister Elizabeth asked.

Jude had been so engrossed in Reece that she hadn't

noticed the nun break away to make her way into the main room. Standing in front of an ornate stone fireplace, she worked to get the attention of the guests. Sister Bernadette stood near, beaming at her and the audience.

"We'd like to say a few words, give credit where due, and then let you all get back to eating and drinking." Sister Elizabeth looked radiant under the glow of the recessed ceiling lights. Flowers near the fireplace splayed in a colorful burst behind her. "I need Drew Winslow and Reece Cavelli, please."

As Drew and Reece made their way to Elizabeth, Jude couldn't take her eyes off Reece, as if he was a magnet. Jude never went through the "school-girl" crush stage during her teenage years. She had only been crushed. Now, any relationship she tried started with a big dose of cynicism. This immediate attraction to a man she'd just met was new.

"I would like to recognize Reece for his hard work and hefty donation of time and talent to get this place finished." She smiled at him. "I've known Reece for years, in happy times as well as sad. Our shoulders bear the burdens and joys of our lives."

Reece ducked his head, nodded, and put a friendly arm around Elizabeth. For a second, Jude thought she saw tears in his eyes.

"He put his heart and soul into this building and, I think, did a tremendous job. Reece, take a bow."

With his arm still around Elizabeth, he gracefully swept her backward into a dip. She seemed surprised at his playful gesture but kicked a leg out under her long black robes and laughed. Sister Bernadette clapped and giggled.

"And don't forget to take a bow yourself," Reece said as he brought her back on two feet. Any tears Jude thought she had seen were gone.

"Thank you for taking care of it for me." Elizabeth was

laughing.

"You go, girl!" Sangria cheered her on, her tray of mushrooms left on a table unattended. "C'mon, Reece, show her some *real* fun."

Elizabeth held up her hand and laughed. "No. I've taken a vow of chastity."

Reece blushed and looked down. He ran a hand through his hair.

Jude took in a sharp breath. He wore a wedding band. Figured.

Elizabeth turned to Drew and addressed the crowd. "Mr. Winslow, one of Trudy's attorneys, would like to read a letter she wrote for this occasion. I'm sorry she's not here to give the speech herself. She'll have to listen from above."

Drew moved to the center of the fireplace. "I didn't know Trudy well, although I wish I had. The more I learn about her, the more impressed I am." He reached inside his jacket and pulled out a letter. "Trudy left a series of letters for me to present during different events. I'm not allowed to open any of them until it's time to read them. Forgive me if I stumble over the words." He tore open the envelope, which bore a wax seal along the flap. Jude wasn't close enough to see the imprint of the seal.

Drew's deep voice began reading.

> *"Dear Friends,*
> *If this letter is being read, it means the Magdalene house has finally opened. Good. It has been a dream of Sisters Bernadette and Elizabeth, as well as my own.*
> *Thank you all for your part in this dream and for giving opportunities to young women who may need help finding their way. God has provided each of us with a gift of life. So, untie*

your bows and take advantage of the blessings put in front of you. Learn to move ahead to find a better life. Cherish friendships both new and old. I wish I could be there in body, not just in spirit. Take care of each other.
   Much love,
   Trudy Wells"

Jude looked around the room, many eyes glistened with tears. As usual, she felt immune and dry-eyed.

Drew folded the letter and handed it to Sister Bernadette, who was mopping a well of runaway tears. Reece had moved from the speakers and glanced at Jude. She caught his eye but looked away. Stepping back, she thought now might be a good time to escape. She'd delivered the paperwork and wouldn't be due back here for a few weeks. Perhaps, by then, the plumbing would be fixed, and Reece wouldn't be around.

She ducked into the kitchen, Elizabeth's voice fading behind as she headed toward the foyer. Just before they made it to the door, Drew blocked her exit.

"You're not trying to run off, are you?" he questioned. Your famous disappearing act?" Smiling, he took her arm and directed her into the dimly lit dining room. "Trudy left a letter for you." He reached in his jacket and produced another envelope. "You're sure you've never met her?"

"She left *me* a letter?" Jude couldn't imagine why.

"Here, open it now. I'm curious." Drew handed the letter over.

"Drew, this whole case is too weird." She waved the envelope creating a slight perfumed breeze. "Why don't you assign one of the new associates to it? I'm too busy to take this much time on an estate case." She shoved the letter into her purse.

"Do you need me to pull you off of other cases?"

"No. That's not what I meant."

"You're on this case..." Drew stopped when Jude's name was called by Elizabeth.

"Jude? Where did she go?" Elizabeth voice carried into the darkened room.

Drew pushed her gently toward the crowd. "Go. I'll see you Monday."

Walking to the entrance of the living room Jude resented the whole affair. She gave a small wave, and resolved not to speak to the group.

Elizabeth indicated for her to come to the fireplace, but Jude shook her head and stayed put. Awkward, as if being called on in school and not knowing the right answer.

"I'd like to introduce my friend, Jude. She's helping us keep up with the house payments." Elizabeth winked but didn't press Jude to join her. Instead, Elizabeth asked Sangria to come forward. "We have a talent in our midst, a beauty with a voice of an angel. Sangria, will you do us the honor and sing?"

Trying to swallow a stuffed mushroom, Sangria bounced next to Elizabeth, wiping grease from her lips with the back of her hand.

"I wanted to sing some blues, but they said I had to sing this song. I'm dedicating this to my babies." Sangria smiled. Then she bowed her head, took a deep breath, and began singing *Amazing Grace* with a voice so powerful the room resonated and echoed with its magic. Time seemed to slow.

Jude stood, transfixed. She felt a shell break inside her. Tiny, like a chick's first attempt to emerge from the shell. Emotion unlocking inside her, Jude fought down a cauldron of feelings listening to Sangria's mesmerizing voice.

"So beautiful." Reece's voice startled Jude.

"Yes." Jude wouldn't look at him but couldn't look at

Sangria in case she gave in to the tears fighting to escape. *Tears?* She never cried.

"I didn't mean to surprise you, I'm sorry. I was just leaving."

"I'm trying to slip out too." She checked her shoes to avoid his eyes. "The home is beautiful."

"Elizabeth is a good construction manager." Reece also seemed uncomfortable. "Um, it was nice meeting you. Maybe I'll see you again?"

Jude forced herself to look him in the eye. "I should be going. It was nice to meet you." She offered a wilted handshake.

Chapter 10

Jude drove home thinking of Reece and her curious attraction to him. It was bad luck he was already married. Besides, he would probably have turned out like all the other men she'd dated. Fun for a while, until a commitment was expected, then, as always, time to go solo.

By the time she got home, she'd dropped the fantasies with Reece and firmly resealed the protective shell that had begun to crack.

Leaving her keys on the dining room table she smiled, remembering them under the chair after throwing them in anger. Glancing at the clock on the mantle near St. Jude, she noticed it was still early, just after ten. Recalling an opened bottle of wine, she poured a glass and pulled Trudy's letter from her purse.

Settling into a chair Tommy jumped in her lap. She absently stroked him as she examined the envelope. The creamy linen paper bore a purple wax seal like Drew's letter. Looking closely, Jude studied the deep imprint of a heart with small flowers entwined along the border. She gulped a mouthful of wine and tore open the flap.

Dear Jude,
I'm not sure if my plans are falling into place as I intended, but I want you to know why I'm in

your life. You are probably aware by now I have ovarian cancer. As I write this, I am undergoing intense chemotherapy with the hopes of reversing this awful disease. I picked up the phone to call you earlier but couldn't muster the courage to go through with it. I'm always so tired now.

As we go through life, people offer kindness to others in many ways: a smile to a worn-out clerk, hot soup and a few dollars to a panhandler, company to an elder. The benefactor often receives more joy in the giving than the recipient.

Some years ago, you provided me with a kindness. I've meant to contact you to thank you directly. But usually, like today, I don't follow through with the phone call for fear you won't appreciate the gesture. Instead, I've helped you out in other ways. Because I was able to afford it, I've provided money to you for school through different venues. I've made sure you've had enough to stay afloat. I learned of you some time ago and wanted to help. From what I know, you have exceeded expectations and become an attorney. You should be proud. If my plans are being carried out, as I asked, you are handling the estate. (I hope you're comfortable with estate law, as I know nothing about executing legal issues.)

I'm sure all this sounds cryptic, but please stay close to Sisters Elizabeth and Bernadette. They are dear friends, and I'm sure you'll enjoy their company.

At fifty-one, I'm too young to suffer with this damned cancer. It's wearing me down. If the treatments don't work (and I guess they didn't if you're reading this), I know there will be much

> *I'll miss. I need to rest now. Thank you for your (anticipated) help with the Magdalenes.*
> *Fondly,*
> *Trudy Wells*

Stunned, Jude turned the letter over hoping for more information. The revelation that Trudy had provided money for her education shocked her. No, that couldn't be. Could it? Jude applied for scholarships and grants and always received more than she expected. And I thought it was because of my solid B average or my great personality, she thought cynically.

Kindness? This totally threw Jude. Had she served Trudy in a soup kitchen? Doubtful, the woman was a millionaire. Was she a rich auntie Jude didn't know about? Maybe Jude had met her at a fundraiser. She didn't think so, because she rarely became close to anyone and usually pulled one of her "disappearing acts" early in the evening. Maybe she was only one of many women Trudy helped. Felt sorry for.

Jude scooted Tommy off her lap and went to the kitchen. She poured another glass of wine, knowing sleep would elude her as she tried to figure out why she'd become a poster child for Trudy's cause.

Chapter 11

The next Monday, Katie buzzed into Jude's office. "Your sister is on the phone again."

"*Sister* Elizabeth?"

"That's the one. Do you want me to take a message? I'm afraid she's trying to convert you, and I don't want you slapping my hand with a ruler every time I make a mistake."

"Go ahead and put the call through. Then get me a yardstick." Jude heard Katie giggle as her phone rang.

"Hi, Elizabeth. That was some party on Saturday."

"We Catholics know how to have fun."

"I hope Sangria got a record contract out of her performance, her voice was breathtaking. I'm not often caught speechless."

"No, just elusive."

"Meaning?" Jude doodled dark circles on a legal pad.

"You left before we could talk. I hoped you could've talked to Sangria and helped her with the documents you left. That, and Reece called and asked about you." She laughed softly. "I told him I'd see if it was okay for him to call."

"What's this, you're pimping for the Magdalene House? Aren't you supposed to save girls from that?"

"Ha! I hadn't thought of that. Pimping? Actually, I'd prefer Madam. It sounds so much better for my reputation."

"All right, *Madam* Elizabeth," Jude couldn't believe she was joking with a nun. "Let him know I would've been interested, but considering he's married, I'll take a pass." Jude's pencil lead shattered on her pad.

Elizabeth became serious. "What do you mean? Reece isn't married."

"Oh." Jude fumbled for words. "You mentioned his wife at the party. I thought…and he wore a wedding ring."

"No, Reece is not married. He was, but his wife died a few years ago. I think he likes to keep the ring, to remember her."

"I'm sorry. Car accident?" Jude set her pencil down.

"No, complications from a surgery." Elizabeth sighed heavily. "I don't know if it's my place to tell you all the details. Well, I guess it's no secret. Megan, his wife, lost a baby at twelve weeks. They had to do surgery to get…," Elizabeth paused. "During a D&C the leg support broke apart." The nun's voice broke. "Megan's leg fell on the doctor's arm. He was using a sharp instrument, which perforated her insides. This is hard to talk about." Elizabeth sniffled. "She died a few weeks later from an infection and loss of blood. Reece was forced to make the decision to take her off life support."

"That's awful."

"Yes, it is." Elizabeth blew her nose. "Megan, Reece, and I were in college together. Megan and I were close friends."

"Were you already a nun?"

"I wasn't then. I hadn't officially taken my vows at that point."

"It's hard to imagine you, you know…"

"Normal?"

"Yeah. No, I mean." Jude dug herself deeper. "You know what I mean."

Elizabeth seemed to enjoy Jude stumbling. "Aren't you the sharp-as-a-whip attorney, able to think fast on her feet?"

"I was before you called."

"I didn't start my religious commitment until my last year of college, as an undergrad. The church helped with my master's. That's when I took my vows."

"Why? Joining a convent seems so archaic."

She paused. "I had a few bumps along the way. I was in and out of trouble. I finally met someone who persuaded me to join. After some false starts in school, the administrative dean in my order encouraged me to pursue engineering while I was a novitiate."

"But, a nun?"

"It was a calling and a true vocation. Believe me, I'd had my own set of problems, long before I met Reece and Megan. I found a few answers in the church. I joined after college."

"Does everybody involved with the church have some kind of crisis in their lives?"

"The church tends to bring people together in bad times. Both Reece and I were able to find some comfort here during Megan's suffering and his difficult decision to remove life support. It solidified our friendship."

"I see."

"You know, Reece has not shown an interest in anybody since he lost Megan. I was happy to hear him asking about you."

"You two seem to get along well. You know, comfortable enough for a relationship."

"I'm a nun."

"You can quit."

"No, I can't. It's my life."

"Are you going to apply for the Mother Superior position?"

"No, High Priestess." Elizabeth laughed. It broke some of the tension. "Can I give Reece your number?"

"I guess so. But I have my own set of issues. He may not want to get involved with me and my problems."

"Who doesn't have a cross to bear? It's how we carry it that makes life interesting."

"Yeah, well, mine is still heavy." Jude's joke sounded more serious than she intended.

Chapter 12
New York

Judith tried to stay away from Mary Toby, although she was fascinated with her brazen spirit. Where did the girl get the nerve to take on Mother Superior? Even after the dress-up incident, Mary continued to push her attitude to the limit.

Judith saw her giggling during an early morning mass before school. Mary huddled around a few other "bad" girls, and she pointed at Monsignor Callen at the altar. She made funny hand gestures, which had the girls trying to suppress laughter.

Judith saw it didn't escape the notice of the old priest, either.

Not long after Mary's dress-up punishment, an announcement was made during gym class. Sister Agnes quietly stood behind Mother Superior, holding a stack of papers.

"Girls." Mother Superior paced. "Beginning next week, the school will now require you to wear shorts under your uniform skirts." The nun looked regal, though menacing. "Sister Agnes will hand out documents that will need to be signed by each of your parents and brought back here by tomorrow. There will be no exceptions to this rule, and violation will result in a school suspension." She looked directly at Mary Toby.

Judith saw Mary sitting confidently, meeting Mother Superior's strict gaze. Mary sat cross-legged, her undies exposed, almost defying the nun to say something. Judith would've withered under a mere glance by Mother. It made her uncomfortable to watch the exchange.

Out of the corner of her eye, Judith saw a figure. She turned and saw Monsignor Callen hovering just outside the gym door. He seemed to hang around the girl's gym class a lot. It creeped her out how often he'd watch the girls while they stretched and exercised. Unconsciously, she pulled a hem over her legs.

"I'll expect these back first thing tomorrow morning." Mother Superior nodded to Sister Agnes, who began passing out the pages. "That will be all. Good day." She strode off, her robes drifting with her movements.

The girls stood up, many brushing dust off their bottoms as they gathered in groups. Some glanced at Mary, whispering, but Judith couldn't hear what they were saying.

"St. Francis is a sissy." Mary spoke to some of her friends loud enough for Sister Agnes to hear as she handed out papers. "I mean who would name a guy *Francis*?"

The young nun shot Mary a disapproving look.

"Mary Toby." Monsignor Callen's booming voice echoed off the gym walls.

Judith jumped.

"Report to my office after school today." The priest glared at Mary.

The few girls that had been standing near her backed away as if she were contagious.

Mary faced Monsignor Callen and crossed her arms. "Fine, okay."

Beneath the bravado, Judith could see the girl shaking, just a little.

The rest of the girls dispersed quickly.

※※※

Judith never knew what kind of punishment Monsignor Callen meted out that day to Mary. The girl just seemed different after, like a light had gone out inside her. After that, Mary rarely spoke to anyone in school. Sometimes the loudest are more easily broken.

Chapter 13

In her office, Jude hung up the phone before realizing she hadn't told Elizabeth about the letter she'd received from Trudy or set a time to meet with Sangria. She smiled thinking they had actually joked about pimping and Elizabeth being a madam. Jude had never spoken to a nun like that before. She thought of strict Mother Superior from her time in parochial school and tried to imagine that stogy old nun a Madame.

A tickle of excitement ran through her thinking about Reece asking for her phone number. Jude wondered if she'd unconsciously intended to leave the unfinished business of Sangria as an excuse to call her back.

No, Jude sighed and turned back to her work, trying to stuff the unfamiliar happy feelings down. It was probably not a smart move to become friendly with a client.

Jude, closing her files for the day, was surprised when Katie stuck her head in the office to say goodbye. It was after five o'clock, unusual for Katie to hang out after hours.

"I got the truck driver's depo transcribed. The mediation is set for December."

"Okay, good. My calendar was clear?"

"Uh, yeah. When is it not clear for work?"

"What's that supposed to mean?" Jude was taken aback by Katie's impertinence.

Katie took a deep breath. "Your whole life revolves around work. I talked to Rick's secretary today. She said he was really upset you didn't go to his sister's wedding. You went to that work party at the Magdalene House."

"Excuse me, since when is my social life so important to you or the office?"

"Well, you know what I mean…"

"No, Katie, I don't. It's nobody's business."

Katie looked down. "You're right, and I'm sorry." She glanced at Jude. "It's just that I care about you."

"Do I need to get the ruler?"

Katie smiled. "Maybe."

Jude's phone rang.

"I'll get it," Katie said as she started to her desk.

"Don't bother, go home. I'll see you tomorrow." Jude waved her off and answered the phone. She watched Katie turn to leave, steamed her social life was a topic of office gossip. Maybe they should solve their own problems before tackling hers.

"This is Jude."

"Hi, this is Reece Dawson. We met the other night…"

Her stomach did a backflip and her face flushed. "Reece. Sure, at the Magdalene House." She stood to close the door and noticed Katie, at her desk, watching intently.

"I forgot my…" Katie stammered.

"Bye." Jude didn't let her finish as she pushed the door shut.

"Is this a bad time?" Reece asked.

"Sorry, my assistant was just leaving." Jude wondered if he'd heard the door slam.

"I'm glad you're still there. I wasn't sure if you left at five."

Jude laughed. "Nah, I'll be here for a while. The sun's still up, I'm just getting started." She sat and leaned back in her chair. "I do have an antisocial cat that needs to be fed, but he can take care of himself for long periods of time. I think he prefers it that way."

He chuckled softly. "I spoke to Lizzie today. She told me you two had talked…"

"And that it was okay for you to call me?" Jude twirled her broken pencil as if playing spin-the-bottle.

"Something like that." There was a long pause. "Um, I was wondering if you'd be interested in dinner."

"I would."

"Really?" His voice rose slightly.

"Really."

"I'm not so good at the dating scene. Lizzie said she told you about Megan."

"Yes. That must have been hard. I'm sorry." Jude wondered what else she could say.

He paused before he asked, "Are you available on Saturday?"

"Yes, I've got nothing planned." Jude jotted the date in her calendar and thought of Katie's remark.

"Okay, good." He took an audible breath. "Wow, that was easier than I thought it would be."

Jude sensed a more relaxed tone in his voice. "We haven't gone out yet, I may still be hard on you."

"Hopefully, I'll be able to take you on." He sighed. "Seriously, this is difficult for me. I hope you understand."

"Sure." She smiled and thought it might be nice to find someone as emotionally screwed up as she was.

⁂

Jude spent the rest of the week working on the truck case. She set up interviews and meetings with the players. She knew the interview with the girl, Tiffany Carmen, would be difficult to get through.

On Friday, Jude was scheduled to go to the accident site

with a reconstruction engineer. He would map out the intersection and provide expert testimony as well as animation and charts of the wreck.

The afternoon was hot and humid, typical for late September in Dallas. Knowing she'd be walking on searing asphalt, she changed into a pair of jeans and sneakers she kept at the office before leaving, she stopped at Katie's desk. "Do you have the Carmen file ready for the expert?"

Katie handed her a thick folder. "This should be everything he'll need. Those pictures of her mother are awful. I can't believe that poor child was pinned under her for so long."

"According to the psychologist, she has no memory of it." Jude put the file in her briefcase. "If she's lucky, she'll never be able to recall it."

"You have a few messages." Katie held up a stack of notes. "Do you want them now?"

Jude put her case down and flipped through each message. "Most of these can wait. I'll try to call them back when I get in later."

"So, who's Reece? You know the other day when you answered your phone? I'd never seen you blush like that before."

"Didn't we talk about this?" Jude snapped, irritated that Katie was probing into her life. "They call it a personal life for a reason."

Katie threw her hands up. "I'm just trying to make conversation. You know, trying to get to know you. Geez, sorry. Rick's secretary called again…"

"You two can make up anything about me." Jude interrupted. "Just, at least, make it interesting." She softened. "I appreciate your concern, but my life is really boring. Why don't you rent a good movie or binge the Hallmark channel instead." Jude forced a smile as she turned to go. She considered talking to Drew about a new legal assistant. Problem was, she'd been through so many. At six months, Katie had lasted longer than most. Why couldn't she just do her job and stay out of Jude's personal life?

At the accident site, Jude waited for the reconstruction expert. Too hot in the car, she decided to walk along the grassy median at the busy intersection and take notes. She thought of the tragedy that had played out less than eight months before. With her phone, she snapped a few pictures of the area and the four-way stop the truck driver ran through.

In the tall dry grass near the street, Jude noticed a small white cross. She went to it as cars flashed by in a wake of hot air. The wooden cross was handmade with plastic roses, bleached from the sun, tied crookedly with a twist-tie. A child's scrawl had written: *I love you mommy. I miss you. Love Tiffany*. Jude drew in a sharp breath. When did her client come out here? She knelt and took a few pictures of the homemade memorial. A hard sadness chewed on her insides. She backed away and watched a few cars speed through the intersection. People were going about their business, unaware of the grisly accident and heartache that had happened there, under the wheels of their cars.

Life goes on, she thought. As does the pain.

Chapter 14

Jude tried to get the heartbreaking image of the little homemade cross out of her head as she got ready for her date with Reece on Saturday. She decided to dress casually in a pair of black slacks, so she'd be ready for anything. She was hesitant to allow a touch of happy anticipation as she waited. The phone rang and the door chimed simultaneously, Tommy dashed under the bed.

Jude quickly answered the phone.

"Hi, babe. Let's go out tonight. Mr. Happy is lonely."

"Rick." She cringed. "Maybe you and, uh, Mr. Happy need to schedule a few therapy sessions. Listen, I'm in a huge rush, I'll call you tomorrow." The doorbell chimed again. "I'll be right there." She yelled toward the door.

"Company?" Rick's tone was acerbic. "Are you going on a date?"

"I'll call you later." Angry he'd question her.

"Jude, answer me." His voice caustic.

"I don't answer to anybody. Especially Mr. Happy. *Ciao*." She hung up the phone and threw it on the bed. He reminded her of a kid that always felt the need to write his name on his toys before he reluctantly shared them.

She ran to open the door but paused and took a breath before she turned the handle. Reece stood on the porch looking handsome in khakis and a denim shirt. He held a bottle of red wine and a handful of flowers, nervously shifting from foot to foot. She wondered if he was as anxious as she was.

"Hi. Please, come in." Jude stood back from the door so he could enter. He handed her the flowers and wine. "Thank you." She was touched by his sweet gesture. "Should we enjoy a glass before we head out?" She smiled and glanced away timidly. "I think I could use one."

"Well, I'm so nervous I was going to bring two bottles, but I drank one on the way." He stepped over the threshold into her living room.

"Then I've got some catching up to do." Jude laughed, happy that he seemed slightly uncomfortable as well. "Please, make yourself at home." He looked better than she'd remembered.

"Nice place." Reece surveyed the living room and entry. "Was this built in the thirties?"

"Very good, 1932 to be exact." Jude's home was a small cottage in Highland Park.

"The crown molding looks original." Reece smiled shyly as he took in the living room. "I'd love a tour."

"Well, don't look too closely, this place needs some work." She headed to the kitchen to put the flowers in a vase and pour the wine.

Jude handed Reece the wine and showed him her house. He inspected the rooms as he followed Jude. "This is beautiful. I hate that so many of these homes are being torn down for those monster zero-lot-line aberrations."

Jude noticed he had become animated when he talked about architecture. "I know how you feel. The house next door was torn down last year. The new house completely blocks my morning sun. Now I just get a great view of my neighbor's kitchen." She turned and looked out the kitchen window. As if on cue, her neighbor brought a stack of dirty dishes to her sink. She waved at Jude through her window.

"See what I mean." Jude waved back. "C'mon, let's sit in the den."

They settled on her couch. Jude sat with her legs crossed and faced Reece. "Have you thought about plans for tonight?"

Reece nodded as he took a sip of wine. "Do you like Italian?"

"Love it. Especially since I'm half Italian."

"Really, with a name like Madigan?" He smiled warmly.

"I'm a mutt, really. My dad is an Irish mix and my mother's Sicilian."

"Your parents must have been very attractive." He ducked his head down and laughed. "Did I just say that out loud?"

"Yes, thank you." Jude blushed. "Your parents must be, you know, nice looking too." She looked at him and they both laughed, which broke the cloud of tension.

Blushing Reece said, "I made reservations at Sorrento's."

"That sounds nice. It's one of my favorites." Jude took a sip. "This is delicious, are you a wine connoisseur?"

"Not really, although I try to avoid the screw-top brands." He drank from his glass. "Elizabeth knows good wines. She and Megan used to go to wine tastings." He looked away.

Jude felt his mood shift like air. She said, "I've enjoyed getting to know Elizabeth. It's strange I'm making friends with a nun. I never expected her to be so down-to-earth and easy to talk to. I still keep waiting for her to make me fall to my knees, pound my breast, and say ten Hail Marys for penance."

"Have you sinned?" Reece's green eyes were radiant.

"Oh, I'm sure I could come up with a few transgressions. Believe me, I manage to punish myself enough without any help from the church."

⁂

Dinner was delicious, warmth flooded Jude from the wine and company. They'd talked non-stop throughout the meal, and she was more relaxed than she'd been in a long time. As they looked at their dessert menus, Reece's phone rang. He glanced at the caller ID. "It's Lizzie." Jude watched him talk while she nibbled on a piece of bread crust. Was it the alcohol that made her feel comfortable, or was it Reece? Whatever the pull, Jude decided to enjoy it.

Reece hung up the phone and looked at Jude. "I'm sorry to do this, but Lizzie needs help. It seems Bandee's boyfriend is causing some trouble there. I can drop you off on the way."

"Could you use company? I don't mind going."

"You sure?" He looked expectantly at her. "That would be nice."

"I need to talk to Sangria anyway. We'll make a night of it." Jude laughed.

Reece was quiet in the car. As they walked to the Magdalene house, he stayed close to Jude but didn't touch her. She was tempted to lean into him. "It looks like you spent a lot of time renovating this place." Jude stopped and gazed at the converted hotel. Feeling shy, she fought the urge to look directly at him.

"I enjoy bringing the beauty out of a building. About half of my clients want me to fix up their existing homes, but others want to start over." He turned to Jude and touched her hair. "I've really enjoyed tonight…"

They were startled by a shadow of a figure that ran, crouched, from the shrubs to the back of the house. The back gate slammed like a shot. Reece pulled Jude close, and they ran to the front door. "Get inside and have Elizabeth call the police." Pursuing the figure, he yelled to Jude. "Stay inside and lock the doors." His voice faded as he rounded the corner.

Jude's hands were shaking so much she could hardly work the handle on the heavy oak door. Before she could manage to open it, the door flew open and Sister Elizabeth stood ready for flight. They both gasped.

Elizabeth looked past Jude. "Did you see anybody?" She ran down the steps to the lawn.

"Yeah, they went to the back." Jude was still shaking.

Elizabeth stopped. "They?"

"Reece took off after him. Call the police! Is everybody okay?"

Elizabeth shook her head. "Don't call anybody, we'll handle it."

Jude yelled. "Reece could get hurt."

The nun walked to Jude, put an arm around her, and called out, "Reece! Come on back. Just let her go."

"Let who go?" Jude pulled out of Elizabeth's grasp.

"Bandee's boyfriend decided he needed her to make some drug money, so she hit the streets." Elizabeth started up the stairs.

Gravel crunched with approaching footsteps. "She didn't quite make it." Reece rounded the building with Bandee, her face covered in heavy make-up, wearing a strappy red dress, not happy about being caught. "Some guy in a Camaro took off when he saw me."

Jude was struck by how much older this girl looked in frosty blue eye shadow and dark slashes of liner than she did when serving wine at the reception.

Elizabeth stepped in front of them. "Bandee, you know the rules. If you leave here, especially to prostitute or do drugs, you can't come back."

She looked at the nun defiantly. "I know. But this place

is worse than prison." She stamped her foot, which was bound in a bright red, glittery stiletto. The high heel sank into the gravel with no effect. She looked down. "Besides, I need the money."

"What do you need money for? And where in heaven's name did you get these clothes?" The nun tried to push a fallen strap back on her shoulder.

"My boyfriend got 'em for me. He told me I looked beautiful." Bandee's painted eyes flashed. "I don't think I'm going to make it here. Me and him are meant to be together. Plus, it's too damned hard being good all the time."

"I'm sorry if it's hard, but we're trying to help." Elizabeth put her arm around her. "You know the alternative if you leave. Would you prefer the juvenile detention center?" She took the girl's chin and made her look Elizabeth in the eye. "Please stay, we'd miss you if you left. But…it's your choice."

Bandee looked away. "I guess here's better than there. Those bull-dyke officers there just can't wait to strip search me."

"Well, in that outfit, they wouldn't have to work too hard. Come on, let's get you inside."

Jude was struck by how gentle Elizabeth was with Bandee. The nun turned to Reece. "Are you okay? This isn't the best neighborhood to get lost in."

"I'm fine. Bandee wasn't moving too fast in those shoes."

"You took a risk running after them," Jude said.

"Were you worried?" He seemed touched by Jude's concern.

"It scared me."

"C'mon everybody, let's go inside before we become mosquito bait." Elizabeth who still had her arm around Bandee, walked to the front door.

Reece put his arm around Jude's shoulders. She held her breath, trembling at his touch. Jude hesitated but nestled close as they went inside.

In the anteroom they found Sister Bernadette, wearing a long robe zippered to her neck. When she saw Reece, she yelped and grabbed her flannel collar. "Heavens! I'm not dressed. Reece, turn around please." She took Bandee from Elizabeth. "What were you thinking, child? And look at that make-up! My goodness, Michelangelo didn't use that much color when he painted the Sistine chapel."

Jude watched the two of them walk up the stairs. Bandee could barely manage the high heels on the steps. Elizabeth ushered Jude and Reece to the kitchen.

"You guys showed up in the nick of time." Elizabeth pulled out a chair from the table. "Can I get you something to drink?"

"I'd love some water," Jude said.

"Make that two." Reece sat across from Jude and watched Elizabeth. "So, how many fugitives break out of this joint every week?"

"That was our first." Elizabeth opened three bottles of water and handed one to him as she sat. "I'm sure it won't be our last. If we can get half of these girls off the streets for good, I'll consider it a success."

"Why would she leave here and risk going to the juvenile center?" Jude asked.

Elizabeth shrugged. "Bandee was raped when she was fifteen—two years ago. Since then, it had been a contest for her to see how many men she can sleep with. It was a bonus when she realized she could get paid for sex. Then her so-called boyfriend sells her to make money for himself." She took a sip of water. "I've never seen anyone with such low self-esteem."

Jude felt a hard stab of recognition. Again she realized, by some twist of fate, she'd come out with her head above water. She wondered how thin the line was between her and Bandee.

Reece shook his head. "What kind of demon would rape a fifteen-year-old? That's sick."

"Probably a priest." Jude blurted out before she could stop herself. The mood change in the warm kitchen was like a bolt of lightning.

"Jude, that's not funny." Reece looked seriously at her. "This is a Catholic home."

Jude sat back in her chair, her face flushing. "I'm sorry…"

Elizabeth stared at Jude but spoke to Reece. "It's okay." She turned to Jude. "Do you care to elaborate?"

Jude shook her head. "No, I…it came out wrong, sorry."

Sister Bernadette, fully dressed in a prim skirt and starched shirt, waltzed into the kitchen with a clean-faced Bandee trailing behind her. "We decided to bake a batch of cookies. There's nothing like baking to clear your head." She twirled happily as she took out utensils and bowls.

Jude watched the young girl who looked incredibly vulnerable without make-up. She stayed close in Bernadette's comforting shadow. "I've never baked homemade cookies before, only slice-and-bake ones. Can we have chocolate chip?"

Bernadette handed her a bag of flour. "Chocolate chip it is!" She winked and leaned toward the teenager. "They're my favorite."

"We'll move into the living room and give you two the run of the kitchen. Just make sure you let us taste the cookies." Elizabeth stood and hugged Bandee.

Bandee looked down and her long red hair fell in her face. "I'm tryin', I'm just not sure I'm gonna make it here."

"I know you can." Elizabeth indicated to Jude and Reece to move out of the kitchen. They'd already started out of their chair as Bandee began pouring flour into a sifter.

Reece walked ahead, and Elizabeth pulled Jude back. "He really seems to like you."

Jude blushed and looked away. "I can't imagine what he sees in me."

"Don't be ridiculous. Why would you even say that? You're gorgeous."

"No." Jude shrugged and looked away, fought down the familiar feelings of insecurity, she diverted. "Something tells me Sister Bernadette is a great cook."

Chapter 15

"Reece, oh Reecie! I have something to show you." Sangria's voice sailed down the elegant stairwell. "You'll be so happy."

Elizabeth leaned in to Jude, "She's infatuated with him."

Sangria ran down the stairs wearing plaid men's style flannel pajamas and a yellow terry cloth robe. She looked tall and elegant in the casual ensemble. "Look what I got." She held up a cylindrical-shaped device then she pushed a button causing it to whir and come alive. "I have a whole set of these, and I want you to show me how to use them."

Just then Sister Bernadette came in, carrying a bowl with cookie dough and spoons. "Sangria! My heavens!"

It took Jude a moment to realize Sangria was holding an electric screwdriver.

Reece laughed. "Sangria, I'll be happy to show you how to use that." He winked. "I hope you have all the attachments for it."

"Yeah, I got the full set." She looked at Sister Bernadette, who was still standing with the bowl in her hands. "It's a screwdriver, Sister. It runs on batteries. You know, automatic."

Elizabeth rolled her eyes. "Bernie, you knew what it was, didn't you?"

Bandee came in licking a spoonful of dough. "It's kinda

small for what you thought it was."

Bernadette shot her a withering glance.

Sangria turned to Reece. "I want to make my babies a dresser. Will you help me?"

"I'd be happy to." Reece took the screwdriver from her. "You'll need a few more power tools though."

"Oh, honey. I got the power." She winked suggestively at him.

Jude wasn't sure how to react to Sangria's attraction to Reece. It seemed harmless, but Jude's hackles raised along her back.

Elizabeth broke in. "Sangria, you remember Jude Madigan? She's the attorney who's going to help you with the custody case for your kids."

"Yeah, I seen you here before. You're going to get my kids back for me? I hate that bitch woman who's got 'em now. She's the devil."

"Did you sign the papers I left with Sister Elizabeth?"

"I haven't gotten around to it." She flopped in a chair next to Reece.

"I can't help you until you sign those releases." Jude said, impatient with Sangria's flippant attitude.

"Sangria, why don't you run upstairs and get them now before Jude leaves." Elizabeth asked.

"'Cause I want to visit with Reecie." She batted her eyes at him.

"I think Reecie will wait a few minutes." Elizabeth pointed to the stairwell.

"All right. Whatever. Like I have time for this." She rolled out of the chair and managed to look seductive in her flannel pajamas. "I just hope I remember where I left 'em."

Jude's patience wore thin. Why should she help this woman who wouldn't help herself? "Look Sangria, if you want my legal advice, you're going to have to jump when

I say. Even so, I'm not promising I can get your kids back. It's important you show some responsibility." Jude chewed on her own bitter words.

"Who made you boss of the world?" Sangria turned and put a hand on her hip.

Elizabeth jumped up. "Jude, I know Sangria will be happy to do what's necessary." She turned to Sangria. "I'll come up and help you find them. This is important."

"I don't get it. I'm their momma. There shouldn't be a problem. Unless you're not a good lawyer."

"If you were such a good mother, then why were they taken from you?" Jude snapped, surprising herself with her harsh response. Jude managed to finish college and law school on her own. She had little patience with someone who wouldn't follow the rules to success.

"The cookies are ready." Bernadette had been listening. "Let's eat them while they're warm."

✦✦✦

On the drive home, Reece was subdued and quiet. Jude tried to make conversation, but even to her, it sounded awkward. "Those cookies were probably the best I've ever eaten."

He nodded keeping his eyes on the road.

"The evening was…interesting. I enjoyed dinner." She noticed he didn't look at her as she spoke. It seemed when things went her way, the rest of the world was out of sync. "Reece, is something bothering you?"

He pulled to the curb in front of her house. "No." When he spoke his tone was flat.

Jude didn't know what to say. "Are you upset because of the way I spoke to Sangria?" The warm breeze mingled with a small taste of autumn.

"Your coldness surprised me." He started out of the car.

"Do you know how bad someone must be to lose their children?"

They were halfway up her sidewalk when Reece turned to her. "I'm sorry. It's...maybe I'm not ready yet."

"Are you sure I didn't do something wrong?"

He ran a hand over his face. "Yeah, maybe. You know, that comment about the priest raping Bandee was out of line. It bothered me."

Her insides twisted. "You're right, and I'm sorry. It's just that..." Jude stopped herself. She was not ready to tell Reece about the old priest. Everyone she'd told had pulled away from her.

"And I didn't think you were very patient with Sangria."

The weight of his words settled in her chest. "Look, I'll admit it's hard for me to see a grown woman unable to care for herself and her children."

"She didn't have an easy life."

"Neither did I, and I managed."

"You have an angry streak in you that's hard for me to understand." He turned to face her. "You know, the church really helped me when I needed it. Even now, I rely on their support." The moon's light cast faint shadows from the trees.

"I would never expect you to doubt your faith. That's not what I meant."

He shook his head. "I thought I was ready to date again, but now I'm not sure."

"You're ready to forgo a relationship because of one comment I made? Now I think you're being selfish." Jude fought to stay calm. She didn't want the evening to end like this. If she was defensive, he'd hightail it.

Reece ran a hand through his hair. "I don't think you understand what it's like to lose someone. I had it all, a loving wife and a child on the way. My life was perfect.

Then, suddenly, it was all taken. In a matter of hours, my life changed forever."

"Do you think you're the only one who's felt pain and loss?" Jude's anger reared. "Maybe you should question God about taking your wife and baby." She turned and looked directly in his eyes. "I've crossed some bridges, too. *I'm* trying to move ahead, not hide behind a sympathetic church telling me it's okay, there's a reason for it, and only God knows why these things happen."

"Whatever you suffered, you seem to have come out of it just fine. Or you hide it well. You appear to be strong."

"Strong? I sure don't feel strong." Jude was anything but. She managed to get through each day like a beaten dog. Put her tail between her legs and fight when the bait was put under her nose.

Reece took in a deep breath and seemed to soften. "You're right. Maybe I'm just scared of my feelings. Somehow, I feel like I'm betraying Megan."

"It's called guilt." Jude wanted to touch his face but kept her distance. "I never knew Megan, but somehow I think she'd want you to be happy."

"I still need to take things slow, you know, sort out my feelings." He gently touched her arm. "If that's okay with you." They walked to her front door.

"It's okay." She looked at his face, hopeful. "It was a good evening, I hope we'll be able to see each…" Jude didn't finish her sentence, she saw Reece's expression quickly change, turn hard. Jude followed his gaze and stared dumbfounded at her porch, which was covered with flower arrangements. In the center was a ring of roses with *Rick Loves Jude* written in it.

"Oh, please." Jude was shocked. "Reece, this isn't what you think."

"What do I think?" He turned and headed to his car.

"I'm sure Katie, my legal assistant, is behind this."

"Well, *she* must really like you." His displeasure was tangible. "It really doesn't matter, does it?"

"Yes." She paused. "It does to me."

"Why, so you can pick and choose men on a whim? Like I said this whole thing has been really hard for me. I don't want to be in competition for a game I'm not sure I want to play."

"Reece. I promise Rick means nothing." She felt the edge between them sharpen.

"Well, he, or *she*, sure went to a lot of trouble for nothing." He stopped and looked at her, his face both stone and sad. He started to say something, but then continued to his car and didn't look back.

Jude sat on the steps, choked down an angry sob, and watched him drive away. Loss and pain balled up inside her, not sure which way to go.

She picked up the floral heart and tore it to shreds. Life was okay being alone, she told herself. She'd always managed to survive. But once, just one time, she wished she knew what it felt like to love and be loved. She threw the remains of the flowers in the bushes.

Chapter 16

The phone was ringing when Jude opened the door to her house. She grabbed the phone. "Jude Madigan, I mean, hello."

A deep voice moaned, "Oh baby, I miss you."

"Who is this?" Jude held the handset away to look at the caller ID. "Rick," she spat.

"I've been terrible since you've dumped me. Did you get my flowers?"

"Did you get my letter?"

He snorted. "Yeah, on your firm's letterhead. How rude is that? And your legal assistant typed it?"

"You seem to talk to her more than I do. Hasn't she told you how I feel?"

"What are you talking about?"

"I like to keep my private life private. I don't want Katie and your assistant to stick their noses in my life."

"I needed some relationship advice. You're like a wild lioness that refuses to be tamed. You keep your distance. Even in bed."

"I hope you didn't tell them that!" Jude stormed to her room to change clothes. Tommy rolled over from his nap, stretched, and yawned.

"I want to see our relationship work. I think we have something special."

"What we had was fun. Now it's time to move on." She

sat on the bed and stroked Tommy's back. "Rick, you deserve somebody that will give you more than I can."

"But I'm happy with you."

She wanted to scream, *get over it*. "Look Rick, I'm tired and going to hang up now." Tommy jumped off the bed and walked to the hallway.

"Are you seeing someone?"

"It's none of your business." She pictured Reece driving away.

"It damn well is my business if I want it to be."

"Rick, I told you upfront I'm not interested in a commitment. You were okay with that, remember?"

"That was before I couldn't have you. I feel like I'm on a hunt."

"Please find someone else. Okay? We were never about a long-term relationship." She took her shoes off and absolute exhaustion folded inside her. "Look, I'm tired. Let's talk another time."

"Katie said you're spending a lot of time with those hookers." He continued angrily.

"Hookers? They're our clients and are important to Drew."

"You don't even do estate law. It has to be something else."

"Whatever it is, it's none of your or Katie's business. Why don't you ask Katie out? You guys seem to have so much to talk about. No, never mind, since *I* seem to be your favorite topic of conversation."

"Barbara told me you dictated the letter and had Katie type it."

"Who's Barbara?"

"My assistant. Hello!"

"Sorry, it's hard for me to keep up with the characters in this soap opera."

"Don't be so dramatic."

"Rick, I've got to go." Tommy stared at her, obviously impatient for dinner. "You'll be fine," she said.

"I know I will, but I worry about you."

"Don't turn this around." Jude had gotten most of her clothes off but couldn't pull her shirt over her head with the phone on her ear. "I'll survive." She said a cursory goodbye and tossed the phone on the bed. As she finished dressing, she wished it had been Reece begging for her affection.

❦

The next morning when she arrived at the office there was a message from Elizabeth on Jude's voice mail. "I had a long talk with Sangria last night, she's ready to work with you. Can she set up an appointment? Call me."

Jude sat behind her desk stirring her coffee, enjoying the quiet of Sunday at the office. She knew little about family law. Maybe she could find an attorney willing to take the girl's cases pro bono and refer them out. Drew should understand. She had a quick urge to talk to Elizabeth about Reece. She dialed the nun's numbers.

Bernadette answered.

"Hi, Sister, this is Jude Madigan."

"St. Jude, how are you this morning?"

"Fine, thanks." Jude imagined the nun's perpetual smile, wishing she had half of the nun's optimism. "It was nice seeing you last night, the cookies were delicious."

"Bandee was excited about making them. Can you believe she's never baked from scratch before? Imagine!"

"I'm not sure I have either."

"That's a shame." Bernadette gasped. "You'll come over and I'll show you."

"Sure. Is Elizabeth there?"

"She is, and she wants to talk to you. You are an angel

for helping these girls with their legal issues. Elizabeth and I can handle their souls, but I don't know the first thing about the law." Her voice lowered. "Sangria really wants her kids back."

Jude heard Elizabeth in the background as Bernadette handed her the phone.

"Hey, I hope we didn't scare you off last night." The nun sounded energetic.

"Nah, I've seen worse." She started to ask if Elizabeth had talked to Reece but instead kept quiet.

"Sangria would like to come in and see you soon. Would that be okay?"

"Yeah. I'll see what I can do." Jude thought about how confrontational Sangria had been. She didn't savor another meeting with her.

"The reason she didn't sign the papers is because she was afraid of doing it wrong. She's not a confident reader."

"Why didn't she say so? It could have saved some arguing."

"I think it's because she needs to come across as strong. She doesn't want others to consider her weak."

"I wouldn't have thought of her as weak, but if she can't admit her problems how does she expect to get her kids back?"

"We're working on it. You know, we try to see the good in people. Although Sangria has issues, her heart's in the right place. She really loves those kids."

"Then how did she lose them?"

"CPS took them."

"They were *taken* from her? That's bad."

Elizabeth sighed deeply. "About a year ago, she was trying to get off the streets and decided to get a real job working deep nights at a nursing home. She wanted to be home during the day and spend evenings with her children, Jared was four and Angel six."

"Please don't tell me she left young children alone during a graveyard shift." Jude sat back in her chair, her gut twisting at the thought.

"She arranged for a sitter, a friend, to get there before she left. They'd had an agreement. This girl had a free place to crash at night if she'd watch the kids. It seemed to be working okay. But one night before Sangria left for work, the girl hadn't shown yet. They talked on the phone and her friend promised she'd be there within an hour. Sangria had no choice if she wanted to keep her job. The kids were sleeping."

"No *choice*?" Jude's tone was heavy with scorn "Did the sitter ever show up?" Jude noticed her hands were shaking.

"No. Apparently, the girl decided to stay out and party all night. Wouldn't answer her cell phone. Sangria was beside herself and told her boss she was leaving, this was about one in the morning, and the supervisor threatened to fire Sangria if she went home. Sangria gave it another hour before she finally left."

"What happened to the kids?" Jude knew if they'd slept all night the offense would've gone unnoticed.

"When she got home, there were police cars and fire trucks in the parking lot. Sangria jumped out of her car screaming for the kids. That's when she saw her youngest, on the ground, being attended to by paramedics." Elizabeth paused. "She was arrested on the spot, couldn't even get to her kids."

"Were they okay? Was there a fire?" Jude felt agitated just visualizing the scene.

"Her four-year-old boy fell off a second-story balcony. He woke up, managed to unlock the patio door in the apartment, and...he fell."

"Oh, no." Jude pictured the scene. "Did he survive?"

"Yes, thank God. He suffered a broken arm and was

hospitalized. Social services took custody of both kids immediately. Sangria has only seen them twice since then."

"I think that's twice too many." Jude sounded cold. She suddenly had a searing thought. What kind of parent had adopted her own daughter? Had she ever been left alone?

"Look, I know all this sounds horrible, and it is. But try to put yourself in her position that evening. She was really trying to get off the streets, the only life she'd ever known. If she lost that job, she thought her only option was to go back to prostitution."

"There are many ways to get help. What about welfare?"

"She didn't know how to get assistance. She tried once, but the forms were too hard to fill out, the instructions too confusing."

"Weren't there people there to help?"

"Not enough. And she didn't know how to ask. I hope the Magdalene Home, and your legal assistance, will point her in the right direction."

Jude blew out a breath. "I don't really know much about domestic law. Who has the kids now?"

"They're split. A foster family has Jared, the youngest boy. And the paternal grandmother has Sangria's daughter, Angel."

"Why wouldn't social services keep the kids together?"

"They wanted to, but her son has a different father. The grandmother couldn't take him but was willing to raise the girl. The kids miss each other as much as they miss their mom."

Jude was silent, a memory of her own abandonment flashed before her. She had no choice but to board the bus out of New York, alone and pregnant. There was no one to help her make decisions, so she was sent to Texas to give up her baby against her will. She, like Sangria, didn't know how to fight the system. Her plans to escape with her baby failed because she was too scared. "I'll see what I can do."

"Thanks. This means a lot."

"What's the story with Bandee? Did she try to leave again last night?" As she asked, Jude wanted to bite her tongue. She'd already committed to more than she wanted to with Sangria and was afraid to hear about Bandee's criminal record.

"Luckily, baking the cookies kept her at home with Bernadette. She came from an abusive home. Her dad beat her and her sisters, and she was raped by a family friend. So she ran away with her boyfriend, who also acted as her broker when they needed money. A friend, Father Dyson, recommended her to the Magdalene Home."

"Broker? I hadn't heard that term for a pimp before."

"It's one I understand they prefer."

"What happened to her mother? Wasn't there any family that could take her in?" I mean, she's only a teenager." Jude thought of her own family.

"No mother, only a drunken stepmother who cared nothing for the kids. Bandee got in some legal trouble after she suffered a vicious beating from her father. Wound up in the hospital but ran away with her boyfriend after meeting with social services. She wouldn't press charges."

Jude insides tightened.

"Her father told her if she left, she'd never be allowed home again—dead or alive." Elizabeth sighed. "Luckily, she has a strong spirit that he didn't break. She wants to succeed but doesn't know how."

Jude crumpled a piece of paper from her desk. Squeezed it as small as she could.

"I don't think she needs any legal help, but you'd be a great mentor for her. I know that may be too much to ask, especially with your busy schedule, but it could mean the difference for someone like her. Someone who still has a spark of hope."

"I don't know, Elizabeth. I've never thought of myself as a role model." She tossed the wadded paper across her office. It landed in the wet dirt of a potted plant.

"Didn't you say you put yourself through school? Maybe you could give her some pointers." Elizabeth's voice threaded with anticipation.

Jude thought of her family, the beatings, and being sent away too young to survive on her own. Could she have made it through school without Trudy's help? Just dealing with *that* new revelation was hard for her to understand. Where would she be now if not for help from others? At least she wasn't on the streets, alone being "brokered."

Elizabeth kept talking. "She already has her GED and wants to register at a community college. She's got what it takes but needs direction."

"Let me think about it, okay? I'm not a 'warm fuzzy' kind of person."

"That's not what she needs. Just spend a little time with her. The next time you're here, talk."

"Have her get some admissions forms from the college. Maybe I can help her fill them out. I'll even donate some money for her education." Jude felt better. No serious commitment, just simple advice, and maybe throw some cash at it.

"Thank you. Anything you can do will be appreciated." Elizabeth changed the subject. "So, did you and Reece have a nice evening? At least before we spoiled it for you."

"Not great."

"Why?"

"Well, it started out fine. But I think I offended him. I don't expect he'll call again." She wanted to confide in Elizabeth, but history dictated to proceed with caution.

"Offend Reece? How? He's so easygoing."

"Well, he left rather quickly." Jude gave her a quick version of last night. "I promise the guy who sent the flowers means nothing to me. I've been working to distance myself from him. The farther I try to get away, the more he tries to push in. Kind of like *Fatal Attraction*."

"You don't have a pet rabbit, do you?" Elizabeth joked. "Look, Reece has a pretty tough hide. I'll bet he was having a hard time dealing with his feelings for you. I think he likes you."

"Not anymore. At least judging from the way he took off last night."

"Do you want me to talk to him for you?"

Jude's heart jumped at the thought. "I don't know. I should be able to fight my own battles."

"This isn't war. Plus, I get the feeling you might have an impenetrable side to you as well."

I don t want to be a pain...well, okay, then, see what he has to say."

Chapter 17

With the truck wreck mediation a month away, Jude spent most of her time working on the case. She'd cloistered herself at home and at her office behind closed doors.

Jude stood over Katie's desk, holding a yellow legal pad with a list of tasks needed for the conference. "Katie, did you get eight-by-tens of the medical illustrations? I need them for the settlement brochure."

"I put them on your desk yesterday. It's the blue envelope on top of your inbox." Since the flower fiasco last weekend, Katie rarely looked Jude in the eye. Nothing had been said about it between them. Rick called Jude the next day and told her that Katie and his legal assistant had "this great idea." He'd given them his credit card and carte blanche. She knew they meant well, but she couldn't get past the hurt look in Reece's eyes. Jude's thank-you-but-we're-breaking-up-letter to Rick had backfired especially after she asked Katie to type it. Probably a stupid move Jude conceded.

Katie became more professional, which suited Jude fine. Jude was glad she never went to Drew with a request for a new legal assistant. Trying to train someone new in the midst of this case would have been a nightmare.

"Thanks. What about the reconstruction expert's report? I needed that today."

"I know. I've been calling his office since last week."

"It's all right. I'll call them myself."

"Do you want your phone messages?" She handed Jude a stack of while-you-were-out memos.

"Thanks."

"Will you need me to work tonight?"

"No, thank you. In fact, when this is over, you need to take a day off for yourself." Maybe she should try to be nicer.

"Really? Thanks."

Drew's voice chirped from her office intercom. "Jude, come up and see me before you go."

"Okay." Jude smiled at Katie. "Why don't you go ahead and leave a little early today."

"Are you sure? It's only four o'clock, we still have a pile of work."

"I know, and it will be here tomorrow. I'm going to shut myself in my office and work tonight." Jude looked forward to the staff leaving so she could enjoy the quiet and be able to concentrate. "At least after I see Drew."

As she headed to Drew's office, she glanced at the employees working in their low-walled cubicles. Most had pictures of their families or drawings done by their children taped to their walls. Jude swallowed a bitter taste and wondered if she'd ever know the joy of raising a child. She remembered handing her newborn daughter to the nun. "Take a deep breath," she told herself, "You're different from the rest of the world, live with it."

Drew waved her into his office. "I hear you're working your butt off on the Carmen case."

"I want to make sure we nail them." She took a seat across from him as he sat at his desk.

"Do you have enough in damages on this kid to justify all the time you're spending? I don't know how much we'll get on mental anguish." He picked up a document from a stack of messy papers and moved it to another pile.

"When they see what this girl went through, both physically and emotionally, I doubt there'll be any arguments on damages," Jude said, nervously picking a fingernail. "In fact, I wouldn't mind trying this case. Make public the trucking company's records. I doubt they'd be interested in the world finding out about their poorly maintained trucks and sleep-deprived drivers. I'm sure a jury would love to know who they're sharing the highway with."

"All right, but let's have a brainstorming meeting sometime tomorrow. I want to see what you've got." Drew leaned back in his massive leather chair.

"Sounds good." Jude watched the late afternoon shadows fall on the Dallas skyline from his office. "Call me when you get in, and I'll come up."

"Okay." He took his reading glasses off and rubbed his eyes. "By the way, Sister Elizabeth called me. She said you've agreed to help out with some of the prostitutes."

Jude was surprised Elizabeth would call Drew. "We spoke earlier today." She looked at her ragged fingernails and wondered what else the nun had said. "I'll start working on their cases as soon as I get more information. In the meantime, I think this truck wreck case should get my full attention."

"We need to keep the women happy. And use the law clerks for any research you need."

"Okay." She stood and turned to go.

"I knew I could count on you." He smiled, and the lines around his eyes crinkled boyishly. "Oh, yeah, I thought I'd let you know that Jack Barrone told me he wants to see you naked."

Jude whirled to face him. "What?"

Drew waved his hands. "Hold up on the sexual harassment complaints. It's because you've been such a hard ass on this case, he thinks you have testicles and he wants to see for himself."

Jude shook her head. "Maybe I should ask the same of him."

༺✦༻

After hours at her computer monitor, Jude's eyes burned with exhaustion. She was tempted to put her head down on top of the piles of papers on her desk and sleep. Instead, she looked out the window and tried to focus on distant office buildings. But only her reflection showed in the darkened glass. Like a goldfish in a bowl—safe in the confines of the bubble, but unable to survive outside.

Checking her watch, she was surprised to see it was almost midnight. Tommy was going to be pissed.

She leaned her head back and thought about the damages her young client Tiffany Carmen would suffer for the rest of her life. The kid was a train wreck. Only fourteen, the physical scars, slashes across her face where shattered glass sliced through her skin, broken ribs, and broken hip, had healed. The emotional scars would bore deep into her psyche for the rest of her life. Tiffany was fearful each time she left the house. Her grandmother said the child was afraid a part of the family car would suddenly fall off, causing an accident and more pain and death. Once, when her grandmother was fifteen minutes late picking her up from school, Tiffany ran to the office screaming hysterically that her grandmother had been killed just like her mother. She threw her backpack and shattered the school's trophy case. Every night she'd cry for her mother. The child blamed herself for the crash because they were going to her gymnastics practice when the accident happened.

Jude quickly organized the file for her meeting with Drew the next morning. As she stood to leave, she wondered if, maybe, she could make a difference in someone else's life.

Chapter 18

The next morning after her meeting with Drew, Jude pulled some of her old law books to look up custody cases. She'd immersed herself in reading and startled when the phone rang.

"Jude Madigan." She wondered why Katie didn't answer the call and was surprised to see it was lunch time.

"Jude, it's Rick." His voice seemed cold, professional.

"Hi?" She leaned back in her chair, not ready to get into an argument about dating. He hadn't called since the flowergeddon almost two weeks ago.

"Fine, thanks. I hear you're the attorney of record for, what's it called, The Magdalene Home."

"Attorney of record? I'm helping out with some legal issues, but…" She stopped, wondering why he would mention the home.

"You guys fixed it up pretty nice." His voice held scorn. None of the pleading lovesick tone he'd had before.

"I had nothing to do with the construction, but I'll pass along the compliment." Jude sat forward. "Why does it interest you?"

"That's why I'm calling. Do you realize how close it is to The Christian Academy? They're not happy about having a bunch of whores hanging around the neighborhood."

Jude laughed. "That's who was hanging there before

the home was renovated. As well as drug dealers and whatever else. In fact, I think if you take the time to cruise the streets nearby, you'll find most of the neighborhood pretty much the same."

"The place is a magnet for more whores. My clients are not pleased about that and want it shut down."

Jude sat straight in her chair. "You're joking. I understood The Christian Academy, offered support during construction. This is a non-partisan home. All denominations are welcome. What's the real reason you're interested?"

"I met with Pastor Rains. He's decided the home might be a problem after all. You know the church has a day care and don't want the kids influenced by the dregs at The Home."

"You're so full of shit."

"The church is willing to buy the property from the estate." He paused. "It would be best for all."

"Not for the women living there. Rick, why are you doing this? Is it personal? Are you trying to get back at me?"

"It's business. You know me better."

"Obviously, I'm not such a good judge of character." Jude wanted to slam the phone down but needed to ferret out his motive. "Why didn't they protest while the home was under construction? They were well aware of what the home would be used for."

"Now that there are prostitutes living there, they've seen an increase of action on the streets. They're willing to buy the home from the estate."

"Rick, you know that's bullshit. Those streets were a bigger problem before the renovation."

"Look, I'm just the hired gun here. I do what I'm paid for."

"Wait a minute, you're a real estate attorney." Jude

began to piece together the real reason. "I know why you want the property. The Academy wants to get their hands on it now that it's been fixed up."

"The Academy is willing to buy the property to get those women out of there."

"So they can cruise the same streets again—outside the gates?" Suddenly, keeping the home protected felt important to Jude. It was now a personal battle with Rick, but she needed to stall for time. "Look, I'll talk to the nuns, but I don't think they'll be willing to move. They're comfortable."

"I know how persuasive you can be, I'm sure they'll listen. In fact, I may be able to toss a bone your way from the commission," Rick sneered.

"A bone? Thanks, but I've got a craving for meat. Ciao!" She slammed the phone down.

Chapter 19

At five o'clock. Jude packed her law books and decided to take an evening off to run and think. Rick's call had thrown a curve ball, and she wasn't in the mood to concentrate on work. She was surprised by the sudden strong feeling to protect the Magdalene Home. No doubt because Rick had added a punch to it. How had he gotten involved with the Christian Academy? Did he seek them out?

Katie was still at her desk. Jude stopped by her cubicle on her way out. "What are you working on? It's time to go home."

"I'm just finishing the depo summaries of the truck driver. I'll be done in a sec. Are you leaving now?" Katie pushed her transcription headphones down to her neck. "You never go home before me."

"I am tonight, and I'm not going to do any work. I'm just going for a good hard run, and a big fattening dinner. My brain needs a break."

"This is a first."

Jude shrugged. "Every now and then I need to re-boot, clear out some clutter. I'll see you tomorrow." She slung her purse over her shoulder and left. At the elevator, she realized she'd left her briefcase in her office. But as the doors slid opened, she knew there would be something else to do if she went back. She walked onto the elevator with a group of people leaving for the day.

It felt strange being out of the building while the sun was still shining. The day was beautiful and the air crisp. November, her favorite time of the year. She rolled down her window and took the long way home.

೧೩೮೩

After a good stretch, Jude jogged toward Armstrong Parkway, a scenic route for her run. Later, she needed to call Sister Elizabeth to let her know about the Christian Academy's offer. A pang of guilt hit her as she wondered if *she* was the cause of Rick's interest to buy the place. No, it was too expensive a deal to use against her. He wasn't that vindictive, was he? She shook off the feeling and picked up her pace.

Dusk had settled, the sunset was a brilliant orange and pink giving the neighborhood a surreal appearance. Crisp leaves swirled under her feet kicking up a sweet smell of decay. She walked the last block home and enjoyed the invigorating weariness of her body. The evening was so pleasant and refreshing, she didn't want to call Sister Elizabeth and break the bad news about Rick's call.

In the kitchen, Jude opened the window over the sink and breathed in the brisk air. She poured Tommy's food into his bowl. He took a cursory sniff, swished his bobbed tail and eyed her with scorn.

"It's what the vet told you to eat." Jude put a hand on her hip. "And it's good for you."

Tommy responded by strolling into the den and jumping on the couch refusing to look at her.

"Don't play hard to get." Jude called after him. "You'll eat it when I'm not looking." She recalled the first time she'd seen him as a kitten. His eyes were plastered shut with an antibiotic gel, his ears were greasy with medicine and pocked with flea bites, and his tail-stump was wrapped with bloody gauze and tape. The vet at the SPCA didn't think he'd survive and tried to talk Jude into choosing another kitten. But when Jude picked up the lethargic, skinny body she knew he needed a home more than the others.

"I'll take him." She'd turned to the vet.

"*If* he survives, he might be blind and deaf. He's really sick." The vet shook her head.

Jude gently put him back under the warming light. "Tommy."

"Um, not anymore. I took care of that too."

Jude shook her head. "I mean, he's like the guy from the *Who's* rock-opera *Tommy*, the deaf, dumb and blind kid."

"Who sure plays a mean pinball?" The vet laughed.

Jude touched Tommy's matted fur and thought of the character who'd been traumatized so much he'd blocked out the rest of the world. She identified with him.

"Come on Tommy, don't make me feel guilty for feeding you a nutritious meal." Jude stood in the kitchen still holding the bag of food. He licked a paw, ignoring her. "Fine, don't eat, see if I care. You could stand to lose a few pounds anyway." She knew she'd eventually give in and feed him a few of the junk treats he liked so much.

Taking a cold bottle of water from the refrigerator, she checked phone messages and sipped as she listened. Elizabeth had beaten her to the punch and asked for Jude to call as soon as possible. There was a hint of panic in her voice. She'd probably already found out the news. Drew called wondering why she wasn't at the office. Her mother left a short message asking if she'd come to New York for Christmas. Jude wanted to hit the streets again at a full run.

Pulling a box of frozen spinach from the freezer and a box of penne pasta from the pantry, Jude dialed Elizabeth. She answered on the first ring.

"Hi, Elizabeth, it's Jude." Before she could say anything else, Elizabeth jumped in.

"I'm so glad you called. I just got a certified letter from The Christian Academy saying they want to shut down the home."

"I know, I just found out this afternoon."

"What's going on? They completely supported us to 'clean up the hood' or so they said. This blindsided me."

"Hang on to the letter, I'll come by and take a look at it tomorrow. Their attorney called me today."

"How did they know to call you? Nobody but us knows you're the trustee."

Jude filled a pot with water and set it on a hot burner. "I'm sure it's in the legal documentation. The estate attorney is not involved in the sale of a property. I know their attorney, maybe that's why he called me." Jude felt a pang of guilt, thinking of Rick's participation as she put her spinach in the microwave.

"Sale of the property? This isn't about buying the home. It's about, let's see what the letter says, 'residents of low moral character within proximity to the Church and the attached daycare'. Give me a frigging break."

Jude smiled at the nun's language. "Honestly, Elizabeth, I think the threat is a smokescreen because they really want to own the property now that you've renovated it."

"Can they really shut us down?"

"I doubt it." Jude threw some olive oil and garlic in a pan to sauté. "We'll still have to answer their requests—hit them head on. Otherwise, they can make life miserable. Do you know if they've bought any of the property around the home?"

Elizabeth scoffed, "How should I know? How would I have known to check? We're here to help women, not work on real estate deals. We've all worked too hard for the Magdalene House to see it whisked out from under us. It doesn't seem fair."

"I didn't bring any paperwork home with me tonight. Let me call you from the office in the morning, and we'll try to meet tomorrow."

"Okay. Speaking of paperwork, did you get the package I sent to your office?"

"No, what package?"

"Oh, no. I hope it didn't get lost. I called you and left word with your assistant to keep an eye out for them. It's Bandee and Sangria's criminal records. I was hoping you could help them get, what's the term, expunged?"

"I didn't get them."

Elizabeth made a nervous clucking sound. "Since Bandee is a minor, those records are confidential. I hope they didn't get lost. I knew I should've hand delivered them."

"I'm sure they're on my desk under a pile of papers. *I've* almost gotten lost in my office. I'll look for them tomorrow."

"Thanks. Also, Bandee has a stack of college registration forms for you to look at. She's really excited."

Jude strained the spinach and dumped it in the pan of garlic. "Maybe we can meet tomorrow evening so we'll have time to take care of everything. In the meantime, I'll find out what's really behind the threat from the Christian Academy."

"Bless you. I feel like a weight has been lifted just talking to you."

Jude felt the weight shift to her conscience as she hung up the phone. She strained the boiling pasta and tossed it into the garlic and spinach. As it cooked, she found a bottle of Cabernet and poured a full glass. Distancing herself from problems had always been a personal strength for her; she could look in from the outside and keep her hands clean. Now she felt a kinship to the nuns and "whores", and a curious need to protect them.

She thought it a strange coincidence that Rick suddenly surfaced on the other side of this issue. If he had a vendetta against her, why did he involve others? She tossed her dinner on a plate, took a big gulp of wine, and tried to forget about the problem for now.

෴

Driving to work the next morning, Jude knew she needed to spend the day on the Carmen mediation and not get sidetracked by any of Rick's real estate antics. She also wished, again, that she hadn't promised the residents of the Magdalene House to help with their personal and legal issues. It was too much to handle out of her safety zone. Instead, she felt put in the line of fire both personally and professionally.

Pulling into the parking garage she found a spot close to the entrance. It was early, so the masses hadn't arrived yet. Riding the elevator, a feeling that she'd forgotten something niggled at her. Probably the briefcase she'd left in her office last night.

Her door was locked, happy the janitorial staff had taken care of that. Entering the office, she noted everything looked in place, just as she'd left it—including the wad of paper in the plant. Jude quickly set out the truck case file and go lost in research. She decided to wait until Drew came in before tackling the issue with the Christian Academy.

The drone of office noise picked up as people arrived. At nine-thirty, Jude went for more coffee and to find Drew. She could tell he was in by the speed with which the employees were working. She stopped to talk to Katie on her way.

"I need to find out some information on real estate law." She briefly told Katie about the Magdalene Home but left any mention of Rick out.

Katie never looked up from her computer screen. "I'm still learning estate and family law. Now I need to look up real estate stuff?" Her fingers moved off the keyboard, but she still didn't look Jude in the eye. "Sure, I mean, I'm sorry. Just a little overwhelmed."

"Just have one of the law clerks bring me some cases about forced sales of commercial properties. I'll figure out the rest." Jude turned to leave. "I'm going to see Drew. Page me if you need me."

"Okay." Katie began to type again, her eyes glued to the computer screen.

Jude wondered what was bothering her usually bubbly assistant. By the time she reached Drew's office, though, all thoughts were back to business.

His booming voice greeted her as she entered his secretary's office. "Jude, I hope you enjoyed your evening off last night. I tried to invite you to join me for drinks with the defense side of your truck case, but you'd already left."

"I'm glad I wasn't available." Jude took a seat in front of his massive oak desk, feeling sheepish she'd left early the night before. "I think it would've been uncomfortable, consorting with the enemy."

He waved his hand. "Nah, this is how you get them to hit the ball into your court."

Jude made a weak attempt at a joke, "Are we playing tennis or trying a case?"

Drew looked over his reading glasses at her. "The more people we keep happy—on both sides—the better result we'll get." He shuffled papers on his desk. "Jack Barrone says he's ready for mediation. He also doesn't think you have the experience for such a big case. I told him he's wrong." He took off his glasses and set them on the pile of documents and looked at Jude as a father to a teen before a big game. "I know you won't let me down."

"I won't." Insecurity bubbled in her gut. She hated feeling like she was always walking into a dark unknown. She'd managed to keep one foot in front of the other. But knew, one day, the shoe would drop and she'd fall on her ass. She shook off the doubts. Jude would hold her head high and, as was her usual modus operandi, pretend to know what she was doing.

"I'll be ready to take him on."

"Good. Let's go over the exhibits. We'll have a meeting later this week. By the way," he picked up a single document from the pile, "I got a letter from Rick Carney. I understand he's working with the Christian Church trying to buy Trudy's Magdalene Home. What the hell is this about?" He tossed the paper on the desk. Floating, it landed sideways on his glasses. "Isn't this the guy you're dating?"

"No." Jude fumbled for words. "We went out a few times, nothing serious." She hated having her personal life brought up by her boss. "Actually, I wanted to talk to you about the Christian Academy's interest in the home. It took me by surprise too."

He glanced at her as if he wasn't sure she was telling the truth. "Have one of the clerks check on sales in and around the neighborhood." He picked up the letter and looked at it intensely. "Rick didn't tell you why this group is suddenly interested in this place?"

"No. I only found out about it yesterday." She wanted to melt into the chair.

"Jude, I don't know what these guys are up to by trying to buy this property. Do whatever you need to, to get these guys to retreat." He looked hard at her. "Make this a priority."

"Yes, sir." Jude felt the sting of dread.

Drew's words rang in her ears as she headed back to her office. Katie quickly hung up the phone when she saw Jude.

"Do I have any messages?" Jude's tone was curt. It was childish to take out her anger on her assistant, but felt a need to be empowered.

"I put some calls into your voice mail." Katie shifted nervously and arranged a pile of papers on her desk.

"Thank you." Jude leaned against her assistant's cubicle and looked directly at her. "Were you able to get information on real estate law?"

"Yes. The books are on your desk."

Something in the way Katie acted bothered Jude. "Is everything okay? You seem nervous about something."

"Me?" Katie laughed, high pitched. "No, I'm just trying to complete the file on the Tiffany Carmen case." She looked away. "I don't want to miss anything."

"Yes." Jude continued to observe Katie. "I've got a pile of work to deal with today, too." She turned into her office.

As she sat at her desk, Jude considered Katie's odd demeanor. She pulled out the heavy Carmen file and surmised, with mixed feelings, that Katie had probably found another job and was waiting until her Christmas bonus before turning in her notice.

Chapter 20

Jude walked into her dark house after a long day—and night. Before she could turn on a light her phone rang. She fumbled for the light as she grabbed the receiver. "This is Jude."

"You don't answer your phone by saying 'hello'?" Her mother's voice cut through her weariness.

"I worked till nine o'clock, my brain is still at the office. How are you?"

"I have some good news." She paused for effect. "Stephen and Frannie are expecting again! Isn't that the best Christmas present ever?"

This would be Jude's brother's fourth baby. She felt little excitement at the news. "After that many kids, isn't it called a litter?"

Jude's attempt at a joke.

"Don't be mean. My grandbabies are blessings," She admonished Jude, but her voice softened. "You know, you should start thinking about settling down and having children yourself."

"I tried once. You wouldn't let me keep it." Jude blurted.

"Judith!" Her mother's voice quavered. "It still hurts when I think about what you went through."

"I'm sorry. It's hard for me, too." Jude squeezed her eyes shut, tried to filter the pain, push it down. "It was a difficult time for all of us."

There was a long pause. "Judith." She paused. "Have you ever tried to find your...you know, your child?"

"You can barely even say it." Jude said harshly, she fought sadness and anger.

"How old is she? Seventeen?"

"Yes." Jude leaned on the kitchen counter and put her head in her hand. Her mother had never brought up her daughter before. Except, after finding Jude, to ask if it had been a boy or girl.

"Do you ever think of...that time? Of her?"

"Mom! I thought we weren't supposed to talk about it. Why all the questions now?"

"Honey, it's just that...she's my grandchild. Like a ghost though, she's there but I can't see or know her. As I've gotten older, I think about her more. Time does not heal all." She was crying, a soft sound, as if she was used to keeping her pain quiet. "I think of her every Christmas, but I've been afraid to ask you about her. You're an attorney, can't you do something legal to find her?"

"Why? So dad can beat the crap out of her, too? Why don't you talk to him about *his* grandchild, or better, his own daughter."

"Oh, Judith, I'm so sorry." She was openly crying now. "Things would have been different if I'd known. If I could've found you sooner."

"No, Mom, I'm sorry." Jude took a deep breath, remembering the severe beating her mother had endured when she'd tried to find Jude. "I shouldn't have said that. I know you would've been there for me." She tried to shift the mood. "But, thanks to Stephen, you've got enough grandkids to keep you busy. And they live near you. That's all good." She hated she'd hurt her mother. God knew the woman took enough grief from her husband.

"I'm sorry I brought it up." Her mother sniffled a little, sounded defeated. Like someone who could duck a blow. She changed the subject. "You know everybody will be here on Christmas. Can you make it this year? You haven't been back, and you've never even met Stephen's kids."

Age was evident in her mother's sorrowful voice. For the first time, Jude wondered how much longer her mother would be around. She wished she could forget about the rape. Bottle the memories, put them in a fast-moving river, like souls riding the currents to be lost in the ocean, and try to recycle the twisted life swirling in her. She also wished she could forgive the priest. And her father.

"Judith? Do you think you can come?"

Her mother's question brought Jude back to the present. "I don't think so. I've really got so much work." Jude wanted to ask her to visit Dallas but knew she'd be needed with the family and her grandchildren. It would be selfish to suggest it. "Another time, maybe."

"We're running out of time. You wouldn't believe how big Stephen's kids are. They'll be grown before you ever see them." She paused. "I understand. I just miss you."

Hard as Jude tried to be immune to sentiment, her words cut.

After they hung up, Jude made a quick turkey and cucumber sandwich, more for need and less for enjoyment. She dumped Tommy's food in his dish and checked her messages: two from Sister Elizabeth, two hang-ups—caller ID listed both numbers as "unavailable". It was almost ten o'clock, and she was too tired to open her briefcase. While she ate, her mother's questions haunted her; *Have you ever tried to find her? Do you ever think of her?*

Jude knew if her mother was aware how often she

thought about her child, how she desperately tried to remember those precious few minutes she'd held her baby, to savor her scent and touch, it would kill her. Before tonight, she'd never given a second thought to her mother's feelings about the baby. Jude intentionally stayed busy, filling the emptiness with work. She stayed on the fast track of her career and wouldn't give in to the painful emotions that fought near the surface, wouldn't give in to the sweet smell of her baby all those years ago.

She put her plate in the dishwasher and headed to her bedroom. As she reached for the lights, she was startled by a noise outside the French doors near her bed. Tommy growled and shot under the bed. Keeping the room dark, Jude breathed deep to calm her racing heart. A shadow moved behind the curtain. Jude's hand went to her mouth to hold back a scream. A man stood next to the glass door, silhouetted by the streetlights. She could only see his shadowed figure through the gossamer curtain. He didn't appear to be hiding. In fact, he seemed to be swaying, trying to stand. A drunk?

His bold demeanor angered Jude. It reminded her of the time she caught a peeping Tom at her window in her college dorm. She stayed calm, slowly took a baseball bat her roommate kept nearby and, with anger she didn't know she possessed, turned and shattered the window on the guy's face. She wished for that bat now.

The figure moved to the door and tried to open it.

Jude ran to her phone. Her hands shook so much she could barely dial 911.

The man knocked on a glass pane. "Jude!" His voice sounded slurred through the door. "It's me, open up."

The police operator came on the line.

Damn. Why was he here? Jude wasn't sure whether to send the police out anyway, hesitated when the operator answered. With everything going on at work, she didn't want to deal with being put on the police blotter and have this become public record. "False alarm, sorry to bother you," she said into the receiver.

Jude hung up but kept the cordless phone in her hand. She yelled through the glass. "Come around front, I'll talk to you outside." She kicked off her shoes. "You're lucky I didn't shoot you!"

"You don't own a gun, you hate them." Rick leaned into the glass. "Why can't I come in this way? I have some great memories of your bedroom."

Jude grimaced at the thought. "Better yet, why don't you call me at work tomorrow when you sober up. We have no business to talk about here."

"Yeah, we do. It's about those whores."

Chapter 21

Jude knew she should send Rick packing but couldn't pass up the opportunity to find out what was behind his motivation to buy the Magdalene Home. "Go to the front."

The night air was chilly with the threat of a strong cold front. She stood on the top stair of her porch and faced Rick. "What do you want?"

"You're not going to invite me in?" Rick walked unsteadily toward her. "Even for a cup of coffee?" He winked, an exaggerated gesture in his condition. "I really miss you."

"Why are you suddenly so hell bent on trying to buy The Magdalene Home?" Jude asked defiantly crossing her arms.

"I told you, those women of ill repute…" He swayed as he waved his arms in the air. It made Jude think of a conductor orchestrating music to have a seizure by. "Those women are ruining the fine neighborhood near the Christian Academy. They want them out."

"And you're involved, because?"

"It's my job." He reached the first step to her porch and stopped.

"That sounds too simple." Jude backed away. "What were you going to tell me that couldn't wait till morning?"

"Here pussy, pussy." Rick leaned closer looking toward the living room window.

Jude followed his eyes. Tommy was watching from the ledge.

"That's one weird cat." Rick stamped his foot, scaring Tommy from his perch. "But then if I had my nuts cut off, I'd have problems too." He snickered through his nose.

"You have enough issues." Jude took another step back. "Why are you here?"

"I came here," he swayed, and almost fell off the step, "to ask you to talk to the nuns. Make them go quietly. You're pretty chummy with them now."

"It's my job." She gave his line back.

"Well, I'd be worried about my reputation if I were you."

"Wait a minute. You tried to break into my home drunk and disorderly, and you're worried about *my* reputation? That's arrogant."

"Those women," he sneered, "all have criminal records. As if it's not bad enough they're whores."

"And the home is there to help them get back on their feet."

"Or back on their backs!" He doubled over laughing.

"When did you graduate from asshole school?" She stood tall.

"You know one of those bitch clap-traps broke into a church and defaced a sanctuary. The Academy doesn't want that to happen to their church. What was her name? Bandana, or something."

A jagged feeling sliced through Jude. "How do you know about that? I don't even have her records."

"They're public records, *hello*. You're an attorney, didn't you learn about that in criminal law 101?"

"Hello, she's a *minor*. How did you get them?"

"That's beside the point." He waved his hand and stumbled. "You know, Jude, I stand to make a lot of money on this deal. We could work together." He raised his eyebrows suggestively.

"Speaking of law school, does ethics class conjure any memories? I don't need the money that bad."

"Everybody needs money." Rick's loopy, drunk demeanor became cold and hostile. "You've always been interested in your career. Well, now's the chance to make a name for yourself. Unless you want to be associated with a bunch of prostitutes."

His tone reminded Jude of her father's scorn and hatred. She decided then to fight Rick with whatever it took to keep the home standing. "I'll start generating paperwork on this case and file a motion for discovery tomorrow. I'd like to find out about your sudden interest." She turned to go but stopped. "And how you managed to open a minor's sealed records."

"You're turning into a royal bitch, Jude." He walked up the steps facing her, any signs of drunkenness gone. "You might as well buy a tombstone for your career. Can you say, 'You want fries with that?' 'Cause that's where you're headed, or better yet, maybe you can get a job whoring with all your new friends."

"I'm not the one selling out."

He reached for her arm and she backed away.

Rick took another step closer. "I'm not selling, I'm buying." The evil he exuded was tangible.

Just then a Highland Park Police SUV pulled in front of the house. The officer stuck his head out the window. "Everything alright, Miss Madigan? We got a call from here earlier and thought we'd drive by."

"Thanks, I'm glad to know you guys are out there. I was just telling my guest to leave." She looked directly at Rick. "Now."

The officer started out of the truck. "I'll be happy to escort him to Central Expressway."

Rick turned and appeared sober. "That won't be necessary, sir."

Jude noticed he'd parked three houses up from hers. As she watched him jog to his car, she began shaking. It wasn't from the cold.

Chapter 22

Christmas cards began to decorate the office, though Thanksgiving was still two weeks away. Many of the employees had already started taking long lunches to get shopping done. Jude had a few cases to settle before the end of December, not to mention the Tiffany Carmen case needed her full attention. She knew insurance companies were more inclined to settle at the end of the year, so they didn't have to pay taxes. She hoped Katie was willing to work overtime.

Morning sun painted her office a butterscotch yellow. She loved the angle of the light this time of year, especially at sunrise. As well as the quiet of the office early morning. Jude sipped coffee, and pulled files from her heavy briefcase. Making a new stack, she began to sort through the other mounds of paperwork looking for the letter Elizabeth sent. Sure enough, she found it with her unread mail. It was opened, as all her letters were, and organized according to date.

Looking at the mountains of files on her desk, she realized how much she had to get done in a short time. It was overwhelming. She fought temptation to a strong "flight or fight" instinct, preferably the "flight."

"One piece of paper at a time," she told herself, and started easy, with the mail. Mixed into the pile she found a Christmas invitation to dinner at the Magdalene House scheduled the week after Thanksgiving, as well as a few early holiday cards and invitations to Christmas open houses hosted by various law firms. "How do people even start thinking about the holidays before November?" Jude wondered. A visual of Reece came to her. She took yellow Post-It® notes and put "decline" on most of the invitations, even though Drew would want her to attend for the good of the firm. She smiled as she wrote "calendar" on the Magdalene reception. She would give the stack back to Katie to respond to.

Finishing with the last piece of mail, she leaned back in her chair and savored her coffee. She didn't get much sleep last night, thanks to Rick's strange visit. She'd stayed awake for hours trying to shake off the image of his shadow through her curtain, and the evil radiating from him. Jude couldn't understand why he had such a strong vendetta against her. Why couldn't he fade quietly into the night like the other men she'd dated?

She set her coffee on the desk and opened the records of Sangria and Bandee. A few of the other resident's records were included, but they were mostly for charges of prostitution. No big secret there.

Sangria's file listed the crime of "child neglect and endangerment," and the enclosed police report summed up what Elizabeth had told her. Jude wondered if she should call a family lawyer who could help sift through those files. Bandee's records were sealed with blue ribbon and fastened with a gold adhesive seal. The file was marked "Confidential". Even though Jude had permission to break the seal, she still felt as if she were violating Bandee's rights. The gold label popped off easily. Too easy.

Most of the reports were for domestic violence calls to Bandee's home. Apparently, her father was a frequent visitor to the local jail. It looked as if the charges were always dropped, and he'd be released. There were medical records and a psychological report on the girl, where the counselor mentioned she thought Bandee's father was sexually abusing her. There was no doubt about physical abuse, but again, no charges had been brought against him.

Bandee had been cited multiple times for loitering and aggressive behavior toward law enforcement. The girl did have spirit and fight. Something Jude could've used when she was younger.

Jude began reading the file about the church break-in. Just as she read the first line, a shadow fell across her desk and startled her. Jude was still on edge from last night.

"I'm sorry, I didn't mean to surprise you." Katie walked to the front of Jude's desk. "What do you need me to start on?"

Jude put the document she was reading on her desk and noticed Katie glance quickly away. "I finished going through the mail if you want to work on that. Then I'm going to complete the PowerPoint presentation on the Carmen case. Is the file in order?"

"Yes." Katie answered. "The expert's final report came in yesterday. That should be the last of it."

"Good. And Katie, I know the holidays are busy, but you know how tough this time of year is. We're going to be pretty crazy trying to settle cases before January."

"Yes, I know." She gathered the stack of papers.

Katie seemed unusually formal this morning. "I'm reading the records of some of the women from the Magdalene Home, and I noticed the seal marked 'confidential' appeared to have been loosened, was it like that when it came in?"

Katie shrugged. "It must've been. I just pull the letters out and clip them to the envelopes, like I always do." She pushed a stray hair behind her ear but wouldn't look Jude in the eye.

"You probably know my files better than I do." Jude

smiled. "But I'm afraid of information leaking out of this office. Drew would have my head on a platter if opposing counsel ever found out our game plan."

"I know," Katie replied.

"Thanks. I'll run my presentation by you later to proof." Jude was struck that Katie didn't ask what prompted the question about the loose seal, she was usually the first to dig into everyone else's business.

"Sure." Katie turned and didn't look back.

Jude took another sip of her cooling coffee and went back to Bandee's file. What got Bandee into the Magdalene Home was an incident at her local church. It seemed she and her boyfriend decided to "covet" each other on the altar one night. The priest, hearing noises, went to investigate and found them in the act. Instead of pressing charges, he called Sister Elizabeth to see if Bandee could be put in the Magdalene Home. However, if she left the home, charges would be filed. That's probably why she was so willing to come back after her attempted 'breakout'. Jude wondered if this girl had been a working prostitute or had only made bad choices. Not surprising, considering her home life. She made some notes and attached them to Bandee's file. She'd set up a time to visit with Sister Elizabeth when she brought her the next check.

The rest of the day, Jude worked on her cases, dictating demand letters and culling through medical records for settlement brochures. By mid-day, she'd begun her presentation on the Carmen truck case. She needed to make sure every hole in this case was solidly plugged. Jack Barrone, the defense attorney, had an awful reputation for skewering and eating young attorneys. Jude did not want to be the appetizer.

Chapter 23

"Do you want to be the first to try the toilet?" Elizabeth, dressed in jeans and an old sweatshirt, curled around the base of a toilet at the Magdalene Home. Using a wrench, she tightened a bolt Jude couldn't see.

"No thanks, I'd rather not be the first to christen the john, especially in case the wires got crossed." Jude leaned against the sink.

Elizabeth lifted her head from behind the porcelain. "Wires? I'm not planning on electrocuting anybody."

"You know what I mean." Jude bent down to see Elizabeth's progress. "I wish I knew more about plumbing and electrical stuff. Now I'm at the mercy of any plumber who comes to work on mine. I don't understand enough about it to know if they're taking me for a ride."

"On a toilet?" Elizabeth joked.

Jude laughed. Enjoying the nun's easy demeanor.

Elizabeth, grunting, sat up and leaned against a claw-footed tub. "I'll be happy to help. I really enjoy this kind of work."

"I'm impressed you know how to do this."

"I have to." Elizabeth returned to the job. "Plus, I want to put the finishing touches on this place by Christmas. We're hosting a dinner with the head of the Catholic diocese." She looked up from the toilet's base. "That is, if we still own the property. What've you found out about the Academy's motives?"

"Well, there's no question of ownership. Trudy's attorneys did a good job securing the property. If the estate doesn't want to sell, they don't have to. However, the Academy could assert outside pressure, you know, create a smear campaign that could make being here miserable."

"We're tough. I'll clog their toilets if they try anything." Elizabeth waved a wrench in the air as if in battle.

"Legally, you guys have the upper hand. Just don't give them a reason to pull out their power tools."

"I don't understand why suddenly they're upset with us being here. They were one of our biggest supporters, happy to get this old hotel cleaned up." Elizabeth pushed a short lock of hair off her face. "Trust me, we're a much better neighbor than the vagrants and drug dealers that were here before."

Jude stepped back from the counter she was leaning on. "Look at this place. Not only have you cleaned it up, you've made it into a work of art." She touched a marble counter and ran her hand along polished oak wainscot. "The detail in this cabinet is exquisite."

"Thank Reece for that." Elizabeth pointed to the basin with her wrench. "He found that here and restored it."

Hearing his name caused Jude's stomach to flip. "How is Reece?" she surprised herself by asking.

Elizabeth smiled. "It's funny, he just asked about you, too."

"Really?"

"Yeah. He keeps showing up here, driving the women crazy. But I know he's only here for the architecture. He loves this old place. Put his heart and soul into it. He's upset about the Academy trying to get their claws into it." She dropped the wrench in a toolbox. "I told him you were helping us fight them."

Jude was tempted to ask if he said anything about her, but instead said, "I can understand why he wants to keep this place."

"How about some coffee?" Elizabeth stood and gathered her tools, then turned and flushed the toilet. "Works like a charm." She laughed. "All this and I can cook too."

"I just hope you wash your hands between projects." Jude followed her out.

The mid-morning light washed the huge kitchen in buttery warmth. The lingering aroma of bacon made Jude's mouth water. Elizabeth poured two cups of coffee and handed one to Jude. "Cream and sugar?"

"A little sugar if you have it."

"Are you kidding? With Baking Bernie living here, we have plenty." She pulled out a bag of brown sugar and poured it into a small bowl. "Try this instead of the white stuff. I think it tastes better."

They took their mugs and sat at the kitchen table. Jude pulled her files from her briefcase. "First, let me get you to sign for this check."

"Thank you for taking care of the money issues." Elizabeth waved her hand and looked around with pride. "I really love it here, and I know we're doing something good." She looked solidly at Jude. "I'd rather focus on taking care of the residents and this place and not have to fight to keep it. That arena is one I know nothing about."

Jude wanted to ask about Reece again but couldn't bring herself to. She kept the conversation to business. "Don't worry. The estate owns this property. And with our firm as trustee, Drew won't let anything happen here."

"I hope not. When Trudy first talked to me about managing the money, she tried to get me to handle the whole bundle. I was afraid if anything happened to me, it would get bogged down in legal issues. Plus, I didn't want to spend my time balancing checkbooks." She stirred her coffee slowly. "She told me about you and thought your firm could deal with the money and legal issues."

Jude shook her head. "I still don't know how I got involved in this mix."

"And I'm still surprised. Trudy acted as if she knew you. Maybe based on your reputation?"

"As a personal injury attorney? Doubt it. In fact, our firm has never handled any type of estate law. After a case settles, we advise our clients to find a financial planner or a law firm that specializes in trusts."

Elizabeth shrugged. "I, for one, am glad she found you." She raised her coffee mug in a toast. "To new friends."

Jude clinked her cup against the nun's mug. "Cheers," feeling a mix of warmth and fear of the unknown.

Bandee, Sangria, and a young woman Jude didn't recognize breezed into the kitchen like children on Christmas morning. Bandee was the first to speak. "Sister Bernadette is ready to drive us to the mall." Her eyes lit up.

Elizabeth's demeanor shifted. "Are your chores done?"

"Yes," the three said together.

"I still wish we could put some makeup on to go out. I feel naked." Sangria ran her hands over her beautiful face.

"You all look gorgeous just as you are." Sister Bernadette shuffled in behind them. "Saint Jude. It's good to see you. You need to stop by more often, not just to bring us money."

Jude wondered how the nun was able to iron her white shirt and gray skirt to perfection. She looked as if her whole body had been put in a press and came out a cardboard nun. Even her short gray hair seemed to have been styled around her modest wimple.

Bernadette clapped her hands. "Okay, girls, you know the rules. I'll drop you off and pick you up at four-thirty sharp. Otherwise, you'll be on your own."

Elizabeth stood and went to Sangria. "We're still working on visitation for you and your kids. Please, don't try to go to your mother-in-law's today. It will only make things worse. Enjoy your day, we'll get you together with them soon."

Sangria's mouth turned to a pout. "But they're my kids. I've got a right to them. Besides, that old bitch overreacted when I went over there last weekend."

"You tried to take your daughter."

"She needs her momma. I mean, you should've seen what she was wearing. She looked like a little black hillbilly." Sangria absently ran her hand along the kitchen counter, wiping up spilled sugar. "That old lady won't let Angel see her own brother. Now what kinda grandmother does that? Even the bitch from CPS thinks they need to be together. And I need 'em. They're a part of me."

"I know. But let's do this the right way." Elizabeth touched her arm gently.

"I'm trying. Hurry, damn it. I miss them. My Angel is goin' to be in a Christmas pageant, and I want to be there—as her momma."

"Sangria, you can't violate the restraining order. We'll get you guys together, hopefully by the pageant." Elizabeth looked at Jude as if to say, 'What's taking so long?'

Bandee jumped with excitement. "Hurry, we only have so much time on parole."

Elizabeth turned to Jude. "Saturday afternoons they have free time." She looked back at the women. "We're trusting you all to enjoy the day and to make sure the home continues to have a good reputation. Right?"

They all nodded vigorously.

"Will you all help Shelby since this is her first outing?"

Jude noticed the plump young woman look down, nervous about being mentioned.

"I'm okay alone." Her voice was louder than her demeanor. She seemed to put on airs of bravado in front of the others. Her cheeks reddened as everyone looked at her.

Jude knew the pain of being called on in class when all you wanted was to blend into the back, unseen.

Elizabeth seemed to notice Shelby's discomfort and put a gentle hand on the girl's arm as she spoke to the others. "Tomorrow, we're going to visit our friends at the retirement community, so let's keep our noses clean."

Bandee rolled her eyes. "Oh boy, bingo and drool."

Elizabeth looked at her sternly. "You can learn much from your elders, grasshopper."

Bandee looked at the ceiling. "I know, but it's so boring."

Bernadette pulled keys from her black, sensible purse. "Child, soon you'll be an old coot like me. Learn to have patience." She jingled her keys. "Come on, last one in the van is a rotten egg!" She laughed as she followed the women out.

Jude looked at Elizabeth. "You're good with them."

"It's my job. I know inside they're good people. They've just gotten on the wrong track. These Saturday excursions are more for them to know we trust them on their own. That they can be responsible." She sat down. "I'd hoped you'd have a few minutes with Bandee and Sangria this morning, but the lure of their free time was too much, I guess."

"That's okay. I'll leave the school forms for Bandee. She can call me if she needs any help. I'm having another attorney look over her criminal records."

"What have you found out about Sangria's custody issues?"

Before Jude could answer, the door opened and the group rushed back in. Bernadette looked angry. "There's a crowd of people outside the gate with picket signs."

Chapter 24

Elizabeth and Jude ran to the window, but the perimeter wall around the home was too high to see the street. "I can't believe they're doing this," Jude said. "I really hoped the issue would go away."

"Life doesn't usually work that way." Elizabeth looked pointedly at Jude.

Bernadette herded the women together. "I wonder if we should stay in today."

"No!" Bandee wailed. "I couldn't sleep last night, I was so excited to go out."

Elizabeth turned to the group. "Sister Bernadette, you all are still going. We're not going to let a bunch of picket signs keep us prisoners. Okay, everybody hold your head up high and don't say *anything* to them as you leave." The nun was bristling with energy. "The only action I want to see from you is smiling and waving. Kill 'em with kindness. Do not, under any circumstances, try to confront them. Show them we're better than they are. Comprende?"

Bernadette smoothed her pressed skirt. "You're right, Elizabeth, we're stronger than that. You all ready?"

The women nodded but looked apprehensive. They filed out, postures stiff, and walked to the van. Elizabeth and Jude followed.

"Go and have fun today. Don't let this upset you. Godspeed," Elizabeth said as she closed the vehicle's door.

Bernadette waved her off as if it wasn't a big deal. "I just hope they stay out from under my tires. My eyesight isn't as good as it used to be." She winked at Elizabeth.

"Bernie, please," Elizabeth warned but smiled.

As the van rolled down the gravel driveway, Elizabeth and Jude walked behind it to the gates. Jude was tense. She hated confrontations. This was not a courtroom where all the facts were laid out. This was a different kind of fight, one Jude knew little about.

"Bernie has been an activist for many good causes—peace rallies, disabled rights sit-ins, you name it," Elizabeth said. "Every time she gets thrown in jail during a protest, she counts it as a badge of honor, a reason to celebrate." She smiled. "I usually stay on the sidelines to bail her out." She looked at Jude. "But for this, the stakes are higher. I hope I can bail us out of this."

The van pulled out of the gate through the throng of twenty or so people. They waved protest signs at the vehicle, which read: "Clean up our neighborhood," and "No prostitutes around our children." Bernadette smiled, waved, and didn't stop. Through the van's window, Bandee looked stricken as she read them. All the signs were professionally printed and each had the Christian Academy's logo on the bottom.

"We know who's behind it." Elizabeth stopped near the gate and nodded toward the group.

"Jude, fancy meeting you here." Rick emerged from the crowd. "Working overtime?" He winked. "Or are you trying out a new profession? I'll pay."

His voice ripped through her. "Rick, what are you doing? Why this?" She waved her hand toward the protesters.

"You know him?" Elizabeth stepped away from Jude. "Did you know they were going to be here today?"

"Of course, not," Jude said" She walked to Rick. "I

can't believe you'd sink so low. This home is operating within their legal rights, as well as firmly owning the property outright. You're out of line."

"That doesn't mean we can't tell you what we think." A large woman with a floral print shirt shook her sign at Jude.

Rick looked smug. "According to my research, your firm is the acting trustee of this place. Your boss, Drew, just might be interested in helping to transfer the title for a more reputable cause."

Jude tensed. Rick certainly knew real estate law better than she did, but she couldn't imagine transferring ownership if the owners didn't want to sell. "You're blowing smoke, Rick," she said, with more confidence than she felt.

"Probably blowing less than in here," he whispered to Jude.

"You're sick." Jude stepped away from him.

Elizabeth stepped closer. "Jude, how do you know him? Who is he?"

Rick laughed. "Sweet Judy was my main squeeze until she started working for you." His voice was menacingly quiet, only the two women could hear him.

"It's not how it looks, Elizabeth." Jude backed away. "Let's go back inside."

Elizabeth hesitated and turned to Rick. "This home is here to help women straighten their lives out. We're not out to hurt anyone. Is Pastor Rains here? I'd like to talk to him."

"No, the good pastor is not here. And I'd discourage you from trying to contact him." Rick said as he backed into the group. "If you have anything to say to him, you'll need to go through me, he said." He leaned closer and pointed to himself. "And my mind is made up."

"Rick, you know as well as I do Pastor Rains can talk

to whomever he damn well pleases," Jude said. She was both angry and scared. "Sister Elizabeth, please, let's go inside and make some phone calls."

"Don't bet on the pastor changing his mind. We've had some long talks about this place, and I assure you, we both see eye to eye." Rick grabbed a protest sign and held it high.

Elizabeth punched a code in a keypad to close the gate. Only the woman in the colored shirt and Rick stood near the gate, but they didn't try to stop it. The rest of the group watched quietly. Elizabeth and Jude headed back to the house. Elizabeth walked ahead.

Jude tried to catch up to her, jogging a few steps. "Let me call Drew and get this worked out. Why don't you call Pastor Rains and set up a meeting with him?"

"How well do you know that guy?" Elizabeth reached the back door and held it open for Jude, although she didn't look happy to invite her in.

"He's that jerk I told you about. The "Fatal Attraction" guy." Jude followed her into the kitchen. Their coffee mugs still sat on the table. "But our past has nothing to do with what's going on now."

"I hope not." Elizabeth picked up her cup and poured it into the sink. "The look in his eyes scared me. Like he came straight from hell." She poured them a fresh cup. "I am a little concerned you two have a, well, past. It seems a little coincidental." She offered the cup to Jude.

Jude shook her head. "You can't think I'd let him sway me."

"No, I don't think that. I just wonder why he's taking out his anger on us."

Jude's coffee churned in her stomach. She marveled at Elizabeth's level of intuition, how she summed up the situation so quickly. Jude sat at the table and looked at Elizabeth. "Maybe you should fire me."

"Don't be silly. I need your help."

"Since I seem to be part of this mess, fire us and re-hire a firm that specializes in estate and financial planning. Maybe they'll back down."

Elizabeth paused and seemed to be considering Jude's offer. "Let me give it some thought. In the meantime, I'll call Pastor Rains." She walked to the bay window in the kitchen and looked at the lawn. "How long did you go out with this guy?"

"I don't want to talk about him." Jude looked away.

The nun continued to look out the window. "I can't see you two together. Granted, I don't know him, but from what I saw today, he has a deep hatred. You should have more confidence in yourself than to date a guy like that."

Jude's defenses stirred. It frightened her that this woman seemed able to see inside her. "This is not about me or him. Like I said, fire me. Or better yet, I quit." She picked up her purse to leave.

"You can't quit." Elizabeth turned to look at her. "Trudy made it clear she wants you to manage the estate. We won't disappoint her."

"She's not here." Jude threw her purse over her shoulder. "Besides, I never knew her. I have no commitment to her. She'd understand, especially if this home is as important to her as you say. Find someone who knows what they're doing."

"This may be a learning experience for both of us. I won't break a promise to Trudy."

"You won't be, I'm the one quitting." She turned to leave but stopped. "Look Sister, I feel like I'm partly responsible for Rick's interest in the home. I don't know why he's doing this, but it may be in everyone's best interest if I bow out. Maybe he'll back off."

"As I said before, life doesn't usually work that way. Walking away from problems never helps. Like hungry kittens, they'll be at our door. I suspect the same with Rick. His anger seems to go beyond what's necessary. I doubt he'll drop the chase."

Jude took her coffee mug to the sink. "I'm sorry. Please let me help you find another firm."

Chapter 25

Driving through the protesters unnerved Jude, especially Rick's smug face as he kept pace with her car. No one tried to stop or confront her.
She went straight to her office. The place was empty, unusual, even for a Saturday. Jude knew a lot of people had planned on taking vacation with Thanksgiving being this week. It would be a good time to study the home's complete file without interruptions.

She wanted to strangle Rick for sinking so low and trying to bring her down. Why was this case suddenly so important to him? There must be a golden egg waiting at the end of the sale for him to have spent so much time and energy to buy the old hotel. He wasn't worth the aggravation. There were enough properties there the Academy could purchase without bothering the Magdalene Home. Surely this wasn't about a broken heart?

She debated calling Drew but it was Saturday afternoon. He probably had family in for the holiday and Jude didn't want him to think she couldn't handle the situation. She poured herself into real estate law, furiously taking notes, all the while wondering why she was working so hard on this case when she'd just quit.

On Monday morning, Drew called Jude to his office. She looked at her watch, it wasn't even nine o'clock, early for him.

He was reading the newspaper at his desk. He folded the paper and looked at Jude over his reading glasses. "Good morning. I heard you had an interesting weekend at the home."

"What did you hear?" Jude asked. She sat in a soft leather chair across from him.

Drew didn't answer. Instead, he pulled a manila envelope from his desk and handed it to Jude. "The Christian Academy has made a generous offer on the hotel the nuns converted. It might be in the estate's best interest to sell. Financially, the estate stands to make a huge amount of money."

"But what about the Magdalene Home? The women living there?"

"They could easily take the trust allotted to them and buy another property. Plus, it would make the Academy happy. I understand they're not pleased with having prostitutes living so close to the church's daycare."

"Since when?" Jude shifted in her chair. "They'd supported the home until recently. Do you know what changed their minds? The neighborhood was a mess before. The Academy cohabitated fine with the drug dealers and vagrants before the Magdalenes moved in."

"Honestly," Drew moved forward, "and confidentially, I think they realized what a goldmine that property turned out to be. The Academy is richer than God, they've been trying to clean up that area for years. They were already considering buying up a bunch of real estate there or finding another location for the church. But now that the hotel is in such great shape, they've decided to stay." He leaned back. "That, and their attorney, your friend Rick Carney, is really motivated to get his claws into the deal. He's convinced the pastor to stay in the neighborhood."

"What about our loyalty to Trudy's estate? You told me to get these guys to back off. Don't we have to protect our client first?"

"I'm having second thoughts on that. As I said, this would make Trudy's estate skyrocket in value. The only problem is that I, the firm, don't have authority. We made a commitment until the end of the year, so our hands are tied until then. But to see the numbers Rick has come up with it would benefit the nuns more than if they stayed.

"Trudy has a few more letters we have to hand out, plus the 'big unveiling' of the final will after Christmas." He rolled his eyes. "Resetting my newfangled alarm clock is less complicated than her will. But we're making a load of money, so I'll follow her wishes, no matter how frivolous. We're forced to stick to this timeline of opening the letters she left." He sat back in his chair. "I've been tempted to crack into the whole file, but she's retained another firm that prevents me from doing that."

"What firm?" Jude thought maybe they could transfer the trust to a group that could better manage the property. "Does this other firm specialize in estate law?"

"It's her bank's legal team. They're watching us like hawks."

"Drew, have you wondered why Trudy chose us? We don't do this kind of law. She seemed to be a more savvy businesswoman than to trust millions to a bunch of personal injury attorneys."

Drew looked over his glasses at her. "Are you saying we're not able to handle this? You know, with caps on punitive damages, we need to expand our cases. Besides, I said she was interested in you, and she's been more than generous with her money. I think we can crack a few books

☙☙☙

to figure out how to handle business and real estate law. Do you need help with this and the Carmen case?"

"No." Jude felt pressure squeeze her insides. "Mediation is set for the third week in December. I'm ready."

"Good. Dictate a memo to me of all the cases you're working. Have it on my desk by end of the day today. If we need to shift some work around, we'll do it. Right now, the two biggest cases we have are the Carmen case and this trust fund. You're lead on both. I don't want anything to get screwed up on either of them," he said.

Jude stood. She wondered how the conversation had shifted so far away from the takeover attempt by the Academy and Drew's sudden change of position. "I'll have that memo to you today," She left his office defeated, like a child leaving the principal's office.

In her office, she found Katie shuffling through papers on her desk. "What are you looking for?"

Katie jumped. "Oh, you scared me. I was making sure you had your mail. I couldn't remember leaving it here Friday." She laughed. "My brain erases after a whole weekend."

"The last stack of mail went back to you to respond to. It's not on your desk?" Jude asked.

"I must've missed it under the mess. I'll get right on it." Katie backed away from Jude's desk, not meeting her eye.

"Do you have an updated client list available? I need to get a memo out today.," Jude said.

Jude followed Katie out to get the list. While her secretary was rummaging through the files, Katie's direct line rang. Jude glanced at caller ID and was surprised to see Rick's cell number on the display. Katie turned and looked at the phone, then glanced nervously at Jude as she answered.

"This is Katie." She stared at her desk. "Hi, Rick. Do you want to talk to Jude?" She nodded. "Yeah, she's right here…standing here." She paused while Rick must have spoken. "Okay, I'll put you right through."

Jude looked hard at Katie. "Take a message."

In her office, Jude closed the door. Katie was talking to Rick? He knew her direct number? Jude didn't want to believe Katie was leaking confidential information. She couldn't be. Katie may be meddlesome but had always been professional. And besides, Jude thought, what proof did she have?

She looked around her desk for information that Katie could have read. Luckily, all the Magdalene documents were in Jude's briefcase. Katie was often in and out of it to find files Jude was working on. Jude always carried it with her, except, Jude remembered with a start, the evening she went home early and left Katie here. She quickly pulled the file and began reading about the Magdalene residents.

All eight of the women at the home had charges of prostitution. Some had more than one offense. A few had misdemeanor drug charges and two had theft charges. Nothing too incriminating. All had been given the choice of jail time or a year at the Magdalene Home. The only offense against a church was Bandee's night-on-the-altar, and those files were sealed. Or should have been. Jude considered Rick's knowledge of Trudy's file. Katie had full access, especially with the research Jude had asked her to do.

There was a soft knock on the door, and Katie stuck her head in. "I proofed the mediation presentation," She said. Stepping into the office. "There were only a few typos I fixed. Otherwise, it looks great." She leaned forward to hand Jude the papers. "Do you want me to get a copy to Drew?"

"No, thanks," said Jude. "I'll put it on a flash drive to give to him along with the charts and illustrations."

"Okay. There are also demand letters on two of the cases you asked for."

"Thanks." Jude took the stack of papers from Katie and put them on her desk. "Katie, how often do you and Rick talk?"

"Not that often," Katie said She appeared jumpy. "It's just after working with his assistant some, I've sort of gotten to know him a little." Her eyes grew wide. "Are you guys still dating?"

"No." Jude grimaced. "Are you and Rick...?" She couldn't finish the sentence.

"No, not really. I mean, he calls me some, but I wanted to talk to you first. I wasn't sure it would be okay with you."

"Honestly, Katie, I'd hate to see you get mixed up with him. The guy's a snake."

"So you *are* still interested in him. He said you were. That's why I wasn't sure if it was cool to, you know, keep talking to him."

Jude looked at the ceiling, frustrated. "Trust me, I am not interested in him. I wish I'd never met him," Her gaze shifted to Katie. "But that's not important. What I'm concerned about is whether or not you're talking about our cases with him. Especially anything concerning the Magdalene Home or Trudy's estate."

Katie looked at the floor and shook her head. "We talk about work, but it's just light conversation. It's not like anything important. He thinks it's funny we're working on a home for prostitutes."

Jude didn't want to say something that would get back to Rick. "Katie, you know that talking about our cases with anyone outside of this firm is grounds for termination. Period."

She looked stricken. "Are you going to...am I...fired?"

"No, you're a good legal assistant, but you should know

how important it is that we protect our client's interests."

"Okay. But I didn't think I was doing anything wrong," Katie said. "I mean, since Drew talks to Rick about this case, I figured it was all right. I didn't mean any harm."

"What do you mean, Drew talks to Rick? What has he said?"

Katie sat down, eager for a good chance at gossip. "Didn't Rick tell you that he wants to buy some buildings there and convert them to a cool artsy retail area? He's trying to get Drew to invest, too. Rick thinks it could be another Uptown or Bishop Arts here in Dallas. You know, trendy condos and retail shops."

Jude let the information sink in. "Where does the Christian Academy fit in?"

"Rick thinks if the church buys the hotel, the property values will go up. It would be hard to rent condos next to a place where prostitutes live." She sounded like an expert.

Katie's motor mouth spilled a wealth of information. "So you guys have talked about this?" Jude asked, trying to stay calm.

Her assistant nodded. "He said I could invest, too,"

"I see." Jude didn't know what else to ask, knowing Katie would immediately get on the phone and start gossiping. "Has it ever occurred to you he might be using you?"

"I'm smarter than that." She smoothed her skirt and looked insulted. "I know how to read people, thank you."

"Katie, it's imperative you not mention the case to him, or anybody, again. I can't stop Drew from talking to Rick, but I can assure you I'll mention this to him about you leaking information."

"Will Drew fire me?" She shrunk down in the chair. "It's almost Christmas." Her voice took on a pleading tone.

"I'm not sure how this is going to play out," Jude said. "But stay away from Rick Carney."

Chapter 26

Jude stopped her car at the gates of the Magdalene Home and opened the window to buzz the intercom. She'd planned to get here earlier, before the winter darkness set in, but she wasn't able to get out of the office until eight o'clock.

The protesters had left a few signs thrown around the perimeter fence, and the dark street bustled with a seedy crowd. Even with the razor cold evening, there were plenty of people out. She opened her car window to ring the home, freezing air assaulted her and the acrid smell of smoke from trashcan fires hung in the wind.

"Hey chickie, lookin' for some action?" Three young men sauntered from behind her BMW. Each wore stocking caps and huge pants slung low around their backsides. "Us pimps are ready for this place to open for business." One of them, a tall, skinny kid, came to her window. "Damn, they got some high-dollar bitches here." He leaned close and set his hands on the open window, so close to Jude she could smell the alcohol on his breath and the filth from his sweatshirt.

Jude froze, fear shot through her. A quick flash of her rape came to her mind's eye. *The priest leaning near, his breath, the unbearable pain...*

With one hand the kid grabbed his crotch and put his head closer. "Come on, whore, how about a freebie." He flicked his tongue at her.

There was no air in the car. Jude couldn't breathe. She leaned away from him and tried, with a shaking hand, to hit the window button. *I can't go through this again.*

He grabbed her wrist. "Don't try to shut me out, bitch. I'm gonna make your dreams come true. Right here, right now." The other two guys moved closer, laughing. "We're all gonna have a good time, then take you for a ride in your shiny bitchmobile."

He viciously twisted her arm and slammed it on the open window edge. Searing pain ripped through her. Jude could feel her body shaking uncontrollably. Her foot barely holding the brake. Still gripping Jude's arm, he reached inside the car with his other hand to grab her face.

A primal need to survive swept through Jude. She threw the car in reverse and hit the gas with her shaky foot. As the car accelerated, she felt her body being slammed to the window rim. The kid still held tight. Then he fell and let go. She wasn't sure if she ran over him, didn't care. Through a veil of fear, Jude saw the gate open. She stomped on the brakes. The kid had been knocked into the street and was lying on his side. The other two took off running. She saw Elizabeth and Bernadette lit up by her headlights. Bernadette, holding a broom in her hands, went to the kid. Elizabeth ran to Jude's car.

"Are you okay?"

Jude couldn't talk, only made hiccupping sobs, but she felt a rush of relief seeing the nun's face.

"Put the car in park. Let me get you inside." Elizabeth opened the door and helped Jude out. Jude noticed all the women from the home were standing inside the gate, watching.

Sangria had gone to the boy in the street, who was sitting up rubbing his shoulder. Bernie held the broom up as if to swat him.

Sangria grabbed him by his hair, pulling the nylon cap off. She shook him hard. "Are you stupid, punk? If you're looking for some action, I'll shove your ugly face up your ass, let you try to find your way out."

He held up his good hand to ward her off. "I didn't do nuthin'. She ran me down."

Bernie stood straight, the broom held next to her. "Oh, I see. You and your friends were walking down the street, and she decided to run over you."

"Yeah, just like that." He tried to scoot away. "We're mindin' our own thing, then, bam, she hit me." He put his hand on his shoulder. "She tried to kill me, man."

"Well, it's too bad she missed." Sangria stood and threw his cap at him. "She would've helped clean some scum off the street." She raised a fist. "Don't fuck with us, punk."

"Honey." Bernadette put a calming hand on Sangria's arm. "Why don't you take everybody inside. I'll take care of him."

"I know how to deal with the streets, Sister. Let me take care of this piece-of-shit. I'll teach him a lesson he won't forget."

Elizabeth called Sangria over to the car. "Do me a favor and drive her car inside. Just pull around back by the kitchen."

She hesitated, looked at the prostrate kid, then the car, her fist still half-raised. "You better beat it, punk. I don't want to see your ugly face here again." Sangria said. She turned and jogged to the car, the kid all but forgotten. "Oh, baby, I've always wanted to drive one of these. Can I take it around the block first?"

Elizabeth kept a supporting arm around Jude. "Please,

Sangria, now is not the time. Just park by the kitchen."

"Better yet, let me run him over again. I'll finish the job,"

Jude saw the scene as if it was a dream, she felt disembodied. The only thing she could feel was a sharp throbbing in her arm.

Elizabeth gave Sangria a warning look as she pulled Jude toward the gate. "Come on let's get you inside,"

The cold bit through Jude's clothes. She wasn't sure if her legs were attached to her body, but she moved under Elizabeth's guiding arm.

"I thought you whores were open," He slowly got to his feet. "You guys're advertising." He waved at a sign the protesters left, leaning against the fence that read, "Prostitutes live here."

Jude heard the kid continue to yell at Bernadette as he ran, limping down the dark street. She wasn't sure but thought she saw the older nun swing the broom at him.

The kitchen was blessedly warm, but Jude couldn't stop shaking. She tried to take a steaming mug from Elizabeth but couldn't hold it. The nun set it on the table next to her.

"You can drink this later. Let me look at your arm," Elizabeth gently pushed Jude's sleeve up. Her lower arm was scraped and starting to swell.

The group of women had moved to the entrance of the kitchen. Bandee emerged and said, "I took a first aid course, let me help."

"Thanks, just get a bag of ice," Elizabeth said. "The rest of you can all go to your rooms or the living area. We'll take a night off from our group prayer meeting."

The young woman Jude saw last Saturday stepped forward and said, "I saw it all, Sister, from my window. Those boys came up to her car, started messin' with her. She didn't run over them."

"I'm sure she didn't." She looked at Jude. "Shelby's the

one who let us know you were here." She turned back to the group. "Let's give her some space, then we'll talk about what happened."

Sangria and Bernadette came in with a rush of cold air. "Oh, that's one sweet set of wheels, Sangria said. "Maybe you can take me for a ride." She put the keys in front of Jude.

Jude nodded, still unable to speak.

"Those boys were out looking for trouble," Bernadette said. "I told them not to come around here again." She set the broom in a corner.

Bandee handed a plastic bag of ice to Elizabeth. "I'll get the Neosporin and something to wash it with." She turned and trotted out of the kitchen.

Jude took deep breaths, air filled spaces that held pain and shock. Push it down, seal it up. She was good at that. "I'm okay," She said and held up her good hand. "I'm glad you came when you did." She shuddered thinking of what could have happened.

"You're not okay." Elizabeth pushed the mug closer to her. "Drink this. It's tea with a shot of bourbon to calm your nerves." She looked to Bernadette. "I think we should call the police."

"No." Jude moved forward. "No police."

"They're a bunch of idiots anyway." Sangria said. "They'd just write a few notes and say you were probably asking for it."

Elizabeth rubbed her face. "Sangria, you're not helping."

"And the police never help either," Sangria said.

"No police." Jude spoke quietly. "The home doesn't need this right now. Not with everything going on."

"You're sure?" Elizabeth asked.

Jude nodded.

Bernadette didn't say anything. She looked between

Jude and Elizabeth as if weighing her options.

Bandee came back with a first aid kit under her arm. "I used to take care of my baby sisters, I know what to do," she said proudly, opening the kit. "First you need to wash the cut." She went to the sink and ran water over a washcloth.

Elizabeth watched the young girl. "You know, Jude, you should just stay here tonight. We have plenty of room."

"No. I'm fine, really," Jude muttered. A flash of Rick's visit at her home the other night made Jude wince. She didn't feel safe there, but it would be too uncomfortable here.

"That really hurts, huh?" Jude flinched as the nun gently turned her arm to assess the damage.

Bandee came over, cradling the wet washcloth. "Here, it's got soap on it." She handed it to Jude.

"Thanks," Jude said.

"You'd make a good doctor." Elizabeth smiled at the girl.

Bandee grinned and swelled with pride. "Make sure you put Neosporin on it so it don't get infected." She nodded, feeling important to be dispensing advice.

Shelby stuck her head in the kitchen. "Psst, Bandee, come here." She appeared afraid to enter the kitchen.

Bandee turned and walked to her. "What?" she whispered loudly. "I'm helping here."

"Is she okay?" Shelby, wide-eyed looked at Jude.

Elizabeth stood up and went to the women. "She's fine. Thanks for your help." She touched Bandee's arm. "Right now, I think Jude needs a little quiet time."

The two girls took the cue to leave. Elizabeth turned to Jude. "I'm going upstairs and check on everybody. Drink up, take a few minutes to collect yourself. I'll be right back."

Jude nodded and looked at her drink, glad to be left alone. She was claustrophobic with everyone hovering. She pulled her arm close to her body. Taking the hot mug with her good hand, she stepped out the back door of the kitchen. The biting cold stung her wet cheeks.

The drink was strong. Jude welcomed the warmth from the heat and the liquor. Now might be a good time to make a quick exit. Leave before anyone noticed. She headed toward the car, but remembered her keys were on the table. She stood between the car and the kitchen, trying to collect her thoughts enough to move. The door opened and Elizabeth came out on the porch.

"You look like you're trying to make a fast getaway." She leaned against a pillar and crossed her arms. "You'll feel better if you stayed here tonight, at least to calm down and get your head back on straight. I promise, no one will bother you."

"It's already a short week at work. I need to go. I don't have time to stay." Jude's thoughts and words were jumbled. "My cat is there, he needs me."

"I don't know if those guys are still out there," Elizabeth said. "They may want to retaliate." She shook her head. "I don't understand. Most of the neighbors, although a little eccentric, have always left us alone. I'm surprised, no, disappointed, this happened. We've always been generous to them." Her voice trailed off as she looked over the fence.

Jude's resolve crumbled. "I don't know. I have so much to do." She took another sip, for warmth, for courage, her hands still shaking.

"At least come in where it's warm." Elizabeth held the door open.

"Okay," Jude said. She slowly made her way to the kitchen but stopped. "Wait, I brought some papers. I need to get them out of the car." She hesitated. "Wait, my keys."

She turned. "I think Sangria left them in the house." Jude still felt disoriented. "On the table, I think."

"I'll get them." Elizabeth ducked into the kitchen.

Jude stood in the yard, dazed, not sure if she should to go to her car or wait for Elizabeth. Maybe Elizabeth was right, Jude thought. I should stay, I can't even think straight. Just then, she heard scuffling noises and whispers outside the fence. Not sure how to react, Jude froze. Her brain and body out of sync. She heard someone scream, "Die bitches!" A fireball sailed over the fence into the yard. The last thing she remembered was loud popping noises as she was pushed to the ground.

Chapter 27

The next morning, Jude awoke in a simple room. The springs of the twin bed squeaked when she moved. Soft morning light filtered through the back of pressed linen curtains that hung over a small window. The only adornment on the wall was a crucifix, which hung over her bed. On a three-drawer dresser, St. Jude peered at her as if she were part of his flock, and he'd watched over her as she slept. Was he there last night, she wondered?

Jude rolled over and pain shot through her arm. She tried to piece together what happened. She pulled back the covers and gingerly stepped onto the chilly wood floor. Her arm throbbed viciously. Still wearing the same clothes she had on last night, she pulled her sleeve up to look at the damage. Her shirt stuck to the open scrapes and Neosporin as she gingerly wrestled the fabric over the injury. Her left wrist and forearm were horribly bruised and swollen.

Inspecting her arm, she remembered the young men trying to yank her from the car. The rest of the evening came back in bits and pieces: Bandee ministering to her, Jude trying to leave, then the fireball. Had she heard gunshots? Jude gasped and frantically checked the rest of her body. Other than her arm, she seemed uninjured. Shaking her head, she thought, *Maybe I'm still dreaming.* She needed coffee. Extra strong.

The floor's chill seeped through her. There was an old space heater in the wall, but Jude didn't want to take a chance of blowing up the place trying to light it. A folded towel sat on top of the dresser, along with a bag of travel-sized toiletries behind St Jude, probably a "welcome kit" for the new arrivals.

She tried to put on her watch but winced from the pain. Instead, she stuck the watch in her purse. The house was quiet, and Jude hoped no one was awake since it was only six-thirty. She took the bag of toiletries and went to find a bathroom.

The floors squeaked with each step. So much for a quiet exit. At the top of the stairs, Jude smelled the sweet aroma of baking. Her mouth watered, though a bit disappointed she wasn't the first up.

After washing, she went downstairs and found Bernadette bustling in the kitchen. Flour dusted the countertop around a large mixing bowl.

"Good morning. How are you feeling?" Bernadette asked. "I am so sorry for what you went through last night." She held Jude's shoulders, careful not to squeeze her injury.

"What happened? My memory is coming back in bits and pieces."

"How about some coffee first? Lizzie just made a fresh pot."

"Good idea." Jude sat at the table soaking in the warm atmosphere, her quick escape all but forgotten. "Did I get shot at?"

"No, thank God..." Before Bernadette could finish, Elizabeth came in from the back door.

"Well, there she is." Elizabeth was dressed in jeans and a white sweatshirt. The air that moved in with her was brisk and frigid. "How's the arm?"

"It's sore and I'm trying to figure out what happened,"

said Jude. "Why can't I remember?"

"You're probably still in shock," Elizabeth said. Bernadette brought Jude a fresh mug of coffee and a tray with cream and sugar. "Here you go, Elizabeth's special brew should wake you up."

"Thanks." Jude took the mug gratefully.

Elizabeth sat across from Jude and sipped coffee. "I'm glad you stayed. I didn't want you out driving, considering everything that happened."

"There were guys who tried to..." she stopped. "Then I was in the backyard and I heard gunshots. That's the last I remember."

"You were already stressed from the attack." The nun smiled. "How are you doing now?"

"I remember the shots and falling or being pushed. The rest is kind of fuzzy."

Elizabeth glanced at Bernadette but spoke to Jude. "Those weren't gunshots. I don't know who was responsible, but someone threw a wad of firecrackers over the fence. Scared the crap out of all of us. You especially."

Jude tried to recall the incident but could only remember the fireball. "I do remember you taking me into an office."

Elizabeth's voice was gentle when she asked, "Who's Father Callen?"

Jude almost choked on her coffee. "What?"

"You said something about Father Callen last night."

Jude's hands shook uncontrollably causing her to splatter coffee on the table. "Just babbling." She looked away. "I don't know..." Jude remembered the only other time she'd been so frightened—when Father Callen raped her.

Elizabeth paused, then dropped the subject. "The firecrackers went off right next to you. I'd be scared, too. Especially with all you'd been through with those guys."

"*Jesus Christ,*" Jude swore.

Bernadette put her hands on her hips. "I hope you're praying…," she said, with raised eyebrows.

"I'm sorry," Jude put a hand over her mouth. "I didn't mean…"

Bernadette waved her off.

Jude worked to fit the pieces of her memory together. "Did I fall?" She rubbed her knee near a torn flap of denim.

"No, I came outside just as the fireball was thrown, and pushed you down," Elizabeth assured her. "At that point, I didn't know they were fireworks."

Jude was afraid to ask. "What else did I say?"

Elizabeth looked at her, and answered, "Nothing."

Bernadette brought a stack of hot pancakes. "I guess we're going to have to raise the terror alert here. I'll put a gauge next to the thermometer."

"Bernie." Elizabeth admonished the older nun but chuckled.

Jude smiled. "It's okay. Actually, it's pretty funny." She was relieved she hadn't said anything else about Father Callen. She looked at the two sisters. "Thank you for taking care of me. I'm sorry I'm so much trouble."

Bernadette clasped her hands. "My goodness, don't be silly. We love taking care of people, that's our specialty. Thank God everybody was all right." She crossed herself, then nodded at the hot plate of food. "Eat. I'm going to wake up the rest of the gang, so grab it now."

Jude's desire to leave before the girls got up crumbled as the aroma of the pancakes sparked a ravenous hunger.

Elizabeth, hands wrapped around her mug, said, "Please, eat. Bernie's going to have the others make their own breakfast." She sipped coffee. "It's part of the program, you know, to teach self-sufficiency."

"So, I'm a guest?" Jude asked as she helped herself to two fluffy cakes.

"Nah, more like one of the family," Elizabeth replied.

She forked a pancake onto her plate. "Just remember to say grace before you eat." She winked.

෴

At home, Jude took her time showering, using the hot water to wash away the night before. She spent a few extra minutes giving Tommy attention before she dressed which was difficult with the swelling and bruising. She opted for a simple long sleeve sweater and easy-on pants.

Jude hated being late to work. As she dropped her briefcase on her chair, she noticed Katie wasn't at her desk. Not unusual, since Katie usually ran the office gossip mill. Jude closed her door, wishing for a quiet morning. She was still shell-shocked from last night.

Jude, absorbed in reading a deposition, jumped as a loud knock interrupted her concentration.

Katie walked into the office and closed the door.

"Do you have a few minutes?" she asked.

Jude set the documents aside. "Sure. What's up?"

Katie sat fidgeting with a button on her jacket, never meeting Jude's eye. "This is really hard for me." She tugged at her hair and looked out the window. "I'm turning in my resignation."

"What?" Jude sat straighter. "Why, Katie?"

Katie finally looked at Jude. "Because you can't tell me who I can and can't talk to."

"Meaning?" Jude was baffled, completely blindsided.

"You said I couldn't talk to Rick anymore. That's a violation of my rights."

"Katie, you're smarter than that. We both know you can talk to anybody you want. My concerns are you discuss confidential information with Rick. *That's* a violation of company policy." She took in a breath. "Are you sure you want to do this? You've been important here."

"I'm sure," Katie huffed.

"Sorry to hear it." Jude felt like she'd been socked in the gut. "Christmas is a month away. Do you have another job?"

"I don't have to tell you." Katie acted like a petulant child.

"No, you don't." Jude sat back and ran a hand over her face, her hurt arm rested in her lap. "I didn't expect this…"

"Well, you said," she pulled a sheet of paper out of her pocket and read from it, 'to stay away from Rick Carney'. As an attorney, you should know that's wrong."

"Katie, I don't care what you and Rick have going. I just don't want you talking about my clients with him." Jude was angry, a little hurt, and sorely tempted to speak her mind. But she knew she'd be setting herself up for a lawsuit if she said the wrong thing. Grabbing the deposition folder, Jude waved a hand at Katie and turned to read the pages. "Don't bother with a two-week notice, go ahead and leave today. I'll see you get paid for the time. If you don't want to be here, then I don't need you."

"Okay, fine." Katie stood up.

"Take your things. I'll call administration about your pay," Jude said. "You realize you won't be eligible for a Christmas bonus now?"

Katie shrugged. "Rick said he'd pay me my bonus plus some. And he's giving me a raise." Katie's eyes widened realizing she'd shown her hand.

"I see. So you're working for Rick?" Jude tried to bite back surprise. She fussed with the spiral binding on deposition pages.

"He made me an offer I couldn't refuse." Katie crossed her arms over her chest.

"Yeah, he's known for that," Jude replied.

"I like Rick. Just because you two have problems doesn't mean I can't like him."

Jude already felt beaten, and having Katie quit like this made it worse. "Personally, Katie, I don't want to see you get hurt. Rick can be a real…" she stopped before she said *asshole*. "Rick can be tough." She looked hard at her assistant. "And so can I, if I find out you've broken attorney-client confidentiality."

Her emotions mixed between anger, sadness, and shock. Katie was nosey but had done excellent work. Jude sighed. "Good luck. Please close the door on your way out."

Chapter 28

Sad and tired, Jude left work at seven o'clock. The events at the home and Katie's resignation had completely drained any reserves of energy. She'd thought focusing on work would keep her mind off the pile of problems. Her injured arm ached, and she felt abandoned without an assistant. She needed Katie, who knew all the files, and dreaded the extra work without her. It would be impossible to tackle hers and Katie's job, but a new assistant, at this stage, would only get in the way. There was no time to train someone. She was also anxious Katie might divulge important information to Rick.

After Katie met with administration, the snotty office manager ran to Drew's office to complain about Jude's propensity for losing good legal assistants.

Drew came into Jude's office that afternoon and told her, after so many legal assistants, maybe she should look inside herself to see where the problems were. "You know, Jude, think of them like a spouse. You have to learn to work through the issues. You'd be up to your ass in alimony if you were married." He laughed at his joke. "Legal assistants are a lot easier to deal with than an ex-wife."

"I'm worried she'll give Rick information about our clients, especially concerning the Magdalene Home," Jude said.

Drew sat across from her. "Why worry about that? It's a trust case. No big secrets there."

"The past records of the residents, for one. And he shouldn't have Trudy's financial information."

"What could he do with the criminal histories of the girls? Hell, you could probably find that by a background search." Drew shrugged. "What difference does it make?"

"He's trying to buy the property out from the estate with devious tactics. He could easily use the women's past as leverage to force them to move." Jude wanted to ask Drew what he'd discussed with Rick but she bit back the question.

"We're all swimming in open waters here," Drew said. "If they don't want to sell, then they don't have to." He became thoughtful. "Even though the area does seem to be a potential goldmine. They may not like it, but I'm going to recommend they sell and move the girls to another area. It'll make everybody rich and happy. Including the estate. That should help the nuns and the girls."

"They don't want to sell, and Rick is putting extreme pressure on the church to buy the property and to turn against the Magdalene's." Jude crossed her arms, and flinched at her injured wrist.

"The church is able to handle itself without Rick," Drew said. He stood. "He's got some financial interest, too—even if his approach leaves something to be desired. The Academy has a huge group of attorneys to take care of its business. Rick is only a small player."

"Then why is he so relentless?"

Drew leaned closer to Jude. "Because he's a good attorney. Doesn't let his personal business get in the way of work. He does what he needs to do to get the job done."

"What's *that* supposed to mean?" Jude felt she'd been insulted. Was she picking up the wrong signals from Drew?

He looked at her with a fatherly demeanor and sat on the corner of her desk. "I'm glad you're taking your job seriously Jude, but don't get too close to the, you know, the girls at the home. It's business, keep it to that. We're here to help, not get involved. Take care of the firm first." He turned professional again. "Besides, our hands are tied until the last of the estate pays out. Oh," he snapped his fingers, "that reminds me, you'll need to deliver another letter by Thursday."

"That's Thanksgiving," Jude said.

"I know. Trudy wants it read during the home's dinner. I can't do it since my family is in town. You could probably just drop it off Wednesday evening and let the sisters read it at their leisure."

Jude was too tired to argue. "Okay. But I was planning on working here all day Thursday, especially since I'm shorthanded." Literally, she thought, as she touched her hurt arm.

"Don't you have plans for Thanksgiving?" Drew asked, becoming paternal again. "You're welcome to join us, but you might have to sit next to my mother-in-law." He shuddered dramatically. "I'm trying to talk my wife into having a separate kiddie table and an in-law table. Outside." He laughed, then spoke gently. "Seriously, Jude. I don't want you working over the holiday. You need to enjoy yourself, and we'd love to have you."

"Thank you, Drew. Really. You know what a loner I am. I probably wouldn't be the best company anyway,.."

"Don't put yourself down. We'd be honored." He bent to take her hand in a show of chivalry and grabbed her injured arm.

"Ow." Jude clutched her arm close to her body. "Sorry, I had a little accident."

"Are you okay? What happened?" Drew pulled her arm out carefully. "Oh, my! You're bruised and swollen. Have you had it x-rayed?"

"It's fine. A little Advil and a glass of wine will take care of it." She slipped her arm out of his grasp.

"How did it happen?" he asked.

"I got my arm stuck in the car window. Pretty stupid, really." She shooed him off. "I'll be okay. Hey, does it work as an excuse to get me out of having dinner with your mother-in-law?" She was reluctant to tell him the truth in case he pulled her off the case. Ironic, since she had wanted nothing to do with the trust before.

"If that's all it took, I'd stick my head in a car door." He joked but looked concerned. "Now, really, how did you get your arm battered like that in a car window?"

Jude didn't answer.

"It's not Rick Carney, is it? Or some other guy?"

"Of course not." Jude was insulted and hurt by his implication. "I think I'm a better judge of character than that."

"I should hope so." He turned to leave. "I can see you don't want to talk about it. I don't know Jude, you seem to have a dark, mysterious side. Don't make me worry."

Dark, mysterious side. Jude couldn't get Drew's words out of her head. She slammed the refrigerator door shut, not hungry, but not satisfied. She felt like someone should blindfold her, stick a cigarette in her mouth and shout *fire!* Maybe it would put her out of her misery. She thought of the Scales of Justice, a woman blindfolded, impartial until the evidence was borne out. Some lawyers would happily put a bullet through her blinded heart to get their way, Jude thought bitterly. Justice doesn't always prevail.

She opened the freezer and took out a pint of ice cream and cradled it in her injured arm. The coolness tempered the pain. She grabbed a spoon and headed to the den to join Tommy on the sofa.

As she passed St. Jude, she stopped and looked at the icon. "Okay, patron saint of lost causes. Get me out of this mess. I've lost my favorite assistant to my psycho ex-boyfriend, my job's going to the dogs, the estate I'm supposed to manage is being threatened, and I have no love life. Everything I touch goes bad." Jude put the empty spoon in her mouth and thought—*maybe I'm the lost cause.*

Chapter 29

A brittle Texas norther had blown in Thanksgiving morning, leaving the air frigid and the skies icy blue, Jude's favorite weather. When she'd called Elizabeth about delivering the letter, Jude tried but couldn't say no to Elizabeth's invitation for Thanksgiving dinner at four o'clock. Jude put on a long black wool skirt, not knowing if her accepting the invite was because her resolve was crumbling or was because she was too tired to make up a good excuse. She secretly hoped Reece would make an appearance, even though he was probably celebrating with his family, or worse, a new girlfriend. It had been two weeks since he bailed.

As she drove through the now familiar neighborhood, Jude felt apprehensive remembering the attack. Elizabeth told her to call when she was within sight of the Home so the gates could be opened before Jude got there, and someone would be outside waiting for her.

As promised, the gates were open. She pulled through the drive and looked, with anticipation, for Reece's car. There was only the Home's van and Elizabeth's small battered Toyota. Disappointed about Reece, she still looked forward to having dinner with the women. There was a strong thread of familiarity with the Magdalenes. She figured her past obliquely gave her a degree of acceptance, even if they weren't aware of it.

Elizabeth stood on the back porch waiting. She looked regal, dressed in her full black habit, the cold wind caught the long fabric like a sail.

The sun's warmth was a contrast to the sharp breeze as Jude opened the car door. A gust almost ripped the envelope, containing Trudy's letter, out of Jude's hand.

"Happy Thanksgiving," Elizabeth said. She helped Jude inside and closed the door. "How's the arm?"

"Much better, thanks. It's turned so many different colors, I had a hard time finding an outfit to match. At least I'm able to use it." As proof, she handed Elizabeth the now wrinkled envelope. "This is from Trudy. And don't you look dignified in full habit."

"Thank you. I clean up every so often." Elizabeth grasped the letter. "I'm looking forward to reading this. We tried to get her daughter Elise here for dinner. At the last minute she decided to stay at school and promised to make Christmas. She's still having trouble with her mother's death." Elizabeth touched the envelope gently. "We're all still hurting."

Jude felt awkward. "Sounds like she was a wonderful person."

"Come on, let's eat," said Elizabeth. "Bernie's been up since four o'clock this morning, cooking."

"She didn't make the girls do any work?"

"They've helped, but we wanted them to enjoy the day. Plus, Bernie's become the turkey commando. No one can get in the kitchen today without suffering mortal wounds."

Jude looked toward the gates. "Have the protesters been back?"

Elizabeth followed her gaze. "No. I figure they're taking the holiday off. Bernie had a good idea, though. She's decided the next time they're outside, she's going to serve tea and cookies, and welcome them in from the cold." She laughed. "It helps to have experience as a frequent protester. She could probably teach them a few tricks."

"Then everybody gets together for a love-in?" Jude asked.

Elizabeth laughed. "Yeah, picture Bernadette in tie-dye habit and a groovy wimple? Woodstock, man." She flashed a peace sign to Jude as they entered the comforting warmth of the kitchen.

Sister Bernadette was also in full Dominican habit, only with a flour-dusted apron over hers. "St. Jude, happy Thanksgiving." She walked to Jude and gave her an affectionate hug. "I'm glad you're here. How's your arm?" she asked, gently rubbing it.

"Much better," Jude said.

"What an awful night that was. Thank God you're all right, dear." She went to the stove and began stirring a large pot of gravy. "You need to relax, go warm up by the fire. Tonight I'm cooking."

Elizabeth smiled. "This is her element. It's torture for her to see others mess with her kitchen utensils every day, it's the ultimate sacrifice for her."

"I'll try to surrender the cleaning duties to the rest of you. Even though it will be hard," Bernadette said dramatically. She went to the refrigerator and took out a tray of appetizers and passed them to Elizabeth. "Take these to the living room. I think the girls have fasted long enough."

"I think all of us have," Elizabeth said, picking out a hunk of cheese and stuffing it in her mouth.

"Sister Elizabeth! Show some manners and good grace," Bernadette said and guided her out of the kitchen.

Elizabeth's easy demeanor relaxed the atmosphere. She and Jude walked into the living room. Five of the girls were there, two playing a game of cards. Sangria and Bandee shared a magazine and Shelby sat alone, staring at the fire.

"I brought munchies." Elizabeth set the tray on a table by the fire. She turned to the girls. "Jude's joining us for dinner."

"Hey, lawyer lady, Happy Turkey Day," Sangria said, helping herself to a handful of cheese and crackers. "Damn…I mean darn, it's about time we get to eat, I'm starving."

"Me too," Bandee stood and hustled toward the tray. "All this sacrificing is hard. I swear I don't understand you Catholics."

With a mouth full of food, Sangria spit out questions to Jude. "Did you get the restraining order lifted? Can I get my kids back? Have they been able to see each other yet?" Cracker crumbs flew from her mouth.

"Whoa," Jude stepped back. "One question at a time." She took a piece of cheese and sat. "Another attorney is helping me with family law. So far, she's working on visitation for you and the kids, to get the two of them together."

Sangria jumped and yelped. "Yes!" Her eyes bore into Jude's. "Wait, visitation? That's all?"

Jude held up her hand. "For now, these visits will be supervised by CPS, but they also want Jared and Angel to see each other."

"Supervised? Like I don't know how to take care of my children?" Sangria threw her cheese and crackers back on the tray.

Elizabeth grabbed the thrown pieces from the platter. "Sangria, you can't act like this." She wadded the food into a napkin. "Tantrums aren't going to help your case."

"These things take time," Jude said. "The restraining order won't be lifted until you complete your…," Jude hesitated, not sure what to call Sangria's sentence at the home, "your time here."

Sangria waved the rolled-up magazine at Jude. "I'm able to take care of them myself. I don't need to be *here* anymore."

"It will work better if we follow the rules. I know you want your kids now, but you'll have to be patient. Set a good example for the court."

"Good example? Now you sound like one of the nuns." She flopped down in a chair. "What about Angel's Christmas pageant? I don't want that awful woman, who thinks she's the grandmother, anywhere near her." She threw the magazine into the fire. Shelby flinched. "*I* want to be the one to take her."

"Sangria!" Elizabeth strode to the fire and calmed the flames with a poker.

"You may have to put up with your mother-in-law for the night," Jude told her. "Be polite. She has the right to be there." Jude looked at Elizabeth for help. "And, I'm sorry, but CPS said if they didn't have the staff to attend, you might not be able to go."

"What?" Sangria sat up in the chair. "That's not right."

Jude saw small tears in the woman's eyes. "We might be able to have a representative of the Magdalene Home attend for supervision instead. We're working on it."

Elizabeth sat next to Sangria. "I'll be happy to go. But we follow the rules, okay? No more outbursts. Maybe you'll get more chances to spend time with your children if you do what CPS wants." She bent closer. "Even if you don't agree with their decisions." She looked at her sternly but gently.

Sangria turned her head away from Elizabeth but nodded.

"What about me? When can I get outta this joint?" Bandee asked. She stood and looked at Jude.

Elizabeth, hands on her hips, looked at Bandee firmly, but smiled and said, "Keep it up, kid, and I'll make sure you get a life sentence here. You'd look good in one of these outfits." Elizabeth stood and modeled her habit.

"Oh, man. Do they come in stripes? Like prison?" Dramatically, Bandee fell to the couch. "This place is going to kill me before I'm twenty. Being good is way harder than being bad."

"Don't be such a drama queen." Elizabeth tossed a pillow at her.

Bernadette came into the room, peeling off her apron. "Dinner is served. Girls, please help pour the water. Sangria, Elizabeth, Jude, you can set the food on the buffet. I'll pour the wine."

Bandee jumped up. "We get wine?"

Bernadette waved her hand and shook her head. "One glass, and only for those old enough."

Bandee stomped her foot. "Do life experiences count? Then I'd be way old enough."

෴

Soft candlelight illuminated the dining room, which mingled with the tantalizing smells of food. The sturdy oak table bore the weight of a cornucopia of food. Turkey, pork, and steaming sides. Suddenly starving, Jude couldn't wait to heap her plate with turkey and dressing.

Bernadette went to the head of the table, as if to hold court. "Before we get started, let's each give a personal blessing and thank God for all the many gifts He provides."

Even though a prayer was expected, Jude could feel the disappointment of the hungry women.

"Elizabeth, would you like to begin?" Bernadette sat and bowed her head.

Instead of clasping her hands in prayer, Elizabeth leaned forward and took Jude's and Sangria's hands. The others at the table took the hands of the person next to them. "I have much to be thankful for." She gave thanks for knowing each woman at the table and expressed gratitude for Bernadette, "helping me in my time of need." The two nuns looked at each other, an unspoken communication passed between them like mist. "And I'm thankful for new friends." She squeezed Jude's hand. Luckily, it was the uninjured one.

Elizabeth looked to her right. "Sangria, you're next."

"Damn. All this food's going to rot before we all get our prayers done." She looked hungrily at the bounty. "Okay. I'm going." She bowed her head. "Please God, send the bitch-whore who's got my Angel to hell, and give me my kids back. Also, tell CPS to stop riding my ass. And please bless my children. Amen."

"Sangria," Sister Bernadette admonished. "Do you want some soap to wash down this dinner?"

Jude bowed her head, but only to hide her laughter.

There was a long pause before Elizabeth turned to Sangria. "Your response was heartfelt but, perhaps, misguided. Also, we never wish for anyone to go to hell."

Bernadette spoke up. "Next. Shelby?"

Shelby wasn't sure how to react. She bordered between shock and laughter. "Please, God. Let there be peace on earth. Amen."

Sangria rolled her eyes. "This ain't no beauty pageant."

"Thank you, Shelby, that was nice." Elizabeth must have squeezed Sangria's hand hard because she gave a little jump.

Jude was enjoying herself. In a way she felt part of this gang of misfits.

"Bandee?" Bernadette nodded at the girl.

"Dear God. Please get me out of here early for good behavior and let me get on with my life before I turn into a wrinkled old maid. I know I'm supposed to suffer, but enough is enough," Bandee prayed. She looked at Elizabeth. "Amen," she added.

The rest of the table offered their prayers and, when the circle came to Jude, she wasn't sure what to say. She hadn't prayed since the rape. It didn't feel natural. "Um, Blessed our Lord for these Thy gifts, Amen."

"Well, *that's* original," Sangria said. "Can we eat now?"

"Sure, everybody dig in," said Elizabeth. "After dinner, we're going to have a special treat, a letter from Trudy." Elizabeth unfolded her napkin and put it on her lap.

Bandee scooped a pile of mashed potatoes. "Are we ever going to get a TV? My eyes hurt from reading so much."

"We don't need a TV." Bernadette said. She watched the women serve themselves.

"Yes we do. Especially if the only entertainment we're going to get after dinner is reading a letter from a rich dead lady," Bandee said and passed the potatoes to Shelby. "Talk about boring."

"That 'rich dead lady' has provided a roof over your head, food to eat, and an education. Be grateful," Elizabeth admonished the girl.

"Well, if I had that much money, I'd at least buy a TV," Bandee said with a mouthful of turkey.

"Don't talk with your mouth full," Bernadette said and served herself.

Shelby kept staring at Jude. "I've never talked to a real lawyer before. They're pretty important, like doctors."

Jude felt awkward, she'd never considered herself a person to be admired. "Anybody can be an attorney. You just have to go to school. One class at a time." She buttered a steaming roll. "You could do it if you really wanted to."

Shelby blushed, which illuminated the freckles on her plump face. "Nah, I don't like school. Besides, I want to be a movie star. You don't have to study."

Jude laughed. "I think it's harder to get into the movies than law school."

The girl shrugged. "I don't know, I was in a movie once. Even if it was porn, it's a good start to being famous." She talked as if she were proud of her venture. "I've always been popular with the boys at school."

"Oh." Jude was shocked. "How old are you?"

"Seventeen." She held her head up as if prepared to defend herself. Shelby continued, "I was the only girl ever to ride on the school's team bus. Of course, the driver didn't know. It was fun."

Bernadette made a *tsk, tsk* sound and shook her head. "Oh child, but such a cost."

"No, no cost. I didn't charge anything back then," Shelby answered. She took a bite of bread. "I didn't know I could make money doing that stuff."

The false confidence masked insecurities Jude knew were part of the girl.

Shelby moved her fork on her plate. "A lot of famous actresses do nude scenes. And I was good at it." She nodded.

Jude didn't know how to respond but felt the food lump in her stomach at the indignities this young girl had suffered.

Bandee spoke up. "And, if we had a TV here, we'd be able to watch you."

༺❀༻

After dinner and dishes, the group settled by the fire. Elizabeth took Trudy's envelope and sat in front of the women. Bernadette was still bustling in the kitchen, setting out pies for dessert.

"Bernie, come on, let's read Trudy's letter." Elizabeth

held up the envelope.

Bandee looked at Elizabeth. "Why can't we call Sister Bernadette, Bernie?"

"I've known Sister Bernadette for many years. It's a special name I use with her. It wouldn't be the same coming from someone else." She smiled at the girl. "Plus, it's not respectful."

Sangria said, "Yeah, just like all we're learning about manners and respect in that, what's it called, equestrian class."

Elizabeth laughed. "Etiquette class. Equestrian is about horses."

"Well, whatever it is, I don't need to be that polite all the time. It makes me sound dumb."

"No, it doesn't. Manners are never dumb." Elizabeth looked at Jude. "It's part of our life skills classes."

Bernadette came in, drying her hands on a dishtowel.

Elizabeth smiled. "Try to sit down for five minutes. For heaven's sake, you have more energy than all of us put together."

Bernadette waved her off. "There's always much to be done."

"Okay, let's read this letter." Elizabeth tore open the large manila envelope. Inside were two sealed letters. She read the front of each. "Oh, look, one for me and Bernie, and one to read aloud."

Bandee sat forward. "Shake it real good, maybe there's a check inside."

Bernadette sat near Elizabeth and said, "She's been very generous. We should be thankful for all she's provided." She tossed the towel over her shoulder and looked pointedly at the girl.

The turkey and small ration of wine made Jude sleepy and content. She took a seat in a chair off to the side of the group and watched the others as Elizabeth began to read.

> *Dear Friends,*
>
> *I hope the home is operating well and you all are happy. Elizabeth and Bernadette are amazing women. Follow their lead and you will go far. Keep them close to your heart, as they were always in mine.*
>
> *Remember that Mary Magdalene was thought, at one time, to be a prostitute, when actually she was a loyal disciple of Jesus. Just as she did, you must rise above speculation and be strong. It is within your power to prevail. This home is merely a means to guide you. At times it may seem easier to take the shortcuts in life, but you will usually suffer consequences if you do. Always maintain dignity, let it come from within your soul.*
>
> *I've often sounded like a broken record to my daughter when I tell her to "do the right thing." You will follow the path for self-worth and confidence if you follow that simple rule. For that, you can always be proud.*
>
> *God bless you all,*
> *Trudy*

Elizabeth was quiet as she folded the letter and handed it to Bernadette. Jude wondered how close Trudy had been with them and what had brought them all together. She wished there was a circle of friends in her life. But that would require Jude to open up emotionally. Something she'd never be able to do.

Bernadette re-read the letter to herself then folded it and put it in her pocket. She looked at the women. "Those are wise words to live by. Do you all understand what Trudy was saying?"

"I didn't know Mary Magdalene was a prostitute,"

Bandee said. She hit Shelby playfully on the arm. "Cool."

Shelby tried to ward off a second hit. "Who's Mary Magdalene?"

Bernadette shook her head. "Child, you have so much to learn. You both do."

Elizabeth opened the second letter. "Bernadette, do you mind if I read this first?"

"No, please do. I'll start cutting the pies. Who wants to help?"

Shelby popped up to follow her into the kitchen. "Can I get the first piece?"

Jude decided to stay for pumpkin pie, then head home. It had been a good day for her. This was the first real Thanksgiving dinner she'd been to in ages. For years she'd begged off any invitations and settled for take-out turkey and dressing and ate alone.

"Oh!" Elizabeth jumped out of her chair clutching the letter. "No...I can't believe..." She looked at Jude, then back to the letter. Her hand went to her mouth, and she shook her head in a state of disbelief. "This can't be." She wiped tears from her eyes as Bernadette came in from the kitchen.

"Are you all right, Elizabeth? What happened?" Bernadette looked around the room for an explanation.

Jude sat straighter, with a sick feeling the news was about her. "Elizabeth?"

Elizabeth shook her head. "I'm sorry, I need to do some prayerful meditation...alone...I-I can't talk about this now." She raced upstairs.

Bernadette followed her. "Sister, what is it? What's in the letter?"

Elizabeth grabbed the older nun's hand and pulled her along. "Come here." She shot a glance at Jude.

Jude fought a knot in her stomach, stood, and walked to the base of the stairs. She overheard Elizabeth whisper to Bernadette. "It's here, in the letter. About Trudy and Jude."

"How?" Bernadette asked as the two walked into a bedroom.

Jude raced up the stairs and put her ear to the door. She only heard muffled whispers. She knocked and quickly opened the door. "What's in the letter?"

Elizabeth shoved the letter into her pocket. "Jude. Not now." Tears streaked the nun's face.

Jude looked at Bernadette and then back to Elizabeth. "What did Trudy say? I have a right to know." Her dinner was bubbling inside her.

"You're right. You do have a right to know." Elizabeth wiped her face. "But we can't tell you now."

Bernadette seemed to be praying silently, broke her trance, and looked at Jude. In a trembling voice she said, "God truly works in mysterious ways. Let him give us strength and guidance now." She went to Jude and took her hand. "When the time is right, we'll talk." She looked at Elizabeth and then back to Jude. "We're bound by a promise of silence until…" she bowed her head, "until Trudy says we can tell you."

Chapter 30

Four days after the Thanksgiving dinner, Jude tapped her pencil on her desk, frustrated the nuns wouldn't tell her what was in Trudy's letter. How does Trudy know me? It was agonizing realizing the answer was in a letter delivered by Jude's own hand. Ethically, Jude would have never opened another's mail, but the temptation to find out the contents was driving her crazy. The nuns absolutely refused to talk to Jude about it. Trudy continued to be a mystery to Jude. Why had this woman made her presence known to Jude now after her death?

"Jude. Are you there?" The office manager's shrill voice squawked on her intercom.

"I'm here." She winced and put her index finger in her ear to quell the shriek.

"When do you want to start interviewing for your new assistant?" There was noticeable scorn in the woman's tone. "You can't 'borrow' one from another associate. We can't afford to lose anybody else."

Jude shot her pencil like a spear at the speaker and said, "Let's just wait until after the holidays."

"After the holidays? Jude, how do you expect to get everything done without an assistant? Drew said he wants your cases covered."

Yeah, Jude thought, *and you want your ass covered.* "If I get desperate we can hire a temp," she said.

"Then you'll talk to Drew?"

"No, I'll be busy working on my cases. Thank you for taking care of it." Jude was tempted to add *because it's your job*.

"You know we don't like to use temp agencies. They're too expensive and usually only have mediocre people."

"I'll try to ride out the storm alone," Jude said. "Besides, it would take too long to train a new person. I may need a little help with my filing and mail. But that's pretty easy."

"Well, all of the other assistants are busy clearing their own cases for the end of the year. Really, Jude, I can't believe you let Katie get away." The manager's voice went up an octave. "Especially since we're paying her for the two weeks *you* told her not to be here."

"I had my reasons, and Drew will support me," Jude said. Even though she wasn't sure at all he would. She hung up with promises to do as much of the work as possible.

She was down to the last few days before the truck wreck mediation and she really missed Katie. Her young client, Tiffany Carmen, weighed heavily on her, but distractions from the Magdalene Home prevented her from giving the case her full attention. And that damned letter with the golden answer gnawed at her insides.

She spent the morning working on exhibits for Tiffany's case, and in the late afternoon switched gears to clear other, smaller files. Other than a few phone interruptions, she managed to get a lot done by five o'clock.

As the rest of the office staff left, she pulled out the Magdalenes' case files. She was looking for another excuse to call Sister Elizabeth and pry information out of her. Again, she cursed the Catholics and their vows of secrecy. Jude managed to get Elizabeth to tell her she couldn't divulge the information until Christmas, three weeks away.

Jude felt like a frustrated kid waiting for Santa Claus.

She dialed the home and figured everybody would be preparing dinner.

Elizabeth answered the phone. "Jude, how are you?"

Jude jumped right in. "I can't eat, can't sleep. What can I do to squeeze the information out of you? Extortion? Bribery? Come and clean your toilets?"

"As a nun, I have a high tolerance for pain and for keeping secrets. I'm bound to silence until Christmas. Please, trust me."

Jude noticed a slight edge to her voice. "Are you tired of me asking?"

"No. Well, yes. You've got to take me on my word. I'm restricted to say anything. I'm sorry I read the letter in your presence. If I had known…" She left the sentence unfinished and changed the subject. "What have you found out about Sangria attending the Christmas pageant? She asks me at least twice a day."

Probably like me asking about the letter, Jude thought. She opened Sangria's file. "The attorney that looked over the case needs you or Bernadette to commit to supervising her at the church's pageant. Once that's done, she'll present it to the court for a judge to okay."

"No problem. Get me the papers to sign, and I'll do it."

"Great. I'll try to get them to you by tomorrow. Things are a little crazy here since my assistant quit."

"You were already burning the candle at both ends. Is there anything I can help you with?" Elizabeth asked.

"No, thanks. I'm hoping to get through this by myself. It would be too time consuming to teach someone new about the cases." She looked over the sea of papers on her desk. "I may need to hire someone to do my filing for me, though."

"How about using one of the residents? Sangria or Bandee could work to pay off their debt to you."

Jude gulped. She envisioned one of the girls dressed inappropriately, pushing the mail cart into Drew's office. "That's nice of you to offer. Hopefully I'll be able to manage. Thanks, though."

"I know you think my idea is unconventional, but listen, we're working very hard to mainstream these girls into respectable jobs."

Jude felt a twinge of embarrassment that Elizabeth had read her so well. "It's a good idea, but I'd feel responsible, making sure they were doing the job. I have enough work to deal with," she said.

"Just so you know, most of the women are educated with at least a high school or equivalent degree."

"I know, Elizabeth, but I still think it would be difficult."

"Don't give up on them. That's a big problem. Many people are afraid to reach out and help. They're good people who were forced to make a living on the street. Give them a chance." She paused. "Didn't Trudy help you?"

"What? I've never mentioned that." Jude's stomach tightened with the realization Elizabeth knew about the financial help Jude had only just found out about. "Is that what was in the letter from Trudy? That she helped pay for my college? That she was an unseen benefactor helping me out of a hole?" Jude fought a swell of anger and a dose of insecurity. "I'd never met the woman nor knew of her assistance. So now, from her grave, she's going to let the world know I couldn't have made it without her?"

"Jude, stop. Please." Elizabeth's voice held a soft, reassuring cadence as if she was used to talking people down from the edge. "Trudy helped many. She believed in paying it forward."

Jude swallowed hard. "Did you take Guilt 101 in nun school?"

"I don't want to make you feel guilty, just vital. You could change someone's life."

Jude sighed. "I should probably fix mine first." She leaned back in her chair and wished this wasn't happening.

"Maybe helping someone else would help you."

"I'll think about it. But don't get your hopes up. It'll probably never get past administration."

"Thank you! I'll say a prayer it works out. God bless you."

"Jude, are you there?" Drew's voice boomed over the intercom.

"I'm here."

"Come see me. *Now*."

"Elizabeth, I have to go. I'll get the papers to you soon."

"Okay, it sounds like he means business."

"Yeah, I better not keep him waiting." She couldn't imagine what set him off. Figured the office manager had told him about Katie's pay.

As she walked into his office, he was pacing the floor holding a fistful of documents. He held them up as she entered.

"Do you mind explaining these to me?" He tossed the papers on his desk.

"What are they?" Nervous energy nibbled at her. Had Trudy written to him, too?

"You know, when I agreed to help this group, it was because they were protected under the Catholic Church. An institution I didn't think would mar my credibility."

Jude thought of the huge fee he'd been so interested in before but didn't say anything.

"My name is becoming a laughing stock in the legal community. People think it's funny my legal firm is associated with a chicken ranch." He turned and took the papers from his desk. "Now I'm helping prostitutes *and* criminals? We're a personal injury firm, we don't do criminal defense."

"Drew, some of these girls have records, but mostly minor infractions. And most are underage. The home is only taking women that can be rehabilitated." She took a breath. "Any criminal records of the minor girls are protected."

"I'm not talking about the girls. I'm talking about the nuns. Those two sisters, have rap sheets longer than my arm." He shoved the papers at Jude. "Maybe they're running a scam."

Jude glanced at the first page in the thick stack. Sister Bernadette had been arrested numerous times. In most of the mug shots, she flashed a big smile, in one a peace sign. Jude read quickly through her record. "Drew, these are for war protests and peace rallies. That's what all these jail records are about. That's not so bad."

"I don't care about the peace rallies. I do care about violent crime."

"What violent crime?" Jude began flipping through the pages, not reading them carefully but visualized Bernadette armed with an assault rifle and gun belt. All she saw were minor protest arrests. "Where did you get these? What made you think to ask for them?"

"I didn't ask for them. Your boyfriend, Rick Carney sent them." He sat down. "Rick thought I might be interested knowing who I was working with."

Jude's anger shot up. "He's not my boyfriend."

"Well, you could do worse in your choice of guys. Rick seems on top of things. He's trying to get the estate to sell to the church. And he's making a good argument." He nodded at the papers in Jude's hand. "The more I'm finding out about these women, the more inclined I am to agree."

"Rick stands to make a lot of money on the deal. He's only looking out for himself. The sisters have worked too hard on that home. It would disrupt the service they're providing."

"I'm sorry, Jude. When I said I'd help this group, I expected we'd do some pro bono stuff, you know, financial contributions, managing the money, community outreach. I didn't expect it to backfire on me. I can't be associated with them anymore, especially in light of the crimes." He nodded toward the records in Jude's hand. "Trudy's money is great, but I don't need it that bad. The reputation of my firm is more important." He looked at Jude.

"What other crimes?" Jude started flipping pages again.

Drew didn't answer, but said, "The nuns can easily set up the home elsewhere. I agree with Rick. It would be a win-win situation for everybody. After the year is out, and we no longer have contractual obligations, we'll transfer the estate to the bank. They can manage the money and pay the home. The group can sell that hotel for a profit and move." He nodded. "And I can wash my hands of the case." He seemed to be talking to himself.

As much as Jude complained about working with the home, she'd also become committed to the girls, even liked them. And to add fuel to the fire, Rick wanted to see the greedy Christian Academy get the hotel. That gave her some resolve to continue helping the girls, if not for any other reason than to piss off Rick. "Drew, let me continue to work with the home. So what if the nuns spent a little jail time for peaceful protests? I think it speaks well of their character. Let's not give up on them."

"Peace protests are one thing, Jude. But Sister Elizabeth has more serious problems, a violent rap sheet. I don't want to be associated with a criminal who was arrested for armed robbery."

Chapter 31

"I'm sorry St. Jude, but Elizabeth is at a retreat this week." Bernadette smiled, her cheeks ruddy from the heat of the stove as she made breakfast in the spacious kitchen. "She left a few days early to pray and sort out some feelings."

Jude sat at the table holding a warm cup of coffee. She'd left early so she could talk to the nuns, in person, about the criminal records Drew had uncovered. "Sister Bernadette, I need to talk to her, and you, about the arrests you've both had. Drew is ready to ditch the deal and I won't be able to help you anymore."

Bernadette waved her hands and beamed. "Oh, that was years ago. What would that ancient history have to do with anything?" She blew on a steaming cup of tea. "Are you sure I can't offer you breakfast?"

"No, thank you." Jude stirred her coffee. "What I'm afraid of is the Academy using the information to pressure you to move."

Bernadette sat across from her. "The protesters have been here every Saturday. Really, they're nice people. I've even made a few friends." The nun chuckled as she strained her tea bag from the water. "You know, we've started to till soil for a wonderful vegetable garden in the back. The girls have worked hard, even getting dirt under their nails." She smiled warmly. "It does my heart good to see them enjoying something so simple." She put her hands around her cup. "I can't wait for spring when they see the product of their hard work."

"Sister, I need to talk to Elizabeth." Jude was frustrated the older nun kept veering the conversation away from the subject. "We've got to address these issues." Jude poked a finger at the papers she'd brought.

"Oh, let's not make a mountain out of a molehill. We are all quite happy here," Bernadette became serious and looked pointedly at Jude. Her voice took on a hard edge. "We're also tougher than we seem. We're not moving." She softened, becoming the sweet caring nun again. "Now let me make you some eggs, child. You're so thin." She leapt up, seeming happy to be able to cook for someone.

"Really, Sister, I'm not hungry." Jude shifted in her chair to face her. "I am concerned about Elizabeth's criminal past. She was arrested for armed robbery. Who am I dealing with here?"

Bernadette turned and looked at Jude as if ready to kindly scold her. "You're dealing with a gentle soul who loves her work and is committed to the church and these girls. All people have a measure of good in them, but some may have been, well, misdirected." She shook her head and sat back down. "I don't want Elizabeth to be hurt over any of this. Goodness, that was years ago."

"What happened? How did she become a nun with a criminal past?" Jude asked.

Bernadette became serious again. "She was a troubled teenager." She waved her hand in the air. "Heavens, weren't we all?"

"Not enough to hold a gun to someone." Jude leaned closer to Bernadette.

"I'd rather have Elizabeth tell you her story. It's really not my place to speak for her. Let me just say she's an angel from heaven who's earned her wings the hard way."

The floor above Jude's head squeaked. The women must be getting up. She wanted to find out about Elizabeth before everybody came down for breakfast. "I've been put in an uncomfortable situation here," Jude said. "I want to help, but these surprises that keep popping up are hard to work through. I've asked an attorney to help me with the resident's criminal histories. I'd look pretty stupid being kept in the dark about everything. If this lawyer finds this stuff out, and she probably will, I'll lose credibility for not knowing the background of people I've asked her to help me with." She sat back in her chair. "Another concern is the Academy's attorneys will probably take this to the media. How will it look if everybody associated with this place has a questionable past?"

"Well, for goodness sake, who doesn't?" Bernadette became slightly indignant. "We learn from our mistakes."

"Then I must be an amazing person," Jude joked.

"Why yes, you are!" Bernadette clapped her hands happily, seeming to miss the irony. "Do you see what I mean? None of us is perfect. That's why God helps us guide ourselves. Within our souls, we can feel it when it's right." She raised an eyebrow. "And, we can feel it when it's wrong, too. We have to be strong enough to continue to take the right path."

"Then how did Elizabeth go from being so bad to being so good?"

Bernadette winked. "Because she has a good soul." She tapped her chest. "Both Trudy and I could see that. That's why we took her under our wing." She looked out the kitchen window. "Did you know Trudy's patron saint was Saint Jude?"

Again, she slipped the main point of conversation under the radar. Jude tried to get back on track. "Did Elizabeth go to jail? Did she hurt anybody?"

"She was only hurting herself," Bernadette replied. "That's why we helped her."

"You and Trudy?"

"Oh, I see what you're doing. You're trying to get me to tell you about Elizabeth." She put a finger to her lips and shook her head. "I won't talk about my dear friend anymore. I'll let her tell you everything." She beamed beatifically. "But you can ask me anything about myself. I'm an open book." The nun spread her hands out.

"Okay, how did you meet Elizabeth?" Jude tried to use her trial skills to get answers.

"Objection! I'll plead the fifth." Bernadette laughed, but then became serious. "We've all had our problems." She made a quote mark with her fingers on the word *problems*. "In fact, when *I* was a young woman starting out in the convent, I fell in love with a seminary student." She put her hand on her chest and looked out the window. "We were madly in love and planned to talk to the monsignor about getting married." She sighed. "Unfortunately, monsignor found out about us before we could tell him. That crotchety old priest laid hard guilt on us." Bernadette shook her head and made a sound halfway between a laugh and a sob. "I cowered, was afraid to change, but my beau rebelled and quit the priesthood. He begged me to come with him." She looked at Jude. "I didn't. I was too scared to buck the system." She reached over and patted Jude's arm. "He was married within a year and became a missionary in Japan. I think they had five kids."

"Sister Bernadette, I'm sorry," Jude said. "Damned Catholic guilt."

"I don't blame the church, child." She squeezed Jude's arm. "God gave me many choices and blessings. *I'm* the one who chose the path I've traveled." Bernadette released Jude's arm and brought her hands together. "I'd made a commitment to the church."

"But you gave your whole life to them. Even the bad priests," Jude spat out before she could stop herself. Surprised the words had come out of her mouth.

Thankfully, Bernadette waved off Jude's comment. "The old priest was doing his job. The road God put me on included that young man and the convent. I had to decide." She stirred her tea. "Part of who Elizabeth is came from what happened to her. It shaped her and made her a whole person. Again, anything she wants to tell you should come from her."

The nun stopped talking when Bandee walked in. The girl was scrubbed clean, her hair still wet from the shower. "Hey, lawyer lady. What's going on?" Bandee asked. She went to the refrigerator and pulled out bacon and eggs. "You here to bring me my parole papers? Am I getting out of this joint?"

Bernadette got up from the table and went to the girl. "You're stuck with us for a while." She smoothed Bandee's thick red hair. "Where else could you go that has so much to offer?" Bernadette took some bowls from the cabinet and handed them to her.

Bandee rolled her eyes. "I just miss my freedom. You guys tell us what to do all the time." She looked toward the food on the counter. "You even tell us what to eat."

"Okay, young lady. You decide the menu for today. I'll sit down and enjoy my tea," said Bernadette.

Jude could see it was a struggle for Bernadette to leave the kitchen to the girl, but she sat anyway.

"Chocolate chip pancakes it is." Bandee began taking utensils from the drawers.

The nun winced and looked away. "And don't make a mess."

Jude grinned. "I thought you always let the residents make their own meals."

"Well, we do. But I like to act as a guide," said Bernadette. She glanced cautiously at the girl. "No, honey, not that spoon, you'll need a whisk." She held her tea tight, her knuckles turning white. "I'm not sure my heart can take this."

Bandee pulled out various ingredients and looked at them curiously. "Don't you have anything instant?" Instead of mixing, she looked at Jude. "Did Sister Elizabeth talk to you about hiring me?"

Her bluntness took Jude off guard. "Well, she mentioned you might be a good candidate to help me with some filing." She didn't want to give Bandee false hope.

"I'd try real hard," Bandee pleaded. "I used to work for a veterinarian. I learn fast." She looked away. "Sister said if I found a good job and I'm responsible, it would help my chances of getting out of here."

"You should take advantage of what the home offers you," Jude said.

"I'm almost eighteen. I'm seeing my life pass before my eyes." She moved bags of flour and sugar on the counter. "I'm going to go to community college. Maybe I'll be a lawyer, you could show me how."

"Bandee, it's harder than that..." Jude's voice trailed off as she thought of her own pathetic youth. "But, yes, if you really work hard you can."

"You just don't want to help me because you think I'm a hooker." She put her hand on her hip. "I only turned a few tricks to help out my boyfriend."

Bernadette had been quiet, watching the exchange. "I think it would be good experience for you to help Jude, honey. But you'll have to act more mature than you're acting now."

"What? Just because I want chocolate chip pancakes?"

Jude laughed. "This goes way beyond chocolate chip pancakes."

"You don't think I can do it."

"I didn't say that." Jude felt backed into a corner.

"You don't have to say it. I can tell. You think I'm too stupid to do the job." Bandee turned back to the food. "And I don't know how to make pancakes from scratch." She started crying.

Bernadette was up in a flash and took the girl in her arms. "That's why I'm here. And I'm sure Jude would love to help you." Bernadette looked at Jude and nodded as if that would fix everything. "We're here to teach you life skills child, so you can reach your dreams." She dabbed Bandee's tears with a paper towel.

Sangria walked in and saw Bandee crying. "Oh, Lord, kid. Are you PMSing again? You need to take some birth control pills or something."

Jude turned away from the women. Her own life had been fractured, yet she'd managed to pull through and get into law school. But she'd shut out life, focusing only on the carrot. Now, although her career was successful, she was still that broken girl raped in the confessional. Emotion, the ability to feel, had stopped there. And she wasn't strong enough to love, or care, again.

Chapter 32

How had it happened? Jude wondered as she sped to the office much later than she'd intended. All she had wanted was an explanation from the nuns about their criminal past. *Pasts*, she reminded herself. The next thing she knew, she'd promised Bandee she'd help her go over her college admission catalog, and *maybe* she could help file at the office. That was the last thing she needed. The chocolate chip pancakes were sitting heavy in Jude's stomach, right next to the worry. She shouldn't have stayed for breakfast. It felt as if someone had stuck a fishhook in her lip and kept reeling her back to the Magdalene Home. *I am such a sucker*, she thought, as she parked her car and raced into the building.

As she got to her office, she found Drew's assistant going through Katie's files. "Can I help you?" Jude asked.

"Oh, good. I'm glad you're here. Drew needs Trudy's estate files. I can't find anything here."

"What does he need out of them?"

She shrugged. "I didn't ask. I was just going to bring the whole file. He's in a meeting with Rick Carney and asked me to come down and get everything. He did try to call you first, but you weren't here yet."

Jude knew why pancakes were called flapjacks, because that's what they were doing in her stomach. "He's meeting with Rick Carney, now?"

"Yeah, they're in his office."

"I'll take it." Jude went to her desk and grabbed the file. She dropped her briefcase, took a huge breath, and headed to see Drew.

Rick and Drew sat together at a small table in the corner of his massive office. When Jude walked in, they both rose and greeted her.

"Jude. It's great to see you." Rick took her hand and tried to pull her close to kiss her cheek. "I've missed you." He whispered near her ear.

Repulsed, Jude turned her head as he moved close. She nodded at Drew. "I have Trudy's file. How can I help you with it?"

Drew made a point to look at his watch. "Jude, we tried calling you this morning."

"I had a meeting out of the office." She continued to stand. "I'd left my phone in the car."

Drew sat down, and Rick followed suit. "Jude, I have some bad news," Drew said. "Apparently you had a run in with some kids at the home?" He looked over his glasses at her. "And you didn't tell me?"

Jude hugged the file close to her chest. She could feel Rick's cold eyes on her.

Drew continued. "I don't have all the facts yet." He glanced at Rick. "But one of the kids got hurt and is bringing suit against the home, Trudy's estate, and," he looked hard at Jude, "you."

Jude was too shocked to speak.

Rick spoke up. "When I found out about it, I wanted to talk to you both as soon as possible. Especially since the suit mentions you." He looked satisfied. Happy even.

Jude tried to find words to wrap around her jumbled thoughts. "How…who? I don't understand. The kids, and I use that term loosely, are suing the Magdalene Home for what?"

Drew shook his head. "Jude, I'm disappointed."

She found a small dose of strength. "May I sit down, please?"

Drew stood. "I'm sorry, of course." He pulled a chair to the small table.

Jude put the file on her lap as she sat and didn't acknowledge Rick until Drew sat down. "Let's start from point A. Who is bringing the suit?" she asked.

Rick pulled a small stack of documents from his briefcase. "Marcus Hall is the kid who's filed a complaint. He claims he was run over by a woman driving a black BMW in front of the Magdalene Home."

"Run over?" Jude looked skeptically at him, but her voice was shaking.

"Do you have an accident report?" Drew asked Rick.

Rick sorted through the papers. "No, I don't see it here. Hang on." He dialed a number on his cell and spoke on his phone. "Excuse me." He held up a finger. "Katie, hi, it's me."

Jude could feel coarse salt rubbed into her emotional wounds.

Rick continued. "Hey, could you fax over the accident report on the Hall case? Yeah, you should know the number." He chuckled politely. "Thanks." He put the phone in his case. "My assistant will fax it over right away."

Jude fought an urge to throw something heavy at him. "What attorney would be so desperate to take this case?" Jude asked. She absently rubbed her healing, but still painful arm.

"Lonnie Ball."

Jude scoffed. "I guess the kid must've gotten his number from a daytime TV ad. He's a real class act."

Rick shrugged. "I know he's slime, but I have to say he is really excited with this case. He doesn't usually get such a deep-pocket defendant. He's going after this with everything he has."

Drew sat forward. "Rick got wind of this through the Christian Academy and wanted us to be aware of it." He took his glasses off and nodded at Rick. "I appreciate the heads up."

Jude knew Rick was up to no good. Why couldn't Drew see through him? She asked Rick. "When was the accident report filed? I don't recall the police being called."

"It's my understanding Marcus Hall filed it a few days later." Rick seemed to enjoy watching Jude squirm. "I guess one of the prostitutes threatened to kill him, and one of the nuns hit him." He raised an eyebrow. "After he was run over."

"He was never run over."

Drew turned toward her. "What happened? I can't believe you didn't tell me about it."

"Trust me, Drew, this has gotten turned around. I don't know what Rick has told you, or how he happens to know all this," she glanced quickly, and angrily, at Rick, "but I was protecting myself. After he leaves, I'll tell you what really happened."

"Jude, Rick is on our side. He came here to help."

She deflected the comment. "What did you need out of the estate file regarding this?"

"We need to be clear on ownership. If a suit is brought against the home, they could put a lien on the property. Since Rick does real estate law, he's going to look over the records."

Rick leaned forward. "We're trying to do damage control before the bank gets wind of this. They could pull the rug out from under the estate."

Jude didn't have confidence in real estate law and didn't know if what he said was true. "Thank you, Rick. Why don't I visit with Drew and we'll call you?"

Drew stood. "Actually, Rick, I do need to visit with Jude about some things. I'll get in touch with you later."

"Fair enough." Rick stood and shook Drew's hand. He offered his hand to Jude, who only nodded curtly at him.

After Rick left, Drew closed the doors to his office. "Jude, I can't tell you how disappointed I am. You were my star associate, what happened?" He went behind his desk and seemed to look down at her. "This case keeps bringing the firm trouble, plus you've lost another good assistant, at a time when we've got to get these cases resolved. Now you're involved in a criminal case?" He sat and his leather chair squeaked from his weight. "One that has brought a suit against one of our clients?" He shook his head. "Lonnie Ball may be an idiot, but he's also a pit bull. Once he sinks his teeth into something he'll never let go. Especially with this amount of money."

Jude sat across from him. "Drew, those kids attacked me." She told him what happened. "I was angry and a little out of it, but I did not run over him. For crying out loud, he *ran* away from the scene. He couldn't have been hurt that bad."

"Did anybody see him attack you?"

"You know, I think one of the girls from the home saw them from a window."

"One of the residents?"

Jude looked away. The way he said *residents* sounded disrespectful. "Yes." She didn't add the girl had also been a porn actress.

"I'm becoming concerned with all the controversy. I've worked too many years to give this firm the good reputation it has. I don't want it to blow up." He waved his hand. "I know I'm partially to blame for taking Trudy's estate. But now, I want it out of this office. It's brought nothing but trouble."

Drew's brass desk clocked ticked. Each pendulum

swing counted a second, but the ticks seemed like minutes. Jude took a breath and said, "I didn't want this case to begin with. But now we're committed. I can't walk away from them." She wasn't sure how she could untangle herself from the women.

Drew rubbed his eyes. "You have until the end of the year to sever your relationship with them. By then, I'll have met Trudy's requests and can hand the estate over to the bank. I don't want that kid's lawsuit to affect this firm. Jude, this is very hard for me to say, but if we're named as a defendant, I may be forced to let you go." He couldn't look at her. "I'm sorry."

Chapter 33

Jude left Drew's office shocked at his words, she fiercely bit the inside of her cheek to keep from crying. Swallowing the bitter taste of blood, she was determined not to lose composure in front of the staff. The Magdalene Home had been the kiss of death for her. Ever since the sisters had come into her life, she'd had nothing but bad luck. Instead of relief, she was giving up responsibility, she felt there was too much unfinished business and promises broken. Walking to her office felt like walking the gauntlet. She told herself she didn't need to be anybody's hero. Life had been easier when she kept barriers up like a protective force field.

Relieved when she reached her office, she closed the door and put her head in her hands. Rick had turned into her worst nightmare and was now honing in on Drew. A strong wave of insecurity welled inside her. What else had they talked about?

It seemed harder to cut and run now that she'd invested so much in the firm and the women at the home.

The phone's ring brought her out of her thoughts. She looked at caller ID. It listed a number only. One she didn't know. She missed Katie. "Jude Madigan," she answered in a strident voice.

"Jude?" A deep voice asked.

She sat at her desk. The voice sounded familiar, but Jude was afraid to guess. "Yes."

"This is Reece Dawson. How are you?"

Her insides jumped. "I'm fine," was all she could get out. *Breathe*, she told herself.

"Sorry to call out of the blue like this. Especially considering how awkward our last evening together was."

He got right to the point. "How have you been?" she asked.

"Fine. I just spoke to Sister Bernadette."

"I saw her earlier today." Jude could still taste blood from biting her cheek.

"I know." He paused. "She told me what's been going on. The attempted takeover by the Academy, the protesters."

"Yeah, it's been tough for them."

"She said you were attacked outside the gates."

"I'm okay. They took good care of me." She cringed thinking about the lawsuit.

"They're good people." His voice took a sudden hard edge. "She also said you've been doing background checks on them, as well as the girls. Bernadette is upset by Elizabeth's past being brought up."

Jude leaned back in her chair as defeat settled in like an old friend. "I didn't look into her past." She spoke softly. "The only background information I asked for was for the women, to help them. Any documents I received about them were from Elizabeth." She turned and looked out the window. "Another source found the other information. And I was more shocked than anybody else."

"Then why were you there this morning asking about her?"

"Her criminal records were brought to my attention in a meeting last night. I did what I could to defend her, but it was hard considering I was totally blindsided. I didn't know anything but what was presented to me, which was her armed robbery charge. Pretty surprising."

"What kind of meeting was it, a nun bashing seminar?"

His tone was severe and took Jude aback. "Reece, I wasn't aware of her background, I never saw it coming."

"Then why bring it up? Why bother Sister Bernadette?"

"Because I'm afraid a group from the Christian Academy will use it against the home." She gave him a short version of the Academy's interest in the property.

"There's enough run-down property in that neighborhood they could buy. Why the home?" Reece's voice softened.

"Think about it. My suspicion is they're impressed with the renovation. They want *that* building. Plus, an attorney is working with them to help his own deal to buy some of the surrounding strip centers, so he can turn a profit when the neighborhood gets 'cleaned-up'." Jude ran a hand over her face. "He's been pretty aggressive in his tactics. He found the sister's background."

"Sounds like it's two against one. Who's this attorney?"

"Just some jerk." Jude said the words before thinking.

"Do you know him?" Reece's voice became guarded again.

"No. Not really." Jude didn't know what to say. "Reece, I don't want to see Elizabeth get hurt."

"Well, her history shouldn't have anything to do with this. It needs to stay buried. Leave her alone."

His words drove the stake deep and she knew she should give up working with the nuns. "I won't bother them anymore," Jude said. "I've been asked to relinquish my work with the home anyway." She sighed. In an odd way she was going to miss the women. "I'd planned to work with them until the end of the year, but maybe it's in everybody's best interest to send the files back today." The last bit of confidence she owned was gone. Would she ever be able to rise above her past? "I'll have them couriered over there later."

"I'm sorry, Jude." He sighed. "I don't want to see anybody get hurt either. Elizabeth is a good friend."

"Yeah, she is....was." Jude closed her eyes to hold in tears.

After they hung up, Jude packed the files and began dictating a letter to the home informing them of her resignation. Halfway through, she hit the stop button on her recorder. "Damn, I don't even have an assistant to type a stupid letter."

She typed the letter herself and sealed the large file, then called for a courier.

Reece's voice continued to resonate. She was surprised he could still stop her in her tracks, especially since she hadn't talked to him in a month. Why couldn't she attract and have a relationship with a man like that? Instead of the usual assholes she dated.

Jude buried herself in her cases. Now more than ever, she needed to prove to Drew she could do the work. If only she could prove it to herself. His threat of firing stung hard.

She'd managed to settle some smaller cases these past months, but the Carmen truck wreck needed to be resolved successfully. What if she let Tiffany down? Seeming to fail at everything she did lately scared Jude. And as much as she didn't want to, she considered passing the case to another attorney. A child's future depended on her.

She combed through the file again, even though she already knew each document by heart. The case was mediating in four days. If she passed it off to another lawyer, she feared they wouldn't have the time to learn everything.

By late afternoon, she decided to talk to Drew about Reece's call and her "effective immediately" termination from the home. He would probably be happy about the decision to sever the relationship sooner rather than later.

As she walked to his office, she tried to get her head around the idea she was no longer working with the women. Instead of feeling lighter, she felt a weight dragging her and she wanted to talk to Elizabeth. Shake it off, she thought.

Drew was on the phone. After he hung up, he waved Jude in. He glanced at her quickly and told her to sit. "You've done well settling most of your cases this month, Jude. But we need to get the Carmen case resolved. No distractions. Especially that impending lawsuit." He tapped his fingers on his desk.

"I've spent all day on Tiffany's case." She hesitated. "I'm ready."

"For the Carmen case, you take anybody's assistant you need. Don't get yourself in a bind because you can't type a demand letter."

His intense manner made Jude nervous.

"Will you be coming to the mediation?" Jude asked.

"I'm scheduled for depositions that day." He shook his head. "But in light of everything, I've considered canceling." He stopped. "Are you confident enough to handle it?"

She wasn't sure at all, but said, "Yes." She shifted in her chair.

"Should I assign another associate to work with you, at least to get through the mediation?"

She shook her head.

"Okay. I'll do what I can to get over there before you ask for the demand."

This was her chance to pass the case to a more competent attorney. She shouldn't let her ego get in the way of this little girl's future, but she couldn't bring herself to say anything except, "I can handle it."

"Good. Now, about the case from that damned kid, I'm going to take care of the initial meetings. You need to stay out of sight."

"Okay." Jude wanted to tell him she'd take care of it, but he was so serious. "Drew, I sent the Magdalene Home a letter of resignation effective today. I got a call this morning…"

He interrupted. "You did what? You can't quit until I tell you to quit. We won't see a dime of that money unless we represent them through the end of the year. What were you thinking?"

"I'm sorry…I thought you wanted me to."

"Did I tell you to quit?"

"No."

"Didn't I tell you we'd handle the case until the first of the year?"

"Yes." Her insides were melting.

"Then why did you take it upon yourself to hand it back without talking to me first?" He ran his hand over his face. "I'm really starting to worry about you, Jude."

"I thought it would be best for everybody involved." She told him about Reece's call. "The nuns are upset about their criminal records being brought up."

"As I remember, this guy Reece is a contractor?"

"Yes."

"And you took advice and counsel from a *builder*?"

"But he's friends with Elizabeth and Bernadette…"

"I don't care if he's the fucking Pope! You talk to me before you break a contract from this firm." He moved forward in his chair and looked at Jude. "I want to get rid of this case too, but we're bound to it until January." He shook his head. "Damn it, Jude."

Jude had never been on the wrong end of Drew's temper. She had an urge to crawl inside herself, just like she did when her father berated her.

"Call the nuns. Get back on track with them. Let them know we'll keep to our side of the bargain. *After* Trudy's requests have been met, we'll terminate." He tapped a pen on his desk.

Jude was afraid to speak, tears waited just below the surface. She could not, would not, cry in front of him.

"Excuse me." Drew's assistant stuck her head in the door.

Jude wondered how much she'd heard.

"I hate to interrupt, but there's a nun and some women in the lobby for Jude." She came closer and said, "They were being kind of loud. Should I direct them to the conference room?"

Drew stood. "No, Jude and I will talk to them."

Jude followed behind and took a deep breath. *It's just a job, she thought. What's the worst Drew could do to me? Fire me? I could sell my house and flip burgers.* Then, with a sick feeling, she remembered the lawsuit from the kid who'd attacked her. She could be held personally liable.

Bernadette, Sangria, and Bandee waited in the reception area. Sangria stood near the ledge of a massive floor to ceiling window. "Damn, I've never been this high before. You can see everything from here," she said. Her short skirt revealed too much when she bent and pressed her body against the glass. "Whoa, I'm getting dizzy!"

Bandee touched the furniture. "Wow! This place is way cool."

Even though the women had made an effort to dress, they still looked out of place in the office. Their skirts were too short and blouses a hint too tight. Bernadette, however, looked crisp and starched.

"Ladies." Bernadette wrangled the two women together. "You remember Mr. Winslow." She nodded toward Drew.

Drew shook their hands. Jude thought Bandee looked much younger here, Sangria looked older. Out of the shelter of the home's walls, Jude thought the women appeared more vulnerable.

Bernadette went to Jude and hugged her. "We got your letter today. You can't quit." She held Jude at arm's length. "We need you."

Drew stepped in. "Jude and I were just talking about that. She'll continue working with you." He looked at the receptionist, who'd been fascinated watching the show. "We'll be in the conference room if anybody needs us."

"Yes, sir." She sat down as Drew directed the group toward a massive conference room.

"Since you didn't quit, does that mean you're going to help me get a job?" Bandee was excited. "Can I work here?"

Drew looked at Jude then at Bandee. "You want to work here?"

Jude heard the receptionist stifle a laugh.

"The lawyer...um, Miss Jude said maybe I could help her out...some." The girl suddenly seemed uncomfortable.

"Well, *Miss* Jude could sure use some help." He held the door to the conference room open and let the women pass.

Jude couldn't tell if Drew was joking or mad as she walked into the room with the others.

Bernadette touched Drew's arm. "Mr. Winslow, Jude has done a good job for us, and has become part of our family."

Jude shifted nervously.

Sangria turned and put a hand on her hip. "Yeah, and you're supposed to help me get my kids back. So, don't be jumping ship on me."

Jude said, "You and your son will be able to attend the Christmas pageant. Those papers were in the stack I sent over today. But your mother-in-law will be there too."

"She ain't my mother-in-law. She's a bitch. Besides, I never married her asshole son."

Drew stood to the side and watched, clearly amused.

Bernadette stepped in. "Sangria, manners please. Watch your language."

Drew laughed. "Don't worry, these hallowed walls have heard worse."

Bandee touched the wall. "These walls are hollow?"

Drew turned to Bernadette. "By the terms of Trudy's contract, we'll be transferring the estate to the bank in January. Jude's available until then. After that, a trustee from Trudy's bank will step in."

"Why can't she continue working with us?" Bernadette looked perplexed.

"After we take care of the lawsuit she's named in, she'll be able to volunteer at the home." He put his hands in his pocket. "But she won't be a representative of the firm."

"That's not near enough time for me to get full custody of my kids," Sangria said. "I've got another year at this place." She crossed her arms. "You're ditching us like the rest of the shit-eating world."

"Sangria," Bernadette whispered, but it sounded like a hiss.

"The bank will be there to help," Drew continued.

"I'll make sure you have someone to represent you," Jude said. She had a hard time looking Bernadette in the eye.

"And I want you to help me be a lawyer." Bandee said.

Drew looked at Bandee. "A lawyer, huh?"

Bandee stood tall. "Yes, sir."

The walls were closing in on Jude. She didn't know how to respond being in the middle. "I'll make sure someone responsible will take care of all your needs." She hated that she was letting them down. "I'll do whatever I can…"

"Jude?" Before she could finish the receptionist paged into the room. "Tiffany Carmen is on line one. Do you want to talk to her?"

Jude looked at Drew. "I'll take it." She excused herself but feared leaving the women alone with Drew.

Jude picked up the phone in an empty office. "Hey, Tiffany."

"Hi, Miss Madigan."

"How are you?" This was the first time Tiffany had ever called her. Usually, Jude spoke to the girl's grandmother.

The girl hesitated before saying, "I got an A in math."

Her voice seemed tiny to Jude.

"You did? That's terrific!" A trace of maternal warmth sparked in Jude.

"I told Grandma, she was happy and all, but I don't know," her voice caught, "it wasn't enough for me." She started crying. "It's never going to be enough. I miss my mom. I want to tell *her*."

"I know you do." Jude didn't know what to say. She had a sudden urge to hug the girl. "She'd be proud."

"I don't know why I called you," she said, through tears.

"I'm glad you did." Jude was happy Tiffany trusted her. "You can always call me."

"It was my first 'A' since, you know, the accident."

"Congratulations. I'm proud of you."

"Grandma says you're going to have that big meeting, what's it called…"

"The mediation?"

"Yeah, that's it." The girl became quiet.

"Tiffany?" Jude asked.

"Yeah." She was crying harder. "It hurts when I think about her."

"I'm going to do everything I can to settle…" Jude

didn't want to talk about the girl's mother as a dollar figure. "I'm going to take care of you. Okay?"

"Okay." Tiffany sniffled.

Chapter 34

By the time she got home the problems with Drew, the women, and Tiffany weighed like an anchor. Frustrated, Jude tossed her expensive suit on the floor and kicked her shoes into the closet. In the shower, the hot water cleared the outer layer of dirt, if only she could clean the inner grime. By the time she crawled into bed, her mind still churned with life out of balance. She wanted order, tightly boxed up, the way it was before the Magdalenes came into her life. But she struggled with an odd kinship with them, and a strange need to help them. Before she met the women, Jude hadn't realized how thin the tightrope was that she balanced on. One false step, and it could have been *her* in the rehab home. Except for Trudy's help. Why? Why hadn't Trudy come into her life before she died?

Then there was the friendship she'd forged with Elizabeth. Jude had been careful to keep a safe distance from relationships. Like magnets with similar poles, she moved away when pushed near, never letting anyone get close. But Elizabeth had a way of boring into Jude. She seemed to be a step ahead of Jude's thoughts. Even though Elizabeth's criminal record confused Jude, she felt, for the first time, trust. Then, like a hatchet throw, Elizabeth had the letter that revealed how Trudy knew Jude.

She turned over and pulled her down comforter to her

shoulder. Tommy jumped next to her and settled in. Jude cradled him and stroked his back, as she lay awake thinking.

Tiffany Carmen's phone call had stirred emotions that Jude tried for years to restrain. When the child wanted to tell Jude about her first good grade since her mother's death, Jude's suppressed maternal instinct sparked, letting a small crack of light out. She had an urge to hug the girl and take the hurt away. Jude had been only two years older than Tiffany when she had to give up her own child. She understood loss and love ripped away.

Sometimes, when she allowed herself the aching luxury, Jude would remember the night she held her newborn. After she delivered her daughter, a nurse quickly put her infant on a portable bed, high enough for Jude to see, as long as one of the three nurses didn't stand in her line of sight. Contractions continued to pulse through her lower body but she wouldn't take her eyes off her new child who looked slippery and wet, like a fish taken from life-giving water. Gloved hands were working on her baby who lay limp on the table. Warming lights illuminated the tiny unmoving body. Jude feared she was dead. One of the nurses walked in front, blocking her view when, suddenly, the baby began a lung filling cry. Jude wept tears of joy and relief.

"May I hold her?" Jude asked, her arms outstretched. Her legs still hung in the birthing stirrups while a nurse attended to her, but nothing else mattered except her child.

The three nurses paused and looked at each other. One of them glanced at Jude and said, "Probably not a good idea, we're still scoring her Apgar." She nodded to another nurse. "Make sure she has enough medicine to make her comfortable."

Later, deep in the night, Jude woke from a drugged

sleep. It took a slow measure of time before she remembered what happened. She was a mother. Her baby had been born. She'd heard, no felt, her child's first cry.

Painfully, she rolled out of bed and stood on shaky legs. She sneaked out of the hospital room in the quiet hours of dark, woozy from drugs. She vowed the two would escape together. Jude held her soft distended abdomen, felt like her insides would fall out as she made her way to the nursery. Soft noises from the babies drew her to them. The room was dark and there were only two newborns in rolling cribs. Jude tiptoed quietly, trying to be invisible. She made her way to the beds, knew her daughter instantly, and went to her. As she picked her baby up a nun came in.

"Oh, my. What are you doing?" The nun ran to Jude and took the infant. Jude noticed she was the same one from the birthing room.

"I want to hold her." Jude began crying. "Please."

"You can't, it's not allowed." The nun looked at the door as if afraid of someone coming in. "The nurses have a strict policy." The baby began fussing a little.

Her daughter was magic. "Can I?" She held her arms out.

"Well. I shouldn't do this." The nun glanced furtively at the door again. "Here, sit down. Just for a minute."

Jude sat in a wooden rocking chair and reached for the baby, as the nun handed her the bundle, she felt deep warmth through the swaddling. Her baby was beautiful. Jude touched her delicate cheek, drank her scent, and wiped away the tears Jude had cried on her angelic face. A tiny peanut hand came out of the blanket and softly wrapped around Jude's finger. Then the baby's eyes found Jude's. Through her tears, Jude's insides bloomed with love. The nun hovered nearby but allowed Jude to hold her baby for almost five minutes.

"Come child, it's time." The nun walked toward Jude,

and reached for the infant.

"Jude cried harder. "No, please. I want to keep her."

"Someday, you'll make a wonderful mother." The nun gently touched Jude's arm. "But you're too young. Think about her future, your future. We've found a loving home for her where she'll be well taken care of. It's for the best."

"But *I* love her."

"And with that love you'd sacrifice anything for her, right?" The nun stroked Jude's hair.

Jude nodded under the touch of the woman's hand.

"And you still have some growing to do."

"But we can be together, I know I'll be a good mother." The raw pain that sawed through Jude made childbirth seem easy.

"She's going to a loving home. Think of your baby."

Jude shook her head. Her words couldn't get around the sobs.

"One more hug, child. Feel her heartbeat," She took Jude's hand and placed it on the newborn's chest. "This is your love, your gift to her." The nun gently took the baby from Jude's arms. "It's time, honey."

"No! Please…" Jude held her empty arms out, begging.

The nun turned and walked out the door.

As soon as the door closed, Jude ran to her room, put her head under her pillow, and cried until there was nothing left. No feelings, no pain, no love.

༄༅༄

Memories, one after another kept sleep away. In the dark of her bedroom, Jude tossed and turned until four-thirty before she gave up and got out of bed. Tommy mewed softly but stayed under the covers. Jude threw on her sweats and jogging shoes and hit the pavement on the cold, cloudy morning. The lack of sleep made her more determined to wear herself out physically. Running full speed, she tried to pound away clinging memories of her lost daughter, of Reece, and other lost opportunities. The inability to love or feel. She ran harder, ran until the only pain left was in her muscles.

When she got to the office the physical and mental exhaustion drained her from the inside out. Luckily, the rest of the day was uneventful. Jude thought Drew might admonish her about the women visiting the office. But after he'd met with them, he left the case in "Jude's hands." She would continue to work with them until January. She expected him to make jokes about Bandee working for the firm, but he'd said nothing. Jude prayed Bandee would find another career interest but didn't want to discourage the girl.

Elizabeth was due back today and Jude planned on calling her, no, harassing her. She looked forward to talking to Elizabeth. Quietly surprised that she'd missed her so much.

Just before five o'clock the phone rang.

"Sorry for taking off like I did." Elizabeth sounded weary. "I try to do a few retreats every year, and with everything going on, I needed the break."

"I understand," Jude said. "Was it like some kind of nun seminar?"

"No, not really. I focused on internal healing. Trust me, I needed it."

I wish you could've taken me with you," Jude said. "The timing wasn't great."

"It never is." She paused. "Bernadette told me that you quit as the home's attorney, were re-hired, and have now become interested in my sordid past."

"Yeah, busy day. And it's more the Academy that's interested in your past." Jude hesitated. "At least I think it's the Christian Academy's attorney who's brought up your records." Jude looked out the window. "I'll admit, though, it has intrigued me."

Elizabeth sighed. "This is a lesson in being good. You can never escape your past."

Jude winced at her words. "Unless you shut out the world."

"I can't do that. My work is helping people overcome their problems. I don't deny what I've done, but I also don't spread it around."

"Can we get together?" Jude wondered if Elizabeth would open up about her police record.

"I think that's probably a good idea. Are you free tonight?" Elizabeth asked.

"Actually, I am." Jude remembered Katie's comment about her having no social life. "Should we meet at a restaurant? Or should I come out there?"

"I don't want to talk here. I've alluded to, but not told, the women about what happened to me all those years ago. They just know I've had my share of issues. You know, to give me street-cred with them." She chuckled softly.

"What about my place?" Jude tried to get a visual of what moldy food was decomposing in her refrigerator. "I'll stop and pick up something for dinner. Any ideas?"

"That sounds good. I'm not picky about food, I'll eat just about anything."

"Okay, leave dinner up to me. Usually, a dangerous endeavor, so I'll make sure someone else will do the cooking."

They decided to meet at seven o'clock, and Jude gave directions. She tried to remember the last time she'd had guests over for dinner and realized she hadn't cooked for anybody since she'd moved in. Almost three years.

Elizabeth broke through her thoughts. "Jude?"

"Yeah?"

"I spent the last few days praying intensely about, well,

everything. And I will not—*cannot*—reveal the contents of Trudy's letter until Christmas. Okay?"

Jude sighed. "Okay. I'll take the truth serum off the menu then."

Elizabeth chuckled. "Yum." But just before the nun hung up, she said, "This retreat gave me time to think. I realized part of life is bringing people together. Small miracles happen that most people don't realize. From now on, I'm going to try harder to be more aware of God's gifts and blessings."

Chapter 35

In her kitchen, Jude carefully opened her oven door to check for cooking utensils or a fossilized casserole she may have forgotten. On her way home, she'd stopped by Central Market and bought pre-cooked beef and chicken, and an assortment of side dishes—recommended by one of their expert "foodies." Before checking out she grabbed a few bottles of wine.

She was excited and nervous to have a guest, no, a friend, over. Luckily, the maid came once a week, and since Jude spent so little time there her place was clean. Except for a few messes that Tommy may have scratched up, her home looked pretty good. She picked up the pile of clothes she'd thrown on the floor the night before and tossed them in her closet.

Tommy sat in a corner in her bedroom and watched coolly. Jude picked him up and said, "We're having company tonight. Can you be on your best behavior?" He responded by allowing Jude to scratch his neck before he bit her hand.

She tossed him on the bed and as she pulled on jeans and a sweatshirt, Jude remembered Elizabeth's cryptic message. *"Small miracles happen that most people don't even notice."* She wondered if Elizabeth had learned something else about the sale of the Magdalene Home. Or, maybe, by some small miracle, Rick had choked on a wishbone. Jude smiled, feeling a smidge guilty for thinking such a horrible thought.

She thought of how much Elizabeth prayed. As much as Jude prayed as a young girl, she wasn't sure she'd even remember how to at this stage in her life, but vaguely recalled the sense of peace she'd felt all those years ago. Her sense of faith had been shattered that awful night in the sanctuary with the old priest a lifetime ago. Before she could walk down the path of that memory, the doorbell rang, sending Tommy dashing under the bed.

Jude opened the door for Elizabeth, who was also dressed in jeans. Jude was reminded of the first day they'd met at the construction site when Elizabeth wore dusty work clothes. Only a few grays sprinkled in her short hair gave any indication of age. Jude figured the nun was only a few years older than her.

Elizabeth held a steaming bag and a bottle of wine. "Bernadette made some homemade bread, still warm, and I stopped for spirits." She walked inside. "Wow, this is a great place. Reece told me about it."

"He did?" Jude's heart gave a little jump.

Elizabeth smiled. "He said he was happy you had the foresight to retain the original cottage and not raze it over like most of the homes around here."

They walked into the kitchen. "I do love this place." Jude leaned against the counter. "How often do you talk to him?"

Elizabeth set the warm bread and bottle of wine on the kitchen table. "Almost every day." She faced Jude. "He still asks about you."

"Really?" Jude didn't want to sound too excited. "Did he tell you we spoke the other day?"

"Yeah, he told me. We had a long talk about that." She held up the bottle of wine. "How about a glass of wine while we talk."

"I'm sorry. My hostess skills are rusty."

"Well, put your hostess skills away, I don't need to be entertained." She smiled warmly. "Just tell me where the corkscrew is."

Jude laughed. "Good, then the pressure's off. I can't remember the last time I entertained." She rummaged through a drawer for a wine opener.

"What smells so good?" Elizabeth went to the oven and peeked inside.

"Precooked specials from Central Market." She tossed an oven mitt at Elizabeth. "It's probably hot enough if you're ready to eat."

Jude poured two glasses and set out plates and silverware while Elizabeth put the food on the table.

Elizabeth unwrapped the steaming loaf of bread. "Sangria is anxious to see her kids. Her mother-in-law agreed to let her spend time with her daughter before the pageant. She'll have both her kids together for the first time in almost six months"

"What about supervision?"

"The mother-in-law will be close but promised not to interfere. She's actually a very nice woman, regardless of what Sangria says. Her main concern is for her granddaughter."

"It's too bad she won't let both kids stay together." Jude sipped her wine and looked at Elizabeth.

"She can't afford both children, and Jared is no relation to her. It would be nice for the kids to see each other, but I can understand why she can't keep both." Elizabeth stood next to a chair.

It made Jude wonder who took care of her daughter. Was she wanted even though she wasn't a blood relative?

Jude took butter from the refrigerator. "Can I get you drunk enough to confess to me about that letter?"

"In due time, Jude," Elizabeth said wearily, as she sipped wine.

Jude didn't question her more. "Please, sit. Oh wait, I know one more thing that's missing." She opened a cabinet and took out some candles. "I've never used these, tonight will be a good time to fire 'em up." She lit the candles and dimmed the overhead lights. The candles bathed the room in warm dancing light.

"Too bad you're wasting all this mood lighting on me and not someone romantic," Elizabeth said.

"Probably why I've never used them." Jude wondered if this might be a good segue to mention Reece.

"We were talking about Reece earlier, and the conversation he and I had," Elizabeth said, again seeming to read Jude's thoughts. "He felt bad about putting you on the spot about my criminal past. He thought you were the one checking into my background."

"Wasn't me." Jude offered a dish of coconut-crusted chicken to Elizabeth. "I really think the Academy's attorney is behind all the bad that's happening." She shook her head. "I feel partially responsible. I'm not sure he'd be so hateful if I wasn't working with you."

"Why, because you used to date? He sounds like he has his own set of problems." Elizabeth scooped some pecan and cranberry rice on her plate. "I'll be happy to talk to him."

"Have at him. Hold a cross over his heart, maybe he'll melt." Jude chuckled. "What else did Reece say?" Jude didn't want the conversation to get away from him again. Elizabeth smiled but, this time, Jude didn't care if she could read her thoughts.

"Well, I don't know if I should say this, but he's wondering if he may have acted too hasty the night you two went out."

Jude suppressed a squeak. "Really?"

"I've been talking to him about you a little." Elizabeth looked at Jude. "But I'm not sure how much to say. Since *you* don't open up to people, I'm not sure I know you." She took a bite of chicken. "I figure underneath that tough exterior lies a hurt woman, or girl. I can't quite figure that part out."

Jude's defenses went up. "I'm fine." She took a big swallow of wine. Elizabeth was quiet, and Jude tried to shake off her x-ray vision. "This is not about me."

"Give yourself credit. You seem to have learned how to live with your problems." Elizabeth offered the loaf of Bernadette's warm bread to Jude. "I think there's more to you than meets the eye."

"Not really. What you see is what you get," Jude buttered a chunk of bread, then quickly changed the topic. "Please know I'm not worried about your past. Surprised, yes, and I'm sorry it was ever brought up. My concern is the Academy will use it and combine it with the women's prostitution history. That could get the neighborhood to rally against you."

Jude didn't mention the pending suit with Lonnie Ball.

Elizabeth laughed. "Considering the crime in that neighborhood, they'd be hard pressed to use any of those charges against us. By the way, how is your arm?"

"It's fine." Jude rolled up her sleeve. "Just a little tinge of yellow and green."

"I'm glad it's healing," Elizabeth sipped her wine and sat forward. "Okay, are you ready to dish?"

"What do you mean?" asked Jude.

"I'll tell you everything about my past. Why I got to the place I did." Elizabeth filled both glasses with more wine. "And you tell me what happened to you."

Chapter 36

Jude swirled the wine and looked at Elizabeth. The candlelight danced and reflected in Jude's glass. She pushed the remains of food on her plate. Should she tell Elizabeth about the rape or keep it safe, out of reach? The few who did know what happened had been sent away, like Sister Agnes, or sent Jude away, like her father. Jude's mother was still in denial, and maybe, to a small degree, so was Jude. For the first time in years, she fought an urge to talk. Her past was like a caged monster straining at the bursting lock. Strangely, she had an urge to talk to Elizabeth. Or was it the Catholic guilt of confession?

"Well?" Elizabeth looked at her expectantly. "It might make you feel better to talk."

Jude looked away. "Every person who's known has managed to hightail it." Jude poured more wine into both glasses. Courage.

"Did they leave you, or did you leave them?"

"Both." The sip of wine burned around Jude's answer.

"All right. I'm here if you want to talk, but I won't force you." Elizabeth tore off a piece of bread, steam puffed from the soft inside, and looked at Jude. "And I promise, I won't take off afterward."

Tommy walked into the kitchen but stopped when he saw Elizabeth.

"I didn't know you had a cat." Elizabeth bent and tried

to coax Tommy to her. He scampered into the darkness.

"He's not very social," Jude said. I'm surprised he came out with you here."

"Maybe he senses I'm a person to be trusted." Elizabeth smiled.

Jude sighed. "Let's talk about you. How can a Dominican nun also be a hardened criminal?"

Elizabeth laughed. "Hardened?" She leaned forward and pushed her plate away. "I did some pretty stupid things in high school."

"As a minor?"

"For some of the mischief. The big heist happened right after I graduated. Technically, I was of legal age," she said, shaking her head. "Sometimes, it feels like I've lived more years, no, more lives, than most."

Jude nodded.

"I came from a pretty normal middle-class home," Elizabeth continued. "Not rich, but we lived in a crummy school district. Both my parents worked. Actually, my mom worked just to send us kids to a Catholic school." She smiled sadly. "A lot of good it did. I started hanging out with some kids from the public school, the ones who took chances. We spent most of our time cruising in cars and listening to music. Man, when I think of how much time I wasted doing crap like that, it really irks me."

"Just kids," Jude thought back to her teen years. She never once "cruised" in a car full of kids. Instead, she was giving birth to a child she couldn't keep, then was shifted from one foster home to another. School was the only anchor in her life. She was "aged-out" and on her own by the time she was eighteen.

"I was a kid with too much time on my hands," Elizabeth said. "With both parents working, I had my afternoons to myself. Mom trusted me."

Jude saw pain flicker across Elizabeth's face.

"That's the hardest part for me, disappointing my parents."

"They must be proud of you now," Jude said, softly.

Elizabeth shrugged. "Yeah, but I really let them down then. Especially after getting busted for armed robbery." She winced. "It even hurts to say it."

"I still can't believe you…"

Elizabeth held up her hand. "Neither can I. Trust me, I'm no Bonnie and Clyde, I never went out that night intending to do what I did, but one thing led to another. The gang of kids I hung out with was becoming a little more adventurous. We'd gone from toilet-papering houses to stealing yard stuff, like potted plants and gnomes. One night, we took a set of lawn lion sculptures. We spray painted them and put them in front of the neighborhood school. Thought it was funny. We never got caught, though the principal suspected a few of us." She took another drink of wine. "Well, there was this one kid that I had the biggest crush on."

"You?" Jude laughed.

"Surely you don't doubt my sexuality?" Elizabeth joked.

"I don't see you as anything but a nun."

"Nuns are people, too," Elizabeth said, in mock seriousness. "Anyway, this guy could snap his fingers and I'd jump. He loved to go drag racing and had taken me along a few times." She looked at the ceiling. "Thank God, none of us got hurt. We were so stupid." She paused. "This is hard for me to talk about." She nervously folded and unfolded a napkin. "He was challenged to race this kid from another school, and, of course, couldn't wait to show him up. School was out for summer, so we were celebrating. This particular night, as usual, none of us had money, and this kid couldn't fill his tank. But he wouldn't back down from the challenge. We decided to pump a tank of gas and take off without paying. When we got to the station, the owner must've suspected we were up to no good. I got asked to be a decoy and go inside to distract the owner."

"How old were you?" Jude asked.

"I'd just turned eighteen." She looked down. "Graduated from high school two weeks earlier. So, this kid handed a gun to me, and I tried to push it away. He said the store owner was watching, so I'd better take it. The next thing I knew, it was in my pocket. I walked into the store and cruised down the aisles, afraid to look at the owner, shaking so hard I could barely move. I was sure he'd seen the gun. He watched me and, through the window, watched my friends outside, but he didn't say anything. I just wanted to find the back door and escape." She shook her head. "I didn't. Then my friend came into the store and went to the counter. I went to stand beside him when, suddenly, he demanded the owner hand over money from the register and yelled for me to get the gun. More shocked than anything, I pulled the gun out to get rid of it, but I was shaking so badly I dropped it on the counter."

Jude noticed tears in Elizabeth's eyes.

"I tried to run out of the store, but the police were there waiting. Turned out the owner called them as soon as we'd pulled up."

"Oh, my god." Jude said. She had a hard time picturing Elizabeth with a gun.

Elizabeth dabbed her eyes with her napkin. "Of course, I didn't put up a fight. I cried all the way to downtown, handcuffed, my hair plastered to my face from my tears and runny nose. I was a mess."

"And because you were eighteen you were tried as an adult."

"Yup." Elizabeth tried to smile. "It crushed my parents, both emotionally and financially. That's what hurts the most, the fact that I betrayed my parents' trust. Even now,

I wonder if they still doubt me."

"What happened to your boyfriend?"

"He was only seventeen, so he did juvenile detention for a year and was out. Clean record. The last I'd heard he was still causing trouble."

"Did you do jail time?"

She nodded and looked at the flickering candles. "Three months. A chaplain counseled me and then introduced me to Bernadette, who introduced me to Trudy."

"You've known them *that* long?"

"Hey, you make me sound like I'm ancient! Geez, I'm only forty-one."

"Sorry, you just seem timeless, wiser than your forty-one years. Is that how you became a nun?"

"Through the grace of God, and good moral support, yes. Bernadette sponsored me and helped me get into school. I didn't pursue religion until I was a junior in college." She smiled. "Bernie was like my surrogate aunt. I don't know where I would've been without her."

"And college is where you met Reece."

"Yeah, and Megan."

"How did Trudy play into this?" Jude thought of the letter.

"She and Bernadette were close. The princess and the pauper. They made quite a pair. Trudy contributed a bunch of money to Bernie's order. Bernie would, in turn, make sure it was used charitably. She called Trudy her personal ATM."

"How did they meet?"

"Through the church."

"Bernadette helped Trudy adopt her daughter, Elise. Not easy, since Trudy was a single woman in her thirties. The adoption agencies prefer young parents, a mom, and a dad. Bernie was her angel." Elizabeth stood and took her plate to the sink.

"Don't bother with that. I'll take care of it."

Jude felt a connection with Elizabeth, and was tempted to reach out and touch her arm. Jude stopped herself. But Elizabeth was someone who'd also experienced difficult times. Elizabeth managed to grow from it. Jude's emotional growth was stunted the night she shut out the world.

"I haven't told that story to anyone in years." Elizabeth rinsed her dish. "Reece and Megan were the only people I'd ever confided in." She turned to Jude. "And Bernie, who already knew the sordid tale. It re-opens some raw wounds."

"I'm sorry Rick found those records. I'd like to shove them up…"

"Whoa," Elizabeth raised her hand. "Yes, it's hard to relive it, but I'm a big girl. I know what's important in life and will survive anything he can dish out." She crossed her arms. "Now, are you ready to tell me your story?"

Chapter 37

Jude picked up the rest of the dirty dishes off the table and brought them to the sink. She saw Tommy lurking near the door, curious about the visitor.

Elizabeth followed Jude to the sink and they rinsed the dishes and put them in the dishwasher. Jude fought a storm of emotions as she debated telling Elizabeth about the night with the priest.

She deflected the thought by asking, "So, Trudy helped with your college, too?"

Elizabeth smiled. "In a roundabout way. When I chose to become a nun, the order paid for my tuition. Trudy funded the order. I was only one of their many causes." She covered a dish with aluminum foil and put it in the refrigerator.

"And you're happy with your choices?" Jude asked.

"This is what I was meant to do. And ironically, if I hadn't been stupid and put in jail, I probably would've never met Bernadette. There was a reason my life played out like it did. Although, you couldn't have told me that during that awful time. I just felt like a total loser."

"That surprises me. You seem like anything but a loser."

"There is something to be said for fate." Elizabeth went back to the table and poured more wine for both of them.

Jude finished wiping the counter, nervous about revealing her story, wasn't sure she should. Elizabeth was a nun. How would she react to the story of the priest? She'd likely keep her loyalties to the church and not Jude, especially since the church had helped who she was. Jude tossed the dishrag in the sink and decided to keep her mouth shut and the cap on the dynamite.

Elizabeth sat at the table. "So, what brought you to this place in life?"

"The usual. School, hard work, good looks, you know." Jude sat and sipped her wine.

The nun looked at Jude, her eyes reflected the candlelight. "Who's Father Callen?"

Jude almost choked on the wine. "What?"

"The night outside the home, with the firecrackers, you said something about a Father Callen. You were pretty upset. I'm assuming he's a priest."

"I don't want to talk about it," Jude leaned back and crossed her arms. Suddenly becoming petulant and defensive. She shot a quick glance at St. Jude on her mantle. "What exactly did I say?" She looked at Elizabeth.

"You kept rubbing your hurt arm and asked if that was Father Callen outside." Elizabeth looked away. "Then, you took a cross off the wall and threw it across the room."

Jude gasped. "I did? I'm sorry."

Elizabeth leaned forward and touched Jude's arm. "Hey, it's okay. I just wish you'd talk about what happened. It seems to be boiling just below the surface. Maybe I can help." Elizabeth squeezed Jude's arm and sat back.

Jude shook her head. "I really threw a cross?" She didn't remember any of it.

"No harm done." Elizabeth continued to look at Jude. "I don't want to force you to talk, but I can speak from experience, it helped me."

"Everybody I've ever told has managed to leave."

"I won't."

"That's what Sister Agnes said, too." Jude looked away.

Elizabeth kept quiet and sipped her wine.

"She was sent away. Oh, just forget it. I'm fine, really. I'm over it."

"You know, I used to be so afraid of driving in areas I wasn't familiar with. I was so scared of getting lost," Elizabeth said. "Then I finally realized there were other roads that would eventually lead back to where I was headed."

"What's this, healing with metaphors?" Jude realized she sounded like an irritable child.

Elizabeth laughed. "In a sense, yes."

"Well, thank you, but I'm not lost."

"No, you're not. I didn't mean to imply you were." Elizabeth sighed. "I'd like to help."

"I don't need any help," Jude said, defensively. "I'm fine. Can we talk about something else?" Her mind swirled with indecision and pressure rose in her chest.

"Sure. But I have one more metaphor for you to think about. Remember, the sweetest part of the fruit is bruised."

"Yeah, well, I usually cut those parts out," Jude said, rudely. She got some childish satisfaction in hurting Elizabeth. The nun was getting too close. Jude's safety net was ripping open, and she needed to get back into safe mode. She wasn't ready. She was afraid. Probably best to keep people away from her secrets. She thought of hollow bones, like a sparrow, light enough to fly away, but crushed if held too tight. Should she risk it?

"Fair enough." Elizabeth drank the last of her wine and stood up. "I guess I'll call it a night. I've got another busy day tomorrow. Are you coming to the Christmas pageant for Sangria's daughter tomorrow?"

"I don't know." Jude stood and crossed her arms again.

"You should come. It's so much fun seeing those kids

dressed up as angels and shepherds singing *Away in a Manger* off key. It adds so much magic to the season."

Jude didn't want Elizabeth to leave. She wavered about opening up but didn't know how. She wanted badly to tell someone she could trust. Would she risk losing this friendship by baring her soul?

Elizabeth walked through the den. "This place is great. That looks like the original crown molding."

"Yeah, it is," Jude followed Elizabeth, holding her wine glass close.

"I love how the molding continues over the bookcases. You never see that anymore." Elizabeth went to the shelves and picked up the St. Jude statuette. "Your namesake?"

Jude nodded. "My mother sent it after…"

Elizabeth gently put St. Jude back. "After what?"

"After it happened." Jude took a large gulp of wine.

Elizabeth quietly stood and listened.

"After the priest…" Jude choked on a sob.

Elizabeth hugged her tight. "Come on, let's sit."

Elizabeth led Jude to the couch where they both sat. The nun grabbed a box of Kleenex and handed it to Jude. She sat close, offering comfort without speaking.

Jude sobbed into a tissue, and set her glass on the table. "My life has been emotionally crazy lately. For years, I've been able to deal with what life's handed out. But I don't know, now everything seems to have hit me at one time, and I'm ready to explode."

Elizabeth nodded.

"First this woman, Trudy, died and came into my life. You guys too. I'm getting sued for defending myself, this guy I went out with is a psycho, and now my professional and personal lives are going down the toilet." She sniffled. "Are you sure Trudy wasn't into voodoo and put a hex on me?"

"I can assure you she wasn't," Elizabeth said. "It took going to jail for me to find myself. I didn't think I'd ever recover from that."

"Well, I thought I had recovered." Jude looked away. "Maybe I haven't." She took a deep breath and remembered that night. "I used to go into the church alone, to get away from my screwed-up family. My father's violent rage." Jude closed her eyes and visualized that night, almost eighteen years ago.

Chapter 38
New York

Judith often sought peace and solitude in the sanctuary. The church in the evening light was magical and she found comfort in the large, gilded Jesus that hung over the altar. The priest's table cast long shadows on the marble floor, and, if she wasn't looking directly at it, Jesus's face seemed to move when the light shifted through the stained glass.

A familiar rustling of robes snapped her to attention. Monsignor Callen walked around the altar into the church. "Judith, it's Friday evening. Why aren't you out with your friends?" He came near and sat in the pew directly in front of her. "A pretty young girl should be taking advantage of her youth." He winked an old rheumy eye and got closer. "You know, when you're as old as me, you'll learn to appreciate young bones." He laughed loudly at his joke. The wheezy sound echoed like a sonic boom.

"I'm happy here, Monsignor." Judith looked down at her hands carefully folded in her lap. Being this close to the priest made her uncomfortable. It was different when he was conducting mass. There was distance when he was behind the altar. It made him seem larger than life. She was able to embrace internal peace during the familiar ceremony. Judith wondered what he must experience each time he blessed the water and wine, the body and blood of Christ. He was much closer to God than she was.

"Well, young lady, maybe you need to make a confession?" He winked again, and Judith felt a stab of fear shoot through her. She *hated* confession. Especially now, alone, with Father in the church, it didn't feel right.

"If you tell me your sins tonight, it will save us both time tomorrow." He leaned heavily over the pew to rub her arm. Since his weight made it difficult for him to lean far enough to touch her, his hand accidentally brushed against her breast. Judith recoiled in shame and crossed her arms across her chest.

"I don't mind waiting until tomorrow." Her small voice trembled.

"I have some time now. You'd really be helping me."

Fear swirled inside her gut. "If it will save you time, then…then I'll do confession now." It was the last thing Judith wanted to do, but she knew better than to question his authority. She hoped they would go into one of the confessionals, she on one side of the screen, he on the other. She felt so exposed here in the open church.

"Come on, child, let's go somewhere more private."

Relieved, Judith stood and he indicated for her to move ahead. She walked in front of him, uncomfortable, she could feel his eyes on her. He didn't stop her as she headed into a small confessional. Before she entered the tiny space, she looked up at the light above the door, expecting it to be green or, she wished, red—which meant it was occupied. Tonight, it wasn't lit at all. It looked black against the chalky wall. She closed the door, and darkness commanded the small space. The waning evening light couldn't penetrate through.

"Forgive me, Father, for I have sinned," Judith began, not sure Monsignor Callen had made it to his side of the confessional. Suddenly, the window slid open. Judith jumped and began again. "Forgive me…"

"Why don't you come on this side with me." Monsignor's voice resonated through the screen. "It's too dark for me to see you there."

"I don't mind the darkness, Father. I'll be quick." Judith could feel her heart pound under her uniform. It seemed uncomfortably warm in the confessional.

"No, I insist. Come over here. No one else is here to hear your sins." He opened his door and shut the screen.

Judith held onto the wall as she stepped into the dark chapel. Monsignor Callen sat cramped on his side of the confessional. He patted his lap. "Here, sit down."

"No, Father, really, I'll stand." Her breath shook around the words.

"Of course you won't. My ears don't work as well as they used to. I insist." He reached out, grabbed her wrist, and pulled her onto his lap. "There, there. This is much better." His laugh changed, turned deeper.

Judith was petrified. He was too close. She could see, touch, and smell him. The odor reminded her of an old person's pillowcase. Her stomach roiled.

He rubbed her arms, his movements becoming more frantic. When he spoke, he seemed short of breath. "Do you have mortal or venal sins to confess?" His hands slid across her breasts.

"I…I…don't know, Father. Can I please come back tomorrow?" Fear synapsed through every nerve like an electric charge.

He reached over her and shut the door. "No, no. We're here." He began to raise his robes, shifting Judith so she could be closer. One hand went under her skirt. She reflexively pushed his hand away and pulled her skirt to her knees.

"No, please. Please let me go home." Terror, and his heavy arm, prevented her from moving.

He took her hand and placed it on his trousers. She recoiled, but he forced her hand to stay. He moved their hands rhythmically, becoming more animated and furious. "Yes, Judith. Good girl."

He broke the bread, gave it to his disciples, and said: Take this all of you, and eat it. This is my body, which will be given up for you.

Judith looked away, looked over his shoulder at an image of Jesus. Then shut her eyes tight, shamed that He would see her like this. When she opened her eyes, she fixed her gaze on the seams of Monsignor's vestment. As he moved her skirt up and tore her underwear away, she stared hard at his robes, surprised there were small rips in the decorative thread. Pain ripped through tender skin, yet she refused to take her eyes off his vestment. How could Monsignor stand on the altar wearing something torn? She wanted to apologize to Jesus for him.

He took the cup. This is the cup of my blood, the blood of the new and everlasting covenant. It will be shed for you and for all so that sins may be forgiven. Do this in memory of me.

Judith no longer felt fear. No longer felt pain. As if her soul had seeped out. There was nothing. A black hole collapsed, burning the last light of its star. She was no longer a part of her body, instead she was on the outside looking in. Somehow, she didn't feel Monsignor Callen's hands on her, his body in her. He was there, but she wasn't.

It was better that way.

Chapter 39

Exhausted, Jude hugged a large throw pillow as she sat on the couch. Elizabeth dabbed her own tears.

"I'm sorry. I…I can't imagine…" Elizabeth's words faded as she leaned toward Jude and held her arm. "That's too much for anyone to bear, much less a fourteen-year-old. You were just a child."

"Not after that night." Jude bit her lip to keep her voice steady.

"Did you press charges?"

"Are you kidding?"

"That was a stupid question, sorry. I know, based on the law of averages, this asshole got off scot free."

Jude gasped at Elizabeth's language. "Sister Elizabeth!" Still, it made her smile. Suddenly the air felt lighter.

"I'm sorry, but I'm angry." She squeezed Jude's arm. "What can I do?"

Jude shrugged. "Nothing. It's done."

"Do you feel better after talking about it?"

Jude wiped her tear-streaked face. "Do I look like I feel better?"

"No, you look pretty bad," Elizabeth joked.

"Thanks." Jude managed a smile. She didn't want to admit it, but she did feel different. Like a door unlocked, opened just a little. Still afraid, she glanced at Elizabeth and wondered if she'd find a way to abandon her. "I know your allegiance is to the church, so I'd understand if…"

"If what?" Elizabeth looked insulted. "Do you think I'd risk our friendship because of what happened? How shallow do you think I am?" She sat forward. "I'm dedicated to the Catholic Church, but what that priest did was wrong. Beyond wrong. I'm sick about it." Elizabeth stood and began pacing.

Jude clutched the pillow and watched Elizabeth. The nun had a serious look of concentration on her face.

"I'm beginning to understand some things now." Elizabeth seemed to be a million miles away.

"Like what? Why I'm screwed up?"

"Would you stop saying that? You're not screwed up." Elizabeth stopped and looked at Jude. "I knew you were a good soul when we first met. I could see it in you."

"And you can tell these things, how?" Jude thought Elizabeth seemed too excited and a little distracted.

"Yeah. A little practice and a lot of experience have taught me." Elizabeth sat down next to Jude. "Seeing someone's soul is like looking at a child and trying to imagine what they'll look like when they grow up. Sometimes you just know." She touched Jude's arm. "We're going to get you through this. The worst part is over. We'll work on healing."

"I don't want anybody to know," Jude said as fear blossomed inside her. "Nobody. I've spent years trying to put it behind me."

Elizabeth paused. "You need to stop blaming yourself, for what happened. It was not your fault."

"I'm Catholic. Guilt runs deep," Jude blew her nose and looked over her Kleenex at Elizabeth.

Elizabeth turned to her, serious. "Jude, you know you couldn't have prevented it. You were only fourteen and vulnerable. That priest betrayed you in the worst way. I know there's a big part of you that questions why you didn't punch him in the nose, run out of the church, and be the winner. He was in a position of authority. You couldn't imagine what his intentions were."

"Do you know how many times I've relived that night and tried to reenact it in my mind? Make the ending different?" Jude asked, looking to the ceiling.

"Actually, I do understand what you're saying," Elizabeth said. "I wish I could've changed the night I got arrested but look where it brought me. I'm doing what I was meant to." She leaned back. "I've managed to realize my dreams. Although you couldn't have told me then."

"And what dream was I going for?" Jude asked sarcastically. Fresh tears threatened to spill.

Elizabeth didn't say anything as she stood. She went to the statuette of St. Jude and held it. She turned to Jude. "I know this sounds preachy but try to gain strength from that night. Learn from it."

"I'd rather just forget it," Jude said, with a taste of meanness, as if hurting Elizabeth would make her feel better. Immature, but rewarding in a small way.

Jude's tone didn't seem to bother Elizabeth. "Treasures come from places you'd least expect."

"I don't feel any enrichment from that experience, thank you."

"No, but you might." She put St. Jude back.

"What's that supposed to mean? I'm thirty-one years old. That's a lot of years to undo."

"Each day is a new beginning," Elizabeth said.

"Oh, great, now you're going to go all zen on me." Jude threw her soggy, wadded tissue on the table. "You're not helping."

Elizabeth chuckled softly. "I'm sorry. You're right." She leaned against the bookcase. "What can I do?"

Jude looked at her skeptically. "Oh, let's see," she said. Maybe you can change the past?"

"How do you think that experience altered your life? Where would you be now if it hadn't happened?" Elizabeth asked.

"What is this, twenty questions for a depressed psychotic?"

"First step, and it's a big one, stop blaming yourself." Elizabeth walked to the sofa. "It was not your fault. You're innocent," she said, with such conviction Jude almost believed her. "Turn it around, the priest raped *you*."

Hearing the words so clear was like a slap in the face to Jude. Elizabeth was right. Even though Jude knew deep inside she hadn't provoked the rape, she blamed herself for allowing it to happen. "But I went into the confessional with him."

"He made you."

"I could've run."

"And go against a priest's orders?"

"It didn't feel right to be there. I should've known."

"You were a child! He forced you."

Jude couldn't hold back the tears. "I'm *sorry*!"

Elizabeth sat next to her and hugged her tight. "You have nothing to be sorry for."

"And then I let them take my baby," Jude sobbed. "My little girl." The pain pulsed in waves deep inside her.

Now Elizabeth was crying as she rocked Jude. "And I'm sorry for that."

Chapter 40

Jude slept until eight-thirty the next morning. She stood in the bathroom and looked at her reflection in the mirror. Her face was swollen and blotchy from crying so much, but for the first time in ages, she'd slept soundly. Finally, a deep, dreamless sleep.

She smiled at herself. "You look like shit," she said as she splashed cold water on her face. The feeling she had was not so much a weight lifted inside her, but a release. Maybe Elizabeth was right, it was time to face it. But as she took a deep breath, she remembered the pain of giving up her child, and couldn't believe she'd said anything to Elizabeth. In a moment of doubt, she wondered if suppression was better. She splashed more cold water on her face. That way she could avoid the deep anguish she felt every time she thought of her baby. But now someone else knew.

She walked from the bathroom into her room and picked Tommy up from her bed. "I don't know how you can sleep so much. Is that what you do all day?" He playfully batted her hand as she scratched his tummy. "Can you believe I told someone other than you about what happened?" He grasped her hand while she tickled under his chin. He looked ecstatic. "You just think you're a tough guy when you're really a big lug." She dropped him on a chair by the bed. He rolled on his back looking for more attention.

Elizabeth had stayed until one o'clock. They'd spent the rest of the evening talking and crying. Elizabeth swore she'd help and wouldn't desert her, but Jude couldn't help feeling a twinge of abandonment when she watched the nun drive away. She hoped Elizabeth would call as promised.

Jude debated about going to Sangria's daughter's Christmas pageant. She wanted to be among friends, but not at a church service. She hadn't been to mass since the rape. Maybe if she stood in the back, near a door.

Jude dressed quickly and headed to the office, enjoying the crisp Texas cold. A crystal blue day, cool with a promising tinge of warmth from the sun. She stopped for a big cup of coffee to help offset the wine she'd had. As she drove, she thought she should call Tiffany Carmen's grandmother to check on the girl. Jude wanted to spend time with her before the mediation. And not by having the child scrutinized by a mental health professional. Tiffany had been through enough since the accident. Jude wanted to see how the girl was doing on her own.

Settling in at work, she reflexively started to close her office door but decided against it. She wanted to hear the office activity. There were two messages waiting from Elizabeth, both checking on her, telling her to call as soon as she got in. Elizabeth sounded a little worried on the second message.

Jude dialed the phone as she stirred her coffee.

Elizabeth sounded relieved when she heard Jude's voice. "Hey, I was starting to get worried."

"I slept in. You know, too much partying last night," Jude chuckled.

"Yeah, we're both animals. How're you feeling?"

Jude sighed. "You name it, like a melting pot of emotions. But good is in the mix. That's a new one for me."

"Well, let's keep working on that."

Jude was reassured Elizabeth still seemed vested in her.

"You are coming to the pageant tonight? I'll be happy to pick you up."

"I'm not sure. I want to, but the last time I went to a church…" Jude didn't finish her thought.

"This might be a good way to segue back. The kids add so much magic to the service. It'll be casual, and I'll be there with you."

"Let me see how much work I can get done today. I'll call you later."

"Okay, but think about it. Plus, I may need some help refereeing Sangria and her mother-in-law."

"That may be worth the price of admission. I'll call you this afternoon."

If Jude could have charted her emotions throughout the day, her graph would've been a series of upward spikes and downward plunges. There were times she couldn't believe she'd actually told another person about the rape and yet felt a sense of relief now someone else shared her burden. Another person to lift the weight Jude had been buried under for years. Then there was the gnawing fear of Elizabeth leaving or telling others. What if the nun decided to cut ties with Jude because of her loyalties to Catholicism? Or thought it would be best for Jude if someone else knew? And, of course, there was work to keep her busy between musings.

Marcus Hall, the kid who was suing Jude, had started moving forward on his case. His scumbag attorney was setting up depositions and interviews.

Drew had been out of the office for most of the afternoon dealing with that. Jude was anxious about the idea of being deposed, under oath. If the case could be limited to the night of the incident, Jude wouldn't be concerned. But she feared the questions about her past. How deep would the attorney dig into Jude's life? They always dug deep.

She did on her cases. It was one thing to tell Elizabeth, and she was still trying that on for size, but the rest of the world knowing scared her more than she cared to admit.

At five, Jude hastily decided to close shop and make the seven o'clock Catholic service. She called Elizabeth and told her she'd be there and she'd drive herself in case she needed to make a run for it. Like a nervous puppy, she went home to get ready.

As Jude dressed, she fought the butterflies in her stomach. *Why the nerves?* The rape happened eighteen years ago, she'd done a lot of growing up since then, no one was going to hurt her tonight. Maybe it was because the memory was so close to the surface now, after telling Elizabeth about it. *Okay, take another step*, she whispered. *Move ahead.*

Parking at the church was impossible. Jude left her car blocks away. Just as she walked past the tower, the church bells rang sharp and loud. She jumped, every nerve on fire. *For whom the bell tolls*, Jude thought wryly. Make it a good omen, not a bad one. She took a deep breath and joined a throng of people entering the church.

Inside, she stood in the vestibule and tried to breathe. In the sanctuary, a mosaic of Jesus hung over the marble altar, keeping watch over the church. Families crowded the pews, saving seats with coats and cameras.

The tiled Jesus above the altar seemed to gaze directly at her, His eyes following her every move. Her stomach was in knots and tears threatened. But there was beauty and comfort in the image and fear. Not sure she could handle mass, Jude turned to the door and was almost trampled by a herd of little shepherds and angels. Children wrapped with sheets and towels tied to their heads. Little angels had pipe cleaner wings, and sparkling garland halos. Parents, some also dressed in costume, tried to keep the flock together. Two little boys made capes of their robes as they played superhero, using their crooks as swords.

"Boys, come here," commanded a mom shooting video while trying to wrangle them back with one hand. "Sorry." She smiled at Jude.

"That's okay. They look cute," Jude said.

The mom rolled her eyes. "They're sure not little angels."

"Hold on, we got one more sweet angel," a familiar voice called out.

Jude turned and saw Sangria pushing her daughter toward the kids. Jude gasped when she saw Sangria had put a long blonde wig on the child and a too-grown-up slip over her white turtleneck. The lacy adult-sized undergarment hung loose on her delicate body.

"Do you think I look pretty, momma?" Angel glanced nervously at the other children.

"You look like a princess," Sangria re-adjusted the wig over the child's braids. "You're going to have all the good things that I didn't have growing up. You'll shine out there."

"The child looks like a tramp," said an elderly woman, who came in behind Sangria. She reached to take the little girl away from Sangria. "She's not going in like that."

Jude figured this was the girl's grandmother.

The room hushed. Everyone stopped and watched. Angel squirmed under the scrutiny. Some of the kids pointed and giggled. Before Jude could move, Elizabeth, her habit billowing like batwings, rushed in holding a white sheet.

"Sangria." The nun's tone was sharp. "Angel should wear the same costume as the other kids." She took the child's hand and led her outside.

"Hey, this is *my* night with *my* kids." Sangria's voice echoed through the sanctuary.

The elderly woman shushed her. "You're going to undo all the good I've worked so hard on. You're a bad influence, woman," she said.

"Outside," Elizabeth ordered the women. "Now." Her eyes caught Jude's and her stern demeanor seemed to soften.

Elizabeth guided them outside. Jude followed. The nun pulled Angel's slip over her head and the wig fell to the ground. "Sangria, I know you mean well, but Angel needs to be dressed appropriately." She wrapped the sheet around the girl, working to not mess up her wings.

"She looks beautiful," Sangria held a long string of pearls. "Put these on, baby."

Angel's big eyes welled up. "I don't want the kids to laugh at me."

"Honey, they're just jealous 'cause you look like a beauty queen."

A young boy Jude hadn't noticed before came up and gave the girl a big hug and said, "Jared thinks Angel looks like a real angel."

Jude was struck by how much the kids looked like Sangria.

Angel hugged her brother back, then let Elizabeth finish the costume.

"Hurry. The other kids are going in." Elizabeth led the girl to the entrance clutching the necklace Sangria had tried to give Angel.

"Mommy, Jared, Grandma, listen for me when I sing," Angel ran to join the others, her pipe cleaner wings lopsided from the quick change.

Through the open doors, Jude could see some of the other kids making room as Angel joined them. She brought up the end of the line and looked for her mother outside.

Sangria, hands on her hips, argued with her mother-in-law. "You don't tell me what's best for my child. I know her better than anybody. She deserves to be a real princess."

"Dressing her like that is wrong." The grandmother was firm.

"She don't need to turn out like me. I want her to be extra special," Sangria said.

"Sangria" Jude touched her arm and nodded toward Angel.

Sangria turned. Angel was still looking and waved to her mother.

"Oh, baby. Momma's coming," Sangria said, more to herself than anybody, and put a hand over her heart.

Elizabeth herded them toward the door. "Come on. Let's all get along for the kids." She leaned toward Jared and said, "I know you're happy to see your sister and mom."

"Yes ma'am, real happy." He took his mother's hand and walked inside with her.

Stoic, Sangria's mother-in-law followed.

Elizabeth turned to Jude and let out a sigh. "How are you?"

"Okay, but I'm not sure I can do this."

"I'll be with you. Are you ready to try?"

Jude shrugged. "I don't know." But she walked with Elizabeth into the crowded church. They stood in the back with throngs of others unable to find a seat.

A thin, older priest had the children seated on the altar. He stood among them smiling and asked them questions. "Does anybody know why we celebrate Christmas?"

Little hands went into the air and voices called out: "It's Jesus's birthday." "Santa comes," and "we get presents."

"Who is Jesus?" The priest grinned and looked at the children flocked around the altar.

"He's God's kid," one of the shepherds said, and the congregation laughed.

"Why did he come here?"

An angel waved her hand. "'Cause there weren't any rooms at the inn." More laughter, including the priest.

"How did Jesus tell us to treat people?" He took another approach.

"You're supposed to be nice to people," a sweet voice called out.

"Have you all been good this year?" the priest asked.

"Mostly." The children giggled.

The priest laughed. "Do you do what your parents tell you?"

"Yes!" Most of the voices cried out.

"Are you nice to your brothers and sisters?"

"Yes. No. Sometimes."

Everybody laughed.

"Do you ask for forgiveness if you don't listen to your parents?"

"I don't know. Maybe."

"Because you know Jesus will help you with your problems."

"Yes!"

"Because God blesses the children."

"And mommies." Angel's voice rose above the others. She scanned the crowd for her mother.

Sangria raised a hand to her mouth as tears spilled down her cheeks.

For the first time, Jude saw Sangria speechless.

The priest's eyes found Sangria in the audience. "You're right. God blesses everybody." Then he turned to the children. "Are you ready to sing?"

"Yes!"

Giggling and holding hands, the children jumped up and scampered to their reserved pews in the front.

Jude looked at Elizabeth, who was beaming as if lit from within, obviously in her element. Sangria hugged

Jared in front of her and kept her eyes on Angel. She waved when her daughter sat down and turned around.

The joyful, infectious mood of the children penetrated Jude's resistance. She relaxed, standing in the back of the church, watching the service. Elizabeth waved to someone, and Jude looked over and saw Bernadette sitting with the women from the home. They all turned to wave back. Jude's heart jumped when she saw Reece, sitting next to Bernadette, lean forward and smile.

Sangria whispered, "Me and Jared are going to sit with them. I want everybody to meet my baby." She took the boy's hand and weaved through the standing-room crowd.

Jude said to Elizabeth, "If you want to sit with them, I'll be okay here. If I need to leave, I want to be close to a door." She tried not to look at Reece.

Elizabeth took a rolled-up church bulletin and playfully hit Jude's arm. "I'm not going anywhere." She looked at the group. "I'm glad Reece made it."

"You didn't tell me he'd be here." Blushing, Jude felt like a teenager.

Elizabeth answered with a smile in her eyes. The children started singing *The First Noel*. The nun took Jude's arm and moved close to her. A swell of happiness broke another chip in Jude's armor.

Chapter 41

When mass began, Jude's memory opened. All the years of Catholic rituals that had wormholed deep in her brain emerged. Even with a few changes over the years, Jude felt an old smoldering ember that sparked recognition of the comfort of the church, as well as the ache. The prayer responses were on the tip of her tongue, though she couldn't get the words out. The children's songs and Christmas play altered some of the usual ceremony. Jude became so engrossed in the songs and the children's acting that she barely registered Reece get up, offer his seat to Sangria, and walk toward her and Elizabeth.

By the time Mary and Joseph reached Bethlehem, Jude heard a voice near her ear.

"Merry Christmas." Reece moved next to her.

Caught off guard, she flushed. "Merry Christmas to you."

Elizabeth greeted him with a smile.

"I love the children's service," he whispered.

Jude nodded, afraid to talk in church, though she liked having him near.

When it was time to take communion, Jude hesitated, she'd feared this moment.

"Are you going?" Reece asked, nodding toward the altar.

"No. I'll wait here." Jude's discomfort was obvious. Only Catholics, free of sin, were invited to communion. She looked at the congregation and noticed only a few remained seated, she shifted aside to let others around them.

Elizabeth moved next to her. "I'll be right back."

Jude watched her join Sister Bernadette and the women. Elizabeth leaned in and spoke to them, but only she and Bernadette went to the altar, leaving the women in the pew. Jude looked away, and, again, felt a connection to the women left seated.

Sinners.

Reece joined the line behind them.

Jude watched him as he waited, thought of the pain he'd suffered losing his wife and child. Then, a spark ignited in her, like a movie playing in her head as she tried to picture her own daughter's childhood. Did she sing in Christmas pageants? Did her parents take her to church? Did she play sports? Music? The sudden questions surprised her.

Though she'd thought of her daughter throughout the years, she'd never tried to imagine the small details of her life. She watched the children sitting in the front. Some were smiling at their parents, others were whispering and laughing with each other. She was desperate to know about her own child. What did she look like? Then Jude had a sickening thought. What if something had happened to her?

She stared at the mosaic image of Jesus and asked silently, *why did you let it happen?* Then, from somewhere deep inside, she thought, *can you help me find her?* She backed away from the image and turned toward the door. People coming back from communion, and others moving to the exit caused Jude to be shepherded into a small room, walled off with stained glass.

In the quiet alcove, a statue of the Virgin Mary surrounded by white roses presided over individual velvet-padded kneelers. A woman lit a candle and went to one of the kneelers to pray. Jude's insides unfolded as she took in the statue. Mary, who sacrificed her own child, her own soul. The embodiment of suffering. Jude's breath caught before she took a step to the bank of candles, lit one, and knelt. The congregation and children's voices softly echoed *Silent Night* in the small room. Jude had to smile a little when she heard, above the rest, Sangria's clear, strong voice.

The day had been a roller coaster of feelings. Every emotion she owned had been twisted and wrung out. For the first time, she'd told someone about the rape. Now, she's attending a Catholic mass. The evening had been rewarding, but the sudden strong desire to know where her daughter was burned a painful hole through her. She stared at the Virgin Mary, unsure how to pray, how to ask for help. Was she strong enough to deal with the answers? Was she strong enough to ask? She'd worked her whole life patching and covering old wounds. Would she survive re-opening what she'd fought to forget?

She continued to kneel, even though mass was over. She allowed the images and questions about her daughter to unfold. The pain was exquisite.

She heard Sangria behind her. "Here she is."

Elizabeth was quieter. "Let's wait outside. People are trying to pray."

"I want her to meet my babies." Sangria's high voice pierced Jude's thoughts.

"Shhh, we'll get together soon," Elizabeth said. "Let's go." Her voice was receding. "You can spend a little more time with your kids."

Angel said to her mother, "I miss you, Momma."

"I miss you and Jared so much," Sangria said. Her voice faded as they walked away.

Jude took one lingering look at Mary and stood. Maybe

she hadn't given Sangria enough credit. It was hard to give up your children. She promised a new resolve to help Sangria. Jude went outside just as the priest was coming in.

"Merry Christmas." He smiled warmly and offered his hand.

Jude sucked in a breath and looked at his outstretched hand. "Merry Christmas." Barely touching his fingers, she sidled out the door.

Outside, people were milling about and pulling up their coat collars. Jude saw Reece talking with the women. Jude caught his eye as she walked to them.

Jared hung on Sangria's leg, and Angel clutched her hand. "Momma, I'm ready to go home. I'll keep Jared better. You can still work. I can take care of me and him," Angel said.

Sangria stood straight. "I'm your momma, sweetpea. I can take care of both my babies just fine." She directed this last comment to Angel's grandmother. "See? They need their momma."

"What they need is supervision," her mother-in-law said.

"I don't like this new school. It's too hard, and I can't wear my cool clothes. The uniforms suck," Angel whined.

"You know we don't talk like that," Angel's grandmother said sternly. "You want your mouth washed out with soap?"

Angel pulled her mother's arm to whisper in her ear. "And I don't like the smell of Grandma's house."

Sangria looked at her mother-in-law. "Don't you go stickin' soap in her mouth." Sangria pulled her kids closer. "Angel, you tell me if she don't take care of you right."

"We do fine," the older woman said, as she raised an eyebrow at Sangria. "She does miss her momma, though. And her brother." She wagged a finger at Sangria. "You get yourself together, then we won't be having this conversation again."

Elizabeth and Bernadette stood close but didn't interfere.

Sangria started to say something, but instead bent and hugged both her kids. "We'll be together soon, babies."

"Then study hard so you can come home soon," Angel said to her mother.

"Study?" Sangria looked quizzically at her.

"Yeah, in school. Grandma said you're in one of those boarding, overnight schools. I don't *ever* want to go to one of those, so hurry and graduate."

Sangria looked gratefully at her mother-in-law. "Thanks." She bent to Angel. "And your grandmother can be pretty smart. Go ahead and mind her. I'll get home as soon as I can. I'm gonna study real hard, so I can get a good job, then I'll send you and Jared to college, too."

Her mother-in-law turned to Angel. "Maybe we can have Jared spend Christmas day with us," she said.

Sangria bent her head. "That would mean everything to them…and me." She wiped away a tear.

"And Sangria, you're welcome too." The woman looked sternly at her. "As long as you do what you're supposed to do, we can help each other." She waved a hand. "But if your grades start slipping…"

"Don't worry, ma'am." Sangria nodded to the nuns. "They'll make sure of it. And so will I."

"All right, then. Angel, say good night. It's late."

Jude noticed Sangria struggled with her mother-in-law telling Angel what to do, but Sangria stayed tight-lipped and hugged her daughter. "We'll be together soon, honey." She and Jared watched them leave. "Oh, lordy, this is hard," she said.

Jared turned to his mother. "I want us to live together again."

"Me too, baby." Sangria hugged him. "You let me know if those people you're stayin' with are mean to you, okay?"

Jarred nodded. "They're okay, just not you and Angel."

Bernadette stood next to Sangria and said, "No one said this was going to be easy. One step at a time."

"I just wish the stupid foster care would keep them together."

"It's in God's hands," Bernadette said as she put a comforting arm around Sangria.

Elizabeth walked to Jude. "You did well in there. I'm sure it was emotional."

"Yeah, but okay. It gave me time to think." Inner turmoil was nipping at her insides. Lighting the candle under Mary's statue and envisioning her own child started an avalanche cascading in her soul.

"Lizzie, should we meet you back home?" Bernadette herded the women together, keys in hand.

"Sure, I've got my car," Elizabeth answered.

Reece stood, quietly watching the group.

Bandee tapped her foot impatiently. "Can we just do something? It's too cold to stand around and talk."

"Come on, ladies, to the nun-mobile." Bernadette was chipper as she led the others. "Sangria, we'll drop Jared off on the way."

"Oh, man. Not another stop," Bandee whined.

After the women left, Reece stood next to Elizabeth and Jude. Jude smiled at him, but turned to Elizabeth and said, "I'm ready to find her."

Elizabeth touched Jude's arm. "Good. I'll help you."

"Find who?" Reece asked.

Jude looked at Reece, took a deep breath, surprising herself, and said, "My daughter."

Chapter 42

A cold gust of wind suddenly whipped around the church, causing Elizabeth to grasp hold of her habit.

Reece looked perplexed. "What daughter?"

"Come on, let's go inside and talk," Elizabeth said and turned toward the church.

Jude hesitated. "Not there. I'm not ready to go into an empty church." She turned her back to the biting wind. "There's a Starbucks up the street." She looked at Reece. "I know all this seems weird. God, I'm still trying to understand it. Elizabeth is the first person I've told, and that was just last night, so bear with me. It's new. I'll explain, but let's go before we all freeze out here."

The warmth of the coffee shop was heaven to Jude. She waited inside for Elizabeth to park and wondered if Reece would follow. She didn't know why she'd even mentioned her child to him, but something had released and changed in her, like petals opening, especially while in the small chapel with Mary looking over her. Somehow by telling Elizabeth what happened, it didn't feel like such a dirty secret. Now it seemed more important to find out about her child. The tectonic shift made her feel like a different person.

Elizabeth came in, her robes riding on the wind. "Whew, I was afraid people might find out what we really wear under these."

Jude laughed. "Some things in life are best not known." They walked to the counter to order. "Do you think Reece will come?"

Elizabeth glanced outside. "I'm not sure. He didn't say anything when he left."

"Oh, well, maybe it's for the best." Jude absently looked at the pastries as they waited. "Suddenly, I want to find out about...about her. Her life. I need to take one thing at a time." She turned to Elizabeth. "And it's okay. For the first time I can remember, finding my daughter is what's important."

Elizabeth was quiet. She only nodded.

"Sister, what can I get you?" the barista asked.

"A chai tea and," she looked at Jude.

"A latte," Jude answered.

While he made the drinks, Jude stepped away from the counter, not wanting to start the conversation there. The barista finished the drinks and handed them to Elizabeth. "On the house. Thanks for all you do, Sister," he said.

"Thank you and bless you," Elizabeth replied. She smiled and accepted the drinks gracefully. She and Jude found a table near the window.

Jude sat across from her. "In a way, I feel like a new person." She hesitated. "I only hope she's okay, that she *wants* me to find her."

Silent, Elizabeth sipped her tea and gazed out the window.

"If you're looking for Reece, I really don't mind if he doesn't show." Jude felt like a chatterbox. "I need to figure myself out before I even think about another relationship. That is, if he'd even be interested."

Elizabeth put her hand on Jude's. "I'm not thinking

about Reece. I can help you find your daughter, but you have to be sure you're ready..." Before she could finish, Reece came in.

"Whoa, it's cold out there." He sat down. "Am I interrupting?" He looked at Elizabeth's hand over Jude's.

Elizabeth moved her hand. "No, we were just talking. You know, 'sista' stuff."

It still surprised Jude he could take away her breath, and words, when she was around him.

"I'm going to get something warm to drink. Anybody need anything?" Reece stood.

Jude shook her head. "No, thank you."

After he left, Jude asked, "What were you saying?"

Elizabeth leaned over the table. "I'm glad you're ready to find your child, but you need to be emotionally prepared for it."

This stopped Jude. She hadn't thought beyond her own needs of having her curiosity settled. Of stopping the emotional bleed. What would her daughter think of her?

Elizabeth went on, "You have to think beyond the past. What kind of relationship do you want to pursue? Do you want her to be part of your life?"

Reece came back with treats. "I couldn't resist a few pieces of coffee cake. Dig in."

"Thanks, my favorite." Elizabeth picked up a fork, took a bite, and looked at Jude.

"If she'll have me, then I'm ready to be part of her life," Jude answered. "Can you really help me?"

"I can." Elizabeth tasted another forkful of crumb-encrusted cake.

"How? Do you know something?" Jude asked. "You seem so sure."

Elizabeth didn't answer, wouldn't look at Jude.

"Why do I still feel like a third wheel?" Reece asked.

Jude looked over at him. "Sorry." She smiled. "I'm just trying to rediscover some things."

"I didn't know you had a child." Reece seemed gentle. "What did you mean when you said you were ready to find her?"

"It's a long story." Jude glanced at Elizabeth. "A painful one." She stirred her coffee as she explained to him she'd gotten pregnant when she was fourteen and was forced to give up her daughter. She left out the part about the priest.

"Fourteen?" Reece sat back. "That's young."

"I was…it was." Jude fought a surge of tears. "I was raped."

"Oh, God." Reece moved closer. "I'm sorry."

Elizabeth, unusually quiet, sipped her drink.

Jude didn't want to cry again. Her eyes and emotions were still raw from telling Elizabeth. "I hadn't told anyone about it until last night." She looked at Elizabeth. "So, forgive me if I'm scattered. All of a sudden it's at the surface when for years I've tried to keep it buried." She closed her eyes. "Now, two people know."

"And you can help her?" Reece asked Elizabeth.

"Yeah, Bernie has connections to the Aurora Home for Unwed Mothers. If it's okay with Jude, I'll have her start making some calls."

"Sure, it's fine with me." Jude wrapped her hands around her coffee cup for warmth. "I hope I'm doing the right thing. It's weird, it's as if something sparked inside me when I was in church. It's like I *have* to find her. To make sure she's okay." She sighed and a soft sob followed. "When I saw those kids singing…" This time she didn't stop the tears. She used a coarse napkin to wipe her face "I am so sick of crying. Reece, it seems like every time you see me, I'm having some kind of emotional trauma."

"It's nice to see you care about your daughter." He

pulled a package of Kleenex from his pocket and handed it to her. "Here, this might feel better."

"Thanks." Jude looked around the coffee shop, self-conscious. "I didn't know I could cry so much." She blew her nose.

Elizabeth smiled. "You're going through a lot. I think you're handling everything well."

Jude nodded as she wiped her nose. "I'm glad for your help. Even as an attorney, I wouldn't know where to start." She wadded the tissue and put it in her pocket. "Maybe we can talk to Bernadette tomorrow." A startling realization hit Jude. "Wait, I don't remember telling you I was at the Aurora Home. Did I?"

"You must have. I don't know." Elizabeth waved her hand. "I mean, if you didn't, you know, that's the only Catholic home in Texas for unwed mothers. It would make sense." She tripped over her words.

Jude tried to remember what she'd told Elizabeth, but she didn't recall speaking the name of the awful place. "Only 'good' Catholic girls are sent there. Or were, when I was pregnant. Now you can get a school pass at your OB's office."

Elizabeth ignored her comment as she chewed another hunk of cake.

"Let me know if I can help," Reece said. "I'll be happy to do what I can."

Jude looked quizzically at Elizabeth but answered Reece. "Thanks. Hopefully, Elizabeth and Bernadette can answer my questions."

Chapter 43

Jude walked into her house and put her keys on the table where she and Elizabeth had eaten the night before. Her mind wouldn't shut down and her gut had a weird feeling. She knew she'd not mentioned the name of the Aurora Home to Elizabeth. As long as she'd tried to forget the horrible place, she'd almost forgotten the name. Perhaps it would stand to reason that Jude would've gone there. She was Catholic, a teenager, but these days girls were openly having babies. The stigma and ostracism were a thing of the past. Lately, it seemed a badge of honor. Still, it was unsettling for Jude.

Tommy paced in front of his food bowl.

"Sorry, another late dinner, kid," Jude said, as she poured his food.

He sat, twitched his bobbed tail, and stared at her, obviously pissed.

"Don't make me feel guilty." Jude leaned down and stroked his back. "Eat."

He only sniffed his food and walked away.

"Aw, come on, you know I can't cook." Jude let him go. "Suit yourself."

It was almost nine o'clock on a school night. Jude thought it was too late to call Tiffany about the mediation. Kids were just getting out for Christmas break. She'd wait and call her tomorrow. With the settlement meeting looming, Jude wanted to make sure Tiffany was mentally prepared to relive the accident. Jude also wanted to protect her from the pain.

She pulled her phone out and checked messages. Drew had called and demanded she call him back immediately. Jude's stomach twisted. She hadn't given her assault case a thought all evening. Had almost forgotten that Drew had been working on it all afternoon. She didn't know how much more she could take. People shouldn't have more than one major crisis in their lives at a time.

The next voice message gave her chills. "Hi, babe," Rick said. "Have you had a chance to talk to the nuns yet? The Academy is ready to pay big bucks for the land. Anything you could do to push this along would help me out."

The only thing she wanted to push was Rick, off a tall building, but she settled for pushing the erase button.

The last message on the machine was a surprise. "Jude, it's me, Katie. Call me at home." Her voice was tentative as she left her number.

Curious, Jude started to dial but stopped after hitting the first few numbers. As she hung up, she figured Katie was probably looking for information. And with Rick still hammering at her, she didn't want any conflict-of-interest problems with them.

Instead, she dialed Drew's number and headed to the kitchen. She pulled out some leftovers from last night and a bottle of water. After the fifth ring, she was relieved he hadn't answered and was ready to leave a message when he picked up.

"Jude, it's about time. Where've you been?" His voice was clipped. "Your cell phone was turned off."

"I had to take care of some things." Jude opened the top of the water bottle nervously. "How did it go today?"

"That asshole, Lonnie Ball, has already filed the suit.

He's ready to start taking depositions."

"Before getting all the information secured? What about discovery?"

"He works differently from real lawyers. His approach is wham, bam, cheap-sex law. I need to get a detailed statement from you and any of the ladies who saw what happened."

"There's not much. I doubt the kid even talked with the police. He likely just went with what Lonnie told him to say." Jude was sick this hoodlum was making her look like the bad guy. "Once the facts are out, he won't have a chance in hell." She didn't want to be deposed, to have her private life raked over, and worry that others would learn what happened to her so many years ago. Her gut clutched when she considered they'd interview the awful foster families she'd lived with. Jude wasn't ready for the world to know about her life. She knew Lonnie Ball would question every move she'd made since birth. The laces of her past began to tighten again "I mean, *he* tried to hurt *me*."

"Yeah, I know. But we'll need the judge to sort everything out. In the meantime, I'm getting the kid's records. Hopefully, he'll have a mile-long criminal past."

"How old is he?" Jude had an awful thought. "What if he's a minor? Can we use anything we find out about him in court?"

"It'll be up to the judge. This is a civil case, not criminal. Since he's bringing the case against you, we should be able to bring anything up. We'll need a good judge. But at this point, we got nothing."

"What about medical?" Jude asked. "I'm sure he didn't go to the hospital that night. Any injuries he tries to claim, I'll bet will be dated after he retained a lawyer."

"I've already thought of that," said Drew. "Believe me, I know how this skunk of a lawyer thinks. I doubt he has many tricks that I haven't already seen—or used."

Jude continued to twist the cap on the water bottle. "I'm sorry about all this, Drew. I can't believe the jerk has turned this around. He really has no case."

"I'm sorry, too. This is not how I want to spend my Christmas holiday. I can't risk having my firm tarnished by this. If we don't act faster than Lonnie, then he'll have us by the shorts. Sit down and write down everything you remember about that night." He sighed.

"Then Jude, we need to talk about your future with the firm. Between this case and the prostitutes, we're taking a hit. I can't have that."

Jude's heart sank as she hung up the phone. How could this punk kid manage to turn the case upside-down? Why had Drew soured so much on the home? He put her in the line of fire, and now he was the one pulling the trigger.

She breathed deeply as she thought of the changes that had happened in her life in mere months. She wondered what Drew would've thought if he'd known she'd spent the evening with the nuns at church.

Her phone rang, she jumped and almost dropped the water bottle. Caller ID listed Katie's number. Tempted, she reached to answer but stopped. She was already in enough trouble with Drew and didn't need to take any more chances hurting her already shaky career. She let the call go to voicemail.

She took a big gulp of water, grabbed a legal pad, and sat on the sofa in the den. She spent the next hour writing down everything that had happened that night. Tommy jumped next to her and tried to make himself comfortable on the legal pad she was writing on. She petted him and pulled the pad out from under his inert body.

"Did you eat?"

He rolled off her lap and lay next to her. Absently, Jude stroked his fur with one hand and wrote with the other. She paused to look at her wrist, which was almost healed. It would be hard to prove the kid had done anything to her since she hadn't sought medical attention. Still, both Elizabeth and Bernadette could testify as to what happened. Who would be more credible than two nuns? Jude sighed. The others, though, might be a problem. It would be hard to consider the credibility of ex-prostitutes.

Jude went to the kitchen for more water. The leftovers still sat on the counter. She tossed them in the trash, no longer hungry. It was hard to keep all her problems in order. She needed to detach from her troubles. Leave her body behind and soar above her life. Move the pieces into places where they belonged.

She poured a glass of wine and lit a few of the candles she and Elizabeth had enjoyed. She put them on her coffee table in the den, turned out the light, and sank into the sofa sipping her wine. Tommy curled into her lap. "At least you still love me," she said as she scratched behind his ears. Prioritize, she thought. She wanted to think about finding her daughter. Wanted to remember some of the good feelings that had started after telling Elizabeth. But it seemed life continued to put up blocks when something positive came along.

Chapter 44

The office was already bustling when Jude arrived the next morning. She'd slept later than usual again. She'd even caught herself humming some of the Christmas music the children had sung the night before. Now, at her desk, with the weight of potential unemployment bearing on her, she wondered why she couldn't get those damned happy songs out of her head.

It was Friday, and probably the last day of school for Tiffany before Christmas break. The mediation was on Monday, and Jude wanted to talk to the girl before the meeting. She called Tiffany's grandmother. The woman answered on the first ring.

"Mrs. Carmen? It's Jude."

"Yes, I was going to call you" the grandmother replied. Her voice was frail. "I'm so nervous about Monday. It's like I have to think about the accident all over again."

"I know it's hard. How's Tiffany?"

The woman sighed. "I don't know. Sometimes she can be the sweet girl she was before the accident. But then she can turn into a demon child, taking out her anger on me and her teachers. I don't want her to get hurt, you know, having to relive it all again."

"Usually, the clients come to the mediation." Jude leaned back in her chair and thought of the gory accident photos and graphic medical illustrations. "But I'm not sure it's a good idea for Tiffany to be there. It would just be a boring, and probably agonizing, day of sitting and waiting."

"Thank goodness." The relief in her voice was audible. "I was afraid you'd need her to testify or something."

"No. This is a mediation, a chance for both parties to try to settle the case before we go to trial. Since Tiffany's been deposed, she won't have to talk about it anymore." Jude paused. "At least not for this meeting."

"We're confused as to what to expect on Monday."

"If you're both available later, I'd be happy to come out and visit. Explain to you and Tiffany what will happen."

"I pick her up from school at three-thirty, we're usually home by four," Mrs. Carmen said. She hesitated. "She doesn't have many friends, so I doubt she'll have any after-school plans."

Jude knew about the bonds of loneliness, and how keeping people away made problems easier to hide. She'd spent her high school years in the library to avoid going to the foster home. "I'll be there a little after four. Can I bring anything?"

"No, thank you. But I do have one request."

"Yes?"

"You must promise you won't hurt her with questions. This is…was…her mother, and my daughter, that's being bartered over. It seems awful to ask for money." Jude could hear her crying softly.

"It's difficult, and I'll be gentle. But I want Tiffany to understand what we're doing and to make sure she has a say in the final decision." Jude remembered having her decisions wrenched from her own arms. "I think she's old enough to realize what's at stake."

"I've lost one child. Don't hurt her, too."

Jude squeezed her eyes shut. "I won't."

Jude decided to face the music with Drew, to find out if he was going to make good on his threat to fire her. She called his assistant and found out he was in. She took a long look at her office before she went to see him.

Drew was in the reception area supervising Christmas decorating. He held a sprig of mistletoe and joked with anyone in kissing distance.

"Get me a headband or something. I'll attach this to it and maybe get lucky. Lord knows I've had enough carrots dangled in front of my nose. I'd like to try something different," Drew laughed. He turned to Jude. "What do you think? Can I get away with wearing this to the Christmas party?" He tucked the sprig behind his ear.

The receptionist laughed. "Maybe at a party with those hookers who were here the other day."

Jude sucked in her breath.

Drew didn't respond, but Jude noticed his shoulders tense. He stuck the mistletoe in his pocket and addressed Jude, "I'm glad you're here, let's talk." He directed her to his office and said quietly to Jude. "Those are the kind of comments I'm not happy with."

"Me either. Do you want me to talk to her?" Jude asked.

"No. I want to forget about the damned case."

In his office, Jude walked in first, and Drew closed the door behind them. Jude wavered between asking him directly about her job or waiting until he swung the ax.

"Please, sit," Drew said, as he took his place behind his desk.

Jude sat in one of the chairs that faced him. Instead of being nervous, she was calm. Maybe the calm before the storm.

"What do you need for the Carmen mediation?"

"Nothing. I'm ready to go." This was ground Jude

knew well. "I know the case inside and out. I'm meeting with Tiffany and her grandmother this afternoon."

He folded his hands over his lap. "I've got depositions scheduled for Monday. I'm going to try to get there. If not, I may send one of the other associates to help."

"No need. I'm confident I can handle it." Jude nervously smoothed the wrinkles from her skirt.

"Jack Barrone has been giving me trouble about the prostitutes, I don't want him picking on you, too."

"Why? We're not working on the Magdalene Home. He shouldn't mention it. If he does, I'll take care of it." Jude wondered if Drew was going to bring up his comment about her future with the firm. Instead decided to hit him head on. "Drew, if you're concerned I can't handle the job, I'd like to talk about it now."

He raised his eyebrows. "Well." He paused and leaned back. "You've been my number one lawyer. But now you seem distracted, unfocused."

She tried to keep a semblance of composure but sitting in front of Drew was unsettling. Suddenly, she didn't trust her voice, afraid the quaking from inside her would erupt like lava, that he would see through her false confident façade.

"Then there is Lonnie's case against the firm," he went on. "It states, in part, that you were working, which puts liability on us. I've never been sued, and this firm has enjoyed a stellar reputation. At least it did until we took that case from Trudy Wells. It's like a curse." He shuffled some papers on his desk. "And I'm concerned you can't seem to keep a good legal assistant. What does that say about you?"

"I hope my reputation, and the fact I've settled most of my cases successfully, would speak for itself."

"That's why this is so hard for me. I don't want to let you go, but you know this firm is important to me." He ran a hand through his thinning hair. "I'm afraid if I don't do something, other firms may see me as not standing behind what's right. Keeping you could be a potential liability here."

"What about innocent until proven guilty?" Outrage and fear swelled inside Jude.

"Jude, were you drinking that night?"

"No!"

"Lonnie is also claiming you were drunk, that's why you drove over the kid. He's also getting some mileage out of the fact it happened while you were going to the home for prostitutes."

"It is not a home for prostitutes! It's a rehabilitation facility." She was tired of hearing people refer to the home as a whorehouse. Jude stood and paced. She wanted to run. She didn't want to accept defeat but knew how cases worked. Even though she was innocent, the facts could get twisted just enough to muddy the truth. Enough to scare Drew into settling the case, to make it go away. But it went against what she knew was right.

She faced Drew. "Come on, where's your spirit? I told you what happened. Why are you sure this kid is telling the truth? Why are you giving in to Lonnie-scumbag-Ball? Your firm, *our* firm, was built on integrity. Where's that?"

He only looked heavily at her.

She continued pacing. "First, you insisted, no demanded, I take Trudy Well's case. And now all the drama that goes with it. I didn't want it." Jude stopped and looked at Drew. "The night I was accosted I went to get information on the women's background, and to talk to them about the Academy's interest in the property. When I pulled up to the gates, those kids were outside, looking for trouble." She stopped and looked directly at him. "You know, Drew, I resisted taking Trudy Well's case, tried to get out of it. But now that I've gotten to know the women,

I want to help them. I'm not ready to give up on them." She continued to look at him. "Don't give up on these women because of me."

"I don't know, Jude. I hear what you're saying, but I worry about losing…" He waved his hand around his office. "I've worked too hard to lose this."

"I think you're being melodramatic." She surprised herself by talking back to Drew.

He eyed her severely but didn't respond.

Jude tried to form her words carefully, but instead blurted out, "You're acting old and complacent. Maybe it would do you some good to be hungry again. Give me my notice if you want, but at least let me finish the Carmen case and the Well's estate."

He continued to stare at her sternly, but his eyes held a new light. "All right, Jude. Prove to me you were attacked that night and you weren't drinking. Mediate the Carmen case but keep me posted throughout the day. Don't make any decisions on the case until we've talked. Give me a good reason why the nuns shouldn't sell the home to the Academy, and, in the interest of the firm, why you think we should help those women. And, above all," he sighed, "keep up the fight."

Chapter 45

Driving to the Carmen home, Jude was surprised she'd gone up against Drew and defended the Magdalene women. As far as her own case, Jude knew Elizabeth and Bernadette would testify on her behalf about the attack. Two saintly nuns on the stand may shake Lonnie a bit. She was concerned about him deposing the women at the home. Of course, he'd subpoena anybody within spitting distance. His style would be less about the facts of the accident and more about the women's prostitution history.

And now, the nuns' criminal past.

Her world had been shaken. Giving up part of herself by telling Elizabeth about the rape had been a soul-baring leap of faith. She was still waiting for the dust to settle. Today was a mix of easy and hard. Jude looked forward to finding her daughter, without the sharp familiar pain she had when remembering the day she was taken. Now, there was a measure of hope.

At four o'clock she parked in front of Tiffany's grandmother's home, a modest, ranch-style house in East Dallas skirting the edges of White Rock Lake. Grabbing her briefcase, she stepped carefully over the broken walkway to the front door. Little had been done for Christmas decorations. An anemic wreath hung haphazardly on the door, and thin strands of colored lights were slung over sparse bushes.

Jude rang the doorbell and glanced around the porch. Dried leaves from a huge maple had piled in a corner, and wood posts were showing signs of rot.

Tiffany opened the door in a rush of energy. "Hey, Miss Madigan."

"Hi, Tiffany." Jude waited to be asked in, but Tiffany just turned and walked inside. Jude figured the open door was an invitation to enter.

The inside of the house was tidy and unpretentious. Jude stepped over the threshold and saw a Christmas tree in the front window. She hadn't noticed it from outside because the curtains were closed. "Hello," she said from the entry as she shut the door.

"Back here," Tiffany called.

Jude followed the voice and found Tiffany in front of the TV in a den near the kitchen.

The girl had started wearing makeup, heavy eyeliner, and glittery eye shadow. She wore a black shirt and black jeans. Gothic? Goth? Jude couldn't remember the term kids used. The child had grown since Jude last saw her. Maybe it was the heavy make-up, but Tiffany looked much older than her thirteen years.

"Hey. I almost didn't recognize you, you've grown so much." Jude sat near her.

"It's still me," Tiffany said. She smiled through the makeup, twisting a lock of hair.

"When did you start wearing makeup?" Jude asked.

"This year." She changed her position on the couch and faced Jude. "Grandma hates it. But she said if I kept my grades up, I could wear it." She crossed her legs and shrugged. "She still won't let me wear it at school."

Jude thought that was a smart decision. "You don't really need it, you're pretty without it."

"*Whatever.* You sound like my grandmother."

Jude decided to drop the issue and said, "Congratulations on your good grades."

"Thanks."

Tiffany's grandmother came in from the back of the house. "I thought I heard the doorbell. Miss Madigan, how are you?"

"Fine, thanks. Tiffany and I were talking."

"Tiff, have you offered our guest something to drink?" Her grandmother fluffed a pillow on the couch.

Tiffany looked exasperated and turned to Jude, "You thirsty?"

"No, but thanks for asking."

The girl shrugged and looked at her grandmother as if to say, *see*.

Jude smiled a little. She was happy to see Tiffany acting like a normal teenager. A little rebellion was probably a good thing. Considering her own teenage years, Jude had never gone against authority and regretted it since.

She got to business and tried not to fight with another flashback. "We'll mediate your case on Monday, and I want you to understand how it's going to work."

Tiffany twirled her hair around her fingers. "I know." She didn't look at Jude.

"I hate you're going to have to think about the accident again. And you don't need to be there if you don't want to."

"What if I want to?" Tiffany asked.

"No. I forbid it," her grandmother said. "I don't want you there."

"Maybe *I* want to go." Tiffany pulled her legs up to her chest, and curled into a ball. She continued to focus on a ringlet of hair.

"She has the right to come," Jude said to the girl's grandmother.

"I won't allow it." Her grandmother was adamant.

"Mrs. Carmen, I agree this may be difficult for Tiffany, and you. But if Tiffany feels like she needs to be there, we shouldn't deny her. It's her case." Jude said. She turned to Tiffany. "Although, I have to say that I agree with your grandmother. It would be a long, boring day. You'll have to sit in a waiting room for hours while the lawyers go back and forth talking."

"Why can't I be with the lawyers?" Tiffany asked.

"We'll have one mediation room, where each side will present their case, then we'll break off to small rooms to talk individually. Since you've already been deposed, you won't have to answer any more questions," Jude said. She sat back. "Unless we don't settle. Then we'll move forward toward trial."

"Do you think it'll settle?" Tiffany relaxed a little.

"Probably. They know the driver was wrong, although they won't admit it. They're smart enough to know a jury would likely pound them after seeing the facts of the case."

"Will they see pictures of," Tiffany curled up again, "...the car and everything?" She'd almost permanently tied the lock of hair she'd been twisting.

"Yes." Jude thought of the graphic images. Tiffany's mother had been crushed and decapitated, her daughter, bloodied and folded under her.

"Do *you* think I should be there?" Tiffany asked in a little girl's voice.

Jude looked at the girl's grandmother, who'd been quietly dabbing away tears. She clutched a box of Kleenex on her lap.

"Usually the clients come, but I think it would be best if you stayed home. I'll call you during the day."

"Why shouldn't I be there?" the girl interrupted.

Jude sighed. "Many reasons. For one, I'm going to be working on the case. If you're there, I'd be worried about you."

"I'd be a distraction?" Tiffany looked at the grandmother affectionately. "Grandma always says I'm a distraction, but in a good way. I think."

Her grandmother smiled and nodded.

Jude put her hand on Tiffany's knee. "I also don't want you to relive the accident again."

"Like I'm ever going to forget it." She looked at Jude defiantly. "I don't even care about the money. I mean, it would be cool to buy stuff. But I'd rather, you know..." she pulled her legs closer to her body. Jude's hand dropped.

"I know," Jude said softly. "I wish she were here, too." She had an urge to hug the girl but stopped short of acting on it. "Tiffany, I won't make any settlement decisions until I talk to you and your grandmother. We'll all decide what's best."

Tiffany looked down, clasped her hands together. "I still miss her so much." She began crying. Then she jumped from the couch and ran to her room. The door slammed behind her.

Her grandmother watched her go but didn't get up. "These tantrums can go either way. She may start throwing things, or just cry for hours. It kills me to see her like this." She looked at Jude as if it had been her fault.

Jude picked up her purse and stood to leave when she heard the girl's bedroom door open. Tiffany came out, her heavy black makeup smeared down her face. "Okay, I won't go. But you promise you'll call me?"

"I promise."

"Here, give the truck driver this," Tiffany said. She held out an envelope. "He didn't even say he was sorry. He didn't even try to help us. I hate him."

"Okay. Is it all right if I read it, too?" Jude wondered what was in the envelope as she put it in her briefcase.

The girl shrugged. "If you want to." She looked at Jude.

"Make sure you kick their asses."

"Tiffany!" Her grandmother scolded.

Jude winked. "I will. *We* will."

Tiffany nodded, then went to Jude and wrapped her arms around her.

For a moment Jude flinched from the girl's affection. Then, slowly, she put her arms around Tiffany and hugged her, too.

Chapter 46

Energized, Jude got back to the office as the rest of the staff was leaving for the day. She sat at her desk and prepared arguments for Tiffany's case, more determined than ever to win. Her legal pad in her lap, she filtered ideas that flowed from her head to her pen. Sentences were scratched through, and bold letters formed an argument she'd present. Jude wanted to make sure any holes in the case were sealed with an answer. Engrossed in her work, she jumped when the phone rang.

"Jude Madigan." She forcefully circled an important paragraph on the pad as she answered.

"Jude, it's me, Katie."

The voice stopped Jude. She set her pad on the desk and leaned forward. "This is a surprise." She didn't know what else to say.

"You were right about Rick. He's a real scumbag. I'm sorry I didn't listen to you before." Katie seemed on the verge of tears.

"Katie." Jude hesitated. "I'm sorry." She was dying to know more but didn't want to jeopardize the Magdalene case by speaking to her. "You know we shouldn't be talking."

"I know. I'm calling from the office, and if Rick walks in, he'll kill me." Her voice turned into a frantic whisper. "Can I call you tonight? Will you be at home?"

Jude wondered if Katie was pumping for information. "As long as you're working for Rick, I can't talk to you. You know that."

"I want to quit, but I can't afford to be without a job! Will you hire me back? Please?"

Jude remembered how betrayed she felt when Katie quit. Even though she wanted her back, the fact she'd worked for Rick would probably backfire, not only on the Magdalene file but hon er other cases. "I wish I could, Katie, but you've now worked on two sides of the same case. It's unethical."

"I can help you. I have information that will surprise you," Katie said.

"That's exactly what I'm talking about. I'll win on the merits of the case. It's safer to play by the rules." Jude's hands were shaking.

"Rick's not playing by any rules but his own. He scares me." Katie whispered. "I think he's on drugs or something."

"I'm hanging up now, Katie. I'm sorry. Good-bye." Jude carefully put the phone back in its cradle. Sidetracked and flustered, Jude had a hard time refocusing on Tiffany's case. She opened her legal pad to a clean sheet of paper and wrote down the time of the call and everything she remembered they talked about. She weighed the decision to tell Drew the next morning—or just forget it. She didn't need to get into any more hot water with him.

She couldn't get her mind off what Katie had said. *Rick's not playing by any rules but his own.* What game? Jude was sorely tempted to call her back so Katie could spill her story but thought better of it.

She worked into the evening finalizing the settlement brochures for Monday and tracking down each expert to make sure they would be available by phone if needed for the mediation.

Throughout the drive home, her mind skittered from one thought to another. Jude couldn't hold on to any one crisis at a time. Questions jumped from problem to problem. *What did Katie know about Rick? Was Rick behind the lawsuit brought by the kid against Jude? Would Drew fire her if Monday's mediation was unsuccessful? Would she disappoint Tiffany?* When she tried to switch off the worries of her office, another question reared up. *What did Elizabeth know about her child?*

Her hands tensed around the steering wheel. Jude often had a recurring dream. She's driving fast. Exhilarating speed on an open highway. Suddenly, as she tops a hill, traffic ahead is at a complete stop. There's no time to react. She always woke before impact, heart racing and unable to get back to sleep.

She eased her foot off the accelerator and decided to take the long, slow way home.

Chapter 47

For most of the weekend, Jude worked on the Carmen case, at home, and at the office. Each detail of the case was a part of her, embedded in her psyche. The evening before the mediation, Jude ran three hard miles, but tension kept pace with her. She was determined to win, *had* to win. She wanted to be ready to take on Jack Barrone and needed to vent steam, didn't want to be a snack for him.

By the time the alarm went off the next morning at six, Jude was already up and dressed.

The mediator's office was a mixed combination of styles. Hunter green carpet and dark oak furniture made it look like most of the law offices Jude had seen. A woman, dressed in a drab suit that tried to be fashionable, led Jude through a beige hallway with store-bought landscape prints. Small conference rooms flanked each side. It was early, so the rooms were empty.

Jude glanced at her watch: eight-fifteen. Forty-five minutes before the meeting started. She was escorted into a large conference room and was surprised to find a young man already sitting at the table.

"Miss Madigan?" He stood and offered his hand. "I'm Ryan Thomas, with Jack Barrone's office."

If anyone looked like they should be named Poindexter, this guy did. Looking at his round, acne-pocked babyface,

Jude couldn't help but think of marshmallows. His brown hair was cut short, and his large eyeglasses slid down his nose when they shook hands. Jude preferred to be alone to set up her presentation. "You're early. Is Mr. Barrone here yet?"

"No, the mediation doesn't start till nine." He looked at his watch. "It's only eight twenty-two."

His movements were so precise, Jude imagined he'd freak out if he deviated from his routine. She looked around the room as she set her briefcase and purse on the table and noticed Ryan had already used the mediator's easels for his own charts. A large screen was pushed into a corner. Jude needed to hook up her equipment to the projector and test the equipment. "If you'll excuse me, I need a few minutes to set up." Jude picked up a phone on an end table to call for more easels.

"I can't leave the exhibits alone," he said, fidgeting with his watchband.

"You're welcome to take them while I set up," Judesaid, her anger flaring. The receptionist answered the phone, and Jude asked for additional equipment and some coffee brought in.

Ryan seemed uncertain of what to do and stood nervously by his charts.

"Please, I need ten minutes," Jude said.

A woman in a navy tailored suit came in, holding easels and a thermos of coffee. "Will two easels be enough?"

"Three would work better if you have an extra. Thank you." Jude had seven charts to display. She could lean some against the wall.

"I'll be right back with cream and sugar." The receptionist put the coffee on the bar and leaned the easels against the wall.

"Perhaps Mr. Thomas would be happy to help you." Jude nodded toward Ryan.

He hesitated and looked at his charts, as if they'd disappear without him, but shuffled out behind the receptionist, casting another nervous glance behind him.

Alone, Jude quickly plugged her laptop into the projector and rolled the screen to a good viewing range of the conference table. While she waited for the computer to boot up, she looked at the defense charts. It listed medical and economic damages considerably less than what Jude intended to ask for. From her briefcase she pulled five books, bound in linen hardcover. These were settlement brochures, which told the story of her client before and after the accident. Expert reports and future damage charts were included. Jude stacked them on a credenza. She'd hand them out after the evidence was presented. She set the easels near the end of the long conference table and put up the graphic medical illustrations of injuries Tiffany and her mother suffered. The economic charts she leaned against the wall facing in.

Jude was glad she'd talked Tiffany out of coming today. The drawing of her mother was especially hard to look at. It showed the decapitation and a multitude of broken bones and lacerations. Her body had been crushed and broken with Tiffany hidden under her. Jude kept the envelope of scene photographs sealed in her briefcase. A chill curled up her back as she thought of Tiffany trapped under her mother's body for almost an hour, waiting to be rescued.

Jude sat at the conference table and cued up her presentation. She'd just finished checking her show when Ryan and the receptionist returned.

Jack Barrone came in twenty minutes late, with an entourage. Jude was irritated, but not surprised at his arrogance. He didn't even look at Ryan when he entered and gave a cursory nod at Jude. "Where's Drew?" he asked.

Sitting at the conference table she made a point to look

at her watch. "He's scheduled for depositions this morning."

"He isn't going to be here?" Jack talked to her but looked out the window. "I don't have time to waste with a rookie."

"Fine." Jude stood and started packing her briefcase. "We can take today off and meet in the courtroom. I have no intentions of wasting my time either." Jude continued to pack hoping her insecurity wasn't apparent.

He looked at his entourage. "Spunky *and* cute."

Jude felt violated even though he was standing ten feet away. "Who's the insurance adjuster?" she asked. Her gaze followed the line of men sipping coffee.

One of the men still pouring a cup of coffee raised his hand. "That would be me." He turned and offered his hand to Jude. "I'm Larry Burnett."

"Nice to meet you, Mr. Burnett. Before we get started, *if* we get started," Jude looked at Barrone, "I want to make sure you have the authority to approve five million dollars."

Larry smirked at Jack. "I don't think we'll need that much today."

"Fine." Jude took her posters off the easels, acting braver than she felt. "If there's not an insurance adjuster here today with that much authority, I'm not going through with this presentation. I'll save it for the jury."

"Excuse me, is it Miss Madigan?" One of the men came forward. "I'm Mark Anderson, owner of Anderson Trucking. You have my assurances we have five million in coverage." He carried himself with confidence, his graying hair contrasted with his youthful face. Jude thought he looked distinguished, without all the bells, whistles, and bluster Jack Barrone flashed. "Let's get on with it."

Jack turned his back on her and spoke to Anderson. "Really, Mark, I was hoping Drew would be here."

Jude bit down and ignored the insult, she asked the men to sit.

"It looks like you're going to give us a real dog-and-pony show," Barrone said and laughed as he took his place at the head of the table, his back to the screen.

Jude tried to calm her shaking nerves. "After the presentation, I'll provide a settlement brochure to each of you, which will list the facts of the case and my demand."

"Why don't you just state your demand, so we won't have to waste time watching an emotional video," Barrone said, rolling his eyes to the ceiling.

Jude walked next to the screen and stood behind him. "If you're ready, I'll begin." She tried to find a level of confidence she could hold on to. Part of her wanted Drew there to deflect Barrone's disparaging attitude, but she also needed to prove, to herself and Drew, that she was capable of settling this case on her own.

She dimmed the lights and hit play.

"Well, I can't see it from here," Barrone said, making no attempt to move.

"Mr. Anderson, are you able to see the monitor?" Jude asked.

He nodded. "Yes, thank you. Jack, why don't you move to this side of the table and stop playing games."

Jude couldn't see Barrone's face, but even in the darkened room, she noticed the bald spot on the back of his head change color.

When the video started Jude sat at the conference table and tried to look busy. She didn't want to watch Tiffany's interview and the family video of the girl and her mother. With her emotions raw, Jude feared she'd cry when Tiffany talked about the accident and her loss. Tears at mediation, in front of these men, would be a death knell for Jude's career.

At the end of the emotionally gripping video, Jude

turned the lights up and brought out the economic damage charts. She took a deep breath and said, "Although we have over six million in past and future damages, the client is willing to settle, today, for four million."

"You can't prove that much in damages." Jack stood and handed his empty coffee cup to Ryan.

"I've given you a copy of Tiffany's medical expenses already. There are future damages included in the brochure." Jude handed each gentleman a copy of the settlement book.

"It's fluff. We have caps on punitive damages, honey," Jack said as Ryan handed him a steaming cup of coffee. He set it on the bound brochure Jude had just given him. She watched a brown stain appear on the linen cover.

"These aren't punitive, they're actual." She clamped her lips shut before she said *honey* back to him.

He scoffed. "You're blowing smoke."

"We can let the jury decide." Jude was firm, though she fought an urge to run.

"Your inexperience wouldn't stand a chance against all the cases I've tried." He sneered. "And won."

"I've got the facts on my side." Jude felt a tremor in her voice. "May I remind you, again, of the driver's logbooks, DOT citations, or the mechanic's records showing the brakes had been bad for over a year?" She waved at charts situated around the room.

"What is your expertise in the legal field, young lady?" Barrone stood over her. "Truck wrecks or managing homes of ill-repute?"

Jude couldn't believe what she'd heard. "What?" She tried to hide her surprise, but he'd caught her off guard.

"Are you helping poor wayward girls become millionaires by filing frivolous lawsuits?" Jack said, his hard eyes locked with Jude.

"What are you implying?" Jude held his gaze.

He looked away. Finally.

"You know this girl has no future medical expenses to speak of," Jack said, pointing at one of the financial charts. "She's fine."

Jude was flustered, couldn't believe he'd brought up the Magdalene Home. She tried to refocus on Tiffany's case. "She certainly has future medical expenses." She went to the illustration of the girl. "Tiffany fractured her spine, her femur, and three ribs. Her future damages are listed. And, she was trapped under her mother's body for an agonizing time before they got her out of the car. The emergency crew didn't even know she was there. They thought her mother was the only one in the vehicle because they couldn't see Tiffany." Jude glared at Jack. "It wasn't until they heard her scream that they found her."

She noticed Mark Anderson was looking through the settlement brochure. "Should I give you a few minutes to go over the evidence that I've presented before we go over your charts?" Jude said.

Mark Anderson closed the book. "Yes, please. I'd like to review this before we talk about settlement."

Jack walked to Anderson and said, "There's no reason to look at that. I'd like to talk to Drew before we make any decisions."

Anderson looked at Jude. "If you'll excuse us."

Jude nodded. "Certainly. I need to make some calls." She collected her briefcase and purse and left the room.

Relief flooded into the shaking spaces in her body when Jude got to the hallway, she took a deep breath, wondering how Jack Barrone could get away with being such an asshole. He knew how and when to drive the nails into her psyche. No woman could ever fit in with his good 'ol boys club.

She went to an empty conference room and considered

putting a glass to the wall so she'd be able to hear the conversation. Instead, she fell into a seat and remembered to call Tiffany as promised. Jude dug through her briefcase looking for her phone. Inside, she found the letter Tiffany had given her. Her heart sank. She'd forgotten about her promise to give it to the driver. It was probably too late to produce it now, at the mediation. It would look like trickery. Plus, Jude hadn't read it yet.

She tore open the envelope. Tiffany had taken care to write neatly, but Jude could still see the little girl through the message.

> *Dear Mr. Truck Driver,*
>
> *My name is Tiffany and you ran a stop sign and killed my mother. I'm trying not to hate you. My grandma says it's wrong to hate. She says I can say I hate what happened. That's what I keep telling myself. The doctor I talk to says I don't remember very much about the accident. But I do. I usually see it when I dream. It still scares me like it just happened. I'm scared to go to sleep. Except sometimes I see my mom in my dreams and I like to sleep on those nights. If I knew what nights I was going to have the bad dream I wouldn't go to sleep at <u>all</u>. There is something big that I remember about the accident. When I was under my mom and it didn't feel real. It was weird, like I was there and I wasn't. Then I heard a voice. The voice said that I could come to heaven if I was ready. It scared me so much I started screaming. That's when the firemen found out I was there. Now I wish I wouldn't have screamed. I wish I would have gone to heaven with Mommy. Everybody says that my Mommy is still in my*

> *heart and I can talk to her. But I want her here <u>with me</u>. I want her to come in and sit on my bed so we can talk about our day like she always used to. I miss her so much. You didn't even say you were sorry!!! Why didn't you stop? That's what I really want to know.*
> *Sincerely,*
> *Tiffany Carmen*

Against her will, tears filled Jude's eyes and she choked back a sob. Taking a breath, she fought to compose herself. *Do. Not. Cry.*

She folded the note, put it in her briefcase, and left to find a restroom. Like a faucet, the damned tears wouldn't stop. The recent emotions for her own daughter paralleled somehow with Tiffany's loss. Both she and Tiffany had suffered. Both were trying to repair the damage.

In the bathroom, she tried to blot the redness out of her eyes and touch up her makeup. She wished her face wouldn't balloon so much when she cried. The door to the bathroom opened, startling Jude.

"I'm sorry." The woman who'd brought the easels came in. "The others were asking for you. They're ready to talk." She hesitated as she looked at Jude. "Are you all right?"

Jude put on a game face. "I'm fine. Let them know I'll be right in." The woman ducked out. "Damn, damn," Jude sputtered, looking at her blotched face in the mirror.

Taking a deep breath, she summoned enough courage to go back in to settle the case. Even though she still felt on the verge of tears. With renewed resolve and extra makeup, she left the bathroom and strode down the hallway toward the empty conference room where she'd put her things. *Chin up, eyes forward,* she told herself and steeled her emotions.

The door to the conference room, where the men were waiting, stood ajar. Jude needed another minute before she faced them, so she stepped into the conference room to get her briefcase, and bumped directly into Ryan, who was walking out of the room.

"Jude," He looked taken aback. "There you are. Mr. Barrone and Mr. Anderson are looking for you."

"I'll be right in." Jude slipped past him to pick up her things. "I have to make a phone call first." She closed the door on Ryan and again fought to compose herself. She did some breathing exercises and a few quick stretches. Even so, she still felt fragile as she opened the door.

Finally, she walked into the conference room. *The lion's den*, she thought as she glanced around.

The conversation stopped when she entered. The men were clustered in groups drinking coffee or looking at the charts. Barrone and Anderson were seated together while Ryan hovered nearby.

Mr. Anderson came up to her. "I'd like to see the full video interview, uncut, of Tiffany and her grandmother."

"He wants to make sure you didn't tell her what to say." Barrone sat at the head of the table, drumming his fingers on the brochure.

Jude ignored Jack and turned to Anderson. "I'll show you more in court. She looked at Barrone. "I'm not providing any more before trial."

Barrone stared at Jude, and she wondered if he could tell she'd been crying.

"I'd like to meet with her myself, to see how she's doing," Anderson said.

"She's already been deposed by your attorneys. I don't want her to go through any additional trauma. Her psychological reports are in the brochure."

"How often do you see her?" Anderson's question was on target. "How do you know she's still suffering?"

Jude paused. "Mr. Anderson, there is no doubt she's suffered and will continue to have problems. The reports…"

"I don't care about the reports. You can hire a doctor to say anything if you pay them enough." His eyes bore through Jude.

She reached in her purse for the letter, hesitated, then brought it out. "I didn't produce this because I…I wanted to save it for trial. It's a note she wrote to the truck driver." She unfolded the note. "I haven't even copied it yet, I just got it from Tiffany on Friday. This is the original." She handed it to Anderson.

Barrone stood up and reached for the letter. Anderson brushed him away and turned to read it.

As he read, Jude tried to keep beat with his eyes, reciting the letter in her head. She watched his face react and remembered the line about Tiffany wanting to go to heaven. She thought of abandoning her own daughter. Suddenly fresh tears spilled down her cheeks. Mortified, she hurriedly excused herself.

"Oh, this is nice. How are we going to talk business if you women can't stop crying," Jack said angrily. He turned to the others. "Just like my wife, every time she wants something, she cries. Typical."

Jude was almost through the door when she ran smack into Drew.

Chapter 48

"Jude! What's the matter?" Drew tried to take her arm. Jude waved him off. She did not want Drew to see her crying. Shoulders rigid, she hurried down the hall to the bathroom. Jude barely managed to make it through the doors before the dam burst. Ducking into a stall, she sobbed as she wadded up mounds of toilet paper to wipe her face. She blew her nose and flushed the sodden tissue, thinking she should jump in along with her career.

She considered staying there for the rest of the afternoon in the hopes the men would leave, and she wouldn't have to face them. After a few minutes, she sighed, walked to the sink, and rinsed off the tears, along with the repaired makeup. Tried to blot more on, but her face was too swollen and mottled. Feeling like a beaten dog, she opened the door and went back to the conference room.

Drew stood against the window ledge talking to Barrone and Anderson. She looked straight at him through her puffy eyes. If she felt like a cur with its tail between its legs, he was like the old hound that lay watch on the porch. His tail might be slapping the floor, but his eyes stayed wary. He nodded brusquely at her.

Jack turned to Jude. "Well, here she is. Are you feeling better?" His tone dripped with sarcasm. "Now that Drew's here, we're ready to talk."

"Don't be an asshole, Jack," Drew said. "Jude, have you presented all the evidence?"

"Yes." She stood tall, but failure blossomed in her chest. "Please, let me apologize for my unprofessional behavior." Jude took a deep breath. "Yes, gentlemen, women cry. And you can expect half the jury will be women, they too will cry when Tiffany's letter is read." She looked directly at Barrone. "Count on it."

Jack Barrone, and most of his henchmen, tried to stifle smirks. Anderson looked coolly at Jude.

Drew stepped beside Jude, and said, "I don't want us to lose sight of Tiffany." He nodded at Jude. "We understand the pain she's going through, so will a jury."

He turned to go but stopped and looked at the others. "I decided a long time ago when these cases *stop* bothering me, I'd get out of the business. It's because we care that we do a good job." He looked at Jude. "Do you have anything else?"

She felt a little stronger. "No." She glanced quickly at Drew and then turned to the silent group. "We'll allow forty-eight hours for this case to settle. Otherwise, we'll move forward to trial. There will not be another settlement discussion." She looked at Anderson. "I'll make a copy of the letter for you. I'll keep the original."

He'd refolded the note and handed it to Jude. "I'd like a copy to take with me today."

Jack waved at his assistant, Ryan. "Go find a copier and make enough for everyone. Then let's get the hell out of here."

After Ryan left, Jude took her charts off the easels and stuffed them in portfolios. She shut down her computer and packed it. Drew and Jack were telling war stories. The tears were gone, and Jude was angry for breaking down. Drew had saved her ass, and she feared, even if he didn't fire her, he'd probably demote her. Give her the easy cases to work on. That's probably all she deserved anyway. She snapped her computer case closed.

Ryan came in with copies. Jude took the letter and wanted to be the first to leave. Laden with her briefcase and portfolio, she said to the men, "I'll expect to hear from you soon." She shook Anderson's hand and then turned to Drew. "I'll see you back at the office."

"Can I help carry anything?" Drew asked.

"No, thank you." She turned, and, with her heavy case biting into her shoulder, walked out.

∽∾∽

Jude sped in and out of traffic on the way back to the office, digging her anger into the accelerator. Her cell phone rang. It was Tiffany. She'd forgotten to call.

"Did you give the truck driver my letter?" Tiffany asked.

"I gave a copy to the man who owns the company. He'll show it to the driver." She slowed her car. "It was a good letter, Tiffany."

"I still wanted to be there."

"I know. But it was kind of boring. You know, just a bunch of lawyers talking." *And crying and yelling*, Jude thought. "We should hear something soon. I promise you'll be the first person I call."

"Okay." Tiffany paused. "Thanks. I still want the truck driver to know what he did."

"He will. I'll make sure of it. Stay strong." She disconnected.

Jude pulled into the office parking lot and unloaded the car. In the elevator, she put her head against the cool, wood-grained panels. Drew and Jack's friendship went back years. Jude hoped Drew wouldn't be so disappointed with her that he'd let her go today. She smiled bitterly, thinking that maybe Sister Elizabeth would have to rescue her from the streets if she was fired.

She didn't know when Drew would get back, so she headed straight to her office. She stopped at Katie's empty desk and leaned the portfolio against the wall. Jude was tempted to call her. If she could get a jump on what Rick was up to, maybe she'd feel better about herself and her career. But it would be wrong, unethical. She sighed.

Jude picked up a stack of mail someone had put on Katie's desk and went into her office. On her desk, she was surprised to find a gift basket laden with every type of chocolate imaginable. Grabbing the gift card, she tore open the tiny envelope. *Happy Holidays. I hope to see you at the Magdalene Home on Christmas day. Reece.*

Jude put the card back in its envelope. After the night at church, she wasn't sure if she was ever going to hear from him again. Tears threatened once more. Why, after all these years, were her normally barren tear ducts on hyper-drive? These last few days she cried when she was happy, sad, or in front of adversaries at work. It was giving her a headache.

"Jude, are you there?" Drew's voice boomed over her intercom.

"I'm here." Jude jumped. She'd just gotten a dark chocolate truffle out of the basket.

"Come up and see me." He clicked off, not waiting for an answer.

Instead of putting the chocolate back in the basket, she opened the foil and stuffed the piece, whole, into her mouth. She grabbed Tiffany's file as she walked out.

Drew sat at his desk with his arms crossed, waiting. She wiped her lips, in case dark coco had smeared across them and sat down.

"Jude, what the hell happened to you today? You need to have a tougher hide than that for this kind of work."

She felt like a kid getting reprimanded by the teacher. "It was that letter. Tiffany gave it to me on Friday. I debated using it for the mediation." She didn't want to tell him she'd only found and read it that morning. "Hearing her, in her own words, saying she wished she would've died, it set me off. I'm sorry."

He shook his head. "Jude, you've never shown that kind of emotion with any of your other cases. You've managed to keep a professional front. I need that. What if you would've done that in trial?"

She nodded. "You're right, I shouldn't have reacted like that. I feel awful."

"Why didn't you show me this letter over the weekend?" He held a hand out. "Let me see it."

She opened the manila file and handed him the note.

Drew put on his reading glasses and leaned back. Jude looked out the window as he read. The Dallas skyline blended into the horizon with the afternoon sun. The bitter taste of the day lingered with the sweet chocolate. When Drew was finished reading, he dropped the letter on his desk. Jude thought his eyes looked glassy.

"Make sure you enlarge that to a poster for trial in case they don't settle. That's some good stuff," he said, thickly.

"Okay." Jude picked up the letter and put it in the file, being careful not to look at Drew as he surreptitiously wiped his eyes.

"They'd be stupid not to settle." He shifted in his chair. "By the way, I was talking to Jack at the mediation. It seems your friend, Rick, filled him in on what happened to you at the Magdalene Home. Rick approached Jack a few weeks ago about investing in his real estate deal."

Jude nervously adjusted her blouse. "Jack said something about the home at the mediation. I wondered how he knew how I was involved."

"It would be smart to get rid of that place. Have you

talked to the nuns about selling the property?"

"They don't want to. And they shouldn't be pressured to sell. Rick is behind the Academy's sudden interest in the building, and the protests." She shook her head. "He can buy the remaining buildings in the area. He needs to back off of this one."

Drew leaned back. "Why don't they just sell? The estate would make a bunch of money, which would go to the nuns anyway. They could buy a new building, and everybody would be happy."

"That building sat abandoned for years. He should've bought it first. The nuns are happy there. They spent a bunch of money and sweat to rebuild it to what it is today. And the Academy was fine with them being there until Rick poked the hornet's nest." She looked at Drew. "They spent months fixing that place up. They're interested in helping the women, not rebuilding another place." Jude knew Drew had a good point. Another time, before she'd become involved with Elizabeth and the women, she would've been the first to recommend selling. Now she wanted to see the women stay. Their hearts were part of the architecture.

"Jude, I hope you're not going to let personal issues with an old boyfriend ruin a perfectly good business deal," Drew said. He put an elbow on his desk and looked over his reading glasses at her.

Her insides coiled. "Drew, you know me better. I don't let my personal life get in the way of work," she said, thinking how she hadn't *had* a personal life before Elizabeth and the women came into it. She wondered, too, if her desire to protect the home came from a need inside herself and Elizabeth's knowledge of her daughter. To upset the nuns could delay finding her child.

Chapter 49

After her meeting with Drew, Jude walked back to her office, relieved he hadn't fired her. A fat envelope from Lonnie Ball's office sat on her desk. She tore it open and found a thick pile of discovery questions. Flipping through the pages were, as she'd feared, questions about her own history. She tossed the papers on her credenza. Most of her responses would be "not relevant to time period." That wouldn't hold him off for long.

She slumped in her chair and called Elizabeth to relay Drew's conversation about selling the property. She'd advise Elizabeth to say no to the sale, but was it the advice of a lawyer or a friend? While Jude waited for someone to answer, she sorted through the basket of chocolate from Reece. She'd just unwrapped another truffle when Elizabeth answered.

"Hey, Sister, it's Jude." She shaved off a layer of chocolate with her teeth.

"This is a nice surprise, I was going to call you tonight."

"Anything new?" Jude savored the rich chocolate.

"We're planning Christmas dinner. Elizabeth paused. "You don't have any conflicts, do you?"

"It's on my calendar."

"Good. I'm looking forward to seeing you around three."

"I don't know if I can wait that long."

"Then why don't you come to dinner tonight? We'd love to see you."

Jude looked at the basket of chocolate and weighed her options. A night of sinful cocoa indulgence, or nutrition with nuns. She decided on nutritious comfort food. "Okay, what time?"

"Around six."

"Sounds good. I'll leave here about five, stop home, and change first." Jude hung up the phone and finished the truffle. She left the office a little early.

At home, she decided to go for a quick run. After, showering, she changed and turned on a few interior lights so she wouldn't come home to darkness. Tommy hung near her legs, and she picked him up. "Can you hold the fort down for a few hours?" He gave her a look that said he knew he'd be alone again. She gave him an extra scoop of food.

Jude considered bringing a bottle of wine but thought better of it. Instead, she grabbed Sangria's file from her case.

The night was cool and crisp. Darkness had come early being so close to the winter solstice. Jude drove cautiously through the dilapidated neighborhood to the Magdalene House. The unlit street was alive with people out in the cold, strolling along the sidewalk or huddled around burning trashcans. All eyes turned toward her as she passed. She shivered remembering the night she was attacked. Trying to ward off the memory, she imagined the area cleaned up and turned into a trendy urban neighborhood.

The gate outside the Home was closed. Jude pushed an intercom button and heard a small ring.

"Hello? Who's there?"

Jude recognized Sister Bernadette's voice. "It's me, Jude."

"Saint Jude! I'm so glad you're here. Now let me see if

I can figure out how to work the gate code."

Jude heard some fumbling and finally, "Lizzie, where are you? I can't open the outside gate. Jude's here."

The intercom turned off and on, and Elizabeth's voice came on as the gate moved. "Open sesame. Come on in. Pull around to the kitchen entrance."

Jude drove along the gravel drive to the back. The kitchen door opened, and Jude saw Elizabeth silhouetted against the bright light.

"It's about time." Elizabeth held the kitchen door open for Jude. "We started without you."

"I'm late? I didn't expect anyone to wait for me." Jude walked in, warmth and enticing smells of food cooking greeted her. Five of the girls were working at the spacious counters. Sister Bernadette aproned and smiling said, "Jude, welcome. Come in and help with the salad."

"I thought you said you started without me." Jude washed her hands and let Bernadette lead her to a cutting board overflowing with fresh vegetables.

Elizabeth grabbed a carrot and took a crunchy bite. "We usually don't start cooking until everybody's here. Bernie thinks if we're all involved in preparing dinner, it brings us closer." She bit into the carrot again. "Plus, we tend to enjoy the food more if we've made it ourselves."

Bernadette eyed Elizabeth and put her hands on her hips. "And how is your part coming along?" she asked.

"Fabulous," said Elizabeth. She looked at Jude. "I'm in charge of the chicken. All I have to do is stick it in the oven and wait."

"Well, at least help Jude cut the vegetables," said Bernadette. "And quit eating until dinner is ready and we've said grace." Bernadette bustled off in a cloud of flour dust.

"Hey lawyer lady, what's cooking?" Sangria yelled across the kitchen.

"Chicken and whatever this stuff is, that's what's cooking," Bandee said as she smiled at Jude.

Both women were working together, sautéing diced squash and mushrooms. Shelby spooned fruit into cups.

"Do you eat such a big meal every night?" Jude asked as she chopped at a celery stalk.

"Yeah, we can't use Hamburger Helper stuff," Bandee said, stirring the vegetables.

"I ain't never seen zucchini helper," Sangria said. She added salt to the pan.

"We think it gives the girls a sense of accomplishment. After a full day of classes, they enjoy cooking to help them unwind." Elizabeth said.

Bernadette supervised each station of food preparation. She gave advice or praise each time she moved to another group.

Elizabeth tore wet lettuce leaves and put them in a large wooden bowl. "When I finish this, I'll check on the chicken." She leaned into Jude. "What's going on? Any news on the Academy?"

"No. Not really." Her feet ached and she was worn to the bone after the stress of the mediation, she wasn't sure she had the energy to tell Elizabeth about her crying jag and Drew recommending selling the property. Instead, she wanted to enjoy the company and warmth of the kitchen. Jude recalled the meeting and Jack's disparaging comments. She tossed the lettuce too hard and shot some greens in the sink.

"Hey, watch out. We want our salad tossed, not thrown," Elizabeth said and ducked mockingly. "Are you okay?"

"Yeah, tough day."

"How was the mediation?"

Jude shrugged. "It could've gone better. We didn't settle."

"How's Tiffany?" Elizabeth took another carrot and ate it.

"She just wants her mother." Jude almost told her about the letter and breaking down after reading it. Instead, she told Elizabeth about Reece's gift. "I brought some real chocolate from the basket to make hot cocoa."

"That sounds delish. You know, he's planning to be here for Christmas dinner. He's asked about you a few times since you came to church."

"Really?" Jude tried not to smile. "Who else is coming?"

Elizabeth tossed the rest of the carrots in the salad. "The usual gang, and we hope to have a few others, too" She nodded toward the women. "Sangria is spending Christmas morning with her kids at her mother-in-law's but she'll be here for dinner. I'm grateful the kids will be together."

"And when will we have time to talk about…?" Jude mixed in the salad dressing.

"You'll know when it's time." Elizabeth leaned against the counter and changed the subject. "I think Reece is looking forward to seeing you."

"I'll be glad to see him, too." Jude felt herself blush. She held up the freshly made salad. "Where should I put this?"

Elizabeth pointed to the dining room. "Set it in the middle of the table. Then you can help with the chicken."

While they ate, most of the women were animated and talkative. Exhausted, Jude was comfortable with sitting quietly and observing.

"Did Sangria tell you she's spending Christmas morning with her family?" Bernadette asked Jude. "Her mother-in-law is making a peace offering."

Sangria grinned. "I can't wait to see my babies open their gifts. Thanks to you all, they'll have real presents this year." She looked at Elizabeth and Bernadette gratefully.

Jude smiled. "The attorney handling the custody issues said as soon as you get released, find a job, and get established, you'll be able to get your kids back full time."

"Yes! Get me outta here. I'm ready." Sangria almost jumped out of her chair.

"With supervision," Jude cautioned.

"Have you thought about going back to school, like Bandee?" Elizabeth asked.

"That would take forever. I want them back *now*." Sangria put her fork down. "My daughter is getting brainwashed by that woman. She needs her mama."

"What classes are you taking, Bandee?" Jude asked.

She shrugged. "The stuff I have to take. Then I want to get a job as a newscaster."

"What about a law degree?" Jude asked, relieved the girl's interest had changed so she wouldn't feel obligated to mentor her.

"I want to try something in television instead. I think it'd be more fun." She looked pointedly at Elizabeth. "Even though we don't have a TV here so I could get some ideas."

Shelby chimed in. "I know a movie producer. Maybe he can get you a job."

"Not porn news." Bandee scrunched her face.

"He probably knows a lot of people." Shelby's chubby face turned red. "And don't knock it, you can make a ton of money."

Bernadette touched the girl's arm. "Shelby, that is not an option," she said. "Bandee needs to take classes. Then God will guide her to her career choice."

"Maybe God can do my homework for me, too," Bandee said and played with her salad. "How many years did you go to college to be a lawyer?"

"Seven," Jude answered. "But it goes fast."

"That's like forever," Shelby said. "You'll lose your looks before you get out." She raised an eyebrow and looked at Bandee. "You'll be so old."

"What can I be if I only want to go for a year?" Shelby looked stricken. "I mean, *that's* a long time."

"You can be a cashier at McDonald's." Sangria laughed.

"Well, *you* didn't go to college," Bandee said indignantly.

"I went to the school of life." Sangria pointed a butter knife at her. "I gots lots of experience."

"We all have areas we can grow," Bernadette said. She smoothed the tablecloth. "God has blessed you all with different skills and talent. He will guide you."

"Yeah, look where he put me." Bandee looked around the room. "Prison."

"This isn't prison," Elizabeth said. "You're lucky to be here."

Bandee rolled her eyes. "Whatever."

After the meal, dishes were done and Elizabeth directed everyone into the den warmed by a cozy fire. Light from flickering candles and the fire gleamed butterscotch over the room. Jude sat alone on a love seat. The others sat in chairs or on the floor. The sisters pulled two chairs together in front of the fireplace.

Elizabeth looked at Jude. "After dinner, we get together as a group and talk." She took in the scene like a mother hen. "It helps the others by discussing our pasts, and our futures. Our dreams."

"Yeah, and we can't have no dreams in our own bed till we talk," Sangria added. She sat on the floor and leaned against a soft couch. "I'm tired. Taking classes here is hard. Now I know what people go through when they go to paroc— whatever school."

"Parochial school," Elizabeth corrected.

"You guys must've been good at corporate punishment with kids." She put her hand over her forehead.

"Corporal punishment," Bernadette corrected.

"That's what I said."

Jude ducked her head trying not to laugh.

Bernadette let the comment go. "Sangria, why don't you lead the prayer tonight."

At the word "prayer," Jude stiffened. As emotional as she'd been lately, she didn't want to pray in front of anyone. She should've known they would spend time talking to God, being a Catholic home. She stood, hoping to slip out unnoticed.

"Jude, please join us." Elizabeth waved to her seat.

"Thanks, but I'm going to step outside for some fresh air. That dinner is making me tired."

"No fair," Sangria said. She stood.

"Sit down, Sangria," Elizabeth and Bernadette said simultaneously.

No one followed Jude outside. She stepped into the yard and held her arms around herself. The cold air was bracing, but Jude's chills came from a deeper place. She remembered the night firecrackers were thrown over the fence, sure she'd been shot at. So much had happened to her since the nuns came into her life. In some ways, it was the first time she'd felt alive. She'd allowed more emotion to surface in a few short months than she had in years. She cringed when she thought of crying in front of everyone at the mediation. "Damn it!" she whispered fiercely to herself as she shivered from the cold.

"Damn what?"

Elizabeth's voice made her jump. She turned to see the nun standing on the porch stairs holding two steaming mugs.

"Jes..." Jude stopped herself. "You scared me. I didn't hear the door open."

"WD-40. Great stuff, but it's probably a mistake to use it here. We need the doors to squeak a little in case someone tries to escape." Elizabeth walked to Jude. "I made hot chocolate from your gift, and I added a shot of bourbon." She handed the hot drink to Jude. "Why'd you come outside?"

"Geez, you Catholics drink a lot of alcohol." Jude's teeth were chattering, and her body shook. "Maybe that's the real reason why the Baptists want you out of here." She held the warm mug with both hands and took a sip. There was more bite from the alcohol than the hot beverage. "I wasn't ready to spill my soul. Sorry."

"No one has to talk if they don't want to." Elizabeth took a drink, set her mug on the stairs, and sat down. "Our evening talks and prayers are helpful. I've learned more about human nature listening to people than in years of living."

"You're a nun, you're supposed to lead an introspective, boring life."

Elizabeth chuckled. "You're right. Introspective, maybe, but never boring. I get much satisfaction out of what I do." She scooted over and patted the step for Jude to join her. "Come on, I think we can handle the cold for a while." A brisk gust of wind stirred the barren branches of a massive oak tree, one of many that lined the perimeter of the property.

Jude sat feeling a little warmer. "I didn't mean to snap at you. Lately, you've become a lifeline for me. It's weird like I'm relying on you." Jude paused. "And you know something about my daughter but won't tell me. Why?"

Elizabeth didn't answer. She sipped her drink and looked away.

"I'm still trying to figure out the connection between you, this place, and my past." Jude turned expectantly to Elizabeth, who sat stone-faced and wouldn't look at Jude.

"You're the first person I've told about the rape and my child. I'm not used to depending on someone."

Elizabeth picked up a handful of gravel and tossed stones into the yard one by one. "I know that was hard for you to say. I'm glad you're in my life too. You know, I haven't told many people about my past either." She threw a big stone, which hit an oak tree with a clunk. "Don't try to get me to talk about your daughter, not yet." She finally looked at Jude and smiled. "I hate to say it like this, but you're just going to have to wait until Christmas."

"I've waited so long already. My daughter. It feels weird to even say it. I've always wondered what happened to her." Jude continued to bait Elizabeth. "It's like I'm missing the other half of me."

"Have you thought of what we'd talked about, you being ready to find out what happened to her? Whether or not she's ready?" Elizabeth sipped her drink. Steam swirled out of the cup like a spirit.

"Elizabeth, what do you know? Where is she? Is she okay?" Jude was desperate for the answer.

"Jude, we've talked about this." Elizabeth looked at her. "I want you to be ready, too."

"I've been ready for seventeen years."

The nun blew on her hot cocoa before taking another sip. "Rick came by the other day. He brought more protesters." Elizabeth magically segued to another topic, not even acknowledging Jude's comment. "After Rick left, Bernie invited them in for coffee." She chuckled. "A few of them came in and are now supporting us. They promised to talk to Pastor Rains."

Jude took a deep breath. She knew Elizabeth wasn't going to break whatever promise she held. "Okay, damn it, I'll wait. But don't be surprised to see me at the break of dawn on Christmas."

Chapter 50

It was after ten o'clock when Jude pulled into her garage. Going through her mail, she found a letter from Katie. Tempted to tear into it, Jude decided it would be better to keep it sealed. She should give it to Drew and let him know Katie was trying to contact her with information.

The money management of the Magdalene estate was moving along. She wished the emotional part was going as well. Bandee's school would be paid for as long as she resided at the home. As soon as Sangria found a decent job, the estate would help find a home for her and the kids. Shelby didn't seem to have any motivation for improvement. She balked at any chance to go to school and showed no interest in a trade. Except for making movies.

Jude thought of Trudy and the letter she'd written. What favor had Jude done for the woman? Jude couldn't remember ever meeting her.

Frustrated, Jude headed to bed, wishing she'd brought the basket of chocolate home instead of leaving it at the office.

The phone's shrill ring woke Jude from a deep sleep. She glanced at the clock as she reached for the receiver; it was five-thirty.

Groggy, Jude sat up. "Hello." Tommy shot under the bed.

"Jude, I'm sorry to wake you, but we have to talk."

"Who is this?" Jude pulled the comforter around her.

"It's Katie." She spoke quickly. "Don't hang up. You need to know Rick's the one who found that kid you ran over and made him file a suit with Lonnie Ball. He's out to get you, Jude."

Even though she was wrapped in her warm bedding, Jude chilled. "What? Why?"

"He's already purchased the property around that hotel the nuns bought and told his investors the nun's home was part of the deal. He's, like, possessed about it." She breathed audibly. "He said it's your fault the nuns won't sell."

"Katie, that's absurd. He knows the nuns own it." Jude tried to shake the last of sleep from her brain.

"Since you're the executor of the estate, he thought you'd easily get them to sell. Now he's afraid the investors may not pay because he hasn't kept up his end of the deal. He's running out of time."

"Why would he do something so stupid?" Jude asked. She leaned over and turned a light on. Tommy jumped back on the bed but looked annoyed.

"He thought he was being smart." Katie paused. "You know, Jude, he's doing background checks on everybody. Even you."

Jude was speechless. What could he find out about her? School grades? College records? A home for unwed mothers? She sat up, fully awake. "Unless I give permission for my records to be researched, he can't get anything."

"Why do you think he wanted Lonnie to file that suit? It gives him a reason to get your background checked."

"Katie, wait…" Jude didn't know how to respond. Jude wasn't sure if Katie was playing her. But there seemed to be a ring of truth to what she was saying.

"He's determined to get that hotel. And you," Katie

said, breathless. "I'm trying to stop him without getting caught. You were right about him, Jude. I'm sorry I didn't listen." She started crying.

Jude got out of bed. The chill in the room gave her body a shock as she reached for her bathrobe. Katie cried a little more while Jude tried to sort the information.

"Jude," Katie sobbed, "that weasel Lonnie Ball is always at the office now. He's so gross in his shiny suits and gold chains, he totally gives me the creeps. He keeps asking for the discovery questions on your case. I waited as long as I could before sending them to you.

"What has Rick found out?" Jude asked.

"I'm not sure. He personally hired the private investigator."

"It doesn't matter what he finds," Jude lied, the words fumbling in her mouth. "He's not getting that home."

"I don't know what to do. Everything he does seems sleazy. Especially working with Lonnie Ball." Katie had stopped crying but still sniffled.

Jude was afraid to say more to Katie. "Look, you know you shouldn't be calling me. At least until you quit working with him. I appreciate your concern, but I don't want you to get into any trouble."

"Even if he's not doing the right thing?" Katie asked. "It seems like if he's not being honest, then you should know."

"If he's doing something illegal, then he won't be able to use it anyway." Jude knew she was only fooling herself. He'd find a way to use any information. "Thanks for letting me know, Katie. Just make sure to keep your nose clean. It would be bad for you if he shifted the blame. You're an easier target."

"If I quit, then can we talk about you re-hiring me?" Katie sounded hopeful. "I just need to wait until my Christmas bonus, then I'll turn my notice in."

"I don't know, Katie. We'd need to find out if we have any other cases with Rick's firm. If so, you can't be re-hired."

"We don't. I've already checked. He only does real estate law. Except for him trying to take over the Magdalene Home, we have nothing else." Katie paused. "And maybe I'll find out why he was so happy after meeting with that investigator yesterday."

Chapter 51

Jude hung up and sat on the edge of her bed. She went over what Katie had said. Rick's obsession had already crossed boundaries beyond what was right. How far would he go?

Tommy had made himself cozy in the warmth of the comforter. "I wish I had your life," Jude said as she pulled the blanket over him, tucking him in.

She decided to take an early morning run, dressed warmly in sweats. Maybe the winter air would clear her mind. She had a nagging, nervous feeing about Rick's investigation. Even if he did find out about her child, what could he do? Still, Jude's stomach twisted at the thought of having her personal life flayed open, especially to him. She was sickened she'd actually dated the asshole.

After her run, and a hot, muscle-relaxing shower, she dressed and drove to the office. It was early, so she decided to take an impromptu detour to the mall for a little Christmas shopping. Something she'd not given much thought to in years, since she usually sent money to her mother for the family, and Katie had bought her office gifts. This year, she felt more vested in the holiday. She had a few more reasons, and friends, to buy for.

She put thoughts of Rick out of her mind as she walked into the mall. Whatever he had found out, she'd deal with it. Right now, she wanted to buy something special for Tiffany. In the teen section of Nordstrom, Jude realized she knew nothing of current trends. The fashions, if that's what they were, made Jude feel old and out of place. Why do teenagers wear thong underwear? Jude wanted an exceptional gift, memorable, so she headed down the escalator to the jewelry department.

After deciding against most of the baubles, Jude honed in on a selection of silver crosses. This felt right. She chose a simple styled silver cross with Tiffany's birthstone embedded in the center. The pleasure of buying a gift for another person put a lightness in her step. She paid for the jewelry, then did a little shopping for Elizabeth and Bernadette.

Wandering the mall for the next hour, she went in and out of stores, enjoying time perusing new fiction in a bookstore. Jude bought a few novels for herself. It had been a long time since she'd enjoyed a good book. She picked up a book of saints for Sister Bernadette and a photography book for Elizabeth.

Laden with bags, Jude twisted her arm to look at her watch, it was almost ten. She'd shopped away the morning, knew she should hurry back to the office, but on her way out, she couldn't resist a bath shop and bought lotions and soaps for the women living at the Magdalene Home. Balancing her gift bags, she got to her car and realized that, for a moment, she had forgotten the world outside. She was actually getting into the Christmas spirit.

As Jude put her bags in the trunk, she remembered Reece and wondered if she should buy him a gift. She debated going back in, but her phone rang. She answered as she got into her car.

"Jude Madigan." She fumbled to put her keys in the ignition.

"Jude, it's Ellen."

"Hey, Ellen," Jude said. She recalled the catty comment about the "prostitutes" she'd made to Drew. "What's up?" She started the engine.

"Mark Anderson's called for you twice. Drew wanted me to track you down so you could call him back."

"Drew didn't talk to him?" The deadline for settlement was tomorrow, why was he calling early?

"I offered, but Mr. Anderson didn't want to talk to him. He said for you to call him when you got in."

"Did he leave a number?" Jude grabbed a pen and paper.

Ellen gave Jude the number. "And Drew wants to talk to you," she added. She put Jude on hold without saying another word.

While on hold Jude listened to a corny version of Jingle Bells. She wondered why Anderson hadn't talked to Drew. He probably figured Jude was an easier target and was calling to lowball her settlement demand.

"Jude, did you sleep late again?" Drew was terse. "Anderson's been calling all morning. The settlement deadline is running out. I expected you to be here for it."

"I went…I needed to do something for Tiffany." She didn't want to tell Drew she'd been at the mall Christmas shopping. "I'll be there in ten minutes." She sped out of the parking lot.

Waiting at a stoplight, she dialed Mark Anderson. He came on the line as the light turned green.

"Mark Anderson."

"Mark, it's Jude Madigan."

"The deadline is tomorrow, I hoped we could get together for a meeting today. I'm leaving town for the holidays," Anderson said.

"Sure." Jude weaved in and out of traffic. "I was moving ahead to file a motion for trial." She smiled a little, thinking of the shopping bags in her trunk. "What time are you available?"

"How does two o'clock work?"

"That's good, can you come to my office?"

"On your turf?" He hesitated. "Fine, I'll see you at two."

Jude sped onto the expressway and got to her building in record time since there was little traffic mid-morning. In the office, she turned on her computer and pulled Tiffany's file out. She called the receptionist to let her know she was in, then called Drew about the meeting.

"Mark Anderson will be here at two, are you available?" Jude dug in her basket of chocolate for a small piece.

"Yeah, I'm here all day," Drew grumbled. "But you take this one. If he gives you trouble, call me. And don't get emotional again."

Jude cringed at the reminder. "I'll be fine," she said. "The demand is now set at five million."

"Send him packing if his insurance adjuster doesn't come, too."

"Yes, sir."

She hung up and pulled out the posters she'd used for the presentation, to refocus her mind on the case. She wasn't ready to think about going to trial yet. Maybe they'd meet her demand so Tiffany could get some closure before Christmas.

Jude reviewed the posters and brochure again. She knew the case so well she could practically recite all the deposition statements. She wasn't ready to start work on another case, so to kill time before her meeting, she played solitaire on her computer and ate chocolate. She called Reece to thank him for the basket of sweets and had butterflies in her stomach as she waited for him to answer. He wasn't in, so she left a message. Before long, the receptionist's voice buzzed in her office. "Mr. Anderson is here to see you."

"Okay, have someone escort him to the conference room, I'll be up in a minute." Before she exited out of solitaire, she made a few moves and won the game. Jude smiled, hoping it was a good sign.

As she walked out of her office, the receptionist called again. "Sister Elizabeth in on the phone. Should I take a message? She's pretty insistent."

"No, I'll take it." She thought it would be good to make Mark Anderson wait a little longer and give him time to look at the gruesome evidence. She picked up her phone. "Hi, Elizabeth, what's up?"

"I know this is a long shot, but have you heard from Shelby?"

"No, why would I?" Jude sat on the edge of her desk.

"You were my last-ditch hope." Elizabeth sounded weary.

"Another break-out?"

"Yeah. But she may have taken a few things with her." She sighed. "I don't know. I hope she's all right."

"I'm sorry, Elizabeth. What can I do?"

"Say prayers for her."

"What did she take?"

"A little money, which is not a big problem. But I'm missing one of my habits."

"Maybe she needed a disguise, one that would give her some credibility," Jude suggested.

"Or, according to Bandee, she's going to make a movie." The nun paused. "I hate to think about that. I knew we weren't getting through to her. But I never expected this." Jude could hear the frustration in Elizabeth's voice.

"Did you call the police?" she asked.

"No. I'm not sure we should. I'm sorry to bother you, call me later." Elizabeth hung up.

Jude tried to imagine where the girl would've gone. She hated Elizabeth was faced with this right before Christmas.

Selfishly, she worried Shelby's escape would delay Elizabeth's revelation about her daughter.

Anderson was waiting, so she shook off thoughts about Shelby. Jude needed a clear head for the meeting. Before she headed out of her office, she stopped and grabbed a large manila envelope from her desk.

"Mr. Anderson. Thank you for coming." Jude entered the conference room with what she hoped was a confident air. She noticed he'd brought two other men along. They stood together by the long mahogany table. Jack Barrone was not there.

He nodded. "Ms. Madigan, good to see you." He moved near the two gentlemen. "I'd like to introduce my insurance adjuster and our in-house counsel at Anderson Trucking." He looked down. "Mr. Barrone won't be…wasn't able to join us today."

Jude wondered about Barrone's absence as she went through the motions of shaking hands and offering everyone a chair. She took a seat at the head of the table.

Anderson sat in one of the leather chairs to her right. "Now, let's get down to business." He opened his briefcase and took out papers. "I've looked through your settlement book and documents and I'm prepared to offer two million."

"Five million." Jude moved up in her chair. "I made it clear that was the demand if the case didn't settle." She ran a finger over a crease in the manila envelope.

"You said four million at mediation." He set the papers on the table.

"That was at mediation. I also told you the demand would go up if you didn't settle."

"Five is excessive." Anderson leaned back and crossed his leg.

"So are Tiffany's damages." Jude took in a deep breath. "I'm sorry, Mr. Anderson, once I give the final demand, I intend to stick to it." Jude was shaking inside.

"You seem optimistic."

"If you've read the economic charts, you'll know the actual damages are over six million. This girl has severe physical and emotional issues."

"Yes, you've made that clear." He leaned back in his chair. "But you also wouldn't let me meet her to find out for myself."

"Your company had many opportunities to meet with her and her psychologist before the settlement mediation. Time's up. We can let a jury decide." Jude played with the flap of the envelope.

The negotiations went on for more than an hour. Anderson's offer crept up until they reached four million, eight hundred thousand. Jude made him promise to donate five thousand to the children's hospital that treated Tiffany. "You donate five thousand, and I'll match it. Out of my money, not Tiffany's."

"If you'll excuse me, I'd like to talk to my colleagues." Anderson crossed his arms.

"Of course. Have the receptionist call me when you're ready." Jude picked up the manila envelope, nodded to the men, and left the room.

In the lobby, Jude caught Drew walking down the hallway.

"How's it going in there?" he asked.

"Fine. They started off low, but they're working up to our demand." Jude could hardly contain a smile. She held the envelope close to her chest.

"Good, that's what I wanted to hear." He put a hand on Jude's shoulder and led her toward his office. "I'm happy Anderson wanted to work with you. I understand he doesn't have Barrone with him. You must've made an impression at the mediation." He patted her arm. "Keep it up."

Jude allowed herself a dose of happiness as she left Drew's office. She didn't try to suppress it this time. Entering the reception area, Jude started to tell the receptionist she'd be in her office when Anderson walked from the conference room.

"We're ready," he said, as he turned back to the room.

Jude followed him. His associates sat in the leather chairs around the conference table. Jude stood at the head behind one of the chairs while Anderson paced. She threw the envelope on the table in front of her.

"This settlement is more than I intended to pay." He rubbed his forehead. "But, considering, I'd like to close the books on this before the holiday." He glanced at his assistant. "I agree to your demand."

Jude nodded and said, "I also want a promise from you that you'll make sure those trucks are maintained for safety and the drivers follow the rules."

"You can't tell me how to run my business." He stopped and looked hard at her.

"No, but I can, and should, report all the violations our investigators found. The DOT would love to hear about them."

"The Department of Transportation has already investigated this accident." He slid a hand into a pocket of his tailored slacks.

"Did the DOT find the ex-drivers that we did? Did they find all documentation I showed you in the mediation?"

"Fine. I agree." He waved a hand in the air dismissively.

"Promise?"

He crossed his arms like a petulant child. "Promise."

"Don't be surprised to find me snooping to make sure

you're complying."

He gave her a cursory look. "You seem terribly interested in my company."

"Are you a family man, Mr. Anderson?"

"Yes. Two boys."

"How old?"

"Fifteen and thirteen. And I suppose this is going somewhere?"

"Just in case you fall behind on your promise, keep these close by. Think of your boys on the roads with ill-maintained trucks." She slid the manila envelope of the gory scene photographs in front of him.

Chapter 52

Jude left the conference room, relieved and happy the case settled. As she walked through reception, she fought an urge to sprint to her office and call Tiffany. Instead, she went to Drew's office.

Drew sat at his desk reading. He looked over his glasses at her. "How'd it go?"

"We settled for four-point-eight million. Pending, of course, Tiffany and Mrs. Carmen's approval." She took a seat in front of his desk. "As part of the agreement, I asked Anderson to donate five thousand dollars to the children's hospital. He agreed."

"You did what?" Drew laid the documents he'd been reading on his desk.

"I promised to match it." She smiled. "Out of my own money, of course."

"Jude, you can't ask somebody to do that as part of a settlement."

"Why not?" She suddenly doubted her decision.

Drew looked out the window. "I don't know." He hesitated, then smiled. "Maybe because I didn't think of it first." He became businesslike again. "Good job, that's more than I thought we'd get. Have you notified the guardian ad litem?"

"Not yet. I'll do that after I call Tiffany and her grandmother."

"Call the guardian first. Then let Tiffany know. How she gets her money will depend on the ad litem's decision." He rubbed his eyes. "I heard Anderson was afraid to take this case to trial. He was impressed by how much you seemed to care about Tiffany."

"How did you find that out?"

He shrugged. "Word gets around."

Elated, Jude headed back to her office. Satisfaction for a job well done followed her like a puppy. Tiffany was taken care of financially for the rest of her life. Jude considered whether or not to visit the girl and her grandmother in person instead of calling. She imagined Tiffany's pleased reaction, but there would be sadness, too. The one person Tiffany would want to share the news with wasn't here. Jude knew Tiffany would happily give every dime back to have her mother here.

On her way to her office, Jude paid more attention to the Christmas decorations hanging in the cubicles. She imagined giving her friends, her *new* friends, the presents she'd bought. Remembering Elizabeth's call earlier, Jude hoped Shelby had a change of heart and had come back with the stolen habit.

Jude turned the corner and entered her office. Rick sat at her desk with his feet on the credenza eating a chocolate from her gift. He stuffed a large piece into his mouth, then licked his fingers. Wrappers littered her desk around the basket.

"Hey, good looking." He raised his eyebrows suggestively. "Who's Reece?" He held the gift card between two fingers.

"What the...how the hell did you get back here?" Jude was astounded.

"Your sweet receptionist, Ellen. I told her I'd wait for you here."

"And she let you?" Jude went to the phone and shoved

Rick's feet off the furniture. "Leave. *Now*." She picked up the receiver and dialed the front desk. "Ellen? Who authorized you to let Rick Carney come to my office?"

The receptionist sputtered a little.

"No one, under any circumstances, is allowed in here without permission," Jude barked, never taking her eyes off of Rick. "You know that."

"But I thought you guys were dating."

"We are not!" Jude slammed the phone down and turned to Rick. "I asked you to leave."

"Hey, don't be a bitch." He stood and sauntered slowly to the door. Instead of walking out, he closed it then turned and faced her. "We've got some business to discuss." He inched closer. "Have the nuns decided to sell?"

Jude backed away. "No, and they won't. Ever." Fear danced up her spine. She felt trapped and regretted hanging up on the receptionist.

"I've missed you. We were good together." He opened his arms.

"Don't make me sick. I said leave—*now*." Jude wished she hadn't insisted on the quiet corner office, away from others.

"Do you know how much money I have riding on that property?" His tone dripped ice. He slowly moved closer, keeping himself between her and the door.

His erratic mood frightened Jude. "I've advised the nuns not to sell." Her voice trembled as she backed away. "Find another deal. Let this one go." Jude gauged the distance to the phone. Unfortunately, Rick stood between Jude and the phone, as well as the door.

"I can't let it go!" He yelled and hit the desk. "You're supposed to help me. I need that property." He crumpled the gift card and threw it to the ground. "So who is this guy? Is he advising you not to sell? Does he do those whores, too?"

Jude recoiled as his eyes flashed with hate. She thought of her dad's fist and cringed like she did when she was young.

"You're the executor of the estate, you can get me that property. Or would you rather give it to this Reece guy?" He pushed the chocolates to the floor.

"You're not making any sense. Leave. Please," Jude pleaded.

"I want you to go with me to visit those bitches. They'll talk to you. Tell them to sell. I'm running out of time"

"No." Even though she knew if she said yes, he'd leave her alone. For now.

"You help me, and I'll help you with the case against Marcus Hall. I can get the kid to drop the case."

"What do you know about that?" Jude didn't want to betray Katie by asking a question she wasn't supposed to know the answer to.

"It's not important. I'll take care of him for you." He ran a hand through his hair.

Jude flinched when his arm came up.

"Scared?" He smiled. "I can make it all better." In one step, he moved behind Jude and wrapped his arms, hard, around her, pinning her.

"Stop!" Jude tried to wiggle an arm out. He moved one of his hands and clamped it over her mouth.

"No, I won't stop. Not until you get me that property." He squeezed her tighter. "And if you don't help me, this is just a taste of things to come." He leaned over and bit the lobe of her ear.

Chapter 53

Jude tried to scream, but Rick's hand held firm over her mouth. Images of her father's abuse surfaced. With him, Jude would acquiesce to appease him. Stop fighting, dodge the blows, and admit defeat. It was the only way he'd leave her alone. Should she let this one go? Isolate herself again? Or take the punches?

Claustrophobic panic coursed through Jude. But a new feeling surfaced. *Fight back*, she thought. *You can beat him*. With all her strength, she exploded back and pushed Rick against the wall. The unexpected force knocked his grip loose. Jude ran to the phone, but as she picked up the receiver, Rick's hand shot out and grabbed hers. Squeezing her injured wrist, he slowly forced the receiver back in its cradle.

"Don't make this hard, Jude." His eyes were piercing. "I know a few things about you that might change your tune."

Rage mixed with fear coursed through her. She gouged Rick's arm with her fingernails.

"Hey!" Rick pushed her away and held his arm. Looking like the school bully who'd been hit back.

"This time, I'm not going to let you get away with this." Jude raced around him to get to the door.

"Stop." Rick's demeanor changed, he almost looked defeated. "C'mon, let's talk. Do you really want me to tell the world about you? It seems like you have a few secrets." He continued to rub his arm.

He moved aside as Jude opened the door and stepped into the hall. She touched her sore earlobe. The skin wasn't broken, but it felt like fire. "I can handle my own problems. You'll have to handle yours." She went to a cubicle and picked up the phone. "This time I'm pressing charges."

"Wait." Rick took a few steps toward her.

Jude picked up a letter opener. Since he was such a wimp about her fingernail dig, she thought, he'd probably shrivel by such a threatening weapon.

"I'll make a deal with you. I won't tell anyone about the kid you gave up if you don't press charges." He held his hands up in defeat, but his eyes held evil victory.

Jude's fight fell apart. He *did* know. Who else had he told? She put the phone in its cradle but kept the letter opener.

"That's a good girl." His smile became more confident. "Now you're thinking."

If she let him get away with the struggle today, she'd be right where she was before. No one would know. It wouldn't be so bad. Jude looked steadily at him but wavered.

"Just help me out here, babe. This deal is my life savings. If I don't get that home, this contract falls apart. I need you."

She listened. He had a way of holding Jude's eyes with his. She really didn't want any confrontations anyway, especially at work. Perhaps she should give up. Did she want the world to find out about her past? Drew and the police would undoubtedly think Rick's anger was a simple domestic dispute. Jude didn't need any more drama, especially in front of Drew. She'd be better off letting the issue drop. Like she always had, run and hide.

"Listen to me Jude." He smiled easily. "You can help. I'll even cut you in on the deal. Talk to those nuns. Tell them how important it would be to the…the community, yeah, the neighborhood. That's all you have to do, convince them to sell, they'll listen." He winked. "We'd make a good team."

Jude hesitated and looked deep into Rick's eyes. A kaleidoscope of emotions swirled in her gut. He must've sensed her giving in.

"Those nuns respect you." He spoke softly, hypnotically, as he stepped closer.

Jude wondered what would happen if he told people about her daughter. What was she afraid of? The fear of exposing herself had been so ingrained she couldn't seem to get past it. Her first reaction had been to crawl quietly away. Why? Because she gave up her child? Was she a failure? She'd been raped. Had it been her fault?

"C'mon," Rick pleaded, "make the call."

She picked up the phone and dialed. "Ellen." She spoke into the phone, watching Rick intently. She squeezed the letter opener, "Get security here now, then call the police."

Chapter 54

Christmas lights dimly flashed muted colors through Jude's darkened living room where she sat. Tommy perched on the windowsill as if guarding his domain. Only three days left until Christmas, and Jude's buoyant mood had tanked. She was surrounded by the gifts she'd bought that morning. Jude cringed when she recalled what happened with Rick earlier.

The security officer who'd gotten to Jude's office first was a complete dud. He'd stood in the hallway, talking on his walkie-talkie to building management about a "disturbance." The police created more of a scene since everyone had raced to Jude's office to check out the excitement. Around the circle of rubber-neckers, Jude pressed charges against Rick. Two male officers took her statement, but didn't appear to take her complaint seriously, probably because Rick acted like such a gentleman. He'd put on an Academy award-winning performance in front of the audience, laughing and joking with the police. He made Jude look as if she was the crazy one.

Drew stood along the periphery, arms crossed and obviously irritated.

Being the center of attention was one of Jude's worst nightmares. After Rick was released, with orders to stay away from the "complainant," one of the officers smiled, leaned into him winked, and said, "She'll cool off soon."

As Jude feared, it was only being considered a domestic dispute at the office.

Drew cleared the crowd with, "Get back to work." But Jude knew she'd provided fodder for the gossip mill for months. This is what comes of taking a stand, she thought bitterly. Drew hadn't spoken to her after.

She'd closed herself in her office to call Tiffany's grandmother about the settlement but decided to wait until the guardian ad litem had looked at the terms and decided how to structure the payments. Rick poisoned Tiffany's victory.

Jude no longer felt happy about telling the girl about the settlement. She no longer felt happy about anything. Her phone rang a few times as she sat in her dark living room. She ignored each call. Sighing, she pushed off the soft couch and stood. In the kitchen, she poured a glass of wine. Tommy trotted behind her. Jude put the phone on speaker and checked messages as she uncorked the bottle.

A few of the calls were hang-ups, with caller ID showing "restricted." Reece called her back and said he'd be in all evening. Was that a lifetime ago that she'd called to thank him for the chocolates? A female officer called, to talk about the charges and restraining order against Rick. The woman also left a number for a domestic abuse hotline. Jude wondered if they had an asshole hotline.

Her mother called to thank her for the Christmas money and asked her to visit for Christmas. "You can meet your niece and nephews," she said. "You're missing so much of the holiday by not seeing the faces of the children on Christmas morning. I called the airlines, there are still seats available. Try to make it this year, honey." Guilt wrung Jude's insides and another flash of pain for missing a certain young girl's Christmas mornings for the past seventeen years.

Drew called to check on her, and Elizabeth asked her to

call when she got in. Jude took her wine into the den, flopped on the couch, picked up Tommy, and turned on the TV. Surfing channels, she caught the end of *It's a Wonderful Life*. The ringing bell when Clarence got his wings made her wonder where her own guardian angel was. She glanced at St. Jude on the bookshelf and tipped her glass to him. "Merry Christmas, patron saint of lost causes. No wonder I'm named after you."

Turning the TV off, Jude sipped her wine in the dark and stroked Tommy. She needed to get back in the saddle and quit wallowing in despair. But, for now, she'd ride the misery out for the evening.

The phone's ring abruptly broke her thoughts. Jude answered before she forgot not to. "Hello."

"I'm surprised you're not at a Christmas party."

Jude couldn't help but smile at Elizabeth's voice. "No, you know how I love those mixers."

Elizabeth laughed. "We'll break you in one of these days."

"What's going on there? Are you all caroling around the fire?"

"Not tonight. After church, we all decided to pack it in early. Shelby's escape has sobered the gang a little. I still can't believe she's gone."

"Did you find your habit?"

"No, and I hate to think about her plans with it. She confided in Bandee. Told her about talking to some low-brow movie producer." She sighed. "Bandee feels awful about keeping quiet."

"Why didn't she say anything?" Jude asked. "You'd think her loyalties would've been with you instead of Shelby, as much as you've done for her."

"She's still a work in progress. Being conflicted between us and friends is normal. Maybe we needed to lose Shelby to get Bandee. God's plan doesn't always go like we think it should. The kid really feels terrible about it."

"You always seem to see the good in life's problems."

"It's my job." Elizabeth chuckled softly. "You know, speaking of problems, I was wondering if you've given any thought to continuing as the executor of Trudy's estate? I hate to think of you giving up at the end of the year. Would you consider working independent of your firm?"

Jude didn't want to think about the deadline. After the new year, she wouldn't have an official reason to call Elizabeth. Would she have the confidence to pick up the phone to say "hi" or would this new friendship slip away? "I was hoping to talk Drew out of transferring the estate to the bank. But I wanted to prove myself to him first." She sighed. "Even though the Carmen case settled, I think, after today, I screwed up any credibility I'd gained with him." She told Elizabeth about Rick's visit and pressing charges against him.

"That's great!" Elizabeth sounded happy about it.

"What do you mean?" Jude asked, offended. "There's nothing great about it."

"The fact you took action and called the police is a huge step. I think you're finally gaining some sense of self-worth."

Jude almost choked on a sip of wine. "Then why did it backfire?"

"It didn't. I'm proud of you."

"Now I'm the firm's psycho. The whole incident made me look hysterical," Jude said. She took a deep breath. "What if I have to transfer as the executor? Aren't you worried about losing the home? Rick has a way of turning things around."

"No," Elizabeth said, slyly. "I have a good attorney."

"For a few more weeks."

"I hope longer." She shifted topics. "Actually, that brings up another reason I'm calling."

"What, you're holding a Dale Carnegie seminar so I can keep working on my self-esteem?"

Elizabeth laughed. "I had a visitor this afternoon. She wants to help us save the home and is concerned about you. We had a nice long talk. She thinks highly of you and is not very fond of Rick."

"My mother?" Jude quipped.

"No," Elizabeth paused. "Katie."

"Katie called you?" Jude almost dropped the phone.

"Yes, she's really very sweet. She wants to go back to work with you and thinks she could be a big help with your job as executor here."

"But she left me to work for Rick." Jude sat up straighter on the couch displacing her sleeping cat who looked at her indignantly.

"And for that she's suffered," Elizabeth said gently.

"Oh, so she gets Catholic points for her pain?" Jude was pissed that everybody around her thought they knew what was best for her.

"I think you know what I mean. She wants to get back in your good graces," Elizabeth said.

"So, a few Hail Marys should take care of it?" Jude sipped her wine. "She's been working on the other side of the attempted takeover of your home. How do you know she's not trying to get information to help Rick?"

"Because I trust her. I think she's sincere."

"Yeah, just like Shelby? You trusted her."

"Shelby needed help but wasn't ready to accept it. Katie wants out of a bad situation and has come to me. I can't stop trusting, Jude. I have more faith in people than that, and I think you do, too."

"Do you ever get tired of being so good?"

"I'm not better than anybody else."

"I wish I had your ability to see the good in life, in people." Jude scratched Tommy's stomach.

"You do. Like I said, you just need to respond to it. Quit shutting it out. I offered to help Katie financially for a while. In turn, she's offered to manage some of the bookkeeping here and help us fight Rick."

"She not only plays both sides, but the middle, too." Jude stroked Tommy and he grabbed her hand and bit it.

"She also wants to help you with the case against Marcus Hall. She said Rick has used some slime tactics to move the case forward."

"Rick uses slime tactics to run his life," Jude said, shutting her eyes. "Did Katie tell you she called me?"

"Yeah, she did."

"Did she say she knew about me giving up my daughter?" Jude asked while Tommy tried to grab her hand again.

"No, why would she?"

"Because Rick found out."

Elizabeth gasped. "I'm sorry, Jude. How? What did he say about it?"

Jude noted her voice changed, seemed guarded. "Just that he wouldn't tell anyone if I'd work on you to sell the home."

"Does he know where she is?" Elizabeth asked urgently.

"I don't know." Jude felt worry settle in her chest. "Oh, no, what if he does know and tries to contact her?"

"I'll take care of it. I wish you would've called me." Elizabeth paused as if collecting her thoughts. "Don't worry about it." Her voice was unconvincing, preoccupied.

"Elizabeth, damn it, when are you going to tell me?"

"Soon," Elizabeth answered, distracted. "Look, Bernie's talking to the women about Shelby. Let me go help her. I know it's hard Jude, but let's wait until Christmas to talk. It's only a few more days." She hung up abruptly.

Jude listened to the empty dial tone, yearning to know about her daughter. *Dammit*, why won't Elizabeth tell her now? The familiar pain of her father's cruel hand, and the loss of her child, enveloped her in the darkened room.

Chapter 55

The next morning at the office, the mood was merry. As was his usual custom, Drew gave each employee a fifty-dollar bill, then sent them to Target to buy toys and clothes for needy children. After, he'd have an elegant lunch catered in.

Jude always evaded the shopping trip and would only make a quick appearance at the luncheon before getting back to work. Katie had always dutifully stayed for the rest of the day, sipping spiked punch at her desk, while the other employees were given the afternoon off. Even though most of the staff openly called Jude "Scrooge." Katie never complained. Maybe, Jude wondered, she'd been too hard on her.

Jude sat in her office and looked at Katie's empty desk, thinking about what Elizabeth had said. Distrust had been a companion of Jude's for so many years, she wasn't sure she could live without it. Was Katie being sincere?

Ellen, with a handful of money envelopes, stuck her head in Jude's office. "Are you going shopping with us?"

"No." Jude could barely look at her, still angry she'd allowed Rick in her office.

"You sure? Drew told me to make sure everybody got an envelope." She fanned the stack out as if playing a card trick.

"I'm trying to get some work done," Jude said, her desk

empty, a steaming cup of coffee the only thing she'd been working on.

"Look, I'm sorry about letting that guy Rick wait in your office." Ellen leaned against the doorframe. "I thought you were still dating."

"No, we're not. And you should've known better. No one outside the firm is allowed to roam the offices."

"I know. Drew really lectured me about it. I didn't realize Rick was such a jerk. He seemed so persuasive, said he wanted to surprise you."

"He did."

"I'm sorry, really." Ellen nervously fanned the envelopes. "Here," she put one on Jude's desk, "shopping always puts me in a good mood. Especially when I'm using someone else's money. Give it back to Drew if you don't want it. But try to go, it'll be fun."

After Ellen left, Jude thought about the gifts she'd bought for the women and the joy she'd felt while choosing their gifts. She wanted to let Tiffany know about the money and give her the silver cross.

She scrolled through her contacts and found the guardian ad litem's number. Because of the holiday, no one was available except the answering service. Jude left a message and asked that someone call her back today. She disconnected and started dialing Tiffany's number, but her second line rang in, so she answered it.

"Jude Madigan."

"Merry Christmas, it's Reece."

Jude felt a tickle in her stomach. "Hi, Merry Christmas." She smiled. "I loved the chocolate, thank you."

"Loved? Past tense?" Reece's baritone voice melted like the dark cocoa.

"It didn't take long. There are a few survivors, but not many." She pinched her eyes as the memory of Rick's destruction flashed. "They'll be history soon." Jude twirled the money envelope on her desk. "You're still planning on dinner at the Magdalene Home, aren't you?"

"Of course. That's one reason I'm calling. Do you want me to pick you up?" Reece asked.

"Sure," Jude said eagerly. "That would be nice." Jude anxiously thought of Elizabeth's promise to tell her about her daughter. She'd planned on getting to the home as soon as she could. "You know, I was hoping to get there before dinner, early."

"How early?"

"Oh, the crack of dawn-ish."

He laughed. "You're like a kid on Christmas morning. I'll warn you Lizzie and Bernadette will put you to work. Why early?"

"Elizabeth has some…information for me, and she won't tell me until Christmas. I'm going crazy waiting."

"What kind of information?"

"About my daughter."

"Really?" He hesitated. "Will I be in the way?"

"Not at all. I just hope she doesn't have bad news." A flurry of concern spiraled inside Jude.

"I doubt she'd do that on Christmas Day."

Relief pulsed in her. "You're right. I just can't wait much longer," she said.

"Why don't you call her and find out how early we can get there? I'm also planning on going to church on Christmas Eve. Care to join me?" He paused. "Maybe we could have dinner, then make it to eight o'clock mass. I'd have you home before Santa makes his rounds."

"That'd be nice," Jude said. She hoped Rick wouldn't do anything to spoil the evening.

She hung up, for once strangely thrilled about Christmas. She was cautiously happy Reece had called. Were things really looking up? She only wished the black cloud named Rick would evaporate forever.

Chapter 56

Jude folded the money envelope Ellen had given her and stuck it in her purse. She looked around her office and decided she wasn't in the mood to start another case anyway. Instead, she'd call Tiffany and try to see her later this afternoon. Then she'd go shopping with the rest of the firm. Scrooge had found his way when confronted with the ghost of Christmas past. Maybe she could put some demons behind her and move forward too. Jude dialed Tiffany's number.

Tiffany's grandmother answered the phone. "Mrs. Carmen, it's Jude. I was hoping to meet with you and Tiffany later. Are you available?"

"Well, yes." Her voice sounded frail. "Unless you have bad news. The holidays are difficult enough."

"No, it's good news. I'll be happy to tell you now, but I'd like to tell Tiffany in person."

"Okay." She sighed wearily. "I guess you've settled the case."

"We've agreed on an amount, pending your and Tiffany's approval."

"It's just that no matter how much you may have gotten, it's not going to bring back my daughter."

"No, you're right, it won't," Jude put her head in her hand. "But if it's any small consolation, the owner of the trucking company has promised to maintain his vehicles better and keep a close watch on the driver's log books. And a donation of ten thousand dollars will be given to the children's hospital that treated Tiffany."

"Oh, my." There was a long pause. "You know, my daughter struggled financially for years. Her dream was for Tiffany to be able to go to college and have more opportunities than she did." Mrs. Carmen cried softly. "I'm sorry, I wish she were here."

"I know Mrs. Carmen. It's bittersweet." Jude didn't know what else to say.

"Well, then." She blew her nose. "Tiffany has been invited to go to a movie with a school friend tonight. I'm happy that she's interested in getting out. She's supposed to be picked up around five. Can you come before then?"

"How about three? I'd like some time to talk to her about this responsibility. This may seem like a windfall, but there'll be some important decisions you both will need to make for her future. Another attorney, a guardian ad litem, will decide how Tiffany will receive the money."

"That will be fine."

"And Mrs. Carmen?"

"Yes?"

"I want Tiffany to know I'll always be here to help her. Just because the case settled doesn't mean we need to go our separate ways. I'd like to see her, you know, as she grows up."

A puff of hope hung in the air. Maybe she could make a difference in the girl's life. Make up for something she'd missed once before.

Jude went to the reception area where the employees were congregating, ready to go shopping. The mood was light, Drew, wearing a Santa hat, held court and handed out the leftover money envelopes to open hands. "Go forth and spend. Think how happy you're going to make some kids on Christmas morning." His eyes twinkled. "Jude, here, take the last three envelopes."

She shook her head. "I have mine already." She reached in her purse and pulled the money out to show him.

"Good," he said. He took his hat off and put it on her head. He leaned closer to her and said, "I'm happy you're going this year." He turned to the rest of the group. "The one with the most toys wins. See you all in a few hours for lunch."

Everybody teamed up and headed to the elevator. No one asked Jude to join them. The rejection stung a little, even if she'd never given anyone a reason to include her. She took off the hat and handed it back to Drew. "Are you going?"

"I may catch up in a little while. I intend to enjoy the peace and quiet while I can. Now get out of here." He waved his fuzzy red hat at the elevator.

She hesitated, wondering if she should talk to him about the incident with Rick. No, it was probably best to let the issue rest. Try to enjoy the holiday. She turned to go.

"Jude."

She stopped. "Yes?"

"You did a hell of a job with the Carmen case."

"Thanks. She's a good client."

"And let me know if Rick Carney gives you any more trouble."

"Thanks, I can handle him." She smiled. "I will try to keep it out of the office though."

"That would be nice."

"Merry Christmas."

He smiled and walked to his office.

℘℘℘

Jude filled a shopping basket to overflowing. She'd run

into some of the other employees and compared purchases. Thoughts of Reece danced in her head as she wandered down each aisle. Finally, she headed to the long checkout lines.

"Boy, you have way more than fifty dollars' worth there." Ellen pulled her cart behind Jude at checkout. "Are you getting your own Christmas shopping done, too?"

"No, this was fun, I got a little carried away."

"I guess Drew gave you more money than us."

"No, he didn't. I'll pay the difference." Jude glanced at Ellen's cart. She'd bought a few toys, but also had mascara and eye makeup in the pile.

"So what's going to happen to Rick?" Ellen took two packages of gum from the checkout stand, tossed one into the cart and opened the other.

Jude wasn't in the mood to talk about him and spoil the euphoria she'd enjoyed today. She shrugged and said, "I don't know."

"He's so cute, I don't see why you don't want to go out with him."

Jude tried to ignore Ellen's meddling. She picked up a magazine and flipped through it.

"Kind of a dramatic way to break up, with the police and all."

"Ellen, I'd rather not talk about him." Jude put the magazine away.

"Sorry," Ellen said with as much sincerity as a brick. Then she stage whispered, "How're those prostitutes? I heard Drew is going to get rid of that case in January." She unwrapped three more sticks of gum.

A few co-workers had pulled up behind them. Jude wished the line would move faster.

"I'll bet you'll be happy to be rid of them." Ellen put the wad in her mouth.

"Ellen, those women are in a rehabilitative home.

They're working to make better lives for themselves. Stop being so judgmental," Jude said.

"Whoa, take a chill pill. I'm just asking." She rolled her eyes at the group and smacked her wad of gum.

Jude didn't like how bold Ellen had become out of the office. She glanced at the others waiting. They were perked, sensing another good gossip opportunity. She turned and tried to ignore their stares and whispers.

She sensed someone come up behind her. One of the legal assistants tapped her gently. Frustrated, Jude turned to her.

"I thought you did a good job on the Carmen case. I feel so bad for that girl."

Jude smiled gratefully. "Thanks."

"You're going to make some kids real happy. That's nice. Merry Christmas." The woman bumped past Ellen and stood behind her own cart, also filled to the brim with toys.

Jude made her purchase, grateful for the kind words from the legal assistant. Jude knew she was an anomaly with people at work and she wondered why, now, what they thought of her mattered.

Chapter 57

"That's almost five million dollars!" Tiffany sank into the couch in her living room. Open-mouthed and wide-eyed, she looked at her grandmother, who sat straight and held her ever-present box of Kleenex.

"It *is* a lot of money." Jude sat next to Tiffany. "I know it's a shock to think about so much and there will be conditions to how it's paid to you and your grandmother."

The girl rapidly twirled her hair around a finger. "I don't know, it's weird. I'm both happy and sad about it."

"That's a normal response." Jude wanted to touch her, to try and offer some comfort.

"Grandma, we can finally buy a computer and…and…" Suddenly Tiffany started crying. "I wish my mom were here."

Tiffany's grandmother nodded and dabbed at her eyes. She whispered, "I do, too."

Jude finally put a hand on Tiffany's shoulder, surprised at the warmth it radiated. "I'm sorry, Tiffany."

Tiffany's eyes glistened with tears. "Mom promised she'd take me to New York, but we never had enough money. Now we do, but she isn't here."

It struck Jude the girl's grandmother offered no hug or physical reassurances. She stroked Tiffany's arm. The girl responded by moving into Jude and hugging her, filling Jude with affection, a good, but strange, feeling.

"Thank you for helping us," Tiffany said through her tears. "I think I'll always cry when I think of her." She sat back. "Did you read the letter to them?"

"Yes, and you know what, it made me cry. You told them what they needed to hear, and, because of that, they're going to keep their trucks safer now."

"I wish they did that before the accident. I'd rather have my mom with me and Grandma."

"I know." Jude tried to imagine what Elizabeth would have said to make her feel better.

"You would've liked her. She was pretty and smart, and she used to tickle my back to get me to sleep." Tiffany stared ahead as if seeing her mother. "I hope I have a dream about her tonight. One of the good dreams, not the scary one." She looked down, a pained expression on her tear-streaked face.

Jude reached into her briefcase and brought out the present she'd bought for Tiffany. "Merry Christmas." She handed the shoddily wrapped gift to her. Jude hadn't tackled wrapping paper for years, and no matter how hard she tried, she couldn't get the edges to fold neatly. The creases were puffed and lopsided. "I'm not a very good wrapper."

Tiffany brightened. "You wrap like me." She smiled at Jude. "My grandma always laughs at the way I do it."

For the first time that evening, the woman smiled. "It takes practice," she said.

Tiffany tore into the present. She gasped when she saw the silver cross. "It's beautiful. Hey, that's my birthstone. Cool." She held the necklace up to show her grandmother.

"What do you say, Tiff?" Mrs. Carmen said. "Don't forget your manners."

"Thank you, I really love it." Tiffany looked at Jude and smiled.

"It's beautiful," Her grandmother said, admiring the necklace.. "Such a thoughtful gift, too."

"You know, Grandma, this cross reminds me," Tiffany said. She ran a finger over the finely etched silver. "Now we can finally buy a stone with mom's name on it for the cemetery." She glanced at Jude. "We wanted to but couldn't afford one."

"That'd be a good thing to do," Jude said, remembering the lopsided hand painted cross that Tiffany had planted at the accident site. "What are you going to do for Christmas?"

"Since it's just Tiffany and me, we're going to have a quiet day here." Mrs. Carmen set her box of Kleenex on a side table. "Maybe we'll go to a movie."

"Did Dad call?" Tiffany gave her grandmother a hopeful look. "He's going to freak when I tell him about the money. Maybe he'll come over on Christmas."

"No, and I don't think you should tell him," Mrs. Carmen said and looked at Jude. "Does he have any say in how she gets it?"

Jude shook her head. "He was never named in the suit. The guardian ad litem will make sure he can't get any control over it. Tiffany, this money is for you and your grandmother. You won't even be able to get all of it until you're older."

"But I haven't seen my dad in a long time," Tiffany said.

It amazed Jude that Tiffany still wanted, even seemed to need, her father's affection. After working on the case, Jude knew what a jerk he'd been even before the accident. The thought of calling her own father was so remote to Jude, she couldn't imagine why this girl still wanted so badly to see hers.

The doorbell rang, and Tiffany jumped up. "That's my friend Hannah!" She dashed to the door but stopped before she got there. "Can I tell her about the money?"

Jude stood. "Probably not. Let it sink in first," she said.

Mrs. Carmen turned toward Tiffany. "You don't want anybody to like you just for your money."

The girl looked hurt. "They won't."

Jude looked at Tiffany's grandmother. Although the comment wasn't meant to be rude, Jude wished the woman hadn't said anything. "Tiffany, you and your grandmother can set up an appointment with the lawyer that will help you get the money. It would be best if you didn't tell anybody just yet," Jude said.

She shrugged. "Okay."

Hannah came in with her mother. Tiffany introduced Jude as "Miss Madigan" but didn't say who she was.

Mrs. Carmen spent a few minutes with Hannah's mother, confirming which movie at what time and when to be home. She put her hand on Tiffany's shoulder and almost hugged her. The girl bounced outside and waved to Jude.

Tiffany's grandmother closed the door and peeked out a small window. "I'm glad she's making friends again." She turned to Jude. "I'm just afraid that something will happen to her, too. Especially now that she'll have all that money."

"If you help her along the way, she'll have enough money to be taken care of the rest of her life." Jude picked up her purse and briefcase. "She needs you and is lucky to have you."

"Her mother wanted Tiffany to experience so many things, to be able to go to college and travel. She was working so hard for that." Mrs. Carmen looked out the window again. "It's ironic she's provided so much, after her death."

Driving home, Jude bristled with nervous anticipation about her own child. How had she been provided for? Had she been raised in poverty? Wealth? What was Jude going to find out in less than two days?

And worse, what did Rick know about her?

Chapter 58

As she drove home, emotions that Rick had found out about her child rubbed like sandpaper. A stab of guilt coursed through her as she wondered if, with her law degree, she could've found out about her daughter. Years ago, after graduating from law school, Jude had called the home for information. They weren't rude but made it clear the adoptive family had requested the records be sealed. At the time, Jude thought there was nothing more she could do. As an attorney, could she have tried harder? She wanted to find her. Had she been too afraid? Subconsciously distant?

Now, Jude couldn't help but fear that Rick had found a way around the sealed documents. He'd been resourceful in finding history on Elizabeth and Bernadette, not to mention her own background. She shivered, not from the winter chill.

It wasn't even six o'clock yet, so Jude decided to go home and enjoy a long run. Maybe even tackle making a real dinner for herself. Since the office was closed the next day for Christmas Eve, Jude considered not going in. She'd shop for Reece then attempt to wrap the rest of the gifts. That alone might take her all day.

After a cathartic run in the cold evening, she pulled off her shoes, left them by the door and went to the kitchen. Tommy paced by his food bowl, looking aggrieved that she'd left him without a single morsel. Jude fed him before tearing open a bag of frozen veggies for herself. She tossed the mixture in a pan and sautéed them in olive oil and garlic. While cooking, she checked her phone messages. She hit speaker and listened to her one message, playing it back twice to make sure she'd heard it correctly.

An Agent Ladd with the FBI asked she call him back tonight "concerning Rick Carney." Jude hurriedly wrote down the number. Why would the FBI be calling about a local domestic dispute?

She immediately dialed the number only to get his voice mail. "Damn." Jude hung up the phone after leaving a brief message. She turned off the stove and walked through the house, making sure every door and window was locked and bolted. Then she armed the security system. Rick had been charged, but not jailed. She doubted a simple restraining order would keep him away.

Even though she was supposed to wait until Christmas, she dialed Elizabeth, needing to hear her calm voice. Again, the call rolled over to the Magdalene Home's voice mail. She felt alone as usual, but this time it bothered her. She wanted to talk to someone.

She froze when the doorbell rang. Tommy scampered to a safe hiding place.

"Chicken," Jude whispered as he ran off, but her insides tickled with fear. She opened a utensil drawer in the kitchen and grabbed a big-handled tool. Holding the phone close, she cautiously went to the door, the culinary weapon clenched tight by her side. "Who is it?"

"Agent Ladd with the FBI."

"What's this about?" Jude spoke through the door.

"Rick Carney. I understand you've filed charges against him. May I come in?"

"How do I know you're who you say you are?" Her fist tightened on the handle. Surprised, she noticed she wasn't holding a knife, but a pizza cutter. *Shit.*

"I'll hold my ID card up to the peephole."

Jude looked out and saw a dim shadow of identification. "Since when does the FBI get involved in simple assault issues?"

"We're interested in much more than that. Look, I can understand you being afraid, but I'd rather not talk through the door. We don't need the whole neighborhood listening. Why don't you call the police and let them check me out. Then we can talk," he said.

"Good idea." Jude looked at the pizza cutter. Unless he was a big pepperoni, she probably wouldn't do much damage with it. She dialed the police and asked them to please drive by.

Ten minutes later, after the police confirmed he was FBI, Jude let him in. She put the cutter on a nearby table by the door.

Jude saw him glance at the weapon and stifle a smile.

"You might want to take some self-defense courses, you know, living alone and all," he said. He nodded at the utensil. "Learn how to use that thing."

Jude blushed. "I thought I'd grabbed something more formidable."

"Sorry, I didn't mean to scare you. Do you mind if we sit down and talk?"

"Sure." Jude directed him to the den since the living room was cluttered with the unwrapped gifts and rolls of Christmas paper.

He was tall and lanky, but his movements were fluid. Jude was still nervous with him there. "What is this about?" She sat on a chair so he wouldn't sit next to her on the couch.

Ladd took a seat on the sofa and put his briefcase on the floor. "We have reason to believe that Rick Carney has created some," he paused, "unusual business deals. Now, you being an attorney, should know I can't get into specifics with you. But I'm interested in how much you know about his current neighborhood plan."

Jude wondered how he knew so much about her. "Why don't *you* tell *me*?" She was guarded. "I can't see the FBI working on a local case like this. Why isn't the D.A. handling it?"

"We're taking over the case."

"Does this have anything to do with the charges I've filed on him? They're only misdemeanors, not federal."

"This will work better if you tell me what you know," he said.

"About what?" Jude sat forward. "The guy's a jerk. End of story."

"Did he ask you to invest in the deal on the southeast properties?" He pulled out a few documents which mapped out the buildings around and including the Magdalene Home.

"Yeah, he asked me, but I wouldn't do it." Jude wished he'd tell her what they were investigating Rick for. "Why?"

"Your name is on some of the documents." He looked intently at her. "As an investor."

"What?" Jude jumped out of her chair. "On what documents? He's been trying to get me to talk the residents of the Magdalene Home into selling to him, but that's all." Agitated, she walked to the bookcase. "He's been harassing me, so I pressed charges against him. Do I need an attorney?"

The agent seemed to relax. "No. Our investigation indicates you hadn't given him money, but I needed to be certain. You are the executor on the hotel property, aren't you?"

"Yeah, so?" Jude hesitated. "I've been trained, as an attorney, not to ask a question I don't know the answer to.

But you're doing that to me." She faced him. "I'm not saying anything else until you tell me what the hell is going on."

"Okay, that's fair." He put the maps back into his briefcase. "How long did you date Rick Carney?"

"I'm sorry, didn't I make myself clear?" She was more nervous than she tried to appear. Trial lawyer training helped. "I don't want to answer anything else."

"Look, this guy may be in a lot of trouble. Do you want to go down with him?"

"For what?" Jude was visibly shaken.

"Have you ever done drugs, Ms. Madigan?"

"Excuse me, but I'm going to have to get an attorney before we go any farther."

He held his hand up. "I'm here to ask you to look over some information. We've done an extensive investigation on him, and we want to make sure you're not involved with his business deals." He pulled some more papers from his case. "Have you ever seen these documents?" He dropped a few pages on the coffee table.

Jude sat down, picked up the papers and looked over them. She gasped when she saw her name forged on what looked like a contract for the property around the Magdalene Home. "I didn't sign this."

"No, it doesn't match your signature, does it?" The agent folded his hands together.

"When have you seen my signature?" Jude asked warily.

He didn't answer. "Do you realize he's already taken money from investors on this deal?"

"I have no idea what he's doing, except making my life and the lives of the Magdalene women miserable."

"This contract also includes the hotel that is now the Magdalene Home. The investors were told that property is part of the package."

"It can't be! The estate owns the property outright. No one with authority has agreed to sell it." Jude was astounded. "I guess that's why he's hammering so hard to get the property. I never thought he'd do something illegal."

"So, that's definitely not your signature?" he asked.

"Send it to a handwriting analyst—if you haven't already."

Again, he ignored her comment. "According to that document, this deal closed two days ago. The investors are going to want possession of the property soon."

"How? This makes no sense." She picked up the papers again. "What bank would close on a deal like this?" She looked up at the agent. "I suppose that's why the FBI is involved. The deal never closed. These are fake."

"That's the main reason," he said. He looked at her. "The other is, he's running a methamphetamine lab on one of the properties."

Chapter 59

After Agent Ladd left, Jude locked the front door. He'd told her the FBI might need her help to testify against Rick, but they likely had enough evidence to use against him. He did warn her to stay away from Rick since he could be dangerous if he felt caged-in by the investigation.

Jude went to the kitchen and warmed up the soggy vegetables left on the stove. She wasn't hungry anymore but thought to eat something nutritious while trying to absorb what the FBI had said about Rick. Tommy ventured from his hiding place to finish his dinner.

"You are such a wimp. What if I needed protection?" Tommy crunched his food and looked at her contently. She poured the remains of a bottle of wine into a glass and took her dinner into the den, then, for the rest of the evening, jumped at each creak and pop the house made.

As she ate, Jude mulled over the information about the meth lab. Rick was obviously enjoying the fruits of his labor, which would explain his erratic behavior. Still, she felt stupid for having had a relationship with him. Astounded that he was such a bad seed. Her taste in men had been questionable, but not destructive.

It surprised her Rick would be so bold as to put her name on a bogus contract. And that he would do anything illegal. How did she not see it coming? Did her relationship compass always navigate to asshole? She hoped the agent had been truthful and not withheld information about her being a suspect. *But I didn't do anything wrong.* It couldn't turn around on her, not now, when she was so close to finding out about her child.

She wanted to call somebody—Reece, Elizabeth—someone who could offer a dose of reassurance. She ran her fingers over the buttons of the phone before deciding not to call anyone. Elizabeth wanted her to wait until Christmas before talking, and Reece would probably run from a woman with so many problems.

She took her half-eaten plate of food to the kitchen sink, gulped the last bit of wine, and decided to take her chances and go to bed. She grabbed Tommy off the couch, her watch-cat to sleep with. Jude would know if someone was coming if he ran and hid. She was tempted to take the pizza cutter with her.

෴

When Jude awoke on Christmas Eve, sun shone around the edges of the window shades, offering a sense of safety by its light. It had taken her a long time to fall asleep fearing another midnight visit by Rick. Her senses were on high alert, and she was jumping at every sound. Hopefully, Rick was on the lam and as far away from her as possible.

She stretched then tickled Tommy, the furry lump. "Thanks for protecting me last night."

Jude decided not to go to the office. Had she ever taken a day off? She brewed a big pot of coffee and enjoyed the newspaper before tackling the gift wrapping.

As she searched for some Scotch Tape, the phone rang. Maybe it's Reece, she thought hopefully. Caller ID showed her mother's number instead.

"Merry Christmas, almost," Jude answered.

"Judith, this is your father."

Jude froze. She hadn't heard his voice in years. "Dad, what a surprise." Even saying the word "Dad" was like a foreign language. It rolled out of her mouth wrong.

"Merry Christmas to you, too. How'ya been?"

"Fine." She felt like a little girl, panicked, afraid to say something that might spark his anger. "How's Mom? Is she all right?"

"Your mother's fine." His New York accent made it sound like, *ya mutha's fine*.

"Why don't you ever come visit? She misses you."

"I've been busy, you know, working a lot."

"Yeah, we got us a real lawyer—*loiya*—in the family. You must take after your old man, with the brains and all. You're not one of those liberal ones?"

"Yeah, I'm one of those."

"That's your mother's side of the family."

"Still good with the insults, huh, Dad?" It was the first time she'd ever talked back to him. How far could his hand reach? And for the first time, Jude wondered what she had been so afraid of?

"Hey, I gotta keep the family in line." He hesitated. "I wanna ask you something. You know a girl named Mary Toby? She's about your age." He paused and sipped loudly on a drink. "Damnedest thing, she said the old priest took advantage of some of the girls years ago, 'bout the time you were in school. She's stirring up some trouble at the church, ya know with the 'Me Too' movement and all…I mean, you never know who to believe anymore." He took a breath. "That'd be terrible if it was true, Judith. Really awful." He paused again, and seemed to want to say something more. After a beat he said, "Here, let me get your mutha on the phone."

Jude put her coffee cup down and wiped away a quiet tear with a sense of odd relief. It was weird. She wasn't scared of him anymore.

Her mother's voice broke through her thoughts.

"Judith, honey. I guess you couldn't get a flight out to visit?"

"Mom, I have too much work. Maybe another time."

"What kind of job makes you work so hard? It's Christmas, for heaven's sake. Stephen's coming today with the kids. I wish you were here, too. It would be nice to have the family together. Goodness, it's been seventeen years since you've been back."

Jude hesitated at her words about the family being together. *Together how?* Jude wondered. Beatings? Bone-numbing fear? Her last Christmas at home she was forced to serve dinner to the priest who raped her. Then her father called her a whore, beat her, and put her on a bus to Texas. She bit words back before saying anything snarky to her mother.

"Judith? You still there?"

"I'm here. I'll try to plan a visit soon."

"You remember the Larue's down the street? They're selling their house, maybe you'd think about moving back here? It's an easy commute to the city. You could be a lawyer here. Find yourself a nice man and settle down. Then when you work a lot, I'd still be able to see you. My old bones don't like flying anymore. But I will if I have to."

Jude wished her mother a Merry Christmas and promised to call when the rest of the family was there. Nothing else was said about Mary Toby and "the old priest." A taut cord of regret pulled at her after she hung up.

She spent the rest of the day doing a fair enough job wrapping the gifts. Tommy jumped in and out of the paper, tearing pieces she'd already cut. "Beat it," Jude said as she crumpled up a wad of torn paper and playfully threw it at him.

She thought of her conversation with her parents. *Parents,* another term she never used. Maybe she should visit her mother. Close the past by seeing the changes in her old neighborhood.

Jude piled the gifts in the living room before heading out for a run. She wanted to stay busy, so the day would quickly turn into tomorrow.

By early afternoon, Jude went shopping and tried to think of the perfect gift for Reece. She didn't even know what size he wore, and besides, clothes seemed so personal. After wandering through some specialty shops, she settled on a gift certificate for an upscale hardware store. Perfect, she thought, and easy to wrap.

Driving home, Jude noticed the afternoon sun slanting long shadows on her street. The brightness contrasted with a sharp line of gray clouds that threatened rain, or maybe even snow, a blue norther. As many years as she'd been in Texas, she couldn't recall a white Christmas. She hoped the clouds weren't bringing an ice storm, she didn't want to get socked in—not this Christmas.

Before she turned into her driveway, she saw a car that looked like Rick's parked a few houses down. Her heart skipped. *No.* Instead of pulling in her drive, she drove, slowly, by the late model Jaguar. It was empty.

The police would probably think she was a nut case if she called them again, but to be safe, she held her phone, ready. Shaking, she drove to the next block, wishing she knew his license plate numbers. She decided to turn down her alley to check the backyard. If she drove fast enough, she could see into her yard between the slats of wooden fence. Everything looked orderly and in place.

Jude returned to the front of her house. The car was

gone. She hoped the vehicle was owned by a friend visiting a neighbor, but tension nibbled at her, and she couldn't relax. Instead of parking in the garage, she left her car in the front driveway. Cautiously, she got out and walked the perimeter of her house. Nothing had been touched.

She checked the front door. Locked. *Okay, I'm sure everything is fine.* She worked to convince herself. She slipped her key in the lock and carefully opened the door. No one jumped out. The pizza cutter sat on the entry table where she'd left it. Jude picked it up and walked through the house. *Breathe.* The house was exactly as she'd left it.

Calm settled in slowly. But Jude was jumping at shadows. Tommy woke from a nap, stretched, and followed her around the house. Jude headed to her room to get ready for Reece. He was due in less than thirty minutes. She dressed in a bright red sweater and black pants. She wasn't sure if she was nervous because of her date, or the earlier car scare.

Jude went to her kitchen and took Reece's gift card from her purse. She walked to the living room, still littered with gifts and wrapping paper, and took a pre-tied, adhesive bow and stuck it on the card. Quickly, she grabbed the mess and threw it into her hall closet by the front door. The mail had been slipped through the door slot, so Jude picked up the pile and took it to the kitchen.

On top of the mail, a hastily folded piece of paper sailed to the floor. Tommy growled low and shot down the hall. Jude picked it up noticing there was no address. Probably another block party notice. Unfolding the page, she read the typewritten message, then gasped and dropped it on the counter. She backed away from it as if it might hurt her, in disbelief she re-read the frightening message:

She's real pretty, looks just like you. If you want to see her GET THE FUCKING WHORES AND NUNS TO SELL!!!!!!!!

Chapter 60

Jude wasn't sure how long she stood in the kitchen staring at the crude note. The doorbell pierced her stupor. She raced to the door but stopped. What if it was Rick? She peeked out and saw Reece standing on the porch holding a wrapped gift. She flung open the door. "We have to call Elizabeth. *Now*."

Reece stepped inside and touched her arm. "What's wrong?" Worry lined his face.

Jude ran back to the kitchen, grabbed the letter, and shoved it at Reece, who'd followed her. She grabbed the phone and dialed while he read.

"It's Rick." Jude gasped. "He knows where my daughter is. He's going to hurt her." She clawed her hand hard through her hair and paced anxiously, waiting for anyone to answer at the Magdalene home.

"How do you know...what's this about?" Reece's eyes followed her every move.

The answering machine picked up. "No!" Jude furiously hung up then dialed Elizabeth's cell number. "*I* don't even know who she is. How could he have found her?" She looked at him pleadingly. "Why?" Elizabeth's phone also went to voice mail. Jude held the phone away from her and wailed, "Answer, Elizabeth, *please*."

"Jude, calm down." Reece took the phone from her. "Tell me what this is about."

Jude frantically told him about Rick, the FBI, the restraining order, his car out front, and now the letter.

"Okay, let's try to think this through," Reece said. "You call the police, or better yet, call the agent from the FBI. I'll try to get in touch with Elizabeth." He handed her the phone, then took out his cell and dialed. He walked to the living room and looked out the window.

Again, Jude got Agent Ladd's voice mail message. "Why won't anyone answer their phones?" She felt helpless as she followed Reece to the living room.

Reece, with his phone to his ear, glanced at her and shook his head, indicating no one had answered. "Elizabeth, it's Reece, call me as soon as you can. I'm at Jude's, and that guy Rick is threatening her…and her daughter. Hurry." He clicked off the phone and turned to her. "Can you page the agent?"

"I don't know." Jude looked at the phone as if it could dial the numbers by itself.

Reece stepped near her. "Here, call the agent back with my phone, and see if you can page him." He handed her his cell. "Let me call the police from your home line. They'll be able to identify the address right away and get here faster." He took the phone from her.

Jude dialed the number. There was an option to have the agent paged. She hit the corresponding button, keyed in her phone number, and added 911 after the last digits. She felt disjointed, unable to concentrate. What could she do to stop Rick? She needed Elizabeth, her lifeline.

She listened as Reece spoke to the police and asked them to call the FBI as well. "Look, not only did this guy break the restraining order, he's threatening her too." He paused to listen to the person on the other end. "I know it's Christmas Eve. Please have someone here soon. Thanks." He hung up and handed the phone back to Jude.

"I'm glad you're here," Jude said. "You probably think

my life is one drama after another." She sat down at the kitchen table and put the phone in front of her. "Please, ring. Please, let her be okay."

Reece pulled out a chair and sat next to her. "I asked Elizabeth about you and your daughter." He put his cell phone on the table. "She wouldn't tell me anything, said that she's sworn to secrecy and didn't want to betray a trust."

Jude only nodded and continued to look at the phone.

"She said she'll talk to you on Christmas."

Jude looked up. "If she's known all this time who my daughter is and didn't tell me...and now, if something happens to her." She wiped away a tear. "My life has been incomplete, and I was afraid to admit it until I met Elizabeth. Now, I'm so close to finding out about my child, and...and she's being threatened by some asshole I let get too close to me."

Red flashing lights pulsed through the front windows. Jude jumped up to let the police in. Two Highland Park Police SUVs, lights blazing, were parked in front of her house.

Reece came into the living room behind her. "Damn, they brought out the full posse."

Jude opened the door as two officers came up the walk. Just as she let them in, Reece's phone rang.

"Hello?" Reece looked at Jude. "Yeah, she's right here." He handed her the phone. "It's the FBI agent."

She took the phone and let Reece talk to the police. "Agent Ladd? Rick is threatening to hurt my daughter."

"What daughter?" the agent asked.

Jude quickly told him about her child and how Elizabeth might know who she is. "And now Rick's found her, and he put a letter in my mailbox threatening to hurt her if I don't get him the property."

"Don't you think you should've told me this before?" The agent sounded irritated.

"I never imagined there would be a connection," Jude said. "I need to make sure he doesn't hurt her."

"All right, we'll track him down tonight. Hang on to that letter and don't touch it again. I'll send someone out to get it."

"And have someone check on the Magdalene Home, I can't get in touch with anybody there."

"Stay there and wait for my call, okay?"

"I will. But you have to call me as soon as you hear something—anything." Jude heard the other line beep in. "Hurry." She disconnected and answered the new call, forgetting she was on Reece's phone. "Hello?"

"Who's this? Is Reece there?"

"Elizabeth? Is that you?"

"Jude? Why are you answering Reece's phone?"

"You have to help me." Jude started to tell Elizabeth about the letter and the threat. But the nun interrupted.

"Jude, we've got a…a…situation here. I need to talk to Reece, now."

"Elizabeth, please tell me who and where she is. I need to find her before Rick does." Jude could hear sirens behind Elizabeth's voice. "What's going on? Are the police there? Elizabeth, tell me, is she okay?"

Reece was suddenly next to her with the police. One officer was holding Rick's threat letter with his bare hands. "No! Don't touch that," Jude cried.

"Jude, I need Reece," Elizabeth yelled.

Before she could say anything else, Jude heard a loud explosion on Elizabeth's side of the world.

Chapter 61

Jude dropped Reece's phone when she heard Elizabeth scream. She put her hand over her mouth and whispered, "They're dead. I heard an explosion..." She looked up at the two police officers and Reece standing in her kitchen staring at her.

Reece picked up the phone and led Jude to the den. "Hello? Hello?" He spoke into the phone. He took Jude to the couch and continued to talk to his cell. "Yes, Elizabeth. It's Reece. What's going on? Are you okay?" He put a hand over his ear. "What? I can't hear you. Was there an explosion?" He stopped, glanced at Jude who stood nervously at his side, and said, "I'll be right there."

The police officers had followed them into the den. "Ma'am, who did you say left this letter?" the older, graying officer asked.

Jude ignored them. "Reece, is everybody okay? What exploded?"

Reece sat on the couch next to her. "I need to go help Elizabeth."

"I'm going with you." Jude started off the couch.

"No, you need to stay here." He pulled her back.

"I can't."

"Jude, Elizabeth asked me to come alone."

"Alone?" Jude was crushed. "She doesn't want me there?" Pain, anger, and fear mingled in her gut.

"I don't know the details, but I'll call you as soon as I can." Reece took her hand. "Stay here, talk to the police and wait for the FBI to call." He stood and turned to the officers. "Please keep an eye out. That guy Rick might come back."

The officer holding the letter nodded. "We'll get some information from Ms. Madigan and watch the house tonight."

"Reece, I can't stay here." Jude stood and followed him to the door. "I'm going crazy."

"The faster I get there, the sooner I can call you," he said. He opened the door and walked out.

Jude stood in the doorway and watched him, feeling completely helpless. She was on the brink of finding out about her daughter. Was she destined to suffer this loss forever? *Merry Christmas Eve.*

"Ma'am?" One of the officers called to Jude from her den. "Do you mind if we ask you some questions?"

Jude started to close the door as a gust of ice-cold wind blew it open. The blue norther furiously blasted in, famous for dropping the temperature thirty, even forty, degrees in minutes. Jude stood and watched Reece drive away, letting the fierce wind rip through her like daggers. Leaves danced furiously along the street and Christmas lights swayed against the force. Was this an omen?

"Ma'am." The police officer broke her thoughts.

Jude pushed the door closed and went to the den. "The guy who left that letter your fingerprints are all over is Rick Carney. I filed a restraining order against him. He wasn't supposed to come near me."

The older officer put the letter on the coffee table as Jude sat down, the sound of the explosion still ringing in her head.

"Who is the 'she' he's referring to in the letter?" the other officer asked. "And why is the FBI involved?"

"The guy Rick….It's too long of a story." Jude pulled the phone next to her. Her sweater itched her neck, and the heels she'd put on for church were pinching her feet. "Can you call and check on a place called the Magdalene Home?" She gave them the address. "Something's going on there. I'm afraid Rick Carney may have done something to the residents. Please."

"That's not our jurisdiction," the graying policeman said, as he sat on the chair next to Jude.

"You can't make a phone call?" Jude asked, exasperated.

"We'll see what we can do." The tall officer looked at his watch.

Jude answered a few more questions before saying. "Look, I can't concentrate now." She picked up the phone again to make sure it was on.

"We'll take a look around outside," one of the officers said. He turned to Jude. "We'll drive by throughout the night." He grunted as he stood. "Merry Christmas."

"Yeah, you too," Jude followed the police to the door. "If you can find out anything about the Magdalene Home, I'd appreciate it."

"Yes, ma'am. Have a good evening."

Jude closed and locked the door. The temperature had turned frigid, and the rolling wind continued to blow.

She paced the den and kept an eye on the phone. Pulling at the cowl of her sweater, Jude headed to her bedroom to change. Quickly, she threw on jeans and a sweatshirt. She picked up the phone on her nightstand to make sure the dial tone was working. *Call me*, she pleaded silently.

Tommy slunk from under the bed, sniffed around and sat looking nervous.

Jude picked up her cat, went back to the den and sat on the couch. Anxious energy mixed with worry, pulsed through her body. Tommy was as jumpy as she was, he leaped from the couch and walked the perimeter of the room cautiously.

Jude stood and glanced at the statuette of St. Jude. She went to it, picked it up. A puff of dust filtered the air as she moved it. Sorrow washed over her. Sorrow for her miserable childhood and regret for missing an opportunity to provide a childhood to her daughter. *Please, St. Jude, help everyone at the home. Help me find my daughter. You are the patron Saint of hopeless causes and of hope."* She wiped the statue with her sleeve and put him next to the phone. *And, please, let her want to know me.* Tears welled in Jude's eyes. It occurred to her, now that she was close to finding out about her, what would she do if the girl didn't want anything to do with Jude? Torment bored like an auger through her. Why hadn't she tried harder to find out about her? How had Rick found her? Would she ever know?

Another violent gust of wind tore through her backyard, toppling a chair on her porch. She jumped at the sound. Tommy's broken tail puffed, and he tore out of the room. Jude took a breath and picked up the phone again. Reece should just be getting there. Anguish washed over her. Why didn't Elizabeth want her there? Elizabeth had been acting odd the past few weeks, not always taking Jude's calls. Lately, it seemed Elizabeth was trying to distance herself, and Jude didn't want to lose the only real friend she'd had. Especially now.

Uneasy, she turned on the TV more for company than entertainment. She flipped through the channels, finding nothing to hold her interest. Other than Christmas specials, the shows were junk. She continued to change channels and passed a news teaser showing a reporter standing in front of a burning building. Jude gasped and quickly cued the channel back.

The wind-whipped reporter stood in front of the Magdalene Home, speaking into a mic while trying to hold her hair in place. "...The police suspect arson but haven't given any details on this five-alarm blaze. You can see the flames behind me." The camera zoomed over her shoulder toward a raging fire, "which completely destroyed an abandoned strip center and part of a halfway house called the Magdalene Home. We have an unconfirmed report there was at least one fatality. We'll keep you updated throughout the evening with the complete story at ten."

A fatality? Jude jumped up and grabbed her coat and cell phone. She couldn't sit and wait anymore. She wished the news camera had turned toward the Magdalene Home. She ran into the kitchen. Where were her damned keys? She remembered she'd parked in front and not used the garage. Jude was running to the foyer as the phone rang.

She ran back to the den and dove for the phone.

"Hello."

"It's agent Ladd. Is this Ms. Madigan?"

"Yes, I just saw on the news that there's a fire at the Magdalene Home."

"Yeah, I know."

"I'm going there now."

"Stay home, you'll just get in the way."

"But they said someone died. Who?"

"I'm here. It looks like Rick's meth lab was either set on fire or combusted while they were working. As far as I can tell, everybody at the Magdalene Home is accounted for. We're trying to ID the body now. But...I don't think Rick will be bothering you anymore."

Chapter 62

Jude fell on the couch and dropped her keys. She muted the volume on the TV as she questioned the agent. "You're sure everybody's okay at the Magdalene Home?"

"I just got out here five minutes ago. One of the officers at your house earlier called." He chuckled softly. "You've had a busy night."

"And I'm going crazy sitting here waiting." Jude pulled her coat closer. "Are you sure it's Rick?"

"I can't go into details, but we'll need to get dental records before we can confirm anything."

Jude put a hand to her mouth. "That's awful, even if he was a jerk. I can't believe this."

"I know. It's a real mess here. It'd be best if you stayed home." He paused. "Look, I'll check out the Magdalene Home and have someone there call you. I need to get back to work."

"Okay, but hurry. I'm going nuts waiting."

"I'll see what I can do. Just stay put."

Jude hung up and tossed the phone on the couch. She paced the den and kept an eye on the muted TV. After fifteen agonizing minutes, she picked up the phone and dialed Reece. It went to voice mail. She dialed Elizabeth, again, voice mail.

That's it I'm going, even if I get in the way. She grabbed her keys and headed out. Damned way to spend Christmas Eve.

The temperature had plummeted to a bone-chilling twenty degrees. But the furious, icy wind was much colder. She turned to bolt her door but had a hard time finding the keyhole because the porch light was out. That's odd, she thought, it should come on automatically when it got dark.

She finally secured the door and dashed to her car. The cold took her breath away. It was hard to believe only a few hours ago it had been a pleasantly cool day. She looked at the sky. Crystal clear, making the stars look closer than usual.

"Hello, beautiful." A thin raspy voice shattered the night.

Jude jumped, then froze as Rick emerged from the dark shadows of her porch. He looked wild and shaky.

"It's too bad you didn't get those bitches to give me the hotel. I'm ruined, thanks to you." He walked toward her, slowly.

Jude noticed his clothes were singed and sooty. He smelled like burnt, what was it, plastic, tires? She couldn't get her feet to run, couldn't get her voice to scream, just stood, paralyzed. Like when she was a little girl.

"I saw your kid." His eyes looked feral. "She's real pretty, just like you. You should've introduced me. We could've had pretty kids together."

Jude's brain knew she should move. *Run.* But the message didn't reach her legs. Fear anchored her.

"Your kid must be a whore too, 'cause she's living at the hotel—*my* hotel, you bitch." Like a ghost he was next to Jude. "That was mine!" He slapped Jude's cheek.

Jude reeled. Her hands reflexively went to her face for protection. She tasted blood. As she righted herself, he hit her again, and she fell to the freezing ground. The dull ring in her head made reality distant, like a dream. Was the crack she'd heard her nose? It was hard to tell through all the blood. Jude tried to roll off the cold dirt, but he kicked her side, knocking the breath and strength out of her.

"I'm fucked because of you." He leaned over her, grabbed her collar, and slapped her again. Blood splattered on his soot blackened face.

Jude felt disembodied, just like when she was young, and her father beat her. It always surprised her that, after a while, the punches didn't hurt. She felt Rick's crushing weight, a hand grasped her throat. The other hand punched her cheek. Something cracked.

"You ruined me, you fucking bitch! You killed my career, and now it's your turn."

The voice sounded far away, like she was in the center of a tornado. The punches came in slow motion. Jude didn't want to cry. He always got madder if she cried. If she was quiet and minded him, he'd stop the beating. The fingers clenched her neck, squeezed hard. This time was different. He didn't let go. If she stayed quiet, complacent, he'd let her go. Her mother should be home soon. She'd make him stop.

The hand tightened.

That's weird, you really do see stars, she thought. She needed air, fought to breathe. She panicked as she tried to gulp air. No, this isn't right. He's supposed to stop by now. She clawed at the hand around her neck.

Her last thought before the blackness were dust motes sprinkling in the light around her statue of St. Jude.

Chapter 63

Beeping noises pinged in the back of Jude's thoughts. *I'm in a hospital. My baby.* She had to wake up so she could sneak her newborn out. This time they'd leave together, no one would stop them. She needed to hold her close again and feel her velvet, tender skin. Needed to kiss her soft cheeks and smell the newness of life. This time they'd get away, the nun wouldn't stop her. She'd take her baby home, be her mother. But first, she had to wake up.

"Jude."

There was a back stairway where no one would see them. If she could only get there.

"Jude, can you hear me?"

Oh, no, someone's coming.

"Are you awake?"

I'll come back for you, honey. I love you so much. God, why did it hurt so much? Jude tried to see who was talking. The light hurt her eyes.

"Jude?"

"Judith, my name's Judith," she mumbled. It was hard to talk.

"Hey, you're in there. She's coming around. Thank God."

"Praise the saints. Thank you, Lord."

Jude couldn't see who was talking. It was too hard to open her eyes. "Is my baby okay?"

Silence.

Jude tried to focus, but light hurt. She shielded her eyes and felt bandages on her face. Wait, this isn't where it's supposed to hurt after having a baby. Startled, she opened her eyes fully.

Two nuns hovered over her bed. *Damn, she got caught again.*

"Take your time, Jude. Breathe."

These nuns seem familiar.

"Jude, it's Elizabeth and Bernadette. We've been worried."

Groggy, but slowly becoming aware of time, Jude tried to remember why she was in a hospital. "Elizabeth? Bernadette?" She remembered the Magdalene Home. Bits and pieces fell into place. "What happened?"

Elizabeth leaned close and brushed away a strand of hair from Jude's face. "You had us scared. Rick Carney paid you a visit last night. Tried to…hurt you."

"Rick?" Her memory was becoming more linear. Christmas Eve. Reece. FBI. Fire. "Wait, didn't something happen to Rick?" She looked at Elizabeth. "Didn't something happen to you?" It felt like she had marbles in her mouth and fire in her throat.

"Slow down, I can't understand you." Elizabeth sat on the edge of Jude's bed. "How're you feeling?"

Jude tried to give a "how do you think I feel look," but her face wasn't cooperating. She reached up and touched her swollen cheek. Bandages swathed and wrapped over her nose and head. There was adhesive gauze on her forehead and tape on her nose. Pain radiated under the wraps and shot around her neck.

"What happened?" she croaked.

Elizabeth glanced at Bernadette. Jude noticed the older

nun clutched a rosary and prayed silently. Elizabeth turned back to Jude. "Rick Carney attacked you last night," she said, wiping away a tear. "Thank God the police got there when they did."

"Rick?" Jude tried to remember. "Wasn't there a fire?" she spit out.

Elizabeth grabbed a tissue and blew her nose. "Fire? Is that what you said?"

Jude nodded, then winced as pain shot up her neck.

"Rick set fire to a drug lab it turns out he was running. Blew up the building. Then he came to the Magdalene Home and tried to burn it down, too." Elizabeth took her hand. "Luckily, that place is built like a fortress. He lit some brush near the kitchen. But the firefighters were already there for the other fire. They put it out right away."

"Body...there was a body?" It hurt to think, much less talk.

"Yes, I'm here, dear." Bernadette walked to the other side of the bed.

"No, not Bernadette! *Body*." The harder Jude tried to talk, the worse her words sounded.

"Body?" Elizabeth asked.

Jude nodded slowly, painfully. She realized her neck was bound by a soft collar.

Elizabeth looked at her wadded Kleenex. "I'm not sure who it was, except some guy who worked for Rick in the drug lab. The police are checking everything out."

"Is everybody okay?" Jude worked to enunciate her words.

"Yeah, we're all fine," Elizabeth said.

"Reece?" It felt like she hissed his name.

"He's fine. He's been here all night kicking himself for leaving you alone. I'm sorry I asked him to come by himself." Elizabeth wiped her wet eyes. "If I'd known this was going to happen, I would've never let him leave you." She looked pleadingly at Jude. "I had a promise to keep, and things got so crazy." She wrung the tissue. "I needed help...I'm sorry."

Jude remembered Reece leaving. Remembered Elizabeth's Christmas promise.

"It's Christmas?" Jude asked painfully.

"Merry Christmas." Elizabeth stood. "That's one reason why we're wearing our habits. Plus, it gives us more clout in the hospital. You know, in case they wouldn't let us visit you."

"Your promise. Tell me." Jude winced, not sure from the physical or emotional pain.

"What?" Elizabeth leaned closer. "I'm sorry, I didn't understand you."

Jude closed her eyes, willed herself to speak clearly. "My baby. You promised."

"I didn't forget." Elizabeth turned to Bernadette. "I also didn't expect all this to happen. I'd hoped we could talk at the Magdalene Home." She looked at Bernadette. "I'm going to let Bernie talk to you."

Just then, a nurse came in pulling a large cart with a laptop computer on it. "Time for your meds, and I need to take your vitals."

"No, it makes me tired." Jude shifted in the bed. "Can you come back later?" Jude fought to enunciate her words.

The nurse looked at her as if she were a child. "I'm sorry if I'm interrupting. But we're already short staffed since it's Christmas. I'm sure your conversation can wait a few minutes." She turned to Elizabeth and Bernadette. "If you'll excuse us."

"Fine, but hurry." Jude flopped her arm out so the nurse could put a blood pressure cuff on. She turned to the nuns. "Stay right outside the door. Don't leave." She was speaking a little clearer.

"Okay. We'll be here." Elizabeth squeezed Jude's toe as she walked out.

After taking her blood pressure, the nurse scanned a barcode on Jude's wristband which caused the computer to whir and a drawer pop open on the cart. The nurse drew up a syringe of medicine.

"I'm okay." Jude struggled to sit up straight, but a piercing slice of pain shot through her ribcage. "Ouch."

"Here, this will make you feel better." The nurse went to her IV and cleaned off a rubber stopper. "The doctor will be here this afternoon. I'm not sure when he'll make rounds since it's a holiday." She plunged the drug through the IV.

Jude immediately felt the coolness of the medicine course through her veins. "I need to talk to them. I need to stay alert."

"Hmmm? I can't understand you." The nurse had turned her back to Jude as she fussed with the med cart. "I'll be back to check on you later." She closed the drawer. "Just use the call button if you need anything."

Jude tried, but she couldn't fight the blackness of sleep.

Chapter 64
New York

Christmas at Judith's house was rarely a happy day. Usually, by mid-morning, her father had polished off a few beers and his mood would turn sour quickly.

Judith fought waves of nausea all morning. She'd been up late because her mother insisted the family—everyone except Jude's father—go to midnight mass. Judith had been exhausted lately and she could hardly stay awake during the service. It had been this way for weeks. Fatigue so heavy she'd barely made it through school finals. She feared she'd gotten mono or some awful virus. But mono was the kissing disease, and she'd certainly never kissed a boy.

Judith was cleaning up the living room after opening presents, stuffing torn wrapping paper in the trash. Her dad sat near, drinking beer and reading the paper. She'd gotten a charm bracelet and some new clothes. Her brother was upstairs closed in his room. Judith wished she could take a nap before the holiday dinner was served.

The aroma of roast pork mingled with her father's cigarettes. A strong wave of sickness overwhelmed her. She dropped her trash bag and ran to the bathroom where she dry heaved for ten minutes.

"Hey, get your ass back in here and clean up." Her father banged on the bathroom door. "The damned Monsignor will be here soon, and this place looks like a pigsty."

Judith froze. Monsignor Callen was coming for Christmas dinner? She splashed cold water on her face and slowly opened the bathroom door.

"What's the matter with you? Are you contagious?" Her father had the newspaper tucked under his arm. "Make sure you clean the toilet. I have to go, and I don't want no germs."

Judith took out the disinfectant from under the bathroom sink and scrubbed the toilet while he watched. The smell was so strong she gagged a few times before she finished.

"You got some kind of stomach flu or something?" Her dad made a clear berth around her as he went in the bathroom. "Don't go getting sick in front of the company." He slammed the door in her face.

Judith wiped her mouth. When did her parents invite Monsignor Callen for Christmas dinner? Why? She went to the kitchen to wash her hands. Her mother was peeling potatoes for dinner.

Judith stood at the sink scrubbing her hands raw, her back to her mother. "Why is Monsignor Callen coming for dinner? That's a surprise."

"I know," Her mother said. "He called this morning, so I invited him. Such an honor. I never expected him to say yes." She moved next to Judith with more potatoes to rinse. "Here, help me with these."

Judith scoured the dirty brown skins. Exhaustion and sickness dragged at her from inside. Lately, she was either sick or tired all the time. "Mom, why do you think he called?"

"I don't know. But we should be grateful the Monsignor is having dinner with us." She glanced toward the living room.

Judith could almost read her thoughts. He mom was afraid Judith's father would be drunk by the time the priest arrived. If he wasn't already. She was sure the beer cans and dirty ashtray would be piled high.

"Honey, make sure the living room is picked up, then set the table. Monsignor should be here in an hour, and I need to get the potatoes done." She dropped the cut spuds in a pot of boiling water.

Judith finished cleaning, then set the table, and quietly crept to her room to lie down. The next thing she knew, her brother, Stephen, was pounding on her door.

He stuck his head in. "Get up, the priest's here, and Dad's pissed you're not downstairs." Stephen ducked out.

Judith could hear him descend the squeaky stairs, but he came back up and closed his bedroom door. She got up too fast and fought another bout of nausea. She sat on the bed until her stomach quit roiling. Finally, still a little woozy, she pulled her hair back and emerged from her room. Taking a deep breath, she headed to the living room.

Monsignor Callen sat in a chair facing Judith's father. The priest looked directly at her as she walked into the room. Icy chills prickled down her spine.

"Where the hell...heck were you? Your mother needs help in the kitchen." Her father slurred. "And we have company."

Judith quickly walked toward the kitchen, her head bowed as she tried not to look at the priest.

"Hey, where're your manners? Say hello to Monsignor Callen." Her dad's eyes were bloodshot and angry.

"Hello, Monsignor Callen," Judith said, nodding politely.

"Kids. I swear we try to raise them right, but I wonder

if I'm not home enough," Her father said. He turned to the priest. "Their mother's too easy with them. They need a strong hand around here." He raised his hand in a slapping gesture at Judith.

"Merry Christmas, Judith," the Monsignor said. He stood and held his hand out to her. His eyes pierced through her.

She froze. She never wanted to see this man again, much less touch him. She caught her father's intense fury and knew she'd pay a heavy price if she didn't shake his hand. Without looking him in the eye, Judith stepped closer, extended a shaky hand, and winced through a fake smile when he squeezed it in both of his.

"Are you having a good Christmas?" the rheumy-eyed priest asked.

"Yes, thank you." Judith almost gagged at his mothball stench. "Merry Christmas to you, sir." She hastily ducked into the kitchen.

"Oh good, honey. I need some help." Her mother was flushed from the heat of the stove. "Stir the gravy before it bubbles over. I need to slice the roast."

Judith took a spoon and stirred the thick, brown sauce. Again, she tried not to throw up. The whole kitchen reeked of food, and the thought of eating anything with that disgusting man made it worse. "I don't feel so good." Judith turned to her mother suppressing a rise of vomit.

"What's the matter?" Her mother put a comforting hand over her forehead. "You don't have a temperature. Go sit down, I'll take care of dinner."

She took a cold washcloth and dabbed her face as she sat and watched her mother put the food on serving trays. "I'll clean up in here while you guys eat," Judith said. Please, I'm not that hungry."

"Judith! Don't be silly. It's Christmas dinner, and the Monsignor's here. You must sit at the dinner table." Her mother continued to work at hyper speed. "Take a few aspirins, you'll feel better."

The kitchen door swung open, and her father entered. "What in the hell are you doing sittin'?" He glared at her. "Damned lazy ass." He turned to Judith's mother. "See, this is what I mean, these kids are good for nothing."

"She's not feeling well," her mother said calmly. "I told her to sit."

"Well, get your ass in the living room and talk to Monsignor, and straighten up." He pulled two beers from the refrigerator and popped them open. "And give this to him." He shoved a foamy can at her.

Judith gagged at the smell and put her hand over her mouth. Luckily, she didn't have anything left in her stomach to lose.

"Jesus, you look just like your mother when she was pregnant. Sick, glassy-eyed. Good for nothing." He took a swig of beer and eyed her closely.

"Now stop." Her mother pleaded. "Let's try to have a peaceful meal." She looked at the can in Judith's hand. "The Monsignor's drinking beer?" her mother asked.

"That's what he wanted. I'm not pulling the good shit out for him," her father replied. He stared hard at Judith as she walked toward to kitchen door. "He also wants more damned money from us. I knew he came here for something. Not only are we feeding him, he's not going to be happy until we're in the poor house. Hurry up, I'm starving." He took a crispy end piece of pork and shoved it in his mouth as he followed Judith out.

As Judith handed the priest his beer, the old man's hand lingered on hers. He smelled like he was rotting from the inside out. She gasped and recoiled. She felt a pop on the side of her head where her father hit her.

"Don't be rude." Her father sat noisily in his chair. "What's the matter with you anyway?"

"Maybe we should ask what Judith thinks," the priest said to her father.

He shrugged. "She'll do what we tell her."

Monsignor took a long sip of beer. "What do you think about separating the boys and girls starting in the seventh grade? Not just in high school."

Judith honestly couldn't care less and felt uncomfortable answering. She was sure it would be the wrong response anyway. "Whatever's best, or what you think," she said. She shrugged and looked down.

The priest looked at her father. "It's amazing how early the boys and girls notice each other these days." He turned to Judith. "You know Mary Toby?"

"Yes, sir. I know who she is." She thought of Mary's brazen behavior and became more nervous. What if she was going to get in trouble for the dress-up episode? Is that why he was here? She shuddered.

"She's been a real troublemaker. You need to stop hanging around her." The priest looked accusingly at her.

"Judith's making trouble?" her father asked.

Monsignor laughed but was serious at the same time. "It's more this other girl. But Judith should separate from that group. Some of them are getting too flirty with the boys. One reason we need more money is to build onto the school, so we can keep the boys and girls away from each other."

Her father eyed her suspiciously. "You messin' around with boys? I better not find out you're a..." He stopped, and looked as if he was trying to think of a word. "...you know." Another word he couldn't say in front of Monsignor.

Her mother came into the living room holding a big plate of meat. "Time to eat. Where's Stephen?" She set the tray in the middle of the dining room table. "Monsignor, we're so happy you're joining us." She walked to the stairs. "Dinner's ready," she called to Stephen.

Judith's brother came racing down the stairs but slowed when he neared his father. Even though Stephen was eighteen, he still cowed around his father.

"Go, sit and eat," her father said gruffly as he pointed to the table. "Judith, help your mother."

Judith followed her mother into the kitchen, took the bowl of mashed potatoes, and brought it to the table. Nausea abated, she suddenly had a wild craving for pork and black licorice. Licorice? Judith hated black licorice.

The meal was the most uncomfortable Judith had ever experienced. She wanted to take her plate of pork into the kitchen and eat alone. Where could she find a store open that sold black licorice?

Finally, after what seemed an eternity, the Monsignor stood, thanked her parents for the meal, and turned to leave. "I've got a few more stops before our afternoon mass."

"We're honored you've joined us." Judith's mother stood and walked him to the door. "Merry Christmas." One of Judith's favorite crystal angel ornaments tinkled its sweet bell when the door opened.

Her father got up and waved. "Yeah, thanks for stopping by." He ducked into the kitchen where Judith heard another pop of a beer can. After the front door closed, he came back into the living area and plopped down on his chair. "Friggin' begger. Eats our food and asks for money. Where does he get the nerve?"

Judith began clearing the table. She wanted to run into the kitchen and away from her father's temper. He was on a short fuse already and could blow at any minute.

She couldn't shake the uncomfortable feeling that Monsignor Callen had come to check on her. Was he concerned she'd told her parents what happened? She felt ashamed. The only person she'd told—or tried to tell—

was Sister Agnes. And it seemed the young nun already seemed to know what happened.

And now she was gone.

That evening, Judith tried to avoid her father, but he looked at her quizzically. It seemed every time he'd notice her, she became sick to her stomach. She wished he'd leave, find an open bar. But it was Christmas.

After the kitchen was cleaned and her mother had left for evening mass, he caught her in the living room. Judith was green with sickness. Grabbing her arm, he shoved her against the wall. She cringed at his temper and held her hands up for protection.

With a cigarette dangling from his mouth he hissed, "If I find out you're pregnant, I'll kill you."

Chapter 65

Jude awoke in the hospital room alone. She tried to piece together last night. She recalled watching the news, struggling to lock her front door in the dark, and heading to her car. She cringed remembering Rick waiting, acting crazy. She shuddered. What if he'd attacked her inside her home?

Where were Elizabeth and Bernadette? They were going to tell her about her daughter before the damned nurse came in and shot her with drugs. Jude pounded the nurse call button.

Finally, a voice answered. "Can I help you?"

"It's about time," Jude said as she tried to sit up in bed. She was angry the nurse had given her medicine, even after Jude resisted.

"We're a little busy. You only need to hit the button once," the nurse said. "One of us will get to you as soon as we can."

"Are my friends here?" Jude sounded like her mouth was full of marshmallows.

The nurse didn't try to hide her sarcasm. "Did they have a reservation? Will you need anything else?"

"Yeah, to go home." Jude shifted and tried to sit on the edge of the bed, but the railings held her in. "If you see a couple of nuns hanging around, send them in. Then get me my discharge papers. Call the doctor if you have to.

Please." Her voice was still raspy, but she could finally speak well enough to make sense.

"Your doctor will make rounds when he gets here this afternoon. It's Christmas, he doesn't want to be called."

"Then find another doctor. I don't know, just flag down the next one that walks by." Jude couldn't lower the railings, so she slid slowly to the end of the bed. She might've made it, but she was tethered to an IV line which wove through a meter plugged into the wall. She looked at the contraption and was tempted to yank it out of her arm.

The door opened, and a nurse came in. "What are you doing?" She ran to Jude, lowered the railing and helped her scoot to a sitting position.

"I have to go to the bathroom," Jude said.

"Good. You look like you're feeling better." The nurse unplugged the IV, wheeled it around the bed and helped Jude stand.

Upright, Jude suddenly felt woozy. "Whoa." She almost fell back.

"Just go slow, you've had some heavy medication"

"How bad is my face?" Jude felt the bandages swathed around her head.

"You were assaulted. Some guy choked you, fractured your cheekbone."

"Choked?" Jude touched the soft collar around her neck.

"Yeah, until you were unconscious. I guess the police happened by and saved you." The nurse held Jude's arm and the IV stand as they slowly made their way to the bathroom. "You're lucky."

"What happened to the guy?" Jude felt sick thinking Rick had done this.

The nurse shrugged. "I don't know. Hopefully, he's in jail. I only know what happened to you because it's in your records."

The bravado Jude had shown before was gone. Shock, pain, and disbelief shrouded her. "Why would he do that?" she asked rhetorically.

"Did you know him?"

Jude nodded as they made a slow go toward the bathroom.

"The paramedics told the ER doc that he was doped up." The nurse pushed the IV pole into the bathroom then helped Jude go in. "Are you okay alone?"

Jude nodded. "Yeah, I'm good. Thanks."

"Pull this if you need me," the nurse showed her a call button attached to a long string.

Jude steadied herself against the wall. "Have you seen a couple of nuns in the waiting area?"

"They were here for awhile. I'm not sure where they went." The nurse handed Jude a towel and washcloth along with some toiletries.

"Can you find out, please? It's very important." Jude took the linens. "Please?" She hoped the group hadn't gone back to the Magdalene Home without her.

"I'll see what I can do." The nurse backed out and closed the door.

Jude took a good look in the mirror and was shocked. What she could see of her face was a palette of reds and purples, disfigured by swelling and cuts. Thick bandages covered her cheek and heavy tape coursed over her nose. Gingerly, she touched her neck and peeked under the collar. Her neck was bruised and bloated. She could almost distinguish finger marks between the contusions. Her hip was black and blue, and her whole body hurt.

She cleaned up as best she could and tried to wrap the hospital gown around her as she maneuvered the IV and her sore bones back to bed. Carefully, she sat on the edge of the mattress, hoping to stay semi-upright in case she needed to fight off another nurse wielding more drugs.

The door swung open, and Drew entered.

"Don't you knock?" Jude asked. Embarrassed, she gathered her gown and blanket, trying to hide the gaping areas.

"Sorry." He strode in, leaving the door open. "How are you? What the hell happened? I told you Rick was crazy." He went to her, put a finger under her chin, and gently lifted it up. "Holy shit. Look at you."

"Ouch." Jude pushed his hands away from her. "I'm a little sore."

"Oh, geez, sorry. It's such a shock."

"How did you find out?" she asked.

"Elizabeth. I was supposed to meet her last night with a letter from Trudy, but Rick was tearing up the neighborhood. Then she called me early this morning and told me about you. Damn."

"Yeah, I'm shocked, too." Jude gently touched her throbbing nose.

"He tried to kill you." Drew sat in a chair next to the bed. "Why? Over that damned property?"

Jude looked down and shook her head. "I guess so, I can't believe it."

"He was doped up. Out of his mind. I talked to the arresting officers. Thank God they drove by your house when they did," Drew said.

Jude could feel tears start, but it hurt too much to cry. "I only remember a little of that. He attacked me in the front yard, didn't he?"

"Yeah." Drew looked away. Maybe he was thinking the same thing she had earlier. What if no one had been around to stop him?

She didn't want to dwell on Rick. She had a quick flash of memory: Rick saying he'd seen her daughter at the Magdalene Home. Was she hallucinating or had he said that? She needed to think, to try to find a way out of here.

"Drew, I feel a little awkward wearing nothing but a hospital gown." She pulled the covers over her leg. "Do you know where Elizabeth went?"

He shook his head. "We keep missing each other's call." He pulled an envelope from his pocket.

Jude recognized Trudy's wax seal on the back.

Drew held it up. "This is for Elizabeth, as soon as I find her."

"I'll give it to her." Jude eagerly held out her hand like a kid at Christmas.

"No, Trudy left specific instructions to hand it directly to Elizabeth." He slipped it back into his pocket as he stood. "I'm going to call her again while you get settled." He headed to the door. "Do you need me to get you a nurse?"

"No, that's the last thing I need. They just want to keep me doped up. I need some clothes and a doctor to release me."

Drew raised an eyebrow. "Maybe you should stay."

"No, I need to get out *now*." Jude felt like a prisoner.

Drew looked at her sternly. "Nothing is open, it's Christmas. Let me call Elizabeth and see if she can bring you something to wear. Can she get into your house?"

Jude looked around. "No, I have the only key. In fact, where are my keys, where's my purse? Oh no, Tommy…" She almost stood up, but the gown slipped off her shoulder. "Do you mind finding some scrubs I could borrow?"

After Drew left, Jude looked around the room. She found her personal belongings in a plastic bag under her bed. Her jeans were dirty but okay to wear. Each stain on her pants had a corresponding bruise on her body. Her sweatshirt was cut in half and caked with dried blood. A lot of blood. Jude felt a hollow sickness. She stuffed the shirt back in the bag and went to the bathroom to put her jeans on.

Drew returned and spoke to her through the bathroom door. "I found Elizabeth, she's on her way. She'll be here in thirty minutes."

"Okay, can you find me a shirt?" Jude said through the door. Her voice was still tender.

"I'll see what I can do."

Jude heard him walk out.

Within fifteen minutes, Drew was back holding a folded t-shirt and a sweatshirt. "Merry Christmas, luckily the gift store was open. Sorry, this was all they had." He held up a pink t-shirt, shaped somewhat like a tent. It had a big arrow pointing down that said, *Baby*. He also offered a royal blue sweatshirt. *Proud New Mommy* was written in bold pink. "The pickings were slim. "The other option was being a proud grandma."

"Perfect." Jude stood by the bathroom door, leaning on the frame. "Well, not really, but it's better than this split-up-the-back number the hospital provides." Jude took the clothes gratefully. "Thanks for coming today. Shouldn't you get back to your family?"

"Only if you don't need me anymore." He stood hesitant at the door.

"On your way out, see if you can throw your weight around. Tell the nurses you'll sue the hospital or something if they don't let me out of here today." Jude tried to muster a wry look, but it hurt too much.

"Yeah, sure." He smiled. "I'm glad you're okay. This scared me." He walked to her and gave her a gentle hug. "Merry Christmas." he stopped at the door. "Call me if Elizabeth doesn't get here soon."

"Okay, thanks for everything." Jude tried to watch him leave but her neck wouldn't work independently. She had to move her shoulders around.

"Oh, wait, Trudy's letter." He pulled the envelope from his pocket. "I need to give it to her." He looked as if he was tempted to leave it with Jude.

"I'll be happy to make sure she gets it." Jude hoped there were answers in the letter.

"I don't know." He stared at it as if it would decide for him. "No, I'd better not. I'll go out to the waiting room and wait. Give you time to get dressed."

"Okay. If you talk to her, please tell her to hurry." Jude was impatient, she'd waited long enough.

As soon as he left, she went to the bathroom with her new clothes. Carefully she threaded her IV bag into the sleeve of the shirt then put her arm in next. It was painfully difficult trying to pull the collar over her bandaged face, but she managed. Dressed, she felt a little more normal.

Jude looked at the time. It was almost four 'o clock. The nurse that came in gave her a funny look when she saw the outfit, and said, "I'm glad you managed to get a shirt on without pulling out your IV." She checked the line. "Um, you're not pregnant are you?" She looked a little nervous as if she might've missed something about her patient.

"No." Jude smiled painfully. "The gift shop was the only store open, and this was all they had. My shirt was…" she stopped, remembering the bloody mess. "Did you call the doctor? I'm ready to get out of here."

"You'll need someone to drive you home. That group of people here earlier left a few hours ago."

"Group?"

"Yeah, a couple of nuns and about five women," she hesitated, then smiled, "and one very handsome guy."

"They were all here?" Jude, said hoarsely, she hoped the "handsome guy" was Reece.

"Some guy named Drew is still here threatening to sue us if you don't go home today." The nurse smiled. "We told him we'd get psych down to evaluate him—you know, make sure he's not a complete nut case."

Jude looked at her. "What?"

"Just kidding. One of the nurses knows him and is giving him a hard time. He *is* trying to get you discharged, though."

"Good. So quit eyeing that IV. I don't want more drugs." Jude did not want to gork out again.

A few minutes later, the door opened and Reece came in. He went straight to Jude, sat next to her on the bed, and gave her a hug. "I'm so sorry I left you last night."

He squeezed a little too tight, her bruises screamed, but Jude was glad he was there. "It's okay. I'm still waiting to find out everything that happened," she croaked.

The nurse slipped out just as Elizabeth and Drew came in.

"You're awake, good." Elizabeth moved to the side of the bed, took Jude's hand, and sat in the chair across from her. "Nice outfit."

Jude waved her off, not wanting to explain it again.

Drew stood at the end of the bed and pulled the letter from his pocket. "Here, Elizabeth. This is the last letter from Trudy."

Elizabeth took it and thanked Drew. "This should help answer some questions, thanks."

"And Elizabeth, if you need us to continue to help the home after the first of the year…" he looked at Jude, "we'd be happy to."

"Thank you." Jude stood, pain shooting arrows through her body, and hugged Drew. "Merry Christmas. You should get back to your family. Thanks for everything."

"Merry Christmas." He waved and left.

Bernadette almost collided with him as she came in, full of energy. "Merry Christmas!" she sang. Oh, Jude, I'm so excited you're awake. We've all been waiting for this day for so long." She clasped her hands happily. "Oh, what a nice shirt! And how fitting."

"It's a little big, actually." Jude smiled at everybody.

"Okay, tell me." She looked at Elizabeth expectantly.

Elizabeth stood and opened the envelope. Inside was another sealed envelope with Jude's name written on it. "This is for you." The nun held it up. "I'm sorry so much has happened since yesterday. We'd hoped you would read this at the Magdalene Home. It's a little cozier there."

Jude noticed Bernadette had her hands together as in prayer, and her eyes glistened with tears.

Elizabeth handed Jude the letter. "We're going to leave you alone to read this. When you're ready, call us and we'll come in. Merry Christmas." She smiled, and her voice caught on a sob.

Reece stood and touched her hair. "I'm not going far. Just to the waiting room."

Jude looked at him intently. "You know, don't you?"

Reece didn't answer. He only smiled slightly.

Then she was alone.

Chapter 66

Jude settled back on the bed. With a nervous hand, she broke the wax seal and pulled the linen paper out. She took a deep breath and read.

> *Dear Jude,*
> *Merry Christmas! Right now, if all's gone as planned, you're sitting in front of a blazing fire at the Magdalene Home enjoying good friends and (hopefully) Bernadette's excellent cooking.*

Slight change of plans there, Jude thought.

> *I wish I would've had the nerve to call you before my illness. The gift you gave me is one that I cherished and loved from the beginning. I'm crying now, just thinking about leaving the blessings I'd been given.*
> *I'm not sure if you've already figured out why I barged into your life after my death. You gave birth to Elise, my adopted daughter. From that miraculous day on, my life had meaning, love, and purpose. Elise completed and made my life whole.*

Jude gasped and put a hand to her face.

> *I understand it was difficult for you to make the decision to let her go that day, but for that supreme sacrifice, I can't begin to thank you. I selfishly kept her for myself, and for that I'm sorry. I know you were only fourteen when she was born, and I knew you needed to find your own way. I don't know how often you thought of her or whether you were okay with the sacrifice you made. But I'm haunted by something you said at her delivery, that you wanted to keep her. You were so young. I thought it would be best for all if you grew up too.*

Jude drew in a breath. How did Trudy know what she'd said that day?

> *Throughout the years I tried to find the courage to call you, but I was so afraid you might change your mind and take her back. Or, and this is difficult to admit, that she would prefer you. I couldn't bear the thought of life without Elise.*
>
> *As the years went on, I kept track of you by various means. Because of what you did for me, I wanted to make sure you were taken care of. I'm glad you've become an attorney—and, in a small way, proud of you.*
>
> *I've asked Elizabeth and Bernadette to get to know you and decide if you're willing and able to take care of Elise. If not, I understand, or, when I'm gone, they'll understand. (I'm crying again thinking about not being there to watch her grow).*

How do you think I feel, Jude thought as she wiped at a spillway of tears.

> *They've both committed to helping guide Elise through her adulthood and I trust them completely. Just as they were there when she was growing up.*
>
> *I told Elise about you. How you gave the ultimate sacrifice of yourself and that you were just a child when she was born. I thank God every day, and I thank you from my heart and soul.*
>
> *My will should be read by the end of the year. If you decide to be in Elise's life, then you will be named in the estate.*
>
> *Again, thank you. She's a beautiful girl and has brought magic to all who know her. Please, love her as I know you can.*
>
> *Much love and infinite appreciation,*
> *Trudy Wells*

Jude's facial bandages were soaked through from tears. Her daughter had been taken care of by Trudy. Now, it seemed so obvious. How could she have missed it?

Her insides were a melting pot. Why hadn't Trudy called? Jude had a flash of anger at Trudy for not reaching out. She softened a little with the stark realization she couldn't have raised a child when she was only fourteen. Maybe Trudy had done the right thing by allowing her daughter to grow and blossom before revealing her.

Tears puddled under the bandages. She was swollen before, now she figured her face looked like a bloated caricature. She needed to find Elise. "Elise." She spoke her name for the first time.

It was a good name.

She pounded on the nurse's button again. "Hello? Is anybody there?" Her voice was hoarse but coherent.

"Yes?" The nurse sounded weary.

"Can you find my visitors? I'm ready for them now," Jude announced excitedly.

"Excuse me, but are you confusing us with the last vacation you took? This is not a cruise ship, ma'am, it's a hospital. And we're busy."

"Whatever happened to customer service?" Jude responded to the impertinent nurse. "Then take out the IV, and I'll find them myself." She needed to talk to Elizabeth and find out where Elise was. "I'm kind of tied to the wall right now."

"Hang on." The nurse clicked off.

"Damn it!" Jude stood on shaky legs and yanked the IV's power cord out of the wall. She expected alarms to go off so the nurses would run in. Nothing happened. "A person could die here and no one would know." Jude shook the stand, hoping for a beep.

The door opened and Elizabeth entered. "You're looking more energetic. Are you trying to arm wrestle or dance with the IV?"

"I'm trying to take it out." Jude turned to Elizabeth as quickly as her bruised body allowed. "Where's Elise? Does she want to meet me? Does she know who I am? Why didn't you tell me?" Jude fired off question after question in a burst of built-up energy. Years of layers peeled away. "Elizabeth?"

"Give me a chance." Elizabeth laughed. "Are you ready to meet Elise?"

"Yeah, for like the last seventeen years." Jude took a few tentative steps toward Elizabeth. "Is she here? Now?"

Elizabeth gently took her arm and led her to the chair next to the bed. "Yes, she's ready to meet you as well. It's not the way we wanted, but thankfully everybody is okay.

That's more important."

Jude's hands flew to her face. "Oh, I look awful! What a horrible first impression. Here," she reached for her purse. "Help me brush my hair. My face is a wreck."

Elizabeth brushed out some of the tangles, but the bandages were hard to get around. The nun got a warm washcloth and gently dabbed at Jude's face. "You look beautiful. Besides, that's not important. Elise knows what happened."

"I hate this is how we're meeting. I haven't seen her for her...whole life." Jude sat straight in the chair and took a deep breath. "I don't care, I can't wait another second." Nerves and anticipation and a dose of hope coursed through her. She looked at Elizabeth. "Do you think she'll like me?"

"That's up to you." Elizabeth squeezed Jude's hand, then went to the door and opened it. She nodded to someone, turned to Jude, and smiled. "Jude Madigan, I'd like you to meet Elise Wells."

Chapter 67

Throughout the years, Jude wondered what her child looked like. She'd imagined this moment forever. Like a flower turning to the sun, Jude faced the door. The young lady that entered the room was beautiful. Jude looked for some of herself in the girl's face. Soft blonde hair surrounded delicate features. Her eyes were Jude's. Thankfully, Jude saw no hint of the priest. Elise was cautious but carried herself with a quiet confidence that Jude had never known.

"Hi. Miss Madigan?" The young lady held out her hand. "I'm Elise."

"Call me Jude, please." Jude stood, took her daughter's hand, and pulled the girl into an embrace. "I've waited so long…" She tried not to cry but couldn't help the flood of raw emotion. She pulled back and looked at Elise. "You're so beautiful." She sobbed.

The girl blushed. "Thank you." She wiped away a tear. "I can't believe we're meeting. My mother told me about you."

"She did?" Jude was surprised. "I've thought about you since the day you were born." Weak, Jude let go of Elise and sat down. "Please sit."

"You have?" Elise sat on the bed.

"Oh, my God, yes." Jude wiped her face with the washcloth. "I'm sorry I look like this. I've daydreamed so many different ways when we'd meet. This wasn't one of my fantasies."

The door opened, and Bernadette came in with Elizabeth. "We don't want to get in the way, but we're as excited as you are." Bernadette stood by the door like a mother hen who'd hatched all her eggs.

"The last time I saw you was the day you were born." Jude reached and touched Elise's knee. "I didn't want to give you up."

"I think I recall that day. We were both trying to make a break out of the hospital," Elise said and giggled.

"You remember? No!" Jude looked at her incredulously. "You were hours old."

Beaming, Elise looked at both nuns.

Bernadette raised a hand. "Jude, I didn't know this until the letter from Trudy at Thanksgiving, but I'm the nun that was with you the day you had Elise. I was in the birthing room, and when you were in the nursery that night trying to make your escape, I was there on Trudy's behalf."

"What?" Jude let her hand drop. "It was you?" She thought of the letter Trudy had left Jude. "So that's how Trudy knew what I'd said about not wanting to give you up." Jude looked at Elise. "I was only fourteen. Sometimes it feels like a lifetime ago, and other times, just like yesterday."

"It broke my heart to have to take her from you. I could see how much love you had for her." Bernadette was crying softly. "But you were so young."

Jude looked at Elise. "I know, I'm sure Trudy was a great mom, I just wish…"

"She talked about you." This time, Elise took Jude's hand. "She said you didn't want to give me up." Now the girl was crying. "I wish we could *all* be together. I miss her."

"Oh, honey." Jude stood, scooted closer to her daughter, and hugged her. "You've suffered a tremendous loss, too. I'm sorry." Sore as she was, she held Elise as hard as she could. "I'm glad we're together now."

Elise nodded and smiled through her tears. "And don't forget Aunt Lizzie and Uncle Bernie. They've been sort of surrogate moms, too."

Jude laughed. "Uncle Bernie?"

Both nuns shrugged and Elizabeth said, "You needed an army to keep you in line."

"Yeah, right." Elise smiled at them then turned to Jude. "Like on my first date. There was mom fussing all over me, then these two, dressed in their habits flashing their crosses like shotguns. The poor guy was so scared he wouldn't look at me all night. At dinner, he asked me if we should say grace over our pizza." She rolled her eyes and looked at Elizabeth and Bernadette affectionately.

"I wish I could've been there." Jude felt a stab of sadness.

Maybe sensing Jude's feeling of being left out, Elise said, "I've made a scrapbook for you. Mom and I started working on it when I was fourteen. That's when she told me about you." She hesitated. "I mean, she always said I was hand-picked, but never went into detail."

Jude couldn't help but feel sad she hadn't been in Elise's life.

"She said that one day we'd meet, and you'd want to see pictures of me growing up." She looked subdued. "She wanted to meet you, but after she got sick…" Elise glanced away.

"We have plenty of time to catch up. I can't wait to see the book and find out about your life, with you and your mom. She sounds special."

"Yeah, she was." Elise looked at Jude. "Do you mind if I call you Jude for now? I'm still, I don't know…"

"Call me anything but Uncle Jude." Jude smiled and squeezed her hand. "I wouldn't expect you to call me mom." Another small stab of pain. She almost said, *not yet anyway*. "I'm glad we've found each other, finally."

Reece poked his head around the door. "I couldn't wait anymore." He moved next to Elizabeth and Bernadette. "Well?"

Bernadette clapped her hands together. "Oh, if there was this much love in the world all the time, we'd be in heaven!" She beamed at everybody. "Okay, who's hungry?"

Before anyone could answer, there was a knock on the door and a doctor came in. "Excuse me, I hope I'm not interrupting." He looked at Jude. "I heard you're ready to get out of here."

"Yeah, and I'm sure the feeling is mutual with the nurses," Jude said. She held up her arm with the IV. "If someone will just take this out, I'll be on my way."

"Not so fast, let me check you first." He pulled a stethoscope from his pocket. "You had a serious accident last night. What happened to your bandages? They're all wet and falling off." He turned to the others. "If you'll excuse us." He looked at Jude and noticed her shirt. "Proud Mommy? You're not pregnant are you?"

"No, not pregnant." Jude looked at Elise and smiled.

Chapter 68

The doctor reluctantly discharged Jude under strict supervision and "what to look for" concussion instructions. Elizabeth and Bernadette promised she'd be well taken care of at the Magdalene Home. How could he resist two nuns, especially on Christmas? He'd re-taped the bandages and said he wanted her back for more x-rays as soon as the swelling went down.

"You took a terrible beating last night." He wrote prescriptions as he talked. "I'm not sure how long it will take for your voice to fully come back. The guy choked you hard. You're lucky no bones were broken in your neck."

Dread surged through Jude as she thought of Rick's attack.

He held out two bottles of meds. "These are for pain and inflammation. Since it's a holiday, I'm going to give you enough samples to last until tomorrow when you can get the prescriptions filled. Take them as directed and don't drive anytime soon." He handed the papers and packets to Jude.

Jude left with Reece and Elise beside her. She made sure to wish the nurses a Merry Christmas. Outside, dusk was settling and the cold was refreshing.

"This is the best Christmas ever." She squeezed Elise's arm.

With the nuns hovering, Jude got in Reece's car and

asked Elise to ride with them. The girl settled in the back seat. Bernadette and Elizabeth stood next to the car door. Jude asked, "Do you mind if we stop at home first so I can get a few things and check on my cat? It's on the way."

"Not at all. In fact, we'll follow you," Elizabeth said.

Bernadette reached in and pulled Elise's coat collar up. "I'm afraid we haven't had time to cook the massive amount of food we bought. But that's okay, we'll have sandwiches tonight and a feast tomorrow." She checked that Elise was buckled in.

Jude winced as she turned to the backseat. "We'll manage just fine, Uncle Bernie." She winked at Elise. "You might enjoy a night off from cooking."

Bernadette waved her hands. "I enjoy taking care of everyone. Now Jude, you get comfortable, and Reece drive carefully. We'll see you there." Bernie backed away and closed the door. She and Elizabeth looked regal in their habits.

Jude watched them leave. "They're both amazing," she said.

"Yeah, they are," Elise also watched them head to the nun-mobile. "Even though they guarded me like a hawk, I was lucky to have them." She turned to Jude. "And my mom always reminded me of that." She quickly wiped a tear away. "This is my first Christmas without her, sorry."

"Don't apologize." Jude reached over the seat and touched Elise's knee. "As much as I hated giving you up, I'm glad you were adopted by someone so loving."

Reece took Jude's hand. "And I'm happy you're okay." He looked in the rearview mirror, then back to Jude, and smiled.

෴

Reece parked in front of Jude's house. The nun's van

pulled in behind them. Jude got out of the car and limped to the front yard. Her knees weakened when she looked at the flattened spot of grass where Rick had attacked her. Her car was still in the driveway, and the house appeared as if nothing had happened.

Reece was quickly at her side. Jude took Reece's arm and waited for Elise. "I can't believe so much has happened."

They walked to the porch, and Jude fished out her keys. Elizabeth and Bernadette sidled next to her.

Bernadette fretted. "I wonder if I should call the girls at home."

"They're fine. Let's show them we trust them." Elizabeth held the door open for everyone to enter.

"Wow, cool house." Elise looked around.

"Sorry for the mess," Jude said as she noticed some wadded-up scraps of wrapping paper Tommy had played with. She turned on lights as everybody went into the den. "Make yourself at home. I'll only be a minute."

Tommy was waiting for her in the bedroom. He did not look happy having been left alone. Jude picked him up and hugged him. "Sorry for leaving you here last night. Did Santa come down the chimney?" Tommy wiggled from her grasp, landed on the floor, and gave her a dirty look. Jude filled an overnight bag with toiletries and clothes and changed out of her scuffed jeans. She decided to keep the proud mommy shirt on. Tommy, sensing another night alone, jumped in the bag. "Do you want to come?" Jude reached down to pet him, but he bounded out and ran under the bed. "I'm going to leave you some extra food. And maybe even a Christmas treat, okay?" Since every bone and muscle in her body hurt, Jude couldn't bend to coax him out. She grabbed the bag and headed into the den with the others.

"St. Jude." Elise held Jude's statuette. "He was my

mother's favorite."

"Yeah, mine too." Jude leaned against the back of her couch and rested the overnight bag on the sofa. Tommy ventured near, looking as if he'd like to shoot a middle paw to her.

"Even though my confirmation name is Bernadette." Elise smiled at Bernadette.

"Really?" Jude asked, surprised. "Me, too."

Bernadette clapped her hands together. "Great minds think alike."

Jude looked again at Elise. Promises and hope threaded through her. Elise caught her gaze and smiled.

"Let me get that bag," Reece offered.

"You know, I have gifts to take, too." Jude went to the kitchen, got a few large shopping bags and asked Elizabeth to help her put the messily wrapped presents in it. She filled two bags and gave one to Elizabeth to carry. "Elizabeth, I owe you so much." Jude hugged her.

"Don't be silly. This has been amazing for all of us."

"No, really. You brought me to my daughter, and you helped me find part of myself."

"I pray you both have many happy years together. Elise is a great kid. And you guys are more alike than you think." Elizabeth turned and herded everybody to the door. "Come on, let's get home."

After the group left, Jude turned to close the door. Tommy sat in the hallway and twitched his bobbed tail, annoyed. "I'll be back early, I promise," she told him. She glanced at the others outside and said to Tommy, "There's someone I want you to meet. Go in the kitchen, there's a special treat in your bowl." Nose up, Tommy trotted around her and took his usual perch in the living room window.

She surveyed the den one last time and her gaze caught St. Jude. She went to the mantle, grabbed him, and tucked him in the gift bag before going outside with the others.

❦

They all arrived at the Magdalene Home at the same time. Jude felt sick when she saw what was left of the strip center across the street. The middle of the building was gone, leaving a charred pile of rubble, only two sides of bisected brick stood. She turned away, realizing someone had died there. She hoped Rick was enjoying his Christmas in a dank cell with a big hairy guy named Chopper.

Before Reece could put the car in park, Elizabeth and Bernadette were opening the door to help Jude out.

"Careful, those steps are high." Elizabeth took Jude's arm "Reece, get the door please."

Bernadette and Elise hovered near as they walked to the kitchen entrance. Jude saw a scorched area along the exterior wall. "Is that what Rick did?"

The nuns nodded and Bernadette said, "Everything's okay now."

As soon as the door opened, the aroma of turkey and all good things wafted from the kitchen. Sangria, Bandee, and the others were all busy cooking and cleaning in a mess of flour, sugar, and dishes.

Sangria turned to them. "Well, it's about time. I thought we were going to have to serve hockey pucks instead of turkey and ham."

Bernadette's hands flew to her face. "Oh, my! Did you all cook? Alone?"

Bandee laughed. "The Fire Marshall was still working across the street, so we figured he'd protect us in case."

Sangria playfully popped Bandee's arm with a wooden spoon. "We wanted to surprise you all. Everything's ready. Reecie, you want to carve?" She batted her eyes.

"Breast or leg? Or," she flipped her hair back, "dark meat?"

"I like it all," Reece laughed and squeezed Jude's hand. "I'll take care of the turkey, you get comfortable." He helped Jude sit at the dining table. Elise sat across from her.

"I'm starving," Elizabeth said and went to help with the food. "Thank you for cooking. I thought we were going to have peanut butter and jelly."

"Merry Christmas to you, lawyer lady." Sangria walked to Jude. "You look awful." She stared at Jude's face. "That asshole. I've got some friends who'll take care of him if you want."

"Sangria, please," Elizabeth said and looked at her sternly.

Jude smiled.

"Hey, you got yourself the best Christmas present ever." Sangria grinned. "And she looks just like you. Damn. At least before you got your face rearranged. Now you'll know what it's like to love your kids. Hey, look at your shirt, did the sisters get you that for Christmas?"

Jude shook her head as she pulled down her shirt for everybody to read. "It's kind of a long story."

Elizabeth handed a basket of steaming rolls to Sangria. "How was your Christmas morning?"

Sangria got misty. "Oh, it was perfect. Angel and Jared were so happy together, and they loved all the gifts. Thank you for letting us be together." She turned to Jude. "And thank you for your help. I'm working hard so we'll be together soon."

After a surprisingly delicious dinner, Jude could taste the effort, everybody settled in front of a roaring fire in the spacious living room. Jude sat next to Elise on the couch, and Reece got comfortable on the floor in front of them. Jude couldn't take her eyes off her daughter. After all these years, they were sitting together. Here, now. Even through the physical pain Rick had inflicted, Jude couldn't suppress a swell of immense happiness, like a touch from an angel's wing. Hope was a seed growing inside her.

Jude shifted on the couch. "I have Christmas gifts for everybody," she said. She started to get up, but Reece insisted she sit.

"Are they in the shopping bags?" he asked gently.

"Yes, by the door," Jude said gratefully.

"Oh, you shouldn't have," Bernadette admonished. "We planned to talk about what we're thankful for. We don't need anything else."

Sangria spoke up. "Well, I'm mighty thankful for all the presents you got for my sweet babies. So don't go letting people think you didn't buy nothing, 'cause you did."

"That's different," Elizabeth said.

Jude pulled out Bernadette's gift and handed it to her.

The nun seemed genuinely surprised. She unwrapped the book of saints. "Oh this is wonderful, I love it!" She passed it around. "Thank you."

Elizabeth was happy with the photography book, and the women loved the bath lotions and soaps.

Bandee held the book of saints on her lap as she sniffed the lotions. "This is pure luxury. We're not usually allowed to have fancy stuff here. Thanks!"

Jude took Reece's gift card out of the bag. "Merry Christmas," she said.

He opened the gift and thanked her by kissing her lightly on the lips. "This is perfect. We can shop together."

Jude turned to Elise. "I didn't get the chance to wrap your gift. Especially since I didn't know I was going to meet you today." She touched her daughter's knee. "This has been the happiest day of my life. I've waited seventeen years to see you."

Elise smiled.

Jude reached into the bottom of the bag and pulled out the statue of St. Jude. Through happy tears she said, "I've had this since I was little. He's taken care of me for many years. Now, it's time for him to watch over you."

Chapter 69

The next few days, Elise and Jude learned about each other. They'd spend time at Jude's, with Tommy, before heading back to the Magdalene Home.

Jude learned Elise had graduated from an all-girls Catholic school and had just finished her first semester in Austin.

"I'll move to Austin. I don't want to lose you again," Jude said early one morning. They were enjoying coffee together in the kitchen at the Magdalene Home. "I can work anywhere."

Elise shook her head. "And I can go to school here. Austin's great, but it's so far from home. You know, with mom gone and us just finding each other, I'd like to move back. It doesn't feel like home there. I'm like a lost soul."

"I don't want you to miss out on a good education because of me," Jude said.

"I can go back." Elise looked out the window. "I wasn't doing that great there anyway. And Aunt Lizzie and Uncle Bernie are here too."

"I'll help." Jude still couldn't believe her daughter was here, next to her.

Elizabeth came in through the back door. A faint whiff of burned building followed her in. "I just talked to Pastor Rains. He feels really bad that he listened to Rick about buying the property. Apparently, Rick had been feeding him some bull about us holding hardened criminals here. He said the city was on us to move these horrible law-breakers to a more secure facility." She rolled her eyes. "That's why the Academy wanted us out of the neighborhood." Elizabeth laughed cynically. "I wish the pastor would've come to us first." She shook her head.

Bandee came in holding the book of saints that Jude had given to Bernadette. She was also carrying a DVD. "I'm sort of glad now that we don't have TV."

Elizabeth turned to her, her eyes lit with interest. "Really?"

Bandee held up the DVD. "Yeah, this came in the mail. It's from Shelby." She put the DVD on the kitchen counter. "I guess she made a movie after all. I feel really bad I didn't try to stop her from taking your stuff."

Elizabeth picked up the DVD and looked at the title. She blanched as she slowly set it down. In bold red letters, the title read BAD HABIT. "Well," was all she said.

∽∾∽

Alone at home later, Jude got a visit from Agent Ladd.

"Come in." Jude opened her door and directed him to her living room.

Agent Ladd looked at Jude's healing face as he settled his lanky frame on the couch. "He really laid into you, huh?"

"Yeah. Broken cheek, sprained neck, and loads of bruises and cuts." She glanced in a small mirror on the wall. "But I'm healing." She wanted to say she was getting better both inside and out.

"You won't have to worry about Rick for a while," Ladd said, as he sat down. "The judge made sure he couldn't make bail, and I can assure you he'll be behind bars for a long time."

"Good, I guess." Jude couldn't help but feel conflicted. "You know, I think it was more the drugs than anything else that made him do what he did."

"You're probably right, but still, what he did was against the law. A lot of laws."

"I know." She touched her bruised neck. "What about the guy who was killed?"

"He was a pusher. Rick was buying from him initially. The guy made sure he was hooked then got Rick to fund the meth lab with him."

"That's awful. Rick was a smart attorney." Jude looked away. "Even if he was reckless."

"We'll need a statement from you, and you'll probably have to be available for trial." He stood. "Is there anything else I can do for you?"

Jude thought a minute. "You know, there's one thing." She told him about Lonnie Ball, and the suit he was bringing against her, accusing her of running over the kid at the Magdalene Home.

Agent Ladd laughed. "Yeah, we know about that."

"When you were checking me out?"

He didn't answer directly. "We don't usually waste time on someone as small as Lonnie Ball, but I'll bet I could train a rookie or two on him. There's enough minor criminal activity that we could scare the polyester pants off him. Don't worry about him anymore, okay?"

Jude nodded. "Thanks."

"Don't thank me, thank your former assistant Katie. She's the one who's helped us secure information on both Lonnie and Rick."

"Katie?" Jude asked.

"Yeah." He went to the door and turned around.

"I should call her."

He nodded. "I'll be in touch."

As Jude heard the front door close, she thought about

Katie. Maybe she needed to cut her a break. Like others, Katie tried to be a friend, but Jude refused to let anyone get close. Maybe it was time to dismantle some walls.

Chapter 70

By New Year's Eve morning, Jude felt almost normal. Her face was still a patchwork of contusions, the bruises turning different shades of green, blue, and yellow. Elise had been at the Magdalene Home for the past week. Jude hadn't asked yet but hoped Elise would consider moving in with her.

That afternoon, Jude drove to the Magdalene Home and found Elise reading in the living room alone.

Jude sat in an oversized chair and asked, "Have you given any thoughts to next semester?"

Elise shrugged. "A little. I called SMU but couldn't get through to anyone. I think I'd like to transfer here."

"That's great." Jude sat back. "I don't want to rush you, but I'd love to have you stay with me. I'm only a few blocks from there."

Elise smiled. "Yeah, I've thought about that too. I wanted to ask you if that would be okay."

"Be okay?" Jude laughed as relief bloomed inside her. "It would be perfect. And Tommy would love to have you there."

"Now that he finally likes me," Elise smiled.

"He knows a good soul." Jude leaned forward and touched Elise's arm.

They'd promised to be part of the big New Year's Eve festivities with the Magdalene women. The group was planning to celebrate Sangria's new job, and Bandee had an announcement she'd planned to divulge before midnight. Bernadette, as usual, was planning the menu, and Elizabeth seemed happy keeping the flock together.

"Now, you make sure Reecie shows up tonight, too," Sangria said, entering the great room. "I may get my walking papers soon, and I know he'll miss me when I'm gone." She fanned her face with her hand. "You are one lucky woman, lawyer lady."

Jude smiled, looked at Elise, and said, "I know."

∽∾∽

Bernadette shoed them off to get ready for the New Year's festivities and told the Magdalene women to take time to reflect and give thanks.

Jude and Elise settled in at Jude's.

"I have scrapbooks of me and Mom if you want to see them." Elise seemed shy.

"Sure," Jude said, wondering at a niggling feeling. Would she be jealous or appreciative?

Elise opened a suitcase and filled her arms with a bundle of lace-trimmed books. They sat close on the couch.

For the first time, Jude saw photographs of Trudy Wells. She did not remember meeting her. One thick scrapbook showed pictures of Elise as a baby, playing soccer, and receiving school awards. A lifetime, bound in one book.

"This one we made for you," Elise said. "My Mom said that you sacrificed by giving me away. It was to help me learn about being adopted."

Jude found comfort that Elise seemed happy throughout her childhood. The awful ache she'd felt for years, wondering if her daughter had been loved, was healing. At fourteen, if Jude had tried to raise Elise, she might have come precariously close to the women at the Magdalene Home.

Elise stacked the books and said, "It's getting late. Should we head to see Lizzie and Bernie?" Elise still seemed a bit uncomfortable with Jude. Tommy stayed close.

"Sure, we'll call Reece on the way. Maybe he can meet us there."

"Jude, I umm," Elise couldn't look Jude in the eye.

"Yes?" Jude wrangled with nervousness. What if Elise decided not to live here?

Elise glanced quickly at Jude. "Who's my father?"

Chapter 71

They were quiet in the car as they drove. Jude thought about Elise's question. She should have seen it coming with a response ready.

They settled on Jude's sofa too far apart for Jude to reach her, although Jude wanted to reach out, Jude told her she'd been raped.

When Elise heard the word *rape*, she cried. "I need to process this," she said as she ran from the room leaving Jude alone.

Ten minutes later Elise ventured back. "So I was conceived of hate?" She held Tommy close, who was basking in her arms.

"But born of love," Jude said. She didn't tell her the man was a priest. That would come later. It must cut deep realizing she was the product of violence.

When Elise finally sat down, Jude explained when it happened, she'd been so innocent and frightened she hadn't known what he was going to do to her. She tried to deny and shut out that awful night. But once her baby began moving inside her, the rape had become insignificant to the love that grew with each kick. "I loved feeling you inside me. But I was so young and naïve, I didn't know how to take care of a baby. Or even myself."

Elise nodded. "I can't imagine being a mom." She let Tommy squirm out of her arms.

"Please know I've questioned and struggled with that decision for seventeen years," Jude added. She petted Tommy who sat between them on the couch. "My childhood had some rough spots." Jude wasn't sure how much to tell about the abuse from her father. "I never went home again after you were born."

"What about your parents? Hey, do I have grandparents?"

"Yes. In New York. You also have an uncle and some cousins." Jude didn't mention she'd never met her brother's children. "My dad wasn't the nicest guy. So, as soon as I could, I left. It was easier for me to leave that life behind."

"Didn't they love you?"

"In their own way. My mother did, but she was afraid to rock the boat in case my father lost his temper." Jude looked out the window. "It's funny, I've never talked about them."

"Didn't you tell them everything?" Elise snuggled with Tommy who'd crawled into her lap.

Jude glanced away. "No. I was always afraid to in case I got in trouble. I figured it was easier to forget about that life." She sighed. Jude realized how hollow her life had been.

"Who said, 'It's better to have loved and lost than to never have loved at all'?" Elise asked.

Jude shrugged. "Shakespeare?"

"I don't know, but my mom used to say that all the time. Especially when we lost a pet. We'd always run out and get another dog or cat from the shelter, even though I didn't want to." She grabbed Tommy close and smiled. "I never thought I'd get over the big hole in my heart after one died. Then, the new dog would lick my hand or something, and, eventually, the pain wasn't so sharp."

"Are you saying you want a puppy?" Jude joked.

Elise shook her head as she stroked Tommy, who was happily content. "You know what I mean. Mom thought it was important to keep yourself open to love, even if it hurts to let it go."

"Your mom sounds like she was a very smart person."

There was a light knock at the door. Jude got up to let Reece in. Tommy, comfortable in Elise's lap regarded Reece coolly.

They settled together in Jude's warm den. Tommy made a fast exit, pissed his comfortable domain had been invaded.

"So, do you feel ready to move here?" Jude asked Elise as she and Reece sat.

"I think so." Elise looked around the room.

"It's a wonderful home," Reece said. "And should give you both time to get to know each other." He looked at Jude fondly. "And it's still spitting distance to the Magdalene Home."

"In case I want to join a convent?" Elise scrunched her nose but smiled. "It would be nice to be close to Lizzie and Bernie."

Jude took Elise and Reece to the guest room. "Tommy may not agree, but this is yours now. Decorate it any way you want. If you don't like the furniture, we'll go shopping." Jude leaned into Reece. "Maybe we can talk Reece into helping out with painting and fixing it up."

Reece put an arm around Jude, and raised his eyebrows. "I'll ask Sangria if I can borrow her fancy screwdrivers."

"Next week, I'm going to get a set of keys made. One for each of you, and for Elizabeth and Bernadette." Jude held Reece's arm close, enjoying the comfort and contentment he and Elise gave her.

Trudy was, in a way, a guardian angel. She'd brought Elizabeth and Bernadette into Jude's life. And she'd raised Elise with love and a generous spirit. She'd also provided

Jude's daughter with more than Jude could have ever hoped to give her. Fate shuffles and deals remarkable a hand.

Chapter 72

By ten-thirty, the big New Year's bash at the Magdalene Home was winding down. Bernadette sat in the living room trying to suppress yawns. "Oh, I'm never up this late."

The rest of the group was in a deep game of Scrabble.

Sangria looked up. "Yeah, this is New Year's, we need champagne. This hot tea just makes me want to pee."

"Then break out the ginger ale," Elizabeth said, as she put down a few tiles and spelled the word 'jump.' "I'm getting tired, and I'm not sure how long my brain is going to work. Bandee, are you ready to make your announcement?"

The girl shrugged. "If you want me to."

Elizabeth stood and stretched. "Come on."

Bandee scooted up in her chair. "I'm going to college." She looked down nervously. "Then I might work here."

Jude smiled. "Bandee, that's great. What are you going to study?"

"I don't know, psychology maybe. Social work and...well," she looked at Elizabeth and Bernadette. "I might, *maybe* be a nun."

"Oh, girl!" Sangria jumped up and gave Bandee a hug. "All the shit you took off of guys, I don't blame you."

"No, I want to help people." Bandee was blushing.

Elizabeth and Bernadette puffed up like proud parents.

⁂

By the time midnight rolled around, Jude, Reece, and Elise were the only ones left in the living room. Fireworks popped outside, at least Jude hoped they weren't gunshots. Reece grabbed Jude and gave her a big kiss, then hugged Elise in an embrace. The three of them sat as the house settled around them.

Jude moved comfortably against Reece's chest. She noticed Elise had nodded off. "Isn't she beautiful?"

"She looks like you." Reece squeezed her gently. "You make beautiful babies. You should think about having more."

Jude tried to suppress a noisy laugh. "So, I'm good breeding stock?" She moved closer. "I've thought about having another baby." She looked at Elise, sleeping. "But I was afraid. Mostly of loving and losing again." She pulled a blanket over Elise's legs. "Elizabeth and Bernadette have helped me outgrow some of my doubts."

"I'd like a sister or brother," Elise whispered sleepily.

"You're awake?" Jude asked.

"No." She giggled. "Sound asleep."

"Come here." Jude pulled her close. The three snuggled together and watched the fire burn.

"Can we go to New York, so I can meet the rest of my new family?"

Jude stroked her hair and glanced at Reece. "I guess so. I haven't been back for over seventeen years. I'm sure a lot has changed."

"I used to go with mom every year. She always wanted to go around Christmas so we could see the decorations. She said they were the same angels and ornaments that were there when she was young."

"We could go together," Reece said, as he looked at Jude for an okay.

"That would be nice." Jude nodded thoughtfully. "You know, there's someone else I know who's always wanted to go to New York."

"Lizzie and Bernie?" Elise tilted her head to look at Jude better. "They used to go with us."

"They would be welcome. No, this is a girl named Tiffany. She's one of my clients." Jude sighed. "She wanted to go to New York with her mother. But her mother's no longer here."

Elise looked away.

"What do you think?" Jude asked.

"I think we should bring her," Elise said. "And you'll come too Reece, right?"

"Wouldn't miss it."

"Happy New Year. I'm going to bed." Elise gave them both a hug and went upstairs.

"I feel like I've come full circle," Jude said, as she watched Elise walk upstairs. "I'm not afraid anymore."

"Of what?"

"Of my dad, of failure. I don't know. Of telling people I love them. I'm slowly figuring out what happiness is."

"You wear it well." Reece kissed her forehead.

"What about you? What do you want out of life?"

"More moments like these."

Jude smiled and let contentment soak in. Silently, she said a prayer of thanks. She imagined a bubble filled with dreams and hope, like when she was a child. She closed her eyes and pictured the bubble, rising to the heavens, then popping, and an angel taking her prayers to God.

The End

About the Author

Award winning author, Jeanne Skartsiaris, spins stories about life, digging into the soul her characters while they deal with real life challenges. Many readers identify with her stories, making them laugh as well as cry.

By day, Jeanne Skartsiaris works as a sonographer in an Ob/Gyn's office. Working in sonography helped her get her BA degree in photography, with a goal to get a Masters in Medical Illustration. After graduation, she was offered a job as a medical/legal photographer for a plaintiff's law firm. Instead of completing the graduate program, she worked as a photographer and art director for seventeen years in the legal community.

She attended creative writing courses at Southern Methodist University. Her novel, "Dance Like You Mean It" is a coming-of-middle-age story. Also the author of YA novels, "Surviving Life" and "Snow Globe." The Magdalenes (due for release August 15, 2023) speaks of shedding the past and reinventing oneself after a trauma.

The Magdalenes won first place in the San Antonio's Writer's Guild in 2019 and received a five-star review with Reader's Favorites in 2019. Dance Like You Mean It was a finalist in the humor category in the 2017 Best Book Awards by American Book Fest and received five stars at Reader's Favorites Awards.

Her books are available on Amazon and other book retailers.

You can find Jeanne on Facebook at: Jeanne Skartsiaris; Instagram at JeanneSkartsiaris; and Twitter, @jskartsiaris.

Printed in the USA
CPSIA information can be obtained
at www.ICGtesting.com
LVHW010213220823
755919LV00023B/205